PRAISE FOR
MATTHEW

"Johnson skips like a stone across the myriad provinces of the spec-fic landscape: time travel noir, Le Guinian psychofable, alternate history—even a glorious coda to the myth of the comic-book superhero. Yet somehow he leaves his own unique footprints wherever he lands. Macabre, whimsical, and touching by turns, *Irregular Verbs* does not disappoint."
     —Peter Watts, Hugo Award-winning author of *Blindsight*

"Matthew Johnson is a clever and thoughtful writer, and an unusual one, too."
                    —Elizabeth Hay, Giller Prize-winning author of
                                        Late Nights on Air

"I tore through this collection. Sharp. Insightful. Smart. When can I have more?"
                              —John Scalzi, author of *Redshirts*

"Matthew Johnson is a twenty-first-century Bester. With each story he deftly takes a single idea and gives it an unanticipated shove, presiding over the resulting consequences as they ripple through character and plot, carrying the reader along to shores of distant wonder."
     —Lawrence M. Schoen, Hugo and Nebula Award nominee

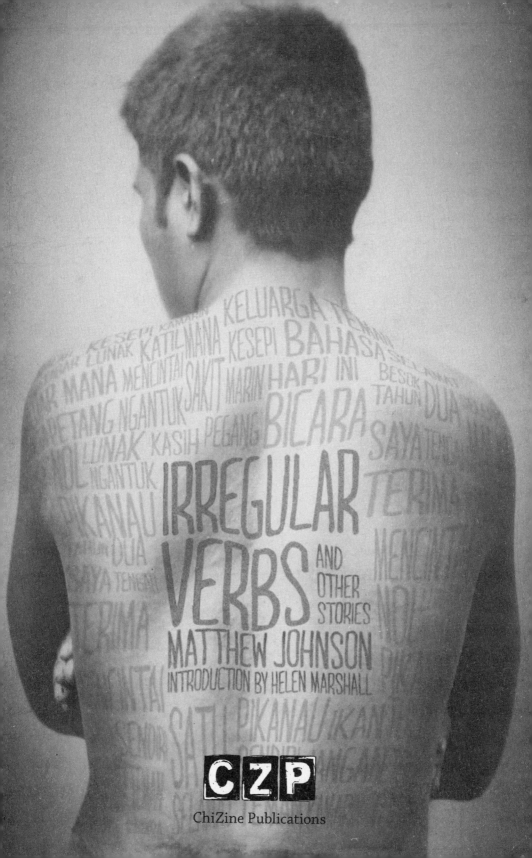

IRREGULAR VERBS AND OTHER STORIES

MATTHEW JOHNSON

INTRODUCTION BY HELEN MARSHALL

CZP

ChiZine Publications

FIRST EDITION

Irregular Verbs and Other Stories © 2014 by Matthew Johnson
Introduction © 2014 by Helen Marshall
Cover artwork © 2014 by Erik Mohr
Cover and interior design by © 2014 by Samantha Beiko

Distributed in Canada by
HarperCollins Canada Ltd.
1995 Markham Road
Scarborough, ON M1B 5M8
Toll Free: 1-800-387-0117
e-mail: hcorder@harpercollins.com

Distributed in the U.S. by
Diamond Comic Distributors, Inc.
10150 York Road, Suite 300
Hunt Valley, MD 21030
Phone: (443) 318-8500
e-mail: books@diamondbookdistributors.com

Library and Archives Canada Cataloguing in Publication Data

Johnson, Matthew, 1972-, author
    Irregular verbs and other stories / Matthew Johnson.

Issued in print and electronic formats.
ISBN 978-1-77148-177-9 (pbk.).--ISBN 978-1-77148-178-6 (pdf)

    I. Title.

PS8619.O482I77 2014   C813'.6   C2014-900782-5

    C2014-900783-3

CHIZINE PUBLICATIONS
Toronto, Canada
www.chizinepub.com
info@chizinepub.com

Edited by Kelsi Morris
Proofread by Klaudia Bednarczyk

Canada Council Conseil des arts
for the Arts   du Canada

We acknowledge the support of the Canada Council for the Arts which last year invested $20.1 million in writing and publishing throughout Canada.

ONTARIO ARTS COUNCIL
CONSEIL DES ARTS DE L'ONTARIO
50 YEARS OF ONTARIO GOVERNMENT SUPPORT OF THE ARTS
50 ANS DE SOUTIEN DU GOUVERNEMENT DE L'ONTARIO AUX ARTS

Published with the generous assistance of the Ontario Arts Council.

Printed in Canada

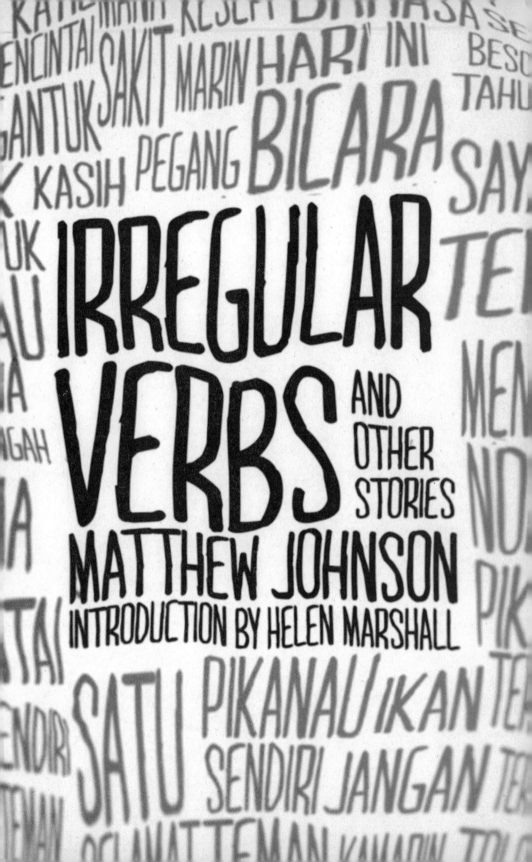

IRREGULAR VERBS

AND OTHER STORIES

MATTHEW JOHNSON

INTRODUCTION BY HELEN MARSHALL

This book is for Megan, of course

Contents

INTRODUCTION | Helen Marshall

Every writer dreams of a perfect language.

I met Matthew Johnson at a local convention in 2010. I remember that period of my life with surprising clarity: at the time, I was a graduate student at the Centre for Medieval Studies in Toronto, the type of scholar that Geoffrey Chaucer might have been describing in the *Canterbury Tales* if you updated the book by some six hundred years, the kid with horse rake-thin and robes threadbare who chose "some twenty books bound in black and red" as the appropriate destination of a university stipend rather than something as practical as a hot meal. Books on medieval siege weapons, *Beowulf*, Aristotelian philosophy, fourteenth-century feasts, Arthurian romances: in short, whole worlds of knowledge that were barely a hair's breadth from the kind of fantasies I had had in my head since I cracked open the *Lord of the Rings* when I was twelve and which I was in the process of rediscovering.

A paradise? Of sorts. But even in paradise there was a shadow.

That shadow was my daily Latin tutorial, a deliberate torture imposed by the administration on all students in the program.

To become a doctor of medieval studies, you see, it was necessary to show mastery over the primary language of the Middle Ages through two brutal exams: the twin gauntlets every student in the department had to run. To prepare, we spent an hour every day for three years—an hour we all desperately *needed* for writing grants, marking essays, preparing conference papers and generally staying afloat in the unkind seas of academia—in a dimly lit office with five or six of our fellow classmates, staring at partially deciphered scribbles we'd made on the texts of John of Salisbury, Osbert of Clare or Petrarch. And all the while we waited—we waited in terror!—for the knotted and nicotine-stained finger of one Professor Rigg to point our way.

"Speak," he would say. His voice was deceptively quiet, authoritative. He would lean back in his chair, an old man, you might think, close to eighty years old, bones that had survived countless Canadian winters, eyes that had looked on and judged practically every tenured professor we knew.

In that moment, I would dream of a perfect language. A language I could summon forth without pause, a language that would effortlessly reveal itself to me and to my colleagues. We all dreamed of this language. Every one of us.

And, one by one, we would open our mouths.

And, one by one, we should shut them. Driven to silence and shame.

Even though we had each studied the subjunctive, we had each separated our gerunds from our gerundives, and made ourselves *maestri* of the passive periphrastic, still, that ancient finger, that low, inscrutable voice obliterated thought.

Every writer dreams of a perfect language. Every writer dreams of a language that obeys, that comes to heel. For some this language is spare and pure, pared down to reveal essential truths without ornament or obfuscation. For others it is devilish and twisting, folding back over itself to create layers of meaning, shades of nuance.

A language that will survive through the ages.

A language that will crack open the hearts of readers like a hazelnut.

Enter Matthew Johnson and his *Irregular Verbs*.

Matthew Johnson never took Latin with me—though when I met him he was as equally conversant on the subject of science fiction as he was on Middle English poetry, a true polymath —but I wish he had: he would have been the quiet student at the back, boyishly good-looking, raised with a keen awareness of Canadian politeness and known for his wry sense of humour. The kind of person you might easily ignore at first glance.

And so perhaps Professor Rigg would have underestimated him, as the rest of us might have. Perhaps Professor Rigg would have pointed that gnarled tree-root of a finger at Matthew Johnson and commanded him to speak.

And, by George, would Professor Rigg have been in for a surprise!

Because here is a writer who can not only untangle the words of the ancients without a hitch—without a gulp!—but can *make something new*. Here is a writer who isn't afraid to speak. And whatever language he chooses becomes a tool effortlessly wielded in the service of his narrative.

Matthew Johnson is one of the very best science fiction and fantasy writers that you've never heard of. Persuasive and insightful, globally aware, witty and wondrously intelligent. He has been praised by the some of the most respected reviewers and editors working in the field, and this debut collection, which gathers together his finest stories, shows that praise is well-earned. Johnson's stories cajole and whisper, they dazzle and delight, but above all they show a complete mastery of the language of genre fiction—not through heavy-handed purple prose but through simple, elegant, evocative language. Language that makes you feel.

Let me start with an example that Professor Rigg might have enjoyed.

In one of the gems of the collection, "Another Country," Romanized Goths fleeing from Attila the Hun's invasion become refugees (or prefugees as they are cleverly designated) in a future where refugees from the Mongol invasions end up in Seattle, Aztecs in Paris, and Romans in Ottawa. They speak to each other in perfect Latin—"Te salute do, amici," Galfridus officially welcomes the new arrivals—and what follows is a flawless story of culture shock and dislocation that demonstrates Johnson's meticulous attention to detail in creating worlds that can only be described as *authentic*.

Understand: what makes Johnson's writing so compelling is

that he knows that the trick to learning any new language is the understanding that languages are not perfect systems. Languages are messy, broken things. They don't always make sense—not on the surface. But in their imperfections—their irregularities—they offer extraordinary revelations.

In the title story of the collection, "Irregular Verbs," Johnson translates the messiness of language into the messiness of loss and loneliness. In the Salutean Isles, language develops so quickly and so personally that the community must meet for one hour every day in order to preserve their common tongue; but after the death of his wife, the newly widowed islander Sendiri begins to forget the private language he had shared with her. Johnson renders the threat of that loss in heartbreaking detail: the irregularities of their marital lingo reflect the subtle but inescapable rhythms of two people with genuine love for one another:

keluarga: to move to a new village
ngantuk: to call out in one's sleep
lunak: to search for something without finding it

Johnson's fragmented dictionary evokes the scope of a life lived together, the desire to preserve that life and the ineluctable knowledge of its passing.

Other stories in the collection show an equally deft hand. "Heroic Measures" might just be one of the best superhero stories of the past decade, delving into the nature of mortality as an unnamed (but instantly recognizable!) wife must decide if—and how—to pull the plug on the husband she had once thought invincible. *This is the kind of care he gets*, she reflects, *after everything*. Likewise Johnson's zombie tale, "The Afflicted"—in which Alzheimer's and senile dementia lead to the all-consuming hunger that evokes the genre—isn't really a zombie story at all, centering not on the monstrous, but on the slow erosion of the human in those we love. These are not stories that walk the well-worn paths of speculative fiction: they are haunting re-inventions that startle us out of complacency. In these pages you'll find time travel and magic, afterlives and fairy tale cottages, gods, dragons, Cold War spies and secret police but nevertheless every single tale in the collection feels startlingly fresh.

"Words are the first step we take to turn intentions into reality," declares Chuck Palahniuk, one of America's great authors of transgressive fiction. Language is the medium out of which writers birth new worlds. But Palahniuk speaks at length in an interview with Andrew Lawless published at *Three Monkeys Online* about how the flaws in language create the reality of those worlds—what he calls "burnt tongue" moments, moments in which he discovers "a way of saying something, but saying it wrong, twisting it to slow down the reader. Forcing the reader to read close, maybe read twice, not just skim along a surface of abstract images, short-cut adverbs, and clichés."

Writers dream of a perfect language. But it is the broken language—the irregular language—that allows one to speak most clearly to the heart. It is that language which fractures the superficial, the easily digested, and the generic.

Matthew Johnson knows this. You can see the truth of this knowledge etched deeply in his stories. Stories like pearls: fashioned around a grit of sand, an irritant, an irregularity, out of which comes great beauty. He offers us new worlds, glimpses of futures provocative and profound, traces of histories that never were.

Here is a writer who is not afraid to burn language.

Here is a writer who is not afraid to dream.

Underestimate him at your peril.

—Helen Marshall
January 2014
Oxford, England

Irregular Verbs

apiluar: to let a fire burn out
gelas: to treat something with care
pikanau: to cut oneself with a fishhook

It is a well-known fact that there are no people more gifted at language than those of the Salutean Isles. Saluteans live in small villages on a thousand densely populated islands; isolated but never alone, their languages change constantly, and new ones are born all the time. A Salutean's family has a language unintelligible to their neighbours, his old friends a jargon impenetrable to anyone outside their circle. Two Saluteans sharing shelter from the rain will, by the time it lets up, have developed a new dialect with its own vocabulary and grammar, with tenses such as "when the ground is dry enough to walk on" and "before I was entirely wet."

It was in just such circumstances that Sendiri Ang had met his wife, Kesepi, and in such circumstances that he lost her. An afternoon spent in a palm-tree shadow is enough time for two people to fall in love, a few moments enough to die when at sea. Eighteen monsoons had passed in between, enough time for the two of them to develop a language of such depth and complexity that no third person could ever learn it, so utterly their own that it was itself an island, without ties to any of its neighbours.

For the ten days of his mourning Sendiri had stayed on the private floor of his house, listening to the fading echoes of his wife's voice. On the eleventh day he descended to the public floor. That was the longest time thought to be safe: any more away from the great conversation, the hour in the evening in which all Saluteans join in maintaining their one common language, ran the risk of leaving a person stranded, isolated by changes in dialect.

His friend Teman was waiting for him, feeding new coals for the brazier to replace those that had burned cold. It was just like Teman, Sendiri thought, to think of a little thing like that, and for a moment the sight of his old friend cheered him a little.

"Apa kabar?" Teman said.

Sendiri just stared, at first not recognizing the words in Grand Salutean. "How should I be?" he asked after a moment. "I'm here, and she's not." As soon as he spoke he regretted it, gave thanks that it was in Teman's nature to chew his words thoroughly before spitting them out.

"That's true," Teman said mildly.

Wincing, Sendiri sat on the reed mat next to his friend. "I'm sorry," he said. "Thank you for coming here, and for the coals. I've gotten very tired of cold rice."

Teman smiled, clearly relieved at Sendiri's change of mood. "It's hard, I know—coming back down. Rejoining the rest of the world."

Sendiri shook his head. "Ten days, to mourn someone who—someone—it just isn't enough."

"A lifetime isn't enough," Teman said, smiling sadly. "But it's all we have."

That night Sendiri realized he had forgotten a word. He had been dozing, half-asleep, the smell of the squid curing in the thatch above reminding him of his and Kesepi's last fishing trip together, when suddenly he could not remember the word for the moment, at the end of the long season before the goatfish run, when you think you will die if you have another bite of dried fish. He couldn't remember which of them had coined it, one of a hundred thousand words they shared, but he knew that it was gone.

That's ridiculous, he thought. It's just nibbling the line. . . . He ran through syllables in his mind, trying to catch a memory that slipped and dodged around him, but it was no use: the hook was empty. He shook briefly, reaching out instinctively across the hammock for the warmth that had once reassured him.

Sendiri cast his mind back, remembering conversations they had had, testing the memory like a tongue probing a loose tooth. Mana adalah jaring— What was that word? Suddenly gaps were appearing in his memories. Where there was a Grand Salutean equivalent, the word from that language slipped in; things for which that language had no words were simply gone. Most frustrating, some were words he knew he had remembered that morning. So far only one in a hundred, perhaps, was gone, but more were joining them.

He had never really thought of a language disappearing before. When his mother had died, he and his father preserved their family language, and when his father had died other people—relatives and neighbours—had known enough of it to keep it alive in his mind. Kesepi's family, though, had been from another village, not witness to their life together, and they had had no children to carry their language on. When it faded from his mind it would be as if it had never been. As if she had never been.

Sendiri sat up, watched the holes in the thatch for the first hint of dawn, cursing the darkness. He would need light for what he had to do, and every moment that passed was his enemy.

Saluteans, on the whole, are not much for writing things down. Their languages are too fluid and mercurial to be caught on paper; only Grand Salutean has a written form, introduced by missionaries of the Southerner to spread his words to the isles and used by village headmen and island chiefs to record debts and proclamations. Sendiri, whose father had been a headman, knew how to read and write, and like most islanders knew how to dry and prepare squid ink to sell to foreigners. Though his and Kesepi's language was as alike to Grand Salutean as a sting ray is to a monkey he bent its letters to his purposes, torturing and teasing the characters until they could record the sounds that would never be spoken again. He began opening the bundles of cold rice, which friends and relatives had left as mourning gifts, to write on their banana-leaf wrapping. Frantically he wrote word after word, pausing only to mix more ink when the bowl was dry. After some hours the house shook, but he did not look up from his work; only when he heard the ladder up to the private floor creaking did he pause, put down the straightened fishhook he'd been using as a quill.

"Sendiri?" Teman's voice called from halfway up. Friends though they were, the private floor was inviolate without an invitation.

"What is it?" Sendiri asked.

"The conversation," Teman said.

Sendiri exhaled sharply, set his work aside carefully. Had it been that long already? The great conversation was held an hour before dusk—he had not even noticed the shadows creeping across the floor. "Just a moment," he said, his joints complaining as he stood.

He heard Teman climbing back down the ladder, waited until he felt the house sway as his friend's feet hit the floor below before heading down himself. Teman waited until he had reached the floor, then the two wordlessly passed along the way to the broad walkway that joined his house to the rest of the village. Below, the receding tide had exposed the mud into which the village's posts were sunk, and the afternoon sun had left it stinking; everywhere nets were hanging to dry, their sharp salty smell burning Sendiri's nose.

At the public walkway all the villagers were stretched out in the line that made up the great conversation. All voices were speaking in Grand Salutean—in most cases, the only time they would speak it that day. Teman's uncle Paman, the headman, moved up and down the line, making small talk and ensuring everyone used the correct form, without words or constructions from other dialects creeping in. All Saluteans know that their gift for languages could easily be a curse: without a common tongue, the separate islands of their speech would drift inexorably apart.

Sendiri joined in the conversation gamely, the words tasting flat and oily in his mouth. What, after all, could Grand Salutean express? Village business, fishing advice, weather talk. Teman had returned to his assigned place in the line, so Sendiri made small talk with his neighbours, two nattering old women, Kiri on one side and Kanan on the other; meaningless prattle of rotting walkway boards and late fish-runs. Finally the sunlight reddened, the walkway fell into shadow, and he could go home. The conversation was over.

Freed, he ran back to his house, felt the mangrove poles that supported it sway as he shot up the ladder. He sat down, spat in the ink-bowl to moisten it, picked up his quill and—what had he been about to write? He scanned the leaf he had left on the floor, hoping to find some clue in what he had written before, saw no connections in the list of words he had been writing. Searching his mind for the words he had inventoried that morning, he found even more were gone. It was more than him simply forgetting them, he realized: the language was eroding, an atoll being washed away by the ocean of Grand Salutean. He would have to forego the conversation, then, until the language was preserved. He laughed. What would be lost? No poetry had ever been written in Grand Salutean. It was a deliberately simple language, shorn of all subtlety, a language of nothing but nouns and verbs; no genders, no tenses but now and not-now, no pronouns but I and not-I. It would do him no harm not to use it for a few days.

keluarga: to move to a new village
ngantuk: to call out in one's sleep
lunak: to search for something without finding it

As the night went on, though, he started to wonder just how long it would have to be. Even with all the words he had lost, he wondered if he could ever write down what was left. He had enough fish oil to burn his lamp for a night, maybe two; more urgently, he was nearly out of banana leaves to write on. Squinting, he made the letters as small as the tip of the hook would allow, and began jotting apostrophes to separate words instead of spaces. Earlier, when he had devised his system of writing, he had not thought about space. Now he cursed his decision to use combinations of letters to represent sounds that did not exist in Grand Salutean, rather than inventing new characters. He was netted now, though. A dictionary had to be consistent, or it was useless; this much he had learned from Grand Salutean.

He kept writing, pushing himself to make the letters smaller and smaller. Hunched over the banana leaf on the floor, his arm held tightly to keep his strokes small, Sendiri's forearm jerked, scratching a line across the floorboard. He swore, drew the quill back to throw it across the room in anger, when he saw that the ink had dried on the wood without smudging. Of course, he thought. What else would be a suitable record of the language he and Kesepi had shared than the other thing that was theirs alone? Excited, he raised his arms to stretch his back, dipped the quill in the ink bowl, and began writing along the edge of the wall. He worked his way inward as dawn came, and the daylight hours passed; he worked in silence as Teman once again came up the ladder, called his name, called again, and finally left. His quill scratched against the floorboards as he followed an inward spiral towards the centre of the room, always trying to increase his pace, to write words down faster than they could be washed away by his mind's tide.

Thunder made him look up. It was dark again: lightning flashed through the holes in the thatch, illuminating the room for a moment. Focused on his work, he had not noticed the smell of rain in the air, the sound as it fell on the roof. Now, in the lightning's flare, he could see puddles sitting on the floor, smudging and washing away most of what he had written. He froze for a moment, rigid with anger; then, too tired even to rage, Sendiri fell to the floor and let himself sleep.

Asleep, he saw himself sitting with Kesepi in their boat, leaning against the palm-stem gunwales on a calm sea. She was speaking, but the words made no sense, and he knew that he had at last forgotten their language entirely. He opened his mouth to speak, then felt something resting in his hand: looking down, he saw that it was the book he had been writing, containing every word the two of them had ever spoken. Flipping through the book, he tried to speak, to say one of the things he wished he had said, but all he could do was string words together. Kesepi, now in a boat of her own, began to drift away. Sendiri called to her, but the words he read from the dictionary had no emotion, and no reaction registered on her face. Even in its perfect state, he realized, the book was just a record, a dead thing without the soul of the language.

He woke from fevered dreams to see Teman sitting on the mat nearby, a bowl of water at his side. His friend rose to his knees and held out the bowl. "Have some of this," Teman said. "I think you've had a fever."

"Thank you," Sendiri croaked, then took a drink. He felt a sharp pain as he sat up; the hook he had been using as a quill had stuck in his side, leaving a black ink spot when he plucked it out. "Why are you—"

"You've missed two conversations," Teman said, "and you were moaning last night, loud enough your neighbours could hear. The talk is . . ."

Sendiri nodded. He knew what the talk would be. Sometimes when a person dies, they take the souls of those they love with them to the sea floor; what's left is just a hantu, a dead, empty shell. To see or even talk to a *hantu* is dangerous, itself an omen of death.

"Maybe I'm not alive," Sendiri said. "All that's worth saving is fading away."

Teman frowned, gestured around at the smudged marks on the floor. "Is that what this was all about?"

"It's useless, I realize that now," Sendiri said. "Even if I had all the words, it would be no more alive than a dried fish." He rubbed the spot where the hook had jabbed him with his thumb. The ink mark was still there, just under his skin. "It needs to live. . . ."

Teman waited for his friend to continue, rose to his feet when he did not. "Well—I shouldn't even be up here. I hope you'll forgive me." He moved to the top step of the ladder, began climbing down.

"No—wait," Sendiri said. "You have to help me. Help me keep her alive."

"But you said—"

"No, please. I have an idea. Help me."

Teman paused at the top of the ladder. "Sendiri—you have to let go. I know how you feel, but you have to let go."

Sendiri picked up the hook he had been using as a quill, held it up to show to Teman. "Please. Just stay—help me."

"You have to come out for the conversation. Today."

"One day. That's all."

Teman took a breath, nodded. "All right," he said.

hadapi: to awake to one's lover's face
cinta: to love truly
mencintai: to love for the last time

At the end of the day, as the shadows reached over the main walkway, Sendiri rejoined the conversation. Many people turned to look, not only because of his absence but because of the black marks that had appeared on his face, arms and legs. Those nearby saw that the marks were letters pricked out under his skin, forming words that meant nothing even to those that could read Grand Salutean. Only he and Teman knew that the words, in fact, covered his whole body, arranged so that their location and position would represent the grammar of the language he and Kesepi had shared: the oldest root words along the spine, verbs on the muscles, every inch of skin recalling the meaning and inflexion of a word.

Despite the small commotion he was causing, Sendiri paid the ink marks little mind. The Saluteans have no mirrors or steel, and their sea is too dark to ever show a clear reflection, so he would never see most of the words Teman had scribed on his skin. That was not important, though. All that mattered was that they would not fade away. That they were, still, a living language.

ANOTHER COUNTRY

Geoff squinted at the figures emerging from the fissure, his period recognition chart at the ready. Not that he needed it, in this case: he was able to fix the new arrivals as soon as he saw their tunics and trousers—late-Empire Romanized Goths, probably fleeing Attila's invasion of lands their own ancestors had invaded a few generations before.

"*Te salutem do, amici*," he said slowly, holding his hands up and palm-outward. The light was fading now, and the four prefugees were looking around apprehensively. The reception room, built around the fissure that had first opened right downtown fifteen years before, had been designed to minimize culture shock, with no modern technology or materials visible.

The fissures had consistency but no logic: prefugees from the Mongol invasions wound up in Seattle, Aztecs in Paris, Romans in Ottawa, and so on. The only thing that was known for sure was that they always brought people from places and times that were much worse than now, periods of tremendous chaos and danger; as a result, the people that came through were wary, and some of the first encounters had not ended well.

"What is your name?" Geoff asked in slow, careful Latin.

The prefugees—a bearded man, a woman with her blonde hair in braids, and two young boys—regarded him cautiously. The man turned back to the woman, said something in a thickly Gothic-accented dialect Geoff couldn't follow. She nodded, keeping her eyes down, and gathered the two boys to her. "Odoricus Aemilianus," the man said. "Where have we come?"

"This is a safe place," Geoff went on. "It is very different from the place you left, but you are welcome."

"How did we arrive here?" the man said, keeping himself between his family and Geoff.

"Good fortune," Geoff said. It was Welcome Services' official answer, and as good a one as anyone could give. "Please—there are many things you have to know, before we can find you a new home. If you'll come with me, my comrades will get you started."

The man looked back over his shoulder, whether at his family or the vanished fissure Geoff didn't know. Finally he made a grunt of assent, jerked his head to order his wife and children forward.

Geoff released the breath he had been half-holding. Ninety percent of what the official terminology called "Delayed Integrations" happened in the initial encounter. Now that that was over he could do the rest on autopilot, supervising the prefugees' processing and initial billeting. When the fissures had first opened, the people that had come through had been seen as a tremendous opportunity, a goldmine for historians and anthropologists; now, in the thousands, they were just more immigrants to be settled and assimilated. This family would probably integrate all right, he thought: the boys looked young enough to pick up English without too much of an accent, and despite the wife's public deference to her husband Gothic women were typically more independent than their Roman counterparts.

He was still thinking about them a few hours later, as he climbed the stairs of an apartment building in Vanier on a follow-up visit to a family he'd welcomed two years ago. More than anything else in modern society, it was the difference in relations between the sexes which prefugees found the most difficult. Women and girls mostly flourished, while men and boys—deprived of the pater familias status even the poorest free Roman male could expect within his family—did less well. At least these new arrivals, unlike most prefugees, still had their father.

Knocking at the Columellae's door, Geoff wished they had had the same advantage. He stepped back, smiled at the fish-eye. A few moments later the door opened inwards a few centimetres before being stopped by the security chain. "Galfridus?" a female voice said from within.

Geoff sighed. "*Ave*, Fulvia," he said. "How are you?"

The door closed briefly, opened again once Fulvia had unlatched the chain. She was a broad, buxom woman in her late forties, pure Roman stock from about five hundred years earlier than that afternoon's arrivals. Her black-and-white streaked hair was done up in a messy bun and she was wearing a simple blue house toga, accented with a long string of fake pearls. "Please, come in."

"Thank you." The small apartment was spotless, as always, but the smell of a thousand meals' worth of anchovies and olive oil—unrelieved by windows that didn't open and a range hood that didn't work—was overpowering. Two armless Ikea couches, in some spots worn through to the stuffing, were perpendicular to the TV, on which the lares sat in a neat pile. The set was tuned to the Latin-language community channel, a Plautus play with the sound off. Between the couches, facing the TV directly, sat an unused armchair wrapped in clear plastic. "How is work?"

"Fine," Fulvia said, brushing a stray hair out of her face. She waved him to the chair. "Someone a maid pretending was, and stealing, so ID cards now we have to get."

Geoff settled uncomfortably into the chair. "Are you going to miss work?"

"No, I'm on my own time doing it. There's a bus I can take, the picture taken to get."

"Good." Geoff accepted a cup of coffee, sipped it carefully. Few Romans ever acquired a taste for coffee, and Fulvia was no exception; she only made it when he came over, and had no idea how much to use, so that it was always either near-water or Turkish-style sludge. "Any other problems?"

A painful look flickered across Fulvia's face before being replaced by a fixed smile. "No, no problems," she said. "A little cake would you—would you like, a little cake?"

Geoff shook his head. His friends in the community told him Fulvia was an excellent cook, well-known for her lentils with chestnuts, but it was his misfortune to always be served prefugees' idea of what moderns ate—an idea in which plastic wrap and microwaves figured strongly. The penalty, he supposed, for being the poster boy for integration. "No thank you." He took a long sip from his coffee. "How is Attius?"

Fulvia grimaced again, showing Geoff that he had guessed right. "In school he's doing well. In Heritage Latin he has top marks in his class."

"Good. Is he still in ESL?" He really ought to know that—prefugees' language status was supposed to be kept updated in Welcome Services' records—but since most of his workload had shifted from first encounters to follow-ups like these, there were simply too many to keep track of.

"No, regular Anglish," Fulvia said.

"Is he making friends?"

Fulvia glanced away. "Some."

"Different kinds of people, or just other Romans?"

"I don't know," she said, her voice quickening. "When they're here, they just go into his room and the counter use."

"The computer."

"Yes. And when I come in they talking stop." She sat down, perching on the edge of the couch nearest to him. "The boys outside, on the walls they write, they into fights get. Maybe in his room he's safer."

"Probably. It can be dangerous out there, for a boy his age."

"He's so sensitive, and smart," Fulvia said. "His father a *quaestor* was, and a poet, did I tell you that?"

Geoff shook his head, though of course she had. "Would you like me to talk to Attius? Make sure he's fitting in okay?"

She looked away, then nodded. "You're not too busy?"

"This is my job, Fulvia," he said. "And I'm happy to do it."

Fulvia held a handkerchief to her face, dabbed at her nose. "Thank you," she said. She rose, vanished into the kitchen, returned a moment later carrying two plastic-wrapped Twinkies. "Here. So you don't away hungry go."

"Do not concern yourself, Geoffrey. This boy of yours is in no trouble." Marcus Apicius was holding court at Mello's, the restaurant that was his in all but name. On the table in front of him sat a plate crowded with fat snails; painted on the cream-yellow wall behind were the words *Hold back your quarrels, if you can. If not, go home.*

"He's Fulvia Columella's," Geoff said. "Do you know the family?"

Marcus popped a snail into his mouth with a tiny silver fork and chewed thoughtfully. "Maybe," he said.

Glancing up at the quote written on the wall, Geoff bit his tongue. "How do you know he's not in trouble, then?" he asked.

"These Columellae, they're an old family, even in my time—a good family, yes? So he's not in trouble."

"That doesn't necessarily follow, you know that," Geoff said. They had both been part of the earliest wave of arrivals, but Marcus remained every inch the old Roman. That was why Geoff was meeting with him: Marcus had always been the man Roman prefugees came to when they needed help of a kind Welcome Services couldn't provide, and he stayed in touch with the community in a way Geoff couldn't hope to.

"But it does, Geoffrey," Marcus said. "Tell me, what do you mean by 'trouble'? Is it running around in a gang, playing tough?"

"I don't know. Probably, yes."

"Then no, he's not in trouble." He speared another snail, dropped it in his mouth and closed his eyes. "Geoffrey, you must have one of these. Do you know we feed them on milk for six days before cooking them? You have to lure the live snails out of the shell, fatten them up until they're too big to get back in."

Geoff shook his head; the strong smell of garum wafting out from the kitchen had taken away his appetite. "Listen, I just want you to ask around—"

Marcus waved a hand—waving him quiet, Geoff thought, until a waiter appeared with another tray. "Geoffrey. I will do this if it makes you happy, but let me explain," he said. The waiter uncovered the tray, revealing a plate ringed with what looked like a dozen perfectly oval white mice.

"Fine," Geoffrey said. "Tell me again how I don't understand the Roman mind. I was only born on a farm on the Tiber."

"And came here when you were, what? Ten? You're a modern,

Geoffrey. You dress like one, sound like one, smell like one." Marcus reached into the salt cellar, pinched and sprinkled across the plate. "'Trust nobody until you have eaten much salt with him,'" he said. "Cicero, of course."

"That's just what I'm saying—a lot of us fit in perfectly well. We're not all determined to relive the last days of Pompeii like you are."

"Ha—you say Pompeii like it was something. In my day it was a fishing village; there were a thousand like it. It was just lucky to get buried alive. But listen, Geoffrey, here is what I want to say. There are two types of Romans, and they are both missing something here. The first type is the everyday sort of man, the worker, and here he cannot work. We had the same problem in my time, of course, but back then we had laws against slaves taking too much of the jobs."

"We don't have slaves anymore," Geoffrey said.

Marcus waved expansively towards the kitchen. "What are you talking about? Look in there, see how many slaves there are."

Geoff frowned. "Marcus—if someone is keeping slaves—"

"No—machines, that do a man's work. Robota, it means slave, you know this; and Capek, he too was a Slav, a slave by nature, as that sheep-fucker Aristotle said. When machines cook and wash dishes and do the work of a hundred, what is an ordinary man to do? He has no money to set himself in trade, so he gets himself in trouble for want of something to occupy him."

"Okay—assume you're right," Geoff said, putting up his hands. "How do you know that's not happening to Fulvia's son?"

"Because he is the other kind of Roman—the kind who is missing his manhood. The ordinary fellow is happy with a day's work for a day's pay, but a man of good family needs leisure, time to give over to a profession. He needs to do his civic duty, contribute to his city, but where is it now? Buried and paved over, infested with Cisalpine rabble."

"So is that what I should tell Fulvia? That Attius can't be in trouble because he's missing his manhood?"

"Well, maybe not like that," Marcus said, cocking an eyebrow. "Listen, Geoffrey, this boy—he's from a good family, he knows with

30

his father gone he has responsibilities. He'll be okay."

Geoff sighed, picked up one of the egg-mice and put it in his mouth. His molars cracked down on something hard and a hot, bitter taste washed through him. "I knew you were putting me on with these," he said, his eyes watering. "Nobody ever ate this, Roman or not."

"Well, not the eyes," Marcus said. "Those are cloves. What are you, a barbarian?"

Geoff was starting up his car when he saw a figure by the restaurant's back door, illuminated by the headlights. Geoff rolled down his window and called his name.

Attius turned, looked at him and bolted for the street. Geoff fumbled with the handle to get out, but by the time he had the door open the boy was gone.

Geoff stood in the parking lot, weighing Marcus' words against what he had just seen. Of course, running wasn't always a sign of guilt, but it didn't look good. Still, Marcus was right about one thing—the idea of a kid like Attius running around with a gang, getting into fights, just felt wrong. He remembered Attius from his earlier visits to the Columellae: a serious kid, well enough integrated, small for his age but mature—not unlike Geoff himself had been. One of his success stories, he had always thought.

The next afternoon Geoff drove to the high school Attius attended. It was a typical mid-sixties monstrosity, modified a dozen times in response to growing and shrinking enrolment; an added ring spurred off of the original square building, with portable classroom trailers clustered around the parking lot entrance. After checking in with the office, showing his ID and passing through the metal detector—this place had as much security as the Welcome Centre—he climbed up to the third floor and started counting down classrooms to 326. He knocked at the door, saw the teacher within glance up from the overhead projector and throw him a look of annoyance.

"Sorry," Geoff said, holding up the call slip the office had given him. The class had erupted in chatter as soon as the teacher's attention was distracted, and he felt the weight of her gaze on him. "I need to see Attius Columella."

"They usually phone," the teacher said, brushing her dark hair away from her face. Geoff shrugged, and she turned back to the class. "Attius, this man needs to see you." Then, to Geoff: "Make sure he comes right back when he's done."

Geoff watched the class as Attius rose, and listened: most of the chatter was in barracks Latin, half the boys in the class wearing toga tops or Not Fallen t-shirts. Attius did not share in either look: instead he wore a short-sleeved red shirt over jeans, and his hair was cut in a modern style.

"My name's Geoff—Galfridius," Geoff said, closing the classroom door. "I've come to see your mother a few times, check on how you and she are doing. Do you remember me?"

Attius nodded. "Is my mother all right?" he asked.

"That's not what I'm here about," Geoff said. He half-crouched, looked Attius in the eye. "Why did you run last night? When I saw you at Mello's?"

"I didn't know that was you," Attius said after too long of a pause. He glanced back at the classroom. "I thought it was some guys who were after me."

"Some guys," Geoff said. "Anything you need to tell me about?"

"No," Attius said quickly. "It was just—you know, these jerks . . ."

"Uh huh." Geoff stood up to his full height. "You saw me before you ran. I called your name."

Looking away, Attius said, "I thought you were someone else."

"Are you working for Marcus? Mr. Apicius?"

Attius said nothing.

"It's important you tell me, Attius. If he's got you mixed up in something—"

"It's not like that," Attius said, scowling.

"Then what's it like? It might not just be you in trouble here . . ."

"What are they going to do? Deport us?" Attius said, looking up at him.

Geoff took a breath. "Not every prefugee has it as good as you and your mother do—you go to school here, you know that. You could lose the subsidy on your apartment, your mother could lose her work permit . . ."

"It's not like that," Attius said after a long silence. "He's just—some of us want better, you know?"

"You're a smart kid, Attius. You can go anywhere in this world if you just stay focused."

"Yeah, in this world. What good is that? I go to college, get a job, turn into a modern like you—what good does any of that do to the ones we left behind?"

Geoff sighed. It was a common enough attitude among the prefugees, especially the young boys: to succeed in the modern world was a betrayal of their own culture and people—better to spend your days drunk on the triclinium, blasting hex-hop on the stereo and dreaming of past glory. He was surprised to hear it from Attius, though. "So what were you doing at the restaurant?" he asked. "He sells you and your friends a little wine, you reminisce about way back in the day?"

Attius looked at him for a moment, then laughed. "No, it's nothing like that," he said, shaking his head. "He's going to take us home."

"Are you crazy?" Geoff asked, pushing open the door to Marcus's condo.

"Do come in," Marcus said. He was wearing a house toga and sandals, took a careful step back from the doorway. "Make yourself at home; I do, but then I live here."

"Don't," Geoff said, pointing a finger at Marcus. "Don't do that—that injured gravitas thing you do. This is important." He paused for breath. Once through the door, Marcus's apartment might easily have been a villa; the tiled floor was inlaid with a mosaic of a dog and the words CAVE CANEM, while three triclinia covered with red silk cushions were arranged in a triangle. Steam was wafting from one of the inner doorways.

"I was about to have a bath," Marcus said mildly. "Will you join me? The tepidarium is a bit small, but there's steam enough for two."

"What are you trying to do? These kids, they don't have enough money to make them worth grifting."

A tiny flicker of genuine concern crossed Marcus's face. "You spoke to Attius, I suppose?" he asked. Geoff nodded, and Marcus crossed to one of the triclinia and sat down. "Well. Have a seat, then, and we'll talk about it."

Geoff moved to a triclinium and sat on it upright, as though it was a bench. "Talk, then."

"Why don't you start, Geoffrey? Just what did he tell you?"

"He said—" Geoff paused, took a breath. "He thinks you can take him home."

"Ah." Marcus reached up to scratch at his jaw; he was, unusually, unshaven, and a shadow had covered his cheeks and chin. "Well. There it is, then."

"Wait," Geoff said after a moment had passed. "You're serious? The fissures don't work that way, you know that."

"Do you?" Marcus asked. "Do you know it, truly? Or have you been told it?"

"It can't work that way. The paradox—"

"Spoken like a modern. Some of us have faith in our gods to bring us home."

Geoff held up a hand. "Forget that for now, I need to understand this. You're going to take a bunch of kids back and then—what? Nuke Carthage, shoot Goths with machine guns?"

"Carthago delenda est," Marcus said, not smiling. "You should know that. We don't need to bring guns or bombs; once we're home, we can build everything we need—enough, anyway. My boys have studied well for this."

"Is your life really so bad? This city is full of opportunities—"

"Can you call it a city?" Marcus asked. "No gymnasium, no theatre, no forum? Where is the life a Roman man should lead?"

"You really believe it," Geoff said. "This whole thing, you really think you can do it." He shook his head. "Just how do you expect to get into the Welcome Centre?"

Marcus frowned, an actor's impression of sorrow. "For that part, regrettably, guns will be necessary. But there's no reason anyone has to be hurt, Geoffrey—"

"You idiot," Geoff said, rising to his feet. "If there's even a chance that you're right, the guards will have orders to shoot to kill—they let one person through and all of history could be changed."

"Regrettable, as I said. But I see no choice, and anyway Mars must always have his due."

"You—I work at the Welcome Centre, Marcus. I could get you in." Geoff turned away. "You didn't even ask me."

For a long time neither of them spoke, both watching each other's faces.

"You, Galfridius?" Marcus said at last.

Geoff took a step towards the door, paused. "I'm still a Roman."

"You might have told the police."

Turning back to face Marcus, Geoff said "I haven't, have I?"

Marcus shook his head. "Will you?"

"Are you—you're really going through with this?" Geoff asked. Marcus nodded. "What I do, it helps our people, here and now. I'm not chasing some crazy revenge fantasy."

"I commend you for it. The great majority of our people benefit very much from what you do."

Geoff began to turn away again, stopped. "I can get you in," he said at last. "Nobody has to get hurt."

"No," Marcus said. "I can't let you. Your job—"

Geoff shook his head. "My job isn't going to get any easier if a dozen Romans get killed breaking into a Welcome Centre. I still don't think this is going to work, but I can at least keep any blood from being shed."

"Are you sure?" Marcus asked, cocking an eyebrow. "We can't afford to have anyone who isn't committed."

"I'll do it—but you're not bringing any kids. That's my condition."

Marcus regarded Geoff for a long moment, nodded slowly. "All right, then," he said. "How soon can you get us in?"

Between visiting the Aemiliani, the restaurant, the school and Marcus's apartment Geoff had been away from the office for most of two days; not an unusually long time, given the nature of his job, but long enough for a pile of message slips to accumulate on his desk.

Flipping through them he found several from Fulvia Columella, on each of which both the PLEASE CALL and WILL CALL BACK boxes were checked. He picked up his phone and started dialling, stopped halfway through.

"Problem?" Wayne said.

Geoff shook his head as he turned in his chair. Wayne's bulky shape filled the doorway, all straight lines and skin so dark it shone; though about half the case officers were resettled Romans like Geoff, everyone from Wayne on up were moderns. "No, just a bit behind."

Wayne did not move from the doorway, regarding Geoff with narrowed eyes. "You've been out a lot. Anything I should know about?"

"Nothing unusual," Geoff said, shrugged. "Why do you ask?"

"Just checking on workload," Wayne said, his tone suddenly casual. He absent-mindedly picked Geoff's stapler up off his desk, pulled it open. "OT budget's tapped for the quarter, you know."

Geoff rolled his eyes, nodded. "I know, I know," he said; then, as Wayne slowly turned to go, "Hey, Wayne—where's your family from?"

"Toronto."

"No, you know—before that."

"Sierra Leone, on my dad's side—his mother came over about forty years ago." Wayne snapped the stapler shut. "Why do you ask?"

"Just curious," Geoff said. "You know much about it?"

Wayne shrugged. "My dad took me when I was about ten."

"You ever think about going back?"

"Nah. Dad used to send money home, when he could."

"How about you?" Geoff asked.

Wayne's brow furrowed into a slight frown. "I've got a family to take care of, Geoff. Wife and three kids—they've all got a life they wouldn't have if my grandma hadn't come here."

"I know," Geoff said.

"How about you?" Wayne asked. He dropped Geoff's stapler back onto his desk. "How come you don't have all that Roman shit like the other guys do?"

Geoff glanced back at his desk; the only personal item on it was the calendar illustrated with erotic frescoes from Pompeii, a gag gift from his colleagues. "Just not my thing, I guess."

"Know what you mean," Wayne said, turning to leave. "You need help with anything, let me know, okay?"

"Sure," Geoff said. He watched Wayne go back out into the hall, counted to ten before turning back to his desk and the problem at hand. It wasn't enough just to get Marcus's people into the building; they had to be there when a fissure was open, when the Centre would be at its busiest. And, of course, even if he got them into the reception room there would be no way to get them back out again other than through the fissure. If Marcus was wrong. . . .

Geoff's phone rang, the call display panel showing Fulvia's number. He briefly considered pretending to be out, keyed the call to go through to his wire. "Hello, Mrs. Columella," he said.

"Galfridius, it's Fulvia Columella." Some technologies seemed forever obscure to the Romans that had come as adults, call display among them. "Did you to my son talk?"

"Yes."

"Well, is Attius in trouble?"

"I don't think so," Geoff said carefully.

"It's only I haven't seen him," Fulvia said, "not since the day you were here. Did he to you anything say, about somewhere going?"

Geoff shut his eyes. "I'm sorry, Fulvia," he said. "I saw him yesterday at school, but he didn't say anything about not coming home." Not exactly, anyway. "Does he ever stay over at a friend's, maybe?"

"I phoned."

"I'll look into it," Geoff said. "Was there anything else you wanted?"

There was a moment's pause before Fulvia said "No. No, Galfridius, thank you."

Geoff nodded—the wire would transmit it—hung up. He should call the school, he thought, find out if Attius had been in class. The thought of school started his mind down a suddenly obvious path, and he opened the second drawer of his desk and took out the emergency handbook. He had been thinking like a bureaucrat, when he should have been thinking like a student: his own high school had been just as paranoid as Attius's, but there had been one thing sure to throw it into chaos.

The warning tone sounded over the PA as the sensors detected a fissure forming. Geoff, sitting in his office, was on call: if his name came up his pager would let him know to go to the reception room. Without waiting for that, he picked up the phone and dialled.

"It's on," he said as soon as the line picked up. "Twenty minutes."

Hanging up, Geoff got up from his desk and stepped into the hall. There was no visible increase in activity, but he knew that forces were mustering to keep the prefugees that would soon arrive in the reception room—and, more importantly to him, keep anyone else out: guards were on alert, doors inside and out automatically locked. He strolled casually to the southwest corner of the building, where most of the offices were unoccupied, checked his watch. When fifteen minutes had passed he reached up and pulled the fire alarm, and a piercing wail filled the air.

Now the halls were busy: it had been months since the last fire drill, and few people remembered where their fire exit was. Geoff heard frantic steps echoing as the inhabitants fled. Only a few passed by him on their way out, and they were too busy to notice he was not following; once the halls were quiet Geoff went to the reception room. The most sensitive place in the building, its doors automatically stayed locked even when the alarm sounded—except when a fissure had formed; nobody wanted prefugees trapped in a sealed room during a fire.

Marcus reached the door just a minute after Geoff did. A half-dozen young men followed him, each in teens or early twenties, all dressed in jacket, shirt and jeans. Geoff scanned their faces, felt only a little surprise at seeing Attius among them.

"I said no kids," he said to Marcus. "We had a deal."

"These are my soldiers," Marcus said. "We couldn't go ahead otherwise." He put his hands on his hips, looked to left and right. "And you, Geoffrey, did you betray me? Are the police waiting for us in there?"

"No," Geoff said.

"Then all our games are played, and we know who is the victor." Marcus cocked an eyebrow, awaiting a challenge.

"What are you waiting for?" one of Marcus's followers said. "Let's go."

Geoff looked at him, then at the other young men, found he recognized them all: each was a success story like Attius, the ones that had managed to overcome the poverty and dislocation. Each one was a boy without a father; each, he now saw, was a boy whom he had failed. "Are you all sure about this?" Geoff asked the boy who had spoken—Gallienus, he was called—moving slightly to stand in front of the doorway. "You know, even if you can go through, we get prefugees from all different periods. You might wind up anytime *ab urbe conditum*."

"We'll manage," Marcus said.

Not looking at him, Geoff spoke to Attius. "You won't have a family, you know, or land of your own. You'll be all alone, and penniless."

Attius looked doubtful for a moment, while Gallienus took a step toward the door. "Not for long," he said. "With everything we know about chemistry, and mining—"

"And everyone knows the Romans loved change," Geoff said. "That's why they invented the steam engine." A few of the boys looked to one another, brows furrowed. "And the compass, and the printing press. They just loved new ideas."

"He's just stalling," Marcus said. "Upset at being tricked, so he hopes to keep us here till the police arrive." He took a step closer, so that he and Geoff were nose to nose. "Step aside, Geoffrey."

Geoff shrugged, moved aside to let the others pass through the doorway and then followed them into the reception room. Inside the light was starting to flicker as the fissure opened; after a moment four dark figures appeared within, three short and one tall.

"Now," Marcus said.

Holding up a hand, Geoff said, "Just a minute. Why don't you see where it is you're headed?"

The figures in the fissure were fully visible now: a woman and three children, each dirty, dishevelled and gaunt with starvation. The eldest was a boy of about ten or eight; he wore a gladius at his belt, so oversized on him that the tip grazed the floor. When he saw the group awaiting them his hand went to the hilt.

"It's all right, little boy," Marcus said, then turned back to the others. "Get through, while it's still open."

The boy looked up at the woman behind him, then moved to stand in front of her and drew his sword with both hands. "Don't worry, mother," he said in deeply archaic Latin. "I'll protect you."

Marcus's followers stood still, uncertain. Attius looked to Marcus, then to Geoffrey. "What do we do?" he asked.

The light of the fissure was starting to dim, and Marcus took a step forward. "He's just a boy," he said, reaching out to seize the sword.

"Not anymore," Geoff said quietly. "He has to take care of his mother now, and his sisters. He's a man." He moved behind Marcus, took hold of his wrist and drew it away from the boy's sword. Then, moving Marcus out of the way, he crouched to speak with the boy at eye-level. "Welcome, friend," he said in the same early Latin the boy had spoken. "What is your name?"

The boy glanced over his shoulder, to where the light of the fissure was flickering. "My name is Quintus Rufinus," he said, working hard to deepen his voice. "Tell me where we are."

"It is a safe place," Geoff said, "far from the dangers you have fled. You must make a choice, though: if you stay here you can never go back." He straightened up to his full height. "Would you like to stay?"

Quintus gripped the hilt of his sword with both hands, looked back at his mother; the fading light flickered on her face as the boy turned back to Geoff, nodded twice.

Geoff's hand paused over the Pompeii calendar, finally picked it up and dropped it into the box containing the few contents of his desk. He took a breath, turned as he sensed Wayne's bulk filling the doorway.

"You leaving, then?" Wayne said, clearing his throat.

"Yeah. Sorry for the short notice."

"Don't worry about me. Where you going?"

"I don't know yet." Geoff shrugged. "I just know these kids need something the Centre can't give them, and right now they're getting it from the wrong place."

Wayne nodded. "Fair enough," he said. "This wouldn't have anything to do with that mess the other day, would it?"

Turning back to his box, Geoff took a breath. "Why?" he asked. "Did you talk to the police about it?"

"Didn't see any reason to—just an unscheduled fire drill, right?"

"Right." Geoff stood still for a moment, turned around once more. "Wayne—could you go through the fissure? Go back?"

Wayne looked at him for a long time before finally speaking. "Would it make a difference?" he asked. "Would you go, if you could?"

Geoff shook his head. "No," he said. "I've got a family to take care of."

Public Safety

Officier de la Paix Louverture folded Quartidi's Père Duchesne into thirds, fanning himself against the Thermidor heat. The news inside was all bad, anyway: another theatre had closed, leaving the Comédie Francaise the only one open in Nouvelle-Orleans. At least the Duchesne could be counted on to report only what the Corps told them to, that the Figaro had closed for repairs, and not the truth—which was that audiences, frightened by the increasing number of fires and other mishaps at the theatres, had stopped coming. The Minerve was harder to control, but the theatre-owners had been persuaded not to talk to their reporters, to avoid a public panic. No matter that these were all clearly accidents: even now, in the year 122, reason was often just a thin layer of ice concealing a pre-Revolutionary sea of irrationality.

On the table in front of him sat his plate of beignets, untouched. He had wanted them when he had sat down, but the arrival of the group of *gardiens stagières* to the café made him lose his appetite. He told himself it was just his cynicism that caused him to react this way, his desire to mock their pride in their spotless uniforms and caps, and not the way they looked insolently in his direction as they ordered their cafés au lait. Not for the first time Louverture wondered if he should have stayed in Saint-Domingue.

The *gardiens stagières* gave a cry as another of their number entered the café, but instead of heading for their table he approached Louverture. As he neared, Louverture recognized him: Pelletier, a runner, who despite being younger than the just-graduated bunch across the room had already seen a great deal more than they.

"Excuse me, sir," Pelletier said. Though it was early, sweat had already drawn a thick line across the band of his cap: he must have run all the way from the Cabildo. "Commandant Trudeau needs to see you right away."

Louverture nodded, glanced at his watch: it was three eighty-five, almost time to start work anyway. "Thank you, Pelletier," he said; the young man's face brightened at the use of his name. "My coffee and beignets just arrived, and it seems I won't have time to enjoy them; why don't you take a moment to rest?" He reached into his pocket, dropped four deci-francs in a careful pile on the table.

"Thank you, sir," Pelletier said; he took off his cap, revealing a thick bristle of sweat-soaked blond hair.

Louverture tapped his own cap in reply, headed for the west exit of the Café du Monde; he lingered there for a moment, just out of sight, watched as Pelletier struggled to decide whether to sit at the table he had just vacated or join the group of young gardiens who were, assuming that out of sight meant out of hearing, now making sniggering comments about café au lait and *créole* rice. When Pelletier chose the empty table Louverture smiled to himself, stepped out onto Danton Street.

It had grown hotter, appreciably, in the time since he had arrived at the café; such people as were about clung to the shade like lizards, loitering under the awnings of the building where the Pasteur Brewery made its tasteless beer. Louverture crossed the street at a run, dodging the constant flow of velocipedes, and braced himself for the sun-bleached walk across Descartes Square. He walked past the statue of the Goddess of Reason, with her torch of inquiry and book of truth; the shadow of her torch reached out to the edge of the square, where stencilled numbers marked the ten hours of the day. He doffed his cap to her as always, then gratefully reached the shadows of the colonnade that fronted the Cabildo, under the inscription that read RATIO SUPER FERVEO.

"Commandant Trudeau wishes to see you, sir," the gardien at the desk said. The stern portrait of Jacques Hébert on the wall behind glowered down at them.

Louverture nodded, went up the stairs to Trudeau's office. Inside he saw Trudeau at his desk, looking over a piece of paper; Officier de la Paix Principal Clouthier was standing nearby.

"Louverture, good to see you," Trudeau said. His sharp features and high forehead reminded those who met him of Julius Caesar; modestly, Trudeau underlined the resemblance by placing a bust of the Roman emperor on his desk. "I'm sorry to call you in early, but an important case has come up, something I wanted you to handle personally."

"Of course, sir. What is it?"

Trudeau passed the paper to him. "What do you make of this?" It was a sheet of A4 paper, on which were written the words *Elle meurt la treize.*

"'She dies on the thirteenth,'" Louverture read. "This is a photostat. There is very little else I can say about it."

"Physical Sciences has the original," Clouthier put in. His round face was redder than usual, with the heat; where Trudeau let his hair grow in long waves, Clouthier kept his cut short to the skull, like a man afraid of lice. "They barely consented to making two copies, one for us and one for the Graphologist."

"And Physical Sciences will tell you it is a sheet of paper such as can be bought at any stationer's," Louverture said, "and the ink is everyday ink, and the envelope—if they remember to examine the envelope—was sealed with ordinary glue. They will not tell you what the letter smells like, or the force with which the envelope was sealed, because these things cannot be measured."

"Which is why we need you," Trudeau said. "Concentrate on the text for the moment: the other parts will fall into place in time."

"I take it there was no ransom demand?" Louverture said; Trudeau nodded. That was why they had called him, of course: his greatest successes had been in finding the logic behind crimes that seemed, to others, to be irrational. Crimes they thought a little black blood made him better able to solve.

"No daughters of prominent families missing, either, so far as we know," Clouthier said. "We have *gardiens stagières* canvassing them now."

Louverture smiled, privately, at the thought of the group at the café being called away on long, hot velocipede rides around the city. "Of course, the families of kidnap victims often choose not to inform the police—though rationally, they have much better chances with us involved. Still, I do not think that is the case here: if a kidnapper told the family not to involve the police, why the letter to us? Tell me, Commandant, to whom was the letter addressed? Did it come by mail or was it delivered by hand?"

"By hand," Clouthier said before Trudeau could answer. "Pinned on one of the flames of Reason's torch—a direct challenge to us."

"Strange, though, that they should give us so much time to respond," Trudeau mused. "The thirteenth of Fructidor is just under two décades away. Why so much warning? It seems irrational."

"Crimes by sane men are always for gain, real or imagined," Louverture said. "If not money, then perhaps power, as a man murders his wife's lover to regain his lost power over her. The whole point may be to see how much power such a threat can give this man over us. Perhaps the best thing would be to ignore this, at least for now."

"And let him think he's cowed us?" Clouthier said.

"The Corps de Commande is not cowed," Trudeau said gently. "We judge, sanely and rationally, if something is an accident or a crime; should it be a crime, we take the most logical course of action appropriate. But in this case, Officier Louverture, I think we must respond. If you are correct, ignoring this person would only lead him to do more in hopes of getting a response from us. If you are incorrect, then we certainly must take action, do you agree?"

"Of course, Commandant," Louverture said.

"Very good. I have the Lombrosologist working on a composite sketch; once you have findings from him, Graphology, and Physical Sciences, the investigation is yours. I expect daily reports."

Louverture nodded, saluted the two men, and stepped out into the hall. Clouthier closed the heavy live-oak door after he left, and Louverture could hear out his name being spoken three times in the minute he stood there. He hurried down the steps to the cool basement where the scientific services were and went into the

Lombrosology department, knocking on the door as he opened it.

"Allard, what do you have for me?" he called.

"Your patience centre is sorely underdeveloped," a voice said from across the room. "Along with your minuscule amatory faculty, it makes for a singularly misshapen skull."

The laboratory was a mess, as always; labelled busts on every shelf and table, and skulls in such profusion that without Allard's cheerful disposition the place would have seemed like a charnel house. Instead it felt more like a child's playroom, the effect magnified by the scientist's system of colour-coding the skulls: a dab of red paint for executed criminals, green for natural deaths, and a cheery bright blue for suicides. In the corner of the room Allard sat at the only desk with open space on it, carefully measuring a Lombroso bust with a pair of calipers and recording the results.

Louverture picked up a skull from the table nearest him; it had a spot of red paint and the words *Meurtrier—Nègre* written on it. "It is not my skull I am concerned with today," he said.

"But it is such a fascinating specimen," Allard said in full sincerity. He had asked Louverture repeatedly to let him make a detailed study of his skull: on their first meeting he had, without introduction, run his hands over Louverture's head and pronounced that he was fortunate to have the rational faculty of the Frank and the creativity of the Negro.

"Could we stick to the matter at hand?" Louverture said.

"Of course, of course." Allard put down his calipers, turned his full attention to Louverture. "My sketch won't be ready for an hour or so, though."

"Never mind that. What can you tell me about the man who wrote the letter?"

Allard picked up the notes he had been consulting, peered through his pince-nez as he flipped through them. "He is most likely not a habitual criminal, so he will lack the prominent jaw we associate with that type. He also likely possesses a need for self-aggrandizement—a man of whom more was expected, perhaps, with very likely a prominent forehead. The need for attention suggests a second child or later, so look for a round skull overall—"

"I wasn't aware you could tell birth order," Louverture said, putting the skull in his hand back on the table.

"You haven't been keeping up with the literature. It was in last Pluviôse's Journal—the mother's parts, not yet stretched with birth, pinch the first child's head, rendering it more pointed than later children. All else being equal, of course."

Louverture nodded. "Yes, of course. And—the race—?" He was accustomed to tip-toeing around the subject; most of his colleagues seemed to feel they were doing him a favour by treating him as white to his face and black behind his back.

"A tricky question," Allard said, apparently feeling no discomfort at the topic. In fact he was likely the least prejudiced man in the Corps, genuinely seeing black and white as scientific categories. "What we know shows significant forethought, which suggests a Frank or perhaps an Anglo-Saxon; the apparent motive, however, is irrational, which of course suggests a Negro. On the whole, I would tend to favour one of the European types. Why? Do you suspect . . ."

"It's nothing," Louverture said, letting the unspoken question hang in the air. It was the reason he had been given the case, of course: the fear that this was the work of irrationalists, believers in religion and black magic. The vodoun murders of three years previous had brought him here from Saint-Domingue, and though they had earned him his office and reputation, he had often heard whispers that like follows like.

"I can give you a sketch for each race, if you like," Allard said. "It will take a bit longer, of course."

"Take your time. The sketch will be of little use until we have a suspect to compare it to."

Allard nodded abstractly, his attention returned to the model head in front of him. "As you say."

Louverture tipped his cap in farewell, stepped out into the hallway and headed up the stairs towards his office, wondering how he might conduct an investigation in which he did not have a single lead. A cryptic threat to an unidentified woman, an unmailed letter delivered by an unseen hand. . . . Clouthier's canvass would turn up nothing, of course; if the culprit did not want a ransom, he might just as easily take a poor woman, or even a prostitute.

By the time he reached his office Louverture had decided that Allard's delay, as well as the no-doubt slow progress of the graphologist and of Physical Sciences, gave him the excuse to do just what he had first proposed: ignore the whole matter and hope the letter-writer went away, or at least provided him with another clue. He was disappointed, therefore, to open his office door and find the graphologist's report sitting on his desk. Louverture settled into his chair, lit the halogen lamp, and began to read. Open curves, large space between letters: male. Confident pen-strokes: written cool-headed, without excitement or fear of discovery. He frowned. That did not square with the notion that the letter-writer was seeking to arouse a reaction from the police, but what other motive made sense? Correctly formed letters: well-educated in a good school. This seemed even more illogical. Anyone who received an education knew that all criminals were eventually caught, save those whose confederates turned on them first. Neat, precise capitals: a man of some authority.

Louverture closed his eyes, rubbed at them with thumb and forefinger. A confident man who nevertheless had a pathological need for attention, and felt neither fear nor excitement in taunting the police—as though the message had been composed and written by two different men. The writer, though, had not been coerced, since the letters showed no fear, so what sort of partnership was he looking at? An intelligent criminal with tremendous sang-froid, paired with an insecure, weak-willed . . . but no, it made no sense. The former would restrain the latter from any attention-getting activities, not assist in them; unless a bargain of some sort was involved, the cool-headed man having to gratify the other's needs in order to gain something he required. Access to something he possessed, perhaps—or someone—

Well, it was a pretty play he had written: all he needed was a pair of actors to play the parts. Louverture tore a piece of paper from the pad on his desk, uncapped his fountain pen, and wrote Imagine two criminals—group like faculties on it. The first criminal, the cool-headed one, would have had little contact with the police, but the second, he very likely could not help it. He opened the bottom drawer of his desk, rummaged inside for a tube labelled LOMBROSOLOGIE; rolled the paper up, tucked it in the tube, and pushed the whole thing into the pneumatic. Standing, he turned the neck of his lamp to point its beam at his bookshelf, then scanned the leather-bound volumes of the Rogues' Gallery there. What would the excitable man's earlier crimes have been? Nothing spectacular, but at the same time something directed at gaining attention. Public nudity, perhaps? Harassment? A man with a wife, a daughter, a sister, perhaps a domestic living in. A man with little self-control, and yet not truly poor, or else how would he have met the educated man he was partnered with? If not poor, though, his neighbours would have complained about the noise that almost certainly came from his house; Louverture took Volume 23, Noise Infractions, off the shelf and added it to the pile on the desk.

He was not sure how much time had passed when he heard the door open. He looked up from the book in front of him, expecting to see Allard with his sketches; instead it was Clouthier. Louverture stood, gave a small salute.

"Officier Principal, what can I do for you?"

Clouthier cleared his throat, brushed at his dark blue jacket with his fingertips. "It's past six. Are we going to see your progress report today?"

"I haven't received anything from Lombrosology or Physical Sciences yet."

"I'm told you haven't given orders to any of the gardiens to search or arrest anyone. Have you spent the whole day reading books?" Clouthier asked, looking around at Louverture's desk and shelves with distaste.

"I've been rounding up known criminals," Louverture said. "Doing it this way saves your men time and energy. Incidentally, are my reports not to go to Commandant Trudeau?"

"To him through me. Public safety is my responsibility, and I must respond quickly to any threat."

"We have almost twenty days," Louverture said mildly.

"If whoever wrote that letter is being truthful. Have you often known criminals to be truthful, Louverture?"

"Why bother to give us the letter and then lie in it? If he wanted to avoid detection, wouldn't it have been better not to alert us at all?"

Clouthier coughed loudly. "It's nonsense to expect him to be logical—if he were a rational man, he'd know better than to be a criminal."

Louverture nodded. "As you say. I'll make sure my report is on your desk before you go—how much longer were you planning on staying tonight?"

"Never mind," Clouthier said. "Just have it there before I get here in the morning."

"Of course. Is there anything else?"

Clouthier seemed to think for a moment, then shook his head, turned to leave. "Just keep me informed."

Louverture waited until Clouthier was out the door, then called to him. "Oh, Officer Principal, I forgot to ask—did your canvass turn anything up?"

With a barely perceptible shake of his head, Clouthier stepped out into the hall. Though he could not help smiling, Louverture wondered whether that had been a miscalculation. It was no secret that Clouthier did not like him, a situation caused as much by his coming from outside the local Corps hierarchy as by his mixed blood. It would be best, he thought, to leave off further teasing of the lion for now. Resolving to restrain himself better, Louverture returned to his desk and began writing his report.

The next morning Louverture was reading over his notes, trying to get them to make sense. He had taken the omnibus instead of his velocipede so that he could read on his way to work, laying the pages on the briefcase on his lap, but the heat and vibration kept him from concentrating. His cap was damp with sweat, but he refused to take it off; he knew from experience how people reacted when they saw his dark, kinked hair emerge from under an *officier*'s hat. Not that there were many people to react this morning, the omnibus being only half-full.

He forced his mind to return to its task. If his theory was right, the second man was undoubtedly the key, but he had not found anyone in the Rogues' Gallery that fit the profile. Could a man with such a need for attention possibly have hidden it all these years? Perhaps he had had another outlet until recently—an actor, for instance, put out of work by the theatre closings. . . .

A sudden jolt interrupted Louverture's train of thought. He looked up from his notes, saw that the omnibus had stopped in the middle of the street; the driver had already disembarked, and the other passengers were filing off, grumbling.

"Excuse me," he said to the man in front of him, "what has happened?"

"It broke down again," the man said. "Third time this month. I'd do better on foot."

Louverture followed the queue onto the sidewalk. A few of the passengers had gathered to wait for the next omnibus, the rest hailing pedicabs or walking off down the street. The driver had the bonnet open and was looking inside; Louverture tapped him on the shoulder. "What is the matter with it?"

The driver turned his head and opened his mouth to speak, closed it when he saw Louverture's uniform. "It's corroded, sir," he said. "Do you smell that?"

Louverture took a sniff; a sharp smell, like lemon but much more harsh, was emanating from the omnibus' hood. "That is the engine?"

"The battery, sir," the driver said. "That's sulphuric acid inside; eventually it eats away at the whole thing."

"This happens often?"

The driver shook his head. "They break down sometimes, but not usually like this. The scientists think it may be the heat."

"And they're sure it's a natural phenomenon? It hasn't been reported to the Corps."

"I suppose," the driver said, shrugged. "Why in Reason's name would anyone sabotage an omnibus? What's to gain from it?"

"Well, I hope they solve the problem soon."

The driver laughed. "Me too. Much longer and I'll need another job—there'll be no-one riding them at all."

Louverture tapped the brim of his cap to the man, stepped over to the curb to hail a pedicab. He could hear the other passengers grumbling a bit when one stopped at the sight of his badge, saw the obvious annoyance of the man inside whose cab he had commandeered. He disliked being so high-handed, but he could not afford to be late: after his little dig at Clouthier the night before, the man would be looking for reasons to undermine him.

His fears were realized when he arrived at the Cabildo at three ninety-five and the gardien at the desk waved him over. "Officier Principal Clouthier is waiting for you in the interrogation room, sir," he said.

Louverture tapped his cap in acknowledgement and went through the big double doors that led to the interrogation and holding areas, hoping Clouthier had not done anything that would make his job more difficult. When he arrived at the interrogation room he saw the man himself, talking to the gardien at the door to the cell.

"Louverture, nice of you to come in," Clouthier said, bursting with scarcely restrained smugness.

"What's this?" Louverture asked, looked through one of the recessed portholes in the wall; he saw, inside, a dark-skinned Negro sitting at the table. "You have a suspect? How did you find him?"

"He was in possession of another copy of the note, along with paper, pen and ink that precisely matched those used to write the letter, according to Physical Sciences," Clouthier said. "So we brought him in."

Louverture took a long breath in and out. "And just how did you find this particular pen-and-paper owner?"

"I had my men search some of the worse areas of Tremé at dawn this morning. I am not afraid to expend a little time and energy, if it gets results."

"And I suppose he vigorously resisted arrest? I ask only because black skin shows bruises so poorly, I might not know otherwise."

"A little rough handling only. Commandant Trudeau directed that I leave the interrogation to you."

"Gracious thanks," Louverture said. "If you'll excuse me."

He nodded to the gardien to open the door and went inside. The suspect was sitting on a light cane chair, his hands chained behind his back; his face, at least, was unmarked. "I am Officier de la Paix Louverture," he said in a calm voice. "What is your name?"

"Duhaime," the man stuttered. "Lucien Duhaime." His eyes darted to the door.

"We are alone," Louverture said. "You may speak freely. Do you know why you have been arrested, Monsieur Duhaime?"

"I didn't—I don't know how that paper got there."

"Someone planted paper, pen and ink in your house, without you knowing?" Duhaime opened his mouth to speak, closed it again. Louverture shook his head. "Well then, how did it get there?"

"I don't. I don't know."

"I see." Louverture sighed. Now there was one man to compose the note, another to write it, a third to deliver it: too large a cast for the play to be believable. Sitting down opposite Duhaime, he realized he still had his briefcase with him; in a sudden inspiration he set it on the table, opened it with the top towards the prisoner, so Duhaime could not see the contents. "I keep the tools of my trade in this case, Lucien. Do you know what they are?"

Duhaime shook his head.

"The most important one is my razor."

Duhaime's eyes widened. Louverture took out his badge, tapped on the image of a razor and metron, crossed. "This razor was given to me by a Monsieur Abelard, but it is not an ordinary razor. Instead of shaving hair, it lets me shave away what is improbable and leaves only the truth." He peered over the open case at Duhaime. "It tells me that you wrote a note with that pen and paper, and placed it on the statue of Reason in Descartes Square, and that we must therefore charge you with suspicion of kidnapping." Duhaime took an involuntary breath, confirming Louverture's suspicion. He took the day's paper from the case, showed the headline to Duhaime. It read *Feu dans le marché: deuxieme du mois*. "Have you seen this? 'Manhunt for kidnapper.' You've cost a lot of time and trouble, Lucien."

"I didn't know anything about a kidnapping. I didn't know!" Duhaime tried to rise to his feet, was restrained by the chain fastening him to the table. "The man, he gave me three pieces of paper, said he'd pay if I delivered them for him. I thought it was a prank."

Louverture leaned back, rubbed his chin. "You've intrigued me, Lucien. Tell me about this man."

Duhaime shrugged, winced as he did so; Louverture saw his right shoulder was probably dislocated. "He was a rich man, well-dressed. A man like you."

"A policier?"

"No, a white."

"A convincing story requires more detail, Lucien," Louverture said, shaking his head sadly.

"He spoke well, though he was trying not to. Clean shaven, with a narrow face. He wore those little smoke-tinted glasses, so I didn't see his eyes."

"And just where did someone like you meet this wealthy, well-spoken man?"

"I have a pedicab. It's good money since the omnibuses started breaking down." Duhaime looked at Louverture's unbelieving eyes, then down at the table. "I stole it."

"Very well. Where did you pick him up?"

"On Baronne street, just west of the Canal. He was going to the ferry dock."

"Would you recognize him if you saw him again? Or a picture?"

"I'll try," Duhaime said, nodding eagerly.

Louverture closed his briefcase, rose to his feet. "Very well, Lucien, we shall test your theory," he said. "You'll remain our guest for the time being, and I'll see your shoulder gets looked at."

"Thank you, *officier*."

"It's nothing." Louverture turned to go, paused. "Oh, one thing more. You said you were given three copies: we found the one you planted on the statue, and one more you had. Where is the other?"

"I was to deliver one every night," Duhaime said.

"Where?"

"The statue, first; second the newspaper; and then Reason Cathedral."

"So you delivered the second last night? To the Père Duchesne?"

Duhaime shook his head. "No, sir. The other paper."

Louverture swore under his breath, turned to the door and knocked on it harshly. The gardien on the other side opened it and he stepped through; Clouthier was still standing there, by one of the portholes in the wall. "We have a problem," Louverture said. "The Minerve has a copy of the letter."

"I'll send a man—"

"It's probably too late. It would have been waiting for them this morning."

Clouthier rolled his eyes. "Assuming your man in there isn't just telling stories."

"He can't read," Louverture said, forcing his voice to stay level. "How do you suppose he wrote the letters? No, he's telling the truth—and by this afternoon everyone will know that 'she dies on the thirteenth.'"

"Perhaps it's a good thing," Clouthier said, shrugged. "It will make people alert; when he strikes, someone will see him and report it to us."

"It will make people panic. With an unfocused threat like this, we'll be sure to get mobs beating anyone they think is suspicious."

"In the poorer neighbourhoods, maybe; we'll set extra patrols in them. But this is not Saint-Domingue, my friend: most of the people here are entirely too rational for that."

"I hope so," Louverture said. Something was nagging at him, some overlooked detail; it slipped away as he probed for it, like a loose tooth.

"At any rate, we still have plenty of time before the thirteenth of Fructidor. Let us hope all the attention doesn't cause our man to move up his timetable."

Louverture nodded, frowned. "Yes, that is strange. Nearly twenty days till then, but only three letters." He turned to the gardien by the door. "Have him moved to a holding cell, and see that his shoulder gets looked at."

The gardien looked from him to Clouthier, who gave a small nod.

"I'd best give the Commandant the news," Clouthier said, then tapped his cap and headed for the stairs.

Watching him go, Louverture wondered how much of his theory could be salvaged. If Duhaime was telling the truth—and Louverture felt sure he was—he had been right about the culprit having a confederate, but he was still left with the impossibility of the letter having been written and composed by the same man. He followed his line of thought up the stairs to his office. When the inescapable conclusion of your assumptions seems impossible, he thought, question your assumptions. His theory depended on at least one of the culprits needing to gain attention for his actions, and the letter to the Minerve certainly supported that; the Père Duchesne would not print it without approval from the Corps. If that was not the motive, though—or one of the motives—everything that followed from it changed; but what other motive could account for everything?

He opened the door to his office, saw four of Allard's sketches sitting on his desk. Two were the ones they had discussed, assuming a single culprit: one version was white, one black. The other two, both white, were a split version of the first, the one having the physiognomy of a cautious, intelligent man, the second one emotional and impulsive. None of them much resembled anyone he had seen in the Rogues' Gallery volumes the night before. He looked them over, wondering if any of them might be the man Duhaime said had hired him. The first two faces were like nobody he had ever seen, impossible configurations of rationality and impulsiveness; the fourth could be almost anyone. The third, though . . . he narrowed his eyes, imagining that man wearing smoke-tinted glasses. He looked a bit like Allard himself, or perhaps one of the men from Physical Sciences. Someone intelligent, certainly. Louverture tried to imagine what his next move would be. Did he know his messenger had been captured? If so, would he find another one, or would his purpose have been achieved with just the first two letters delivered? Would he be lying low or enjoying the chaos that the story in the Minerve would surely spark? No way to know without understanding his motive, and the more Louverture stared at the sketch the more he doubted that this man was seeking a thrill.

Louverture rolled up the sketches, his head starting to feel like a velodrome from the thoughts whizzing around in it. He was missing something, he knew that—some detail, just out of his reach—and he knew that chasing it around and around would not make it appear. Time to do things Clouthier's way: he would have photostats of the sketches made, give them to gardiens assigned to where Baronne crossed the canal and to the ferry dock. Perhaps he could even make some of those snickering stagières pretend to be pedicab drivers, in hopes the culprit would come to them seeking another messenger. He imagined the man was too smart for that, but all it would cost was time and energy.

Cheered, Louverture headed off to the photostat room. Clouthier could hardly complain about this; just to be sure, he would take part in the stakeout himself—at the docks, he thought, where the breeze off the river would make the heat more tolerable. He would be sure to salute all the pedicab drivers dropping off their passengers.

Early the next morning Louverture sat up suddenly in bed, seized by a sudden thought. Two pieces that had not fit: the thirteenth and just three letters to be delivered. If he was right, the two together made up a very important piece indeed, but he could not be sure without a great deal of work—and books that were in the office. He dressed quickly, went downstairs and mounted his velocipede, riding through the empty streets in the dark. Fortunately the rest of the city was still asleep; absorbed as he was by the new lines of thought opening up, he would not have noticed an omnibus bearing down on him. As it was he nearly startled the night guard to death, suddenly appearing in the pool of light cast by the sodium lamps in Descartes Square and skidding to a stop mere metres from the door of the Cabildo. He flashed his badge and rushed up to his office. Hours of reading and calculation later he picked up the speaking tube to call Commandant Trudeau.

"Well, Louverture, here we are," Clouthier said when the three of them assembled, some minutes later, in Trudeau's office. "I take it you are going to tell us you've settled the case by doing figures all night?"

"Not the whole case, no, but I think you'll want to hear it. Tell me, Officier principal, do you know the old calendar at all?"

"The royal calendar, you mean? No, I never studied history. Why?"

"What day of the month is it by that reckoning, do you suppose?" Louverture asked.

"What does it matter?"

Trudeau was smiling, nodding to himself. "May I venture a guess, Officier Louverture?"

Louverture nodded magnanimously.

"Then if you are right, the timetable has been moved up—or rather, it was further along than we knew."

"What do you mean?" Clouthier said, frowning deeply; then, eyes widening, "Oh—so it is the thirteenth today, by that calendar? Of Thermidor, or of Fructidor?"

"Augustus," Trudeau said, with a glance at the bust on his desk. "Very good, Louverture, though I'm afraid this makes things a great deal more serious."

Clouthier ran his head over his shaved scalp. "But I don't understand. Even the English gave up that calendar years ago. Who would still use such an irrational system?"

"Irrationalists," Louverture said with a faint smile. "And the day is no coincidence, either. Thirteen was a very powerful number to pre-rational minds, associated with disaster. Whatever they have in mind may be bigger than even murder."

"You think it is the vodoun again, then? Is this all part of some irrational magic ritual?" Trudeau asked.

Louverture spread his hands. "I don't know. The number thirteen, the royal calendar—yes, that is common to all of those that hew to the old religions. But the letters, no. The vodoun, the Catholics, the Jews, they all rely on secrecy to go undetected."

"Perhaps the letter-writer is not a threat, but a warning?

58

Someone inside this group who wishes to prevent whatever they are planning to do?"

"Then why not tell us more? And why the letters to the Minerve, and the cathedral?" Louverture chewed his lower lip. "If you'll pardon me, that is, Commandant."

Trudeau waved his objection away. "Of course, Officier. Speak freely."

"Moreover, we still have the reports from Graphology and Lombrosology. These tell us the letter-writer is an educated, rational man."

"How can he be a rational irrationalist?" Clouthier put in.

"How indeed?" Trudeau said. "It seems that we resolve one paradox only to create another."

"Commandant, I'm sure I can—"

"I'm sorry, Louverture," Trudeau said, putting up a hand. "Please do not take this as a lack of faith in you, but I am handing this matter over to Officier principal Clouthier. What you have discovered tells me that we must take immediate action."

"But we have no motive! No suspects!"

"We know where our suspects are," Clouthier said. "All the irrationalists—we know where they live, where they have their secret churches. We found your friend Lucien easily enough, didn't we?"

"But—"

"Officier Louverture, I'm told you've been here since one seventy-five. You've rendered great service to the Corps today, and you deserve a rest."

Louverture clamped his mouth shut, nodded. "Thank you, Commandant," he managed to say. With a nod to each of his superiors he rose and left the room.

The sun was beating down outside, causing Louverture to realize he had forgotten his cap at home; as well, his abandoned velocipede was gone. Shading his eyes with his hands he quick-stepped across the square, then ducked into the Café to pick up a Minerve and found a shady spot to wait for the omnibus. The headline, predictably, read *Elle meurt la treize*; further down the page, another story trumpeted

Une autre sabotage aux théatres: la Comedie Francaise ferme ses portes. He folded the paper under his arm, unable to cope with any more irrationality. To whose benefit would it be to sabotage all the theatres, without asking for protection money?

"She's not coming," someone said. He turned to see an older black man in a white cotton shirt and pants, sweating profusely; he had obviously been walking a long way in the sun.

"I'm sorry?" Louverture said.

"The omnibus. She's not coming; broke down at Champs Elysées." The man shook his head. "Sorry, son," he said, continued walking.

Louverture mouthed a curse, scanned the empty street for pedicabs. He supposed that driver had been right in thinking he would be out of a job soon. It was almost like a sort of experiment to see how often buses could break down before people stopped taking them, the way people had stopped going to the theatres. . . .

A terrible, inescapable thought hit him. Desperate to disprove it Louverture set out at a run. His face was red by the time he arrived at the theatre, a very hot half-kilometre away; he banged on the stage door with a closed fist, catching his breath.

"We're closed," a voice came from inside.

"*Corps de commande*," Louverture said. He imagined he could hear the man inside sighing as he opened up.

"What can I do for you?" the man said. He was tall, about a hundred eighty centimetres, with a long face and a deeply receding hairline, wearing black pants and turtleneck. He was quite incidentally blocking the doorway he had just opened.

"May I come in?"

The man's eyes narrowed as he stepped aside. "You say you're with the corps?"

Louverture realized that he was wearing neither his cap nor his uniform, and that his hair was showing. He took out his badge, showed it to the man. "Officier de la paix Louverture. And you are?"

"Gaetan. Gaetan Tremblay. I'm the stage manager. At least. . . ."

Stepping inside, Louverture nodded, held up his copy of the Minerve. "What can you tell me about last night?"

"The cyclorama dropped," Tremblay said. "That's the backdrop that—"

"I know. Was anyone hurt?"

"No—but with all that's happened at the other theatres, people just panicked."

"May I see?"

Tremblay led him down the black, carpeted hallway to the backstage entrance, lit the halogens that hung above. In the pool of light that appeared Louverture could see the fallen cloth, as wide as the stage, gathered around a thick metal pole that sat on the ground. A slackened rope still extended from the far end of the pole to the fly gallery above; the rope from the near end was severed, lying in a loose coil on the floor. "We lowered the intact side so it wouldn't fall unexpectedly," Tremblay said.

Louverture picked up the snapped rope, ran it through his fingers until the end reached him. The strands were all the same length, except for one, and only that one had stretched and frayed. "Has anyone examined this?"

Tremblay shook his head. "I told them it was an accident, but you know how superstitious actors are."

"That will be all I need, then," Louverture said, waited for Tremblay to lead him back out the maze of corridor.

"Officier," Tremblay said when they reached the door, "do you think if we close for a while—the people, will they—"

"Forget?" Louverture pushed the door open, blinked at the light outside. "Of course. With enough time, people can forget anything."

His mind raced as he ran back to the Cabildo. A paradox was not a dead end, he had forgotten that: it was an intersection of two streets you hadn't known existed. He smelled sulphur as he reached the square, saw smoke rising from near the courthouse. The gardien at the door levelled a pistol at him as he neared.

"Keep back, please," the gardien said.

Louverture raised his hands. He could not recall if he had ever seen a gardien draw his gun before. "I'm Officier Louverture," he said, slowly dropping his right hand. "I'm reaching for my badge." He fished it out carefully, extended it at arm's length.

"Go in, then," the gardien said, "and you might want to get a spare uniform if you're staying."

"What's going on?"

"A bomb. In the courthouse."

"Sweet Reason. Was anyone killed?"

The gardien shook his head. "It missed fire, or else it was just a smoke bomb—but they found two more just like it at the Cathedral and the Academie Scientifique."

"Excuse me," Louverture said, waving his badge at the desk man as he went inside.

"Louverture!" Commandant Trudeau said, looking up from the charts on his desk. "I told Clouthier you wouldn't be able to stay away." Clouthier, his back to Louverture, nodded absently. "Quite a mess, isn't it?"

"Commandant—Officier principal—I think I understand it now," he said. "I think I know who is doing this."

"Which group of irrationalists?"

"Not irrationalists; scientists. It's an experiment."

Trudeau looked confused, the first time Louverture had seen it on his face. "Explain."

"A series of larger and larger experiments. The theatre accidents, the omnibus failures—they were done on purpose, to test how much it takes to change people's behaviour. The notes, and the bomb probably too—they were to test us."

"Test us for what?"

"To see how much it would take to make us react irrationally, see every accident as sabotage, every abandoned briefcase as a bomb. Perhaps we too are just a test for a larger experiment."

"But the notes," Clouthier said, turning to face him. "Who were they threatening?"

Louverture glanced out the window, at the statue in the middle of the square. "Reason," he said. "She dies tonight."

"I'm sorry, Officier, but this makes no sense," Trudeau said. "What would be the motive?"

"I'm not sure. Jealousy, a wish to possess reason for themselves alone? Or perhaps the motive is reason itself. Perhaps they simply want to know."

"This is ridiculous," Clouthier barked. "He wants us chasing phantoms. We know who the irrationalist leaders are; arrest them, and the others will follow soon enough."

"And how will people react when they see the Corps out in force, with pistols? Will they remain rational, do you think?"

"I've ordered a *couvre-feu* for eight o'clock," Clouthier said. "People will stay inside when they see the lights are out."

Louverture closed his eyes. "As you say."

"Will you join us, Louverture?" Trudeau said, his attention back on the maps on the desk. "We can use another man, especially tonight."

"Is that an order, Commandant?"

There was a long pause; then Trudeau very carefully said, "No, Officier, it isn't. Go home and get your rest—go quickly, and show your badge if anyone questions you."

"Thank you, sir."

Louverture went down the stairs, pushed through the gardiens assembling in the lobby; noticed Pelletier, saluted him. Pelletier did not answer his salute; perhaps the boy did not recognize him without his cap and uniform, and at any rate he was talking to the gardiens stagières around him. Not wanting to interrupt, Louverture stepped outside.

The sun was nearly down, but the air was still hot; Reason's torch cast a weak shadow on the number eight. Heading for Danton Street, Louverture saw a man approaching across the square. He was wearing a dark wool suit, despite the weather; a top hat and smoke-tinted glasses.

Louverture looked the man in the eyes as he neared, trying to read him; the man cocked his head curiously and gazed back at him. The two of them circled each other slowly, eyes locked. When they had exchanged positions the man doffed his hat to Louverture, his perfectly calm face creased with just a hint of a smile, and then turned and did the same to the statue of Reason. Louverture knew that look: it was the one Allard wore while measuring a skull. The man found an empty bench, sat down and waited, as though he expected a show to unfold in front of him at any moment.

The bells in the Cathedral of Reason rang out at eight o'clock, and the sodium lamps in the square faded to darkness. The lights were going out all over town; Louverture did not suppose he would see them lit again.

Beyond the Fields You Know

The boy was called Calx. He did not remember his real name.

He was not sure how long he had been at the House. He did not know how long it had been since he had seen his parents; their names, too, were long gone, scraped away by toil and hunger. But he remembered their faces, and his bedroom with the biplane wallpaper and the Elmo sheets—and he remembered the Gnome with the Silver Key.

The little man had appeared at the boy's window one night, when his parents thought he had gone to sleep. He had told the boy that there were people who needed his help, and he could have an adventure besides. All he had to do was take the silver key and open the door at the back of the linen closet.

The boy had not known there was a door in the linen closet, but sure enough when he went to check it was there. He had stood for a long time in the hallway, staring into the dark interior just barely lit by the hall nightlight. The floor chilled him through the feet of his flannel pajamas and he thought about going to get dressed, but he did not know just what you should wear on an adventure. Would he need boots? Should he wear a jacket, a sweater? Surely they would be able to give him the right kind of clothes when he got there—and besides, he had a feeling that if he went to his room the door would be gone when he got back.

The key, a funny long knobby thing that was not at all like his parents' keys, fit snugly into the keyhole and turned smoothly. The boy pulled sheets and towels out of the closet, tossing them to the hallway floor to clear the way. There was no handle but the door opened anyway, a crack of light surrounding it and then brightening the whole closet. It was bright on the other side, too bright to see what was there with eyes that had been straining to see in the dark.

Squinting, the boy climbed up into the closet and squeezed through the narrow doorway. He was so excited he did not even notice the door closing behind him.

On this day Calx had been scouring shields. There was only one way to do it: first you had to pull off any stones that had been stuck to them, and the larger clumps of earth; then with a wire brush you took off the mud that was stuck right to the surface. Mrs. Marmalade would only give you one bucket of water for the whole job, no matter how many shields you had to clean or how much you pleaded, so you had to save it for the very end, parcelling it out in spit-drops. Then it was time to scour them, taking red rust off the iron shields and green rust off the bronze ones; for this there was coarse sand and again, finally, as little water as possible. It was hard work, because most of them had been in the ground a long time, but there were worse jobs. It kept you inside, and you were alone except for the strange reflections that sometimes danced in the torchlight on the polished bronze shields.

He could see his own reflection, now, in the shield he had just finished cleaning. His wild hair he recognized—it had sometimes grown that way at the end of a summer, when it went months without being cut or even brushed—but the gaunt, jagged face was not the one he had known from school photos or seen in the mirror while brushing his teeth. He reached up to his cheek, felt the three scars that ran across it and remembered the day he had received them.

The first things he had seen on coming through the door that night had been a great grey-white rabbit, twice as tall as he was and dressed in a checked waistcoat, and a hedgehog the size of a large dog who was wearing an apron and a ruffled cap.

"Hello," the rabbit said, in a voice like the people on the English TV shows the boy's father liked to watch. "I'm Mr. Jacoby, and this is Mrs. Marmalade."

"Hello." The boy pulled himself fully out of the small passage and straightened up. He looked around, saw a room with grey stone walls and a low ceiling. There was a stone hearth in the far wall, where a fire was burning low: the floor was cold, much colder than it had been at his house, and he was suddenly very conscious of being a small boy in his pajamas. "I came because—the Gnome with the Silver Key said—"

"Mrs. Marmalade, take this boy to the dormitory please," Mr. Jacoby said. Turning to the boy he said, "We'll get you to work in the morning."

Mrs. Marmalade walked over to the boy, whuffling with each awkward step. She smelled of earth and rotting vegetables. He felt a sudden shock of fear as she looked up at him and he saw her face more clearly: it was not a human face at all, not a storybook face, but just a hedgehog's face with beady eyes and sharp teeth. Lice were crawling on her hairy snout, and every now and then her long pink tongue darted out to draw one into her mouth.

"I've changed my mind," the boy said, turning around to get back into the passageway. It was gone, the rough stone wall showing no signs it had ever been there. "I don't think I want to go on an adventure after all."

"Let's get you off to bed," Mr. Jacoby said, putting a paw on the boy's shoulder. "It'll all seem better in the morning."

The boy shrugged off Jacoby's grasp. "I want to go home," he said, his voice cracking as he began to cry. "Do you hear me? I want to go home."

He was thrown into the wall by the creature's paw, and raised a hand to his cheek to feel blood running from the deep scratches there. He had not known rabbits had claws.

There were other boys there, boys who had been brought here as he was, and in time he learned a bit about why they were there. There was a war going on, that was clear, though none of the boys knew anything about who the sides were or what the war was about. The House was a good way away from the front, but not so far that it was not occasionally rocked when one side or the other started blasting.

The war had been going on for a long time, so long that the whole country around was a cemetery—some graves the tombs and barrows of the honoured dead, others filled-in trenches where men's bodies lay where they died. The boys' job was to search these graves for weapons and armour that could be used to equip the men at the front. Sometimes these men would pass through the House— though they were not all men, and not all of them were even things Calx could have imagined if he had not seen them. He had learned to avoid them all, no matter how friendly they acted or normal-looking they looked: they lived in another world, one more brutal even than the House.

Each day every boy was sent to work for either Mr. Jacoby or Mrs. Marmalade: Mr. Jacoby supervised the boys who searched the graves, while Mrs. Marmalade oversaw the keeping of the House. At night the torches were put out and the boys allowed a few hours' sleep, but more often than not they would stay awake a while longer, savouring the only time they had to themselves. Sometimes there were fights, as boys lashed out at each other for the slights and insults of the day. Other times they would stay awake and talk, trying to preserve what memories they could of their other lives. Most often they talked about how they had come to the House.

A boy called Skell was talking tonight. "It was a little blue mouse that got me," he said. "Told me my parents weren't my real parents, said I was really missing royalty. I was supposed to be the High Prince of the Vespertine Kingdom."

Calx rolled over, trying as every night to find a position in which he could not feel the stone floor beneath him. "I never even asked," he said. He sat up and looked around at the other boys: the low fire in the mess room outside cast enough light that he could see their outlines, like shadows. "The Gnome with the Silver Key just said come with me, we'll have an adventure."

Rufus laughed. He was one of the biggest of the boys, with red hair and freckles, and the nearest thing Calx had to a friend: they had each defended the other more than once in barracks fights, and it was Rufus who had taught Calx to keep his distance from the visiting soldiers. "Hard sell, you were," he said. "Mine had me at 'Hello.' I never supposed there was anyplace worse than home."

In the morning the boy went out with Mr. Jacoby. They had to leave early, before sunrise: with the more recent battlefields nearer the House picked clean, they had to range further away to the bogs, a country of streams and damp earth that had been burial grounds since long before the war. In his right hand, as usual, Mr. Jacoby held a tarnished gold fob watch; the other held the end of a long silver chain. The chain was a leash, its other end looped around the neck of a wight.

"The wight's sniffed out a spell, down there somewhere," Mr. Jacoby said. There was a dark pool that might have been a flooded pit grave, or else a blast crater. "You pull it out and bring it back."

Calx's eyes flicked over to the rabbit, then at the creature whose leash he held. You couldn't look directly at a wight: they had no shape, only movement, like gesture drawings done in charcoal. They were trackers, used to sniff out forgotten magic in the old battlefields—not to mention wayward boys.

"We'll be waiting for you at the House," Mr. Jacoby said. He glanced at his watch and then turned, loping away at an unhurried pace and followed by the chained wight.

Calx peered into the pool. Its water was opaque in the near-dark, but he knew there must be a dead person in it whose arms the wight had found. He took a moment to find a dry spot near the pool and then pulled off his shirt and pants, folded them carefully and placed them in the lower branches of a willow.

He dipped his big toe into the pool, regretting it immediately; then he closed his eyes, took a half-dozen deep breaths and then jumped feet first into the water. It was even colder than he had thought, and he shuddered as he pushed his hands up against the water, forcing himself deeper. He counted in his head, steamboats for seconds the way his mother had taught him, to know when he should give up this attempt. Before long, though, he touched something solid, freezing mud squeezing itself between his toes. He crouched down and began to feel around the bottom of the pool, looking for whatever it was the wight had scented. There was something hard beneath the mud, armour or maybe a shield— though that probably meant there were weapons as well; he would have to retrieve them all before he could go back to the House.

His fingers found the round edge of a shield, and he began to pry it out of the mud when something brushed his arm. At first he thought it was only a branch, but a moment later he felt it closing around his wrist. Blind in the darkness, he felt in the movement of water a shape rising up out of the mud; something that felt like needles roamed over his chest, searching for his neck.

Calx let out a gasp and it rose in a stream of bubbles. With his left hand he reached for the arm of whatever it was that had grabbed him, but there was no moving it: he might as well have been trying to shift a tree trunk as it moved upwards towards his throat. He forced himself to count to keep calm, one steamboat, two steamboat, while his other hand dug desperately through the muddy ground for a weapon.

He felt a hot pain in his palm, drew his hand back and then immediately reached out again to find whatever had cut him. The hand was at this throat now, not that he could breathe anyway. He cut his hand again, running it down the blade until it found the hilt; his fingers, numb from the freezing mud, scrambled to get a purchase on the weapon. Three steamboat, four steamboat . . . Finally it pulled free and he swung it at the arms that held his wrist and throat. The water slowed the blade, but by finding the space between the arms he was able to get enough leverage to cut at them.

Immediately the hands released him; as quickly as he could he drew the sword close, so its point faced straight out and its pommel touched his heart. Then he drove it forward with as much force as he could muster before launching himself upwards. There was no air left in him to make him buoyant: unable to stop himself, he opened his mouth and breathed in a mouthful of water. He felt phantom touches on his ankles as he rose, afraid with each kick that the hands would grasp him again, but finally he broke the surface. He pulled himself to the shore, kicking furiously to get himself out more quickly, and then puked the rank bog water onto the ground.

And then it was over. The water of the pool was smooth, as though nothing whatsoever had happened. He felt an urgent need to pee; he let out a bitter laugh—he was still conditioned by a dimly remembered rule against peeing in pools—then turned back to the water. His hand, though, wouldn't let go of the knife. Awkwardly he used his other hand, sending the spray half into the water and half on the shore, and then held the knife up to examine it more closely. It was maybe a foot and a half long, with a slight curve to the blade, and despite its time in the water the steel still shone. The edge was wickedly sharp: the cut it had made in his palm was nearly a half-inch deep, though it was no longer bleeding. The hilt fit into his palm snugly, like a prop sword moulded to the hand of an action figure.

With difficulty he put on his shirt—cutting his right sleeve several times as he tried to pass the sword through it—and then his pants. He looked around. It was only a few hours since dawn, but the sky was already a dull grey: the sun had been used up in some great spell earlier in the war, and now like any other vet it rose unsteadily for a few hours each morning before settling back, exhausted, onto the horizon.

As the terror and excitement of what had happened ebbed he felt he could not take another step, never mind walk the miles between here and the House. Better to play dead, then. There was no question of actually fleeing—where would he go?—but enough boys actually did die on these jobs that Mr. Jacoby would usually wait a day or two before sending the wights out after you. There would be a beating at the end of it, of course, but it would be worth it for a day and a night or more of nothing but sleep.

Calx looked around, casting a suspicious glance at the still surface of the pool. The spot where he had left his clothes would be the most comfortable place to sleep, but it was too exposed: aside from the wights, there were any number of things that roamed the battlefields, and even this far from the front he might still be hit by a falling blast. He wandered around for a few minutes until he found a stretch of muddy trench where a stream had been dammed or diverted, and then crouched down to make sure it was deep enough to hide him. Out of reflex he lay down on his right side, but the knife in his hand made that impossible. He rolled over and curled himself up, the blade held tight to his chest like a teddy bear.

A shock awoke him, a painful tingling that felt as though he were grabbing the prongs of a power plug. When he opened his eyes he saw a wight nose-to-nose with him: it touched him and he felt another jolt, forcing him to scramble away from it and rise to a crouch.

"Heel," Mr. Jacoby said from above him, giving the creature's chain a yank. It stretched towards Calx and then receded, coming to rest at the rabbit's side. "Did you think you could get away from us, boy?"

Calx shook his head silently. He was not sure how long he had been sleeping, but he did not feel any better rested.

"Come up here. Let's see if you at least found something."

He climbed up the muddy bank, keeping his distance from the wight. His arm was very heavy as he lifted the knife up to show it to Mr. Jacoby.

"What, did you get that down in the bog? Doesn't look like much." He reached out his paw. "We'll see what the wight thinks. Here, give it—"

Then Mr. Jacoby was lying on the ground, a bright red slash where his throat had been. The wight was screaming: as soon as the rabbit's paw released the silver leash it took off, flowing across the bogs like water, like a shadow.

Calx looked down at the knife. He did not entirely remember killing Mr. Jacoby, but he didn't not remember it: anyway there was his blood on the blade. He reached up with his left hand to feel his scars, which were burning on his cheek.

He thought for a bit about what had happened. He could not escape the fact that he still had to go back to the House: as much as he hated it, it was the only place he knew. Besides, he thought, he could not abandon the other boys. Now that he had something that frightened even the wights he could get them out of there: between the scraps that each of them had overheard there must be some way to take them safely away from the fighting, or even home.

Crouching, he wiped first one side of the knife and then the other against Mr. Jacoby's dirty white fur, until there was no more blood and the blade shone. Then he straightened up and started back towards the House. It was still light, more or less, when he got there, so he climbed up into a barren tree and half-dozed until all the lights were out. He had snuck outside enough times, either to get away from a fight that was heating up or just to pee, that he knew which door opened silently: inside was dark as could be, but his feet knew the way to the dormitory. He found Rufus by the sound of his snoring and gently shook him awake.

"'S still dark," Rufus said.

"Shh," Calx said. "It's me."

There was a brief silence. "Calx?" Rufus asked. "Gone a long time. Jacoby just done beatin' on you?"

"Mr. Jacoby's dead."

A longer silence. "Wha'd you mean, dead?"

"I killed him. With—" Calx took a breath. "It was easy."

"What sort of bloody nonsense are you talking?" Rufus said. "D'you know how much trouble we're going to be in? When Mrs. Marmalade finds out—"

"I'll kill her, too, if I have to," Calx said.

"You're mad." For a moment the only sound was Rufus's breathing, fast and ragged. "Do you really think that's all there is to the House, those two animals? The higher-ups will find out soon enough. You don't know, I've seen them come through here. I know what they're like."

"You don't understand," Calx said. "We can be free. We can all be free."

"You," Rufus said wearily, "are mad." Calx could hear him rising to his feet. "I'm going to go tell Mrs. Marmalade what's happened, before we all get—"

There was no sound at all for a long time, until finally Calx reached his left hand out in front of him. He could feel Rufus's arm:

it was still warm, but it was not moving. He ran his fingers over Rufus' form until they touched blood, hot and sticky, and he knew he could not free the boys, could not live amongst them anymore. He could not go home. He stood up and went back out into the hall, where a dim light beckoned him to the mess room. The last embers of the fire still glowed, giving off just enough light to see by. He sat at the foot of the hearth and held the knife in front of his face, tilting it up and down to see himself fully. At last he recognized his reflection: it was what he had seen, sometimes, in the shields he had polished.

Peter stepped out the door, closing it as slowly as possible. He held his breath as the lock clicked, but after a few moments had passed he decided no-one had heard it. It was a clear October night, the stars bright above and the air just starting to get cold: he felt a little overdressed in his quilted jacket and the hiking boots he had gotten for his birthday. He wondered, too, about the bag he had packed. The Elf with the Bells on His Shoes had not said anything about needing supplies, but then he supposed you could always use a flashlight and some peanut butter sandwiches.

The treehouse loomed above him, looking much taller than it did in the day. He threw his backpack over his shoulder and climbed up, his heart racing. He couldn't believe he was about to meet his long-lost twin brother—but hadn't he always known, in his heart, that it was true—that there was someone more like him than Tyler, with his smelly shoes and his messy room and his incomprehensible baseball statistics? And, of course, to learn that he and his twin were wizards—but that their powers only worked when they were together—it all made perfect sense—

He slowed his climb as a rank smell reached him. He swallowed and pulled his head up into the treehouse. In the moonlight he could see that the Elf with the Bells on His Shoes was there—but he had been cut nearly in half, his chest and belly opened like a zipper. He was hanging from one of the thick branches that supported the treehouse.

Before he could stop himself Peter threw up, half-digested

remnants of his dinner falling on the treehouse floor. When he looked up he saw something that looked like a scarecrow stepping out of the shadows. Its tattered shirt hung on its shoulders as though they were a wire hanger; its face was white, and its hair was caked into spikes with mud and blood. The knife in the scarecrow's hand gleamed in the moonlight, and Peter pressed his thighs together to keep from peeing himself.

"Why did you do that?" Peter asked. "He said I was—he was going to take me away from here."

The scarecrow stood still for a long moment, looking at Peter as though it knew him. "I did you a favour," it said, and then it was gone.

What You Couldn't Leave Behind

The client looked like all the rest, dressed for travel in cargo pants and a crumpled shirt, hauling his suitcase like a ball and chain. He was wearing the confused, overwhelmed look most of them have: dragging his steps, peering into each of the shop windows as though part of him knew that he wasn't headed anywhere good.

"Hey, pal," I said. He glanced around, then over in my direction with a who-me look on his face. "Yeah, you. Looking for something?"

He frowned. "Um, I—they say I'm—"

"Dead. Yeah. Get used to it. Know what's coming next?"

He shook his head. "No, they—they just said, go on to Departures."

I jerked my head at the chair in front of my desk, and after a moment's hesitation he sat down. I could see the relief on his face as he let go of his suitcase. "Pretty heavy, huh," I said.

He nodded. "Yeah. You know, I don't remember packing it. Do you think they'll let me take it with me?"

"Don't worry, you packed it." I held out my hand. "I'm Beau Sutton—call me Buddy. Please."

"Adams. Roger Adams."

"Coffee, Roger?"

He glanced over at the Starbucks, reached into his right pocket and drew out a pair of copper coins. "I don't think I have enough money."

"My treat." I unscrewed my thermos, poured us each a cup, then drew my flask out of my pocket, waved it at him. He nodded, so I unscrewed it and poured a nip into each of our cups.

"Thanks." Roger blew on his coffee, took a sip. "So, uh—what do you sell, here, exactly?"

"I don't sell. I'm a detective."

He raised his eyebrows. "Really? What kinds of crimes do you handle?"

"Murders, mostly." I took a long sip of coffee, hot and strong. "Yours, for instance."

Okay, I admit it: I time that to hit right when they have a mouthful of coffee. "What? No, no—I wasn't murdered. I died from—I don't know what from, but I wasn't murdered. I died in the hospital."

"All deaths are murders, Roger. The question is who pulled the trigger and how."

"But how can that matter now? I mean, I'm dead, aren't I?"

"Do you know what happens after you leave here, Roger?" He shook his head. "You go on to the airport, and they put that briefcase on a scale. If there's too much in it—I mean, if it's heavier than a feather—then you get right on another flight and start all over again. Maybe as a tree, maybe a pigeon, but probably just another dumb guy, making all the same dumb mistakes."

"And if it's light enough? What then?"

I shrugged. "Then you find out what."

"So—" He shook his head. "Why are you still here, if you know all this? You an angel or something?"

I cocked an eyebrow, took off my fedora to reveal my halo-free head. "I emptied out my suitcase a long time ago, but I decided to stay here for a while, help guys like you."

"I already said, I can't pay much."

"Don't worry about it. What you have is enough."

"So how do I make my suitcase lighter?"

"Like I said, I solve your murder. That's what you're hauling around in there: your fears, your desires—all the things in your life you can't let go of. I find the one that had such a hold you let it kill you, and then you'll be able to leave them behind."

Roger took a long breath, released it. "I guess. Sure—I mean, it sounds better than starting all over again." He reached down for his suitcase, hauled it up and held it out to me.

Taking the case, I popped it open. Inside were a set of jars—not jam jars but clay tubes, each topped by a lid carved into a little statue. "Once I start, I won't be back till I'm done," I said. "I may be a little while, but don't worry—I haven't failed a client yet."

He nodded. "Thank you," he said. "So what do you do first?"

I uncorked the first jar. "Round up the usual suspects."

The Jackal's place stank of beer and stale smoke. Once-opulent oak and leather booths sat under a layer of grime, their original colour barely recognizable; on the wall a sign reading PLEASE NO PIPES OR CIGARS had been angrily defaced. From outside tiny shafts of sunlight crept in tentatively through windows that had once been stained glass but were now just stained.

I went up to the bar, elbowing aside a guy who was wide enough to need two stools. The barman was pulling a pint. I watched him pour it, working the tap with forearms like Popeye's. I slipped one of the coins Roger had given me out of my pocket and put it down on the bar, to catch his eye when he turned my way.

"What's your poison?" he asked, putting the mug of dark amber beer in front of the man I had pushed aside. The barman was a heavy guy, too, all soft except for those pistons he used to pull the pints with. His head was mostly bald, and it just sloped outward from the dome top to his jowls and then his shoulders, not bothering with a neck. He wore an apron that bore the stains of a thousand different meals.

I picked the coin up again before he could grab it, turned it so it caught the light. "The Jackal around?" I asked.

The barman's pig eyes narrowed. "Maybe," he said.

"Could you find out?"

He reached out for the coin in my hand, took it like a frog snatching a fly. "Yeah, he's here," he said. He jerked his head at the kitchen door, moved aside so I could get to it. "Go on in."

I worked my way around the bar, squeezed into the barman's side past a man who was attacking a plate of steak and eggs like it was Juno Beach. The kitchen doors swung aside as I pushed through them, letting me into a crowded room where steam and smoke were fighting for supremacy. A pair of short-order guys worked the grill, each skinny as a rail. Neither one looked at me or at each other, but kept their eyes fixed on the job in front of them. They didn't say anything either, except to swear now and then under their breath when a grease fire flared up.

"You got a reason for being here?" a raspy voice asked me. Peering past the smoke I saw the Jackal sitting at the waiter's table. He had a high forehead and sunken cheeks, eyebrows that climbed right up his head. A plate sat in front of him, crammed with just about everything that might go on a grill or in a fryer, and handy by his elbow was a double-pint glass of beer. He had tucked a little white napkin into his collar so that it looked like an ascot.

I held up my wallet, flipped it open and then quickly closed it again. "Health inspector," I said.

The Jackal gave a barking laugh. "You think you're the first guy to try that?" he said. "I pay good money so I never have to see a health inspector, so whoever you are, you ain't him."

"You got me," I said. I put my wallet away. "I'm here about a guy."

"Unless his name's Fish or Chips, you're in the wrong place."

I shook my head. "Roger Adams," I said, watching his eyes. "That mean anything to you?"

"What about him?" the Jackal asked.

"He's dead, for starters."

"Huh." The Jackal's knife and fork were still in his hands, the blade of the knife slipping rhythmically in and out of the tines of the fork. "Why are you telling me?"

I shrugged. "Word is he used to spend a lot of time here," I said. "As who wouldn't, a quality place like this?"

"Hey," he said, pointing his knife at me, "maybe this isn't one of those joints where you get a half-dozen peas on a silver plate, but people who come here, they go away happy. Satisfied." To make his point, he speared a slice of fried ham with his fork and stuffed it into his mouth, working his sharp jaw up and down. It went down like you had dropped it in a bottomless pit: for everything he ate the Jackal was nothing but skin, bone and gristle.

"Maybe you don't ever see a health inspector, but how would it go down if those guys out front heard somebody had died from eating here?" I asked. "You understand, I don't care if it was you who killed him or somebody else. But I have to find out."

"You think you can scare me?" the Jackal said. Flecks of half-chewed ham sprayed onto his shirtfront. "Half the guys out there know they're gonna die with a fork in their hand." He swallowed. "I think I've had enough of this conversation."

The mixed smell of grease and sweat was starting to get overpowering. I took a step closer, pulled his plate across the table before he could stop me. "I don't want to make this a quarrel," I said.

He dropped his fork on the table, reached spastically towards the plate. "Hey," he said, "a man's gotta eat." He looked over at the short-order guys: each one had his back to us, focused on the grill in front of him.

"Roger Adams," I said. "Seen him lately?"

The Jackal started to stand up and move towards me, but I took a sidestep away, keeping the table between me and him. He reached out at me again, trying to stretch his arm longer, then finally sat down. "He used to come in all the time," he said, "but I haven't seen him in ages."

I looked him in the eyes, nodded. "So where's he been?" I asked, holding the plate just out of his reach.

"Falcone's," he said, his eyes fixed on the plate. "You know, the strip club on third? I heard he's there almost every night. Was, I mean."

I held the plate a few seconds longer, just until I started to enjoy it. Then I handed it back to him, turned away before I could see him start to gorge himself. Suddenly I wanted to get out of that place and breathe some fresh air, or at least what passes for it around here. I pushed back out the kitchen doors and past the barman, keeping my mouth shut as I squeezed by all the customers perched over their groaning plates.

WHAT YOU COULDN'T LEAVE BEHIND

Finally I was outside again. I risked opening my mouth, took a cautious breath in and waited to see if anything came out. My throat caught for a second, and I closed my eyes. There was a noise behind me, but before I could do anything I felt a crack on my skull and after that the lights stayed out for a while.

When I woke up I was in Heaven. Well, maybe not your Heaven but mine: my head was in the lap of a soft, young brunette, her teardrop-shaped face hovering over me. Her hair was pulled back and she wore a pair of glasses with tortoiseshell rims, which she was holding onto with her right hand to keep them from falling.

"Are you all right?" she asked, her voice quiet.

"How long was I out?"

She shook her head, leaving a blurry trail that told me I wasn't quite back in condition. "I don't know how long you were unconscious before I found you," she said. "It's been about ten minutes since I brought you back here."

Reluctant as I was to leave the nest I had found I drew myself up onto my elbows. She had laid me on a long couch, cracked brown leather patched with electrical tape. All around were shelves full of books, paper and hardcover mixed pell-mell. "Where's here, exactly?"

"This is my shop, Foy's Books. I'm Zoe Foy."

I sat up, groaning as my head protested the move, and extended my hand. "Pleased to meet you, Ms. Foy," I said. "Buddy Sutton. You spend a lot of time dragging drunks out of alleys?"

"But you're not a drunk," she said quickly. After a second she took my hand and squeezed it. Her hand was warm. It felt nice. "I mean, you do smell a little like one—but I know the look of the guys that spend all their time at the Jackal's. I see enough of them, it's right across the street."

"So you're just a good Samaritan."

Her mouth went tight. "I just—I thought—"

"It's okay," I said, patting her on the arm. It felt nice too. "You just get suspicious, in my business, especially after a knock on the head. I shouldn't snipe at you for doing a good deed."

"I understand," she said. She was smiling now, her face sunny again. "So what business is that, exactly?"

"Well—"

A jingle came from the other side of the shelves. "Oh, that's the door," she said, standing up. Standing had a good effect on her, especially from my perspective. She held up a finger. "You hang on. I'll be right back."

I watched her go around the bookshelf, counted ten and then stood up. As quietly as I could, I moved to the nearest shelf and peered through it. The room was a big one, and probably had first been a warehouse: only the shelves divided it into corridors. They were all used books and shelved without rhyme or reason, mouldy encyclopedias next to last year's bestsellers. I was just about to sit down again when I heard a scream.

A few quick steps took me to the other side of the bookshelf and down the hall towards the door. Zoe was in front of it, frozen. Past her, standing in the doorway, was someone in a long dark overcoat. Before I could get a look at his face I caught sight of a gun barrel rising up to level with Zoe's heart. There were still at least ten steps between me and her.

Instead of running, I threw my shoulder into the bookshelf nearest me and heaved with all my might. The shelf creaked for an endless second and then fell my way, throwing hundreds of books into the air. A shot broke the air and Zoe screamed again as I fought my way through the paperback rain. She was crouched on the floor now, her arms thrown over her face to protect her, and the man in the dark coat was gone.

"Do you know what that was about?" I asked, helping her up. A book on the shelf above her had been blown to bits, a copy of Gray's Anatomy shot through the heart.

She shook her head. She was crying, breathing in gasps. "I can't imagine what," she said. "I've never seen that man before in my life."

"It was a man? What did he look like?"

"I didn't get a good look," she said, turning away. "He had a hat on, the light was behind him—he was clean-shaven, about your height. That's all I know."

I reached up to stroke the stubble on my cheek. Clean-shaven, about my height—that narrowed it down to about a million guys, just in Bardo City. "All right," I said. "I guess this was about me. Somebody probably saw you pulling me in here."

"What should we do?"

"You stay here and close up," I said. "I'm going to go register my displeasure."

She grabbed my arm with both hands. "I can't stay here," she said. "Not now."

I looked back into the store, then at her. "Do you have a car?" I asked. She nodded. "Okay, then. You're going to stay in it."

She nodded again, two quick jerks.

I took a step towards the door, paused. "Before we go—do you have a copy of the Lotus Sutra, the 1903 British Buddhist Society edition with the missing line on the fifth page?"

"I don't think so," she said, throwing a glance at the pile of books on the floor. "Is it important?"

"Probably not." The door jingled as I opened it for her, and I threw a quick glance left and right before stepping outside.

The lights were on at Falcone's, neon dancers flickering onto the sad sacks slouched around the door. When the engine cut I opened the door, turned to Zoe. "You coming?"

She frowned. "I thought you wanted me to stay here."

"Right. Sure, I forgot." I got out of the car, fixed my gaze on the bouncer at the door to the club. "If I'm not back in twenty minutes send a rescue party."

"Don't you carry a gun?" she asked.

I shook my head. "Bad karma." I shut the car door behind me, cut into the line right in front of the bouncer. He wasn't that big a guy, an inch or so shorter than a grizzly bear.

Somehow without taking a step he filled the space between me and the door. "There's a cover."

"I'm not here for the floor show," I said. "I need to see Falcone."

"What's your name?" he asked. I told him, and he flipped through a little pad that he held in his left hand. "Not on the list," he said.

"I understand," I said. "But I need to see Falcone. He'll be sorry if he misses me."

The bouncer nodded slowly, then brought his right hand up in a fist against my jaw. Somebody somewhere was uncorking a bottle of champagne. "I don't think so," he said.

I took a step back, stopped myself. "Okay," I said, stepping back up to the bouncer. "But I need to see Falcone."

"No," the bouncer said. He put his hand on my chest, flat, and pushed. When he saw I wasn't going anywhere he swung back and socked me in the stomach. "No," he repeated.

A cough flew out of me, spattering blood in his direction. I straightened up, kept my hands at my sides. "I need to see Falcone," I said, my voice a bit slurred.

He drew his fist back, and I flinched. He paused. "You gonna swing back?" he asked. I shook my head. "You one of those guys who likes getting beaten on?"

I shook my head again, regretted it. "I need to see Falcone," I said again.

A look crossed his face, pity or maybe disgust. His fist was still drawn back, but his posture had gone slack. After a minute he shook his head slowly, stepped aside. "Go in, then," he said. "You tell Falcone those lumps were from me."

"Sure," I said. "Thanks for the comp." The way my jaw was rattling, though, I don't know if he understood me.

Falcone's was a classy place, the kind where they spray the girls with a mister instead of just letting them sweat. Nina Simone was on the speakers, singing "Please Don't Let Me Be Misunderstood" good and slow, and there was a girl at each end of the T-shaped stage following her rhythm. It was a little bit like the Stations of the Cross: you could get up and walk from clothed to undies to nude if you didn't feel like waiting.

I let my gaze drift from the stage and looked around the room. It was full of the same guys I had seen outside, slouched and embarrassed. They sat at the stage if they could, or else close to it, staring at the girls without blinking. A few of them chatted up the waitresses, dancers on their off-shifts, and every now and then one would slip the girl a bill and the two would vanish up the back stairs.

Fratelli Falcone was sitting at a table near the back. Unlike his customers he faced away from the stage: he knew the dancers were there. A girl sat on either side of him. One of them was buttoned up in a shirt, jacket and tie, like a Catholic schoolgirl. The other was dressed about the same but the effect was different, with the tie loosened, the shirt halfway undone and the skirt about six inches further north.

"Buddy," Falcone said, spreading his arms wide as I came near him. He had a sharp face, with a nose you could use to climb mountains. A walking stick leaned against his knee and he wore a brown cape with a fringe like feathers. "So long since we've seen you."

I looked at one girl then the other, and finally tried to stare Falcone in the face. "Not my scene anymore," I said.

"Oh? And what are you into now?"

I raised my hand to my still-aching jaw. "Being beaten up," I said, "but to tell you the truth I'm getting tired of it. So how about we get right to business: what does the name Roger Adams say to you?"

Falcone gave a slow, wide shake of the head, taking in a good look at each girl. "That is not a name I know," he said. His voice was oilier than the grill at the Jackal's. "Buddy my friend, I think you have been working too hard. How would you find a visit to the Champagne Room? On the house of course."

Despite myself I looked at the two girls: the first looked away demurely, while the second locked eyes with me and ran her tongue across her lips. I shook my head. "Another time," I said.

"These are my best girls, Buddy," Falcone said. He sounded disappointed. "It's never just business to them, they are very talented at making it seem natural." He took his hand off the girl to his right and waved it in the air, looking for the right word. "Genuine."

"Is that what happened to Roger?" I asked. "Did he get too tight with one of these girls? Is that what he can't let go?"

"Please, Buddy. You know as well as I that, in my business, discretion is—"

Before he could finish speaking his eyes went wide. I congratulated myself for watching them, instead of the many more interesting things in the room: they gave me just enough warning to dive out of the way. Falcone had a few more seconds than I did but nowhere to go, and when the shot came a big red splotch opened up on his chest.

I prayed the shooter was as distracted as I was and turned around, staying low. He was in the doorway, a dark shape in a long coat and hat turning away.

"Hey!" I shouted. "You're gonna shoot me, make it stick!"

He didn't slow. Swearing under my breath I stood up, checked on Falcone. He was dead. His two girls were comforting each other, and it took me a minute before I remembered why I had come.

To my relief Zoe was still in the car. She looked startled when I opened the door. "What happened to you?" she asked.

"Which part?" I asked.

She reached her hand up to my cheek and I flinched. "You might have cracked your jaw," she said.

"Why don't you kiss it better?" I said, sitting down next to her.

She smiled and gave me a kiss. It was just a peck on the cheek, but you would never confuse it with the kiss you'd get from your grandmother. "So where to now, shamus?"

I shook my head. "You go home," I said. "I don't know whether that guy was gunning for me or Falcone, but now I know he wasn't after you. Better you go where it's safe."

"I can't stand the thought of re-shelving all those books," she said. "Besides, you need a driver. You're in no condition to walk."

I mulled it over for a minute. "Okay," I said. "You know how to get to One Padmasambhava Place?"

"City hall?"

"Falcone wasn't a very nice guy but he was well-connected. Nobody would take a shot at him without the mayor's say-so."

She frowned. "He won't be in his office at this hour."

"That's what I'm hoping for."

After what had happened at Falcone's Zoe wasn't too happy to be staying in the car, but she wasn't crazy about breaking into city hall either. I left her outside to watch the door while I slipped in the back way and up the stairs to the mayor's office.

I slipped the pick from my coat pocket and worked the lock. The stencil on the door read HON ROBT. BOONE, MAYOR, and when I got it open I saw that name repeated a dozen times or more on plaques, awards and honorary diplomas mounted on the wall. Pictures of the mayor with dignitaries and people so famous even I had heard of them filled what was left of the space, and the marble-topped desk was cluttered with trophies, mementoes and even a bust of the man himself. It made me wonder how a guy ever got anything done in a place like that, surrounded by his own name and face.

It wasn't the mayor's face I was interested in, though, but his brain: that is to say the files he kept in the room beyond. The mayor's life had been one long climb up an endless ladder, and you don't get to be boss of a town like Bardo City without having the dirt on everyone else in it. If he had his hooks into Roger, the reason would probably be in there.

I switched on my flashlight, played it over the filing cabinets. They were unlabelled, so I got the top drawer of the first one open and started to flip through the folders. They were full of a lot of juicy material, things that would surprise you about people you think you know, but nothing about Roger. I was just starting to think that I had had a few better ideas in my life when I heard a noise from the office.

"Who's there?" a voice called. I froze, trying not to breathe too loudly. A second later the office lights went on. "Come on out," the voice said. "I know you're in there."

I sighed, walked out into the office with my hands up and saw the mayor standing there. He had a long face and he looked like he needed a shave, but it wasn't going to happen: his kind hadn't shaved in a million years and weren't about to start now. He had on a shaggy blue coat, its arms trailing down past his knees, and bright red pants. Standing behind him was a taller guy, thin and with about as much expression as an ice cube. He was dressed in a long grey coat, smooth except for the lump in the right pocket.

"Nice night for a party," I said as the tall guy patted me down.

"Just what do you think you're doing here?" the mayor said, hunching forward. His wide nostrils flared as he took a long whiff of me. "Do you have any idea who I am? What I can have done to you?"

"Since I'm in your office, I'd guess that I do," I said. I turned my head to the guy who had been frisking me. "What's your story?"

"He does what I tell him," the mayor said. "That's all you need to know. Who are you?"

I shrugged. "A monkey's uncle."

The mayor hissed at me, his fangs showing. There was a noise from out in the hall, and the blank-faced guy turned towards it and then back to the mayor. "Should I check it out?" he asked.

"Sure," the mayor said. He showed his teeth again. "He's harmless."

I waited until the mayor's stooge had left before I spoke again. "Let's cut the games," I said. "What did you have on Roger Adams?" I watched his little eyes for a reaction. "What was it you offered him? Fame? Power?"

"Listen," the mayor said, grabbing me by the neck, "I don't know who you think you are, but I'm asking the questions here. So why don't—"

There was a shot out in the hall, and we both froze. Still holding my shirt the mayor turned his head around. Zoe appeared in the doorway, a dull grey pistol in her hand. A moment passed before she levelled it at the mayor and fired. The shot hit him in the back and threw him into me, both of us toppling to the ground.

"Oh my God," Zoe said. "Buddy, are you all right?"

With effort I lifted the mayor's body off of me, climbed to my feet. I patted my chest all over, feeling for blood. "Bullets don't always stop at the first body, you know," I said.

"I'm sorry," she said. "I just saw him holding your neck and I thought—"

"Where'd you get the gun?"

She looked down at the pistol still in her hand, took a deep breath and dropped it. "I saw those men going into the building, so I came up to see if you were all right," she said. "The man in the coat found me, he drew his gun—I was so scared, I just grabbed it and—"

"You took a big risk," I said. "You should have stayed in the car."

"I wanted to, but I just couldn't—couldn't stand the thought of losing you." She kissed me once, quickly, and then again. "But it's all over now. You're safe, and I guess with the mayor dead your case is over."

"I guess so." I kissed her again, then took her hand in mine, raised it to my lips and kissed it. "Now that I know you killed Roger."

She tried to pull her hand away but I held it fast. "What are you talking about?"

"Did you meet him at Falcone's?" I asked. "That's why you wouldn't come in, wasn't it, even when I was going to let you? That's why you shot Falcone, before he could tell me anything." I kissed her hand again. "Powder burns, angel."

"I just shot two men," she said. "I saved your life."

"Sure. But you had those burns before, in the car." I reached out with my free hand, stroked her cheek. "You met Roger at Falcone's, but it wasn't sex, was it? Oh, maybe at first, but that's not why he couldn't let go of you. He let go of his gut, of sex, his ego—but he couldn't let go of love."

She turned her head away. "What are you going to do with me?" she asked. "Turn me over to the police?"

"And risk that sweet neck?" I shook my head. "All that matters is I know. He can let go of you, now, and move on."

"And me?"

"You'll move on, too," I said. "Everybody's looking for love."

My office had never looked so much like home as when I got back. Roger was still sitting in the chair in front of my desk, his fingers interlaced, looking nervous.

"What happened to you?" he asked.

"Slightly more complicated case than usual," I said, lowering myself into my chair. "Don't worry, I worked it out. You should be able to go on now."

Roger let out a held breath, got up and picked up his suitcase. A frown crossed his face.

"What is it?" I asked.

"It's still heavy." He held it out to me. "Here."

I took the briefcase from him, felt its weight in my hand. I put it on my desk, popped it open: it was empty, but still felt like it was packed with bricks.

"You said it would be lighter," he said.

"It should be." I furrowed my brow, trying to work things out. "Tell me, Roger—you ever hear of a thing called tape echo?" He shook his head. "That's when you record on a tape more than once, and a little bit of the old recording doesn't get covered up. Well, that can happen with souls, too—if you've been through here a few times, you might have something from a past life still stuck in there."

"But if it's not even mine, what can I do about it?"

I held my hand out palm down, holding him still. "I think we're about to find out," I said. A dark shape had appeared in my office door: a man about my height in a dark coat, wearing a broad-brimmed hat that cast his face into shadow. A gun was in his hand.

"Who are you?" Roger said, turning around.

"Quiet, Roger," I said, keeping my eyes on the gun. "Why don't you let this guy go," I said to the intruder in a carefully level voice. "This is just about you and me, isn't it?"

The man said nothing but moved closer, keeping the muzzle of the pistol pointed my way.

"Get out of the way, Roger," I said.

Roger moved aside as the man took another step in my direction. I took a breath, snapped my hand out and jabbed at the switch of my desk lamp. The man blinked in surprise at the sudden light and I saw his face.

He was me.

I had intended to grab the gun while he was dazzled, but I was more stunned than he was. The barrel was level with my forehead. "Who are you?" I asked.

"Open the desk," he said with my voice. I was frozen. He pressed the gun to my head. "Open it."

Feeling my sweat run around the ring of cold metal I reached down to my desk drawer, pulled it open.

The man with my face pulled the gun away, just a few inches. "Look inside."

With effort I pulled my gaze away from the pistol aimed at me, looked down. A jar like those that had been in Roger's suitcase sat there, a clay tube with a top carved in the shape of a cat's head.

"What's going on?" Roger said, his voice cracking. "Aren't we already dead? Who is this?"

I looked myself in the face, suddenly unafraid. "You're what I couldn't leave behind, aren't you?"

"You said you'd cleared your own suitcase," Roger said. "That you just stayed here out of compassion."

"No—not compassion," I said. "Curiosity. I realize that now." The man with my face smiled, nodded. "That's what I couldn't let go, why I stayed here—the puzzle. Wanting to know how it all works out." I laughed. "I'm just as much of a sap as you are, Roger."

The man with my face lowered the gun, tapped it against the jar. I nodded, and he grabbed the lid with his free hand. I took the base and we each pulled, and when it had popped open he was gone.

I took a deep breath, picked up Roger's suitcase. It was light, lighter than a feather. "Here," I said, handed it to him.

He took it by the handle. "It's empty," he said. "But does that mean you're—we're—"

"This part of me stayed here," I said. "That part of me—the part that couldn't let go—wound up as you."

He took a step for the office door. "So we're—free? Both of us?"

"Come on," I said. I flipped the sign on my door to CLOSED, stepped out into the corridor and locked up. The two of us started to walk down the street, towards the airport. "This looks like the beginning of a beautiful friendship."

When We Have Time

"We have to tell her."

Kevin shook his head. "We don't. She'll never know. It'll just—she won't even notice it."

"We'll know," Jen said, crossing her arms.

It was true, of course. He looked over at Heather in the living room, wondering if she was able to hear everything they said. So far as he could tell she was still engrossed in her Ed-U-Tutor, but he always had the feeling that she knew a lot more than she ever showed.

She looked so much like Jen. Jen always said she looked like him, of course; Heather was a backwards mirror, each of her parents seeing the other in her face.

"I can't. I don't think I could make her understand."

"I know. Do you think I'd have brought this up if I wasn't ready to tell her myself?" Jen kissed him on the cheek, turned away. He watched her, unable to make the few steps that would let him follow from the kitchen to where their daughter sat.

"Heather, can I talk to you a minute?"

"Just a second, mom." Heather clicked a button on the 'Tutor, saving her work. If she heard the strangled sound in her mother's voice, she gave no sign of it. "What's up?"

It was impossible that she was ten. He knew he was biased,

but to Kevin she had always sounded as mature and self-possessed as someone twice her age. He didn't get to see her that much, of course; she was usually asleep by the time he got home from work. He had thought, maybe, that that would change now that he wasn't working. Now he would never know.

"There's something I—your father and I have been meaning to tell you," Jen said.

Heather raised an eyebrow. "If it's about boys and girls, the 'Tutor already told me."

Jen smiled, despite herself, and Kevin felt himself doing it as well. "No, that's not—that's not it. It's about—well, you know how your father isn't working anymore."

"I know. But Dad'll find something soon."

"Of course he will. But for now there are some things, things we were paying for that we can't afford to anymore. And you—do you know how you came to be with us?"

How you came to be with us; what an awkward way of saying it, Kevin thought. But then, everything about this was awkward.

"I told you," Heather said. "The 'Tutor—"

"No," Jen said, an unmistakable choking coming into her voice. "You didn't, not that way. We—you know your father and I have always been very busy, working very hard. To keep this house, buy you clothes and things."

"Yes . . ."

Kevin pulled the photo album from the shelf over the phone. The leatherette spine cracked like it was new when it opened; he couldn't remember the last time he'd looked at it.

"Well, you see we never had quite enough time—for you. I mean, to have you. There was never a time when either of us could stay home, never mind spending a few weeks off my feet."

"I don't understand."

The baby pictures were getting hazy, indistinct. The ultrasound was already gone, replaced by a snapshot of that trip to Algonquin Park they'd never taken.

"We really, really wanted to have you, Heather, you need to know that. So we went to—you know that machine in the kitchen, that makes sure you have a lunch, even if we forget to make you one?"

Heather nodded, not understanding. "You always forget," she said.

"Yes, I know, honey." Jen took a breath, plowed on. "Well, when we decided we wanted to have a little girl, we went to someone who had a big one of those machines. Big enough so that instead of making sure you had a lunch, it made sure we had you."

The picture of Heather on her first bike flickered and disappeared. Kevin could already feel the memory of it doing the same thing, another one rushing to fill the vacuum in his mind. An office, beige wall-to-wall and a pine desk.

"This is one of our most popular packages," the man in his memory was saying. Light from the window shone off the gold lettering on his coffee mug, TIME SOLUTIONS. "Especially among couples your age. You don't have to worry she'd be singled out in any way."

Jen looked over at Kevin, shifted her weight in her chair. "I don't understand," she said. "Would she be—different?"

The man frowned, his solid features coming slowly into focus as the memory grew stronger. "No more than—I'm sorry, Ms. James, I forgot this is your first time in here. No, your child won't be different in any way. All we'll do is pinch off a little pocket of time—let's say, five years ago—and make that the time when you had your child; then we re-attach the pocket to our time, and so far as the world is concerned you have a five-year-old daughter."

"Just a minute," Kevin remembered saying as he flipped through the papers in front of him. "What's the monthly fee for, then?"

"To keep that pocket attached to our time," the man said, a note of impatience in his voice—the sound, Kevin thought, of a teacher explaining something for the tenth time.

Heather's voice called Kevin back to the present. "So I'm not—not—" He knew she was close to tears, confused and frustrated.

"You're real, Heather. You have to remember—have to know that. It's just that—well, once you were in our lives it didn't seem so urgent to have you. So long as the machine kept working, we forgot that you had come to us any differently from anyone else's baby. And so long as we could keep paying the man with the machine, it didn't matter. But now that your father's out of work—"

"So I'm going to—I'm going to—"

"It's not like dying, baby," Jen said. "You'll just—disappear—but when your father finds a new job we'll bring you back again. It'll be just the same as before."

"What if there's a power failure?"

"We have enough backup power to run this facility for a month," the man said. "And if worst comes to worst, we can always start over."

"But would it be her? The same her, I mean?" Jen asked.

The man sighed; he had, Kevin now remembered, a walrus moustache that quivered when he breathed out. "Ms. James—every child is a miracle. To expect to repeat a miracle . . ."

"But I'll be—will I be—?" Heather's voice sounded hollow, somehow. He couldn't blame her.

"You'll be you, honey. You'll be you." Jen put her arms around her daughter and held her, and held her, and held her, and held nothing at all.

Kevin walked over to her, put a useless hand on her shoulder. "I'm sorry," he said. "I should have helped."

"S'okay," his wife said. "It's—better it was just me. Easier."

He said nothing at all for a while; then he crouched down so he was pressed against her back, and held her. "I'm sorry," he said again. "I couldn't—I couldn't have. I'm glad you could. You're right; she needed to know." He kissed her on the top of her head, his tears falling into her hair. "I don't know what I'd do without you."

There was a rush of imploding air, and an absence; just then, he remembered something else he'd never had time to do.

The Wise Foolish Son

The flames are almost to the river, now, and on the other bank we can see our brothers' homes burning. We had thought ourselves safe here in the north, far from the enemies of our people, where only wild men live. Who is it here that can hate us so much?

An old man is speaking. He is the only one who speaks the language of the men that live in the forests beyond the river: he, perhaps, can tell us what is happening.

"Once there were three sons," the old man says. It might be the light of a campfire flickering against his bearded cheeks, and not a city burning. "The oldest was wise, the second foolish, and the third son was wise-foolish.

"Do you know what that means? We call a man wise-foolish when he has a foolish mind but a wise heart. This boy was like that, and his name was Dasat."

The old man pauses, and we bite our tongues. We are not children, we want to say, to be told such stories, but his are the only answers we have. "The three boys' father was poor, so he had nothing to give but his blessing. The oldest son did not ask for it, for he was wise enough to know he did not need it, nor did the second son ask for it, for he was foolish enough to believe he did not need it. So it was left for Dasat, wise-foolish, to ask his father's blessing, and this is what his father said:

"'Three things I have given you, my son, though you cannot see them. The first is your good heart, the second the good manners I have taught you, the third the earth that belongs to all. With these three things surely you can win everything you seek.'

"'Thank you, father,' Dasat said, and set off to seek his fortune.

"As he left, though, his mother stopped him, and gave him a piece of bread wrapped in a handkerchief, saying, 'Take this, and hungry though you be, always leave a few crumbs tied up in the handkerchief; if you do, it will be a piece of bread again the next day.'

"In those days we Kamanai neither timbered trees nor cleared land for farms, for fear of Mokos whose soil it was. So Dasat followed the crooked path through the woods, and though he went from house to house there was no fortune for him in any of them, nor even shelter; for in those days the men of our land lived apart from one another, and owed one another no obligations. Before long came winter, the time when Birun, the God in the Tree, dies. The time when the Lord of Lightning goes mad."

The hairy man shhed loudly and then sat cross-legged on the ground. He began laboriously turning a wooden pole so it dug into the earth, stopping every few seconds to fan smoke from the pile of fragrant leaves over the hole, and humming: "A-hmm-a-HM-ah, forgive us, Mokos, lady of dark soil and dark winters, this wound; A-hmm-a-HM, forgive us, Lord of Lightning, our trespass against your daughter." Finally the hole was deep enough for the pole to stand upright. The hairy man stood and allowed the others around him to begin raising the tent around it.

Guessing it was safe to speak again, Dasatan said, "Still a good bell before sunset."

Balat stepped hard on the still-smouldering leaves and ground his foot into them. "Door needs to face south," the hairy man said, in broken Kavatai. "Need the sun to tell east and west; how can you tell south without east and west?"

"In your language," Dasatan said, shaking his head. "My father wants me to get better at it, since none of you know trade signs. Where I come from, we tell north and south by the stars."

Balat gestured to the forest canopy above. "If you can see the stars, it's a bad place for a camp. No shelter from the wind. Nothing to keep snow off your tent."

"It's spring."

"It's never spring," Balat said. He grinned, an expression with no mirth whatsoever. "Only winter and summer. But summer pays for all."

Dasatan said nothing. He had grown up never wearing anything more than a tunic and cloak, and he felt himself slumping under the unfamiliar weight of the jacket Balat insisted he wear. It was a dreadful thing, weighing at least a stone, crudely stitched together from wild sheepskins and still smelling strongly of the piss that had been used to tan it.

He hated it. He hated this whole country—the endless red birch trees that hid the sun for bells at a time; the nameless winds that crept under his jacket and tunic and froze his blood; the mosquitoes that rose in a humming cloud each time he entered a new stretch of forest, ready to suck the life out of him; the constantly expanding list of rules, against everything from breaking the soil to touching steel; the stinking tents and the stinking men he needed to lead him to the only thing that made coming here worthwhile.

That last reminded him of something he could get done while waiting for the tent to be raised. He looked around and saw the other ai Kavatai standing together in a knot, their backs to him. No-one was pushing them to learn the language, and they tried their best to avoid the pale, hairy ai Kamanai. He walked over to join them, braced himself to stand tall under their contempt. "Time to earn your keep, Yavan," he said.

A short man, clad in a black robe with patchy silver filigree, turned around. The robe failed altogether to hide his stomach, which bulged out of his otherwise thin frame, and he had a head that was nearly bald except for a half-dozen long black hairs. The stone at his staff tip glinted red in the sunlight as he waved it dramatically, drawing his thick eyebrows together in a frown. "Did your father never tell you not to mock a boltforge, boy?" Yavan asked.

"He did, but I'm sure he wasn't thinking of you," Dasatan said. One of the other ai Kavatai laughed. Good: if they had someone else to mock they would find it easier to follow him. "If you were any kind of real boltforge you wouldn't be out here, with us. Do you think Tivakar spent his nights huddled under a skin tent, cheek-by-jowl with ai Kamanai?"

Yavan locked eyes with him, gave him a menacing look—Dasatan felt a moment's anticipation; a snake with only one fang still has venom, after all—then looked away. "Laugh if you will, but I get a finger from each hand of what we bring home. I'll be spending my nights with more pleasant companions soon enough. Where will you be?"

He let the question hang, since everyone already knew the answer. His father might have put him in charge of these men, but unlike them he had already risen as far as he could ever go.

His point won, Yavan drew a broad cloth from nowhere and lay it on the ground. "Pour out today's goods and I shall, as you say, earn my keep."

Dasatan untied the bag at his belt, emptied it onto the black cloth: a dozen stones, ranging from yellow to dark red. Yavan lowered his staff, amber-tipped and twined with copper wire, to hold it near each of them in turn. This was the reason he was on the trip, the one working he could do well: in his hands the stone at the tip of his staff would glow in sympathy with the stones that were true amber, the blood of the god. If they had even a moderate haul one finger of it would fetch a small fortune from real boltforges, and after that Yavan would indeed have a comfortable life, for a long or a short while according to his tastes. Dasatan, on the other hand, would be here again next spring, or on some other road.

"Come on," Dasatan said once the stones had been sorted. He would transfer the true amber to his private pouch, the one worn under his tunic, when he was alone. It was nearly dark, and a cold wind had begun to blow. "Let's get inside. You, too, Yavan—unless you'd like to stay out here to draw the lightning away from the tent?"

"So," the old man goes on, "Dasat knew there was no fortune to be found in the houses of the people, and if he did not find shelter soon he would freeze. Finally he had no choice but to go into the deep forest, though it is a dangerous enough place in the summer and worse in the winter.

"He made his way slowly into the forest, for the paths were few and overgrown. When the sun was high he stopped and ate nearly all the piece of bread his mother had given him, being sure to save the last few crumbs. Just as he was folding up the handkerchief, though, he heard a cheep-cheep-cheep, and saw above him a tiny bird resting wearily on a bare branch. It was all red but for a single black feather on each wing.

"Remembering the good manners his father had taught him Dasat took off his hat and said, 'Good day, gentle bird; is there any service I can give you?'

"The bird raised its wings, and Dasat could see it was thin and weak under its feathers. 'I am one of the Day Birds,' the bird said, 'who help to pull the sun across the sky from east to west. I fell from my yoke, and have been chasing after my flock ever since. I am now very close, as they are right overhead, but I am so desperately hungry I fear I will never catch them without something to eat.'

"Dasat, of course, had only those few crumbs left in the handkerchief, and if his mind had been wise he would have kept them; but his heart made him say 'Noble bird, I would be glad to share with you the little I have.' He opened the handkerchief, and the bird hopped into his palm and ate up all the crumbs that were left.

"'Thank you,' the bird said, 'for such is all the meal I need.' With that, he leapt up into the air and shot off away, so that soon he was only a spot on the sun. Dasat continued on into the forest, wondering what he was to eat now that the last crumbs of bread were gone.

"Further into the woods he saw the lights of a house."

The worst of it, Dasatan thought, was that your feet were always wet. For whatever reason the amber was always found in damp places—swamps, riverbeds, and so on. There were even tales of places, much farther north and west than any Kavatai had ever been, where it was trawled right out of the sea in nets. It would be easier if the ai

Kamanai would collect it themselves, so he could just buy it from them, but to them that was sacrilege: they would lead him and his men to where the amber was likely to be, but no more. That meant bells of wading through water and mud, looking for the telltale blue soil in which the stones always sat—just as the Lord of Lightning, whose spilled blood the stones were, made his home within the Blue Sky Lord's domain.

The memory of the previous day's exchange with Yavan was still sour, and Dasatan had allowed himself to stray out of sight of the others. He followed a stream, shallow but cold, similar to places he'd made good finds in the past. Looking down at the water he did not at first notice the sudden darkening, but could not miss the thunder that broke the air. He turned—they had all been instructed by Balat to return to camp if they heard thunder—but though it was just past midday it was nearly too dark to see. He felt a cold, wet kiss on the back of his neck, then another. Snow: within a moment it had filled his eyes and mouth, blinding and choking him. Before ten heartbeats had passed the world around him was gone, replaced by a solid white wall. He cursed that he should die here, not at sea like a true Kavatai: killed not by the Wind of Ill Fortune or even the Wind of Roasting Hazelnuts but by a cold, nameless wind—a wind as dirtborn as he was.

Dasatan tried to shout, but the snow held his voice close. He stumbled forward, thinking only to get up and out of the riverbed before his feet froze in the water. Never mind finding the others: he needed to get to shelter before this wind and snow killed him. He ran for the distant outline of a group of trees, hoping there would be some protection from the storm beneath them.

He leaned back against the thin, papery bark of one of the trees, closed his eyes. There was no use even trying to start a fire while the wind was blowing. Far above, thunderbolts cracked as the Lord of Lightning took his strides across the sky. There would be good amber to be found here next year, if he lived that long.

Long heartbeats later the keening in the air faded and then stopped. Opening his eyes Dasatan saw that the storm had passed, only little orphan-winds remaining to blow the fallen snow along the ground. He looked around and saw nothing but tree after tree. The blowing snow had obliterated his footprints, so that he could not tell which way he had come. The sky was still grey, the sun hidden: he fished in his pouch for his skystone before realizing that knowing south, east, north and west would do him little good in finding his way back to the others. All he could do was keep moving, call out often in case he was near them, and hope. Picking a direction at random he set off, making sure to stay in the shelter of the tall birches in case of another storm.

After some time he saw a light in the forest, and began to walk towards it.

"As he got closer, Dasat saw that it was no ordinary house. The walls were made not of wood but of bones, the roof not thatch but hair. There were no windows: what he had thought were firelights were the glowing eyes of the skulls that sat at each corner of the house. A garden lay in front of it, but the plants that grew those were such as Dasat had never seen, and the grass moaned as it waved in the wind. At the foot of the path sat a strange little man, with dark blue skin, a white beard, and a peaked red hat, and so still that Dasat was not even sure he was alive until he spoke.

"'Who are you, Kamanai?' the little man said. 'Do you not know where you tread? Turn back, now, before it is too late.'

"Dasat was surprised to hear the little man speaking, but he remembered his manners. 'Beg pardon, Little Father,' he said. 'My name is Dasat. I am come seeking my fortune, but tonight I hope only for shelter and a fire.'

"'You speak properly,' the little man said, 'so I will give you a warning: this is a terrible house. Flee now and you may be safe; stay any longer and death is sure to take you.'

"'If I leave here tonight she will take me no matter what, for I am out of food, and winter is coming,' Dasat said. 'If you could spare anything, even the tiniest crumb of bread, I would be on my way.'

"'I am bound to give nothing away for free,' the little man said. 'But here is a bargain for you: if you will gather wood for me you may stay here, and I will bring you some food each day. But you must never, ever go into the house.'"

It was no more than a gathering of tents, each smaller than the one Balat had erected the night before; still there was a fire-glow from them, a draw Dasatan could not ignore. His hand hovered over his sword hilt as he neared the tents, then drew away as he remembered Balat's warning against drawing steel—an insult to the Lord of Lightning, he had said. Though Dasatan did not put much stock in these superstitions, he needed to make a good impression. The ai Kamanai were wild men, living not in towns but in camps scattered through the forests, and few were even as hospitable as Balat and his followers.

A squat, red-haired man emerged when Dasatan was a pole from the nearest tent. Dasatan could not understand him when he spoke, hearing only the man's sharp tone: the dialect was different from the one he knew, and he realized now just how slowly Balat had been speaking for his benefit.

"I am Dasatan, of the ai Daneyanim," Dasatan said as carefully as he could. "Have you seen or heard any others like me, or some of your people, moving in a group?"

"No," the man said, keeping his broad bulk between Dasatan and the tents.

"Well, might I warm myself by your fire?" Dasatan asked.

"No."

Dasatan took a breath. "I need only to warm myself so I can go and find my companions. I can pay you if you wish."

The man's thick eyebrows rose. "Pay?"

Smiling, Dasatan unhooked from his belt the sack of trade goods he used to pay Balat and the other ai Kamanai he had hired. Trinkets, really: coral necklaces from Kadain Kisak, silk scarves from Sherez. "I have jewellery that would please any woman. Ribbons, and thread—"

"Pff," the man said, and spat into the bushes off to his right. "Do you think me a bachelor, to have to buy a woman's kisses?" He waved the pouch away. "There is nothing here I want. Go."

"If I go now I will freeze to death," Dasatan said, forcing the words past his teeth.

The man shrugged. "So what is that to me? Who are you to me? No kin of mine."

"I could be warm by now," Dasatan said, unable to keep his voice calm any longer. "It would cost you no more to let me stand by your fire than to stand here and argue with me."

The man leaned in towards Dasatan, his eyes narrowing. "You are no kin to me. I owe you nothing. You have nothing I want. Go."

Without even thinking of it Dasatan felt his hand fly to his sword hilt. Flame all these primitive superstitions, he was past worrying about offending the locals. The man's eyes widened for a moment as the short steel blade cut the air.

A heartbeat later—or two, or more; he was sure his heart had stopped—Dasatan lay on the ground. His sword had fallen a rod away from his numb, twitching fingers.

"Go home, stranger," the man said, turning away. "Or die, if that is your destiny. It is no matter to me."

"So Dasat spent his days in the forest, looking for fallen branches to feed the fire in the house, and as the snow rose about him and the cold winds blew he would cast his eye more and more to the firelight glowing inside. No matter how close he came to the house, though, he could never feel any of the fire's heat, not even when he touched the walls, and his little skin tent grew colder and colder. He never went in, though, and he never saw the woman the little man had said lived there.

"One morning he woke to find that the wind had blown his tent open in the night, and snow had drifted in. It had nearly buried him, and he felt as though he would die if he did not get warm. As he stepped out of his tent he saw, again, the eyes of the skulls glowing with firelight. He did not even stop to remember the little man's warning, but went right up to the door, opened it and stepped inside.

"At first all he knew was that it was warm, and he felt the ice in his blood and the frost on his eyelashes melting away. Then he saw the inside of the house.

"All around, hanging from the ceiling, were iron hooks, and hanging from each was the empty skin of a man, curing into leather. A great stone mortar sat on a huge wooden table, and in it sat a dozen thighbones waiting to be crushed. At the middle was a stone chimney, and in it sat a great iron pot, and out of the pot came the sweet smell of boiling man-flesh. The little blue man with the red cap was running around the pot's rim, holding a wooden spoon and stirring it around in the soup. When he saw Dasat he stopped.

"'What are you doing, little Kamanai?' he cried out. 'Do you know not where you are? This is the house of Mokos, the daughter of the Lord of Lightning and Moist Mother Earth, the lady of dark soil and dark winter. Those plants you saw in the garden were souls she was waiting to harvest, and this house is made from the bones and hair of the ones she has already taken. When she returns at sundown she will smell that you were here and find you. Why, oh why did you come into the house?'"

"Can you stand?"

Dasatan opened his eyes. He had no idea how long he had been lying on the ground: he remembered nothing more after falling than crawling away from the camp, looking for somewhere to sleep where he would be sheltered from the wind. Though his vision was still blurry he could see a woman reaching down to grab his wrists. "I don't know," he said.

"Try." The woman was shorter than most ai Kamanai, with long, straight brown hair; like all the others she wore wool trousers and a sheepskin jacket, but hers looked as though it had swallowed her. She grunted with effort as she helped him up, and he could see just enough of her arms to see that it was mostly bone and gristle doing the pulling.

He stood cautiously, shocks still jumping through his arms and legs. "Who are you?" he asked; then, remembering his manners, "I am Dasatan, a trader for the ai Kavatai."

"My name is Ayusha," she said.

"You seem more hospitable than the rest of your family," Dasatan said, looking around for the man he had spoken to earlier. As he tugged his tunic down for modesty he felt his loincloth was cold and damp, and he was embarrassed to realize he had wet himself.

"They are not my family," she said. "Nor yours. That is why we have to leave."

"All right," he said. He spotted his sword lying among the wet leaf-litter, reached for it cautiously.

The hair on the back of his arms rose as his hand neared the hilt. "You might as well leave that," Ayusha said. "This land is the Lord of Lightning's, and he loves iron more than anything."

Not answering, Dasatan reached out for the sword; a spark jumped from the pommel to his hand. He jumped back, waved his hand to shake the tingling out.

"Let's go, then," he said.

"Dasat sat and waited for Mokos to come and eat him, too cold and tired to do anything else. Before she came, though, a black shape came fluttering down the chimney; the little man in the red cap tried to snatch it, but it dodged out of his grasp and landed on Dasat's shoulder. It was a bird, all black save for a single red feather on each wing.

"'Who are you, little bird?' Dasat asked, curious in spite of his despair.

"'I am one of the Night Birds, who pull the moon across the sky,' the bird said. 'I am here to repay the kindness you paid to my brother. Listen carefully: there is no sense in trying to run or hide from Mokos, for she can smell out human flesh anywhere around the world.'

"'Then I am doomed,' Dasat said.

"'Do not lose faith. When Mokos first comes home she will be an old crone, and very hungry, and will be keen to eat you. But for two bells each night, just before dawn, she is a beautiful maiden: if at that time you can get her to promise not to eat you, you will be safe until the next night. If you do this every night until spring comes you will be free to leave.'

"There was a wind at the shutters, and the bird fluttered its wings nervously. 'I must be gone before she comes,' it said, and fluttered back up the chimney.

"A great wind blew into the house, and with it came an old woman. She had hair like coarse rope, skin grey as a winter sky, and teeth sharp as knives; on each hand were five iron nails. This was Mokos."

"If they're not your family, why are you here?" Dasatan asked after the two had walked through the forest for half a bell or so. There was no path that he could see, but Ayusha seemed to know where she was going.

"They were supposed to be," she said. "I was to marry one of the sons of the man you spoke to. But my own mother and father died last winter. Without family I had nothing to give."

"So they just abandoned you?"

"No—they gave me this jacket, and let me follow them to their forage grounds, so long as I keep my camp out of sight." She stopped, bowed slightly. "Here it is."

Dasatan saw only a small clearing in the woods, made by the trunk of a fir tree that had fallen and been caught by the crook of another. Only after a moment did he see that there was a thin wall of sticks piled against the tree on the windward side, and a small fire pit in the dirt under its pulled roots. "This is your home?" he asked.

Ayusha said nothing.

"Well, thank you," Dasatan said, "but I really just need to find my companions again. They'll be making camp soon—"

"They are gone," Ayusha said. "Svatyslan, the man you spoke to—he would have been my father-in-law—he went looking for them after you came, to warn them off his forage grounds. They are nowhere around."

So they had just left him. No surprise, really: they owed him nothing, and he didn't think his father would much mourn his loss. Dirtborn, roadbound, and now abandoned in the woods beyond the world; Yavan was laughing now, he supposed.

He reached down to his belt, patted the pouch with the true stones in it. At least losing him would cost the smug bastard something.

"Here," she said, reaching down into a leaf-covered hole in the shade of the fallen tree. "You'll need something to eat. Aren't you hungry?"

Dasatan rubbed his head, fingertips still buzzing. He hadn't thought about food since the snow started to fall; now that he did, he realized he was starving. "Yes," he said. "Please."

She stood, passed him a handful of dried black berries covered with a light fuzz. "They're good, really," she said.

"Thank you," he said, took one into his mouth and let it soften on his tongue. It was good, sweet and tart, but hardly made a dent in his newly discovered hunger. "Um—is there —"

"Anything else?" she said. "Here." She reached back into the hole, drew out a small mushroom and handed it to him.

He looked the thing over. With its sickly white flesh and dirt-brown cap, it was much less appetizing than the berries had been. "Am I supposed to—eat this?"

"No," she said; hungry though he was a wave of relief washed over him. "Go see if you can find some—it grows in clearings and on stumps. Don't pick any with pink or red on them, though."

Dasatan looked down at his hands. This whole episode had the quality of a dream, and he half-wondered if he was still lying on the ground by the tent. "I'm not sure I—"

"I'm hoping," Ayusha said, "that you're going to bring in more food than you eat; that you're worth my letting you share my shelter and fire. If you want to convince me of that, you'd better get started."

"The old woman wrinkled her nose as she looked around the cottage. 'I smell human flesh,' Mokos said. 'Where are you, my little morsel?'

"Dasat was terrified at the sight of her, but he remembered his manners. 'I am here, grandmother,' he said. 'I am sorry to have come into your cottage without asking, but I was very cold and wanted only to sit by your fire.'

"'Well, that may be and it may not,' Mokos said, 'but I'm going to eat you either way. Now be a good boy and hop into the pot.'

"Dasat looked into the deep iron pot, merrily boiling away as the little man ran around it with his spoon. He had, as I said, a foolish mind and a wise heart; there was no way he could trick Mokos, so he thought how he might slow her down by kindness. 'You wouldn't want to put me in the pot, granny,' he said. 'I'd make terrible stock, with so little fat on me. I'd boil away to bones in no time.'

"Mokos looked him up and down. 'So you would, sonny, and I must say it's mighty fine of you to say so. It's few of you that shows such concern for granny. So up onto the hook you go to hang, for if you're not fit for stock then you must be game.'

"Dasat looked around at the hooks hanging from the ceiling, and all but one of them had a man hanging from it, drying like venison. 'You wouldn't want to hang me, granny, for I've been out in the snow all winter; I'd get mouldy before I aged properly.'

"Mokos sniffed him up and down. 'So you would, sonny, and I thank you again. Since you're so helpful, tell me how I should eat you if I'm not to boil or to age you?'

"Dasat made as though he were thinking about it. 'You should wait to have me for breakfast, granny,' he said. 'For the only fat left on me is just a strip around my belly, and that's good for bacon; the rest of me you can fry in the grease and cook in an egg-cake.'

"At that Mokos's eyes lit up, and her long red tongue, with hairs on it like a cat's, shot out and licked her lips. 'That's the thing to do, and no doubt about it,' she said. 'You're a breath of fresh air, you are, and I thank you again. Oh, if I can only wait until breakfast!'"

"Skylord!" Blood welled up from Dasatan's fingertip. He shook his hand and sucked at the thorn in his flesh, then swore again as the cloth full of berries fell to the ground. "Oh, sweet Sisters . . ." He knelt down, felt a dozen other brambles scratch him as he tried to retrieve the berries he had collected earlier. It was a given, he had learned, that the useless or poisonous plants were the most accessible, while anything worth eating was protected by an army of tiny swords. These ones, tiny strawberries, at least didn't have thorns themselves, but were inevitably found in the middle of a patch of thistle. At least he could tell now which berries were edible; Ayusha's rejection of all but two of the mushrooms he had gathered that first day had been as humiliating as anything in his life.

"What's the matter?" her voice called from the other side of the thicket.

"Nothing," he said, gathering the fallen berries as quickly as he could.

"Are you sure? You sounded hurt."

"I'm fine." He straightened up, gathered the corners of the cloth together and tied them securely. "You don't need to—"

"What's this?"

"I said I was fine," Dasatan said.

Ayusha looked around at the dark, bare earth on his side of the bramble. "What happened to all the plants here?"

"I pulled them."

She frowned. "Why?"

"To plant things. Berries, whatever."

"The dark soil is sacred to the Lady," Ayusha said in a tut-tutting voice. "We take what grows from it, but we don't dig into it."

"I know," Dasatan said. "That's why I'm covered with scratches from head to foot, from picking wild berries. That's why we have to spend dawn to sunset rummaging for whatever food your former family hasn't picked yet. There's little enough life in this land in the spring—have you thought about what we'll do when winter comes?"

"We'll survive."

"Are you sure of that?"

"Don't be angry," Ayusha said, looking down. She was nearer, now: swaddled in the bulk of her jacket she looked even smaller than she was, like a child.

"I'm not angry. Not at you . . . but your people, the way they are—unfriendly and superstitious—"

A spark returned to her eyes as she met his. "Are you sure it's superstition?" she asked, pronouncing the word carefully in Kavatai; it did not exist in her language. "You've felt the Lord's power, why do you doubt his daughter's?"

"I've seen what boltforges work with amber. I know that power exists."

"And planting fruits, you've done this before?"

He picked up a fallen branch he'd selected as a digging stick.

"No. But I've seen it done, by the people we buy from. It doesn't look so hard." Ayusha crossed her arms, said nothing. "What? You make a hole in the ground, put in some seeds, put water on it, and keep the weeds off."

"How foolish my people must be, not to have thought of this before."

"Not foolish. Just—uncivilized. It's not your fault; all the people of the world were the same, before we taught them better, and we needed the Powers to teach us." He took the digging stick in both hands, raised it, and slammed it into the black earth. It made no impression; he might as well have been striking rock.

"Problem?"

"No-one's ever cut this soil before," Dasatan said. He begun to spin the stick in his palms, the way he had seen Balat plant the tent pole. "It's like baked mud."

"Dasatan . . ."

"No, wait—I've got it." He paused to let out a long breath, went back to spinning the stick. After a hundred heartbeats had passed he stopped. Less than a finger's depth had been dug into the dirt; at this rate a single row would take him all day.

"The Lady protects her realm," Ayusha said quietly. "I do not know what weak gods you worship in the south, Dasatan, but ours demand respect. Now, please—we have to get back to our gathering, and waste no more time on this."

"No," Dasatan said. "We just need something harder to cut the soil—my sword—"

"Do you want to go through that again?"

"Flame it!" he shouted, throwing the stick away into the brush. "This stupid country! With its stupid gods and stupid superstitions and stupid people and—what kind of home is this, where it's winter for ten moons a year and you can't even grow beans? How are people supposed to live here?"

"Dasatan, listen to me." He had been ignoring the rising annoyance in her voice; now it was unmistakable. "All I'm asking is that you help me gather enough food to get us through this year and the winter. Then in the spring, when your people come again, you can go back with them and leave me to all this. All right?"

Dasatan laughed, knowing it would make Ayusha angrier but unable to stop himself.

"What?" she asked, her cheeks reddening.

"They're not my people. So far as they're concerned I'm no more a Kavatai than you are. That's why I'm here, when all my brothers and sisters are at sea. The only reason they might try to find me is because I was carrying the—" He stopped, seized by a sudden thought. 'You said the Lord of Lightning loves iron, that's why I can't touch my sword. But I know he loves copper even more—that's why the boltforges use it in their workings—and Yavan carried a staff with copper on it all the time, and he never worried about it . . ."

Ayusha rubbed her forehead with her palm. "Can we please just get back to—"

"No—no, this is a good idea," he said, shrugging out of his jacket. "We need to go back to the shelter, get my pouch with the amber in it. Then we need to go back to Svatyslan's camp—my sword should still be there."

"All right," she said, forcing the words through her clenched teeth. "Will you at least tell me what we're doing?"

He shook his head, stayed silent as they got his pouch and went to where his sword lay, afraid one of the gods up here—more attentive, it seemed, to mortal concerns than the ones he knew back home—might hear his plan. On the way there he pulled a handful of resin off a pine tree, tapped it between his thumb and forefinger until it became tacky.

"Now will you tell me?" Ayusha asked when they found the sword, looking around nervously for Svatyslan and any of her other former relatives.

"Watch," he said. He crouched down over the sword and laid his jacket over it; then, carefully, he rolled the jacket so the sword was inside. Even through the thick sheepskin he could feel a tingling, and he held the bundle as gently as he could as he turned it so the sword-hilt was up. With his free hand he fished a piece of true amber from his pouch, stuck the ball of resin to it, and pressed the stone to the pommel of the sword.

This was the test. He took a breath, seized the sword hilt. Nothing.

Dasatan took his jacket off the sword, raised it to his lips and kissed the blade. "May the smith who made you forgive me," he said to it, "but you're a plow from now on."

"So the two of them sat, waiting for the night to pass. Dasat began to wonder if the Night Bird's words had been true, and watched the sky outside, afraid that dawn might come too soon.

"His heart jumped when he saw a first ray of light in the east; when he looked back a change had come over the cottage. The pot was now full of good porridge, and wild herbs and fat shining fish hung drying from the hooks. He looked over at Mokos and saw that she was now a beautiful maiden. Her skin was gold as the sun, her hair green as spring grass, dotted with wildflowers.

"'Will you promise not to eat me till tomorrow?' Dasat said, the words pouring out of his mouth in a rush.

"Mokos laughed, and her laughter was like summer rain. 'That was not very polite of you,' she said. 'I will grant your wish, though I hope it will be asked a bit less hastily tomorrow night.'

"Soon enough the dawn came, and both the cottage and Mokos became fearsome once more. Though Mokos was angry at not being able to eat her breakfast she nevertheless kept her word, and went out of the house till sunset."

It was easier, Dasatan had found, if you used your imagination. You could imagine that the rock-hard clod of earth that had to be broken was Yavan's head, for instance, or that the stinging weeds that had to be pulled were Svatyslan's lungs.

The plants he had sown—some of them—were starting to come up, accompanied by a much larger number of weeds seeking to take advantage of the earth he had cleared. He had abandoned the idea of planting berries when Ayusha told him how long their bushes took to grow, sown instead wild buckwheat, leeks and onions. Before long—not too long, he hoped—they'd be able to eat some of them.

He stood, rested his weight on his blunted sword. It had become an all-purpose tool now—weed-digger, plow, brush-cutter—but he imagined it would still cut Kamanai flesh if Svatyslan or one of his family were to come and challenge his right to farm this plot. He hoped they would.

"Dasatan!" Ayusha's voice called from the other side of the bramble. "Are you finished with your garden yet?" Kamanai didn't have a word for farm; garden was the word they used for the few herbs they grew outside their tents. "I found a patch of reedmace downstream. Come and help me pick it."

"Just a moment," he said. He drove the point of his sword into the dirt so it stood upright, and removed the amber from the pommel: the thought of a Kamanai trying to steal it without the stone drawing the lightning out made him smile. "How far downstream?" he asked.

Ayusha emerged from the brambles, holding the broad gathering-cloth they used for larger plants. She was thinner than when he had first met her, even her round face looking drawn and sharp. He knew that if he were to look in the water he would see the same in his face.

"Just past where we went last week." He sighed. That walk down the river had taken them most of the day. "Well, we've got to go out further—Svatyslan has left little enough food, and we've picked just about all of it. If we moved the shelter . . ."

"Let's go," he said. "Reedmaces have lots of seeds. Maybe we can grow some here."

"It's not damp enough for them."

"We can try."

They walked in silence to the river's edge. He wondered if another Kavatai would even recognize him now: legs covered with scars—his tunic was long gone, and there were no Kamanai trousers for him to wear—hands and nails so dirty no amount of washing would get them clean.

"Hold on," he said as they reached a spot on the stream where rocks made a natural weir. He had built a fish trap out of branches the day before.

"Well?"

"It's broken. I'll have to find a way to make it stronger."

"It wasn't the fish that broke it," Ayusha said darkly. "It was Svatyslan, or one of his sons. Fish are sacred to Birun; they don't want you bringing them bad luck. Keep this up and they won't let us stay in their grounds anymore."

"It's bad enough they keep trampling my plants. I should be watching them now, not spending all day picking reedmace."

"You're spending enough time on that as it is—working too hard, and I can't gather enough food for the both of us."

"Then go," he said, tossing the sticks away and watching them run downstream. "Anyway, I'd like to see them try to make us leave now."

"Then maybe you could beat someone else with your sword, make him let us use his foraging grounds."

"You don't beat someone with a sword," he said. "You cut them." He shook his head, dissolving the visions of Svatyslan's throat blooming red as his blade cut across it. He was no warrior, but it wouldn't be hard; for all their strength, without iron or steel the Kamanai were just brawlers, homeless savages with no more ambition than to take over another family's foraging grounds. No wonder they sat on treasure and traded it away for trinkets.

"Mokos will get us all soon enough," Ayusha said, though Dasatan wasn't sure whether she was talking about his sword or their own empty bellies.

"The next night came, and again Mokos wanted to boil or hang Dasat, and again he convinced her to wait till breakfast, and again she changed for those two bells; this time she was more reluctant to grant his wish right away, still upset over his hastiness of the night before, and so he had to tease and flatter her a bit before she would promise not to eat him. So it went, he courting her to gain her promise, which came nearer and nearer to dawn each night; but always his wise heart convinced her to spare his life.

"Finally the sun outside returned and the snow melted, and when the door opened that night the smell of spring came in. When it was two bells before dawn and Mokos had changed once more, she had a sad look on her face, like the sun behind a cloud. 'What is the matter?' Dasat asked her.

"'Winter is over today,' she said. 'Today you may ask to leave my house, and if you are wise you will never come back.'

"Dasat began to ask for just that, but found that he could not. Something was in his way; some part of him was keeping the voice in his mouth. It was his heart, his wise heart.

"In all those weeks, courting Mokos for two bells before dawn each night, Dasat had fallen in love with her.

"'If I can ask you one boon,' he said, 'then I will ask this: let me stay here with you, as your husband. Then I will make this house our home and let all the men of Kaman see your beautiful face. Then they may see that there is love in this land, that it is fit to be a home.'"

"Come on. Try it." Ayusha had to admit the buckwheat pottage wasn't the most appetizing thing in the world, but it was certainly no worse than many of the things they ate. "Don't worry, there's plenty. And about time, too."

There was plenty, plenty of almost everything Dasatan had sown; it was as if the soil, never broken, had thrown out all the life it had in it in one burst. But it had almost come too late: he had had to work it all day for the last moon, and she had had to range further and further for what little there was to forage.

Dasatan took a mouthful of the pottage, swallowed. He was so thin, now, she imagined she'd be able to see it sinking to his belly. "Too hot."

"Sorry," she said, and blew on the scoop.

"No—not the food. Too hot." He reached up to wipe sweat from his forehead.

Ayusha frowned. "It's the food," she said. "Your body's probably not used to it by now."

He nodded his head weakly. "That must be it." she said.

She carefully fed him the rest of the pottage. "You need water to go with that. I'll fetch you some, all right?" He didn't answer but gave a small smile. She rose, looked back at him—his eyes were closed, now, his face flushed and sweaty—grabbed his waterskin and headed for the stream. She had seen this fever before: it would pass so long as he had rest, water and food. Thank the Lady, they finally had that last.

She reached the bank of the stream and knelt to fill the waterskin, ignoring the remains of Dasatan's broken fish-trap. They could forget about her almost in-laws, now: they didn't need them anymore. Rising carefully—she was as weak as he was, and found she often lost her balance—she headed back to the shelter.

"Dasatan?" she called. He was sleeping, now, and looked more peaceful. Wondering if the fever had broken she put his hand to his forehead. Yes, it was definitely cooler.

She held her palm two fingers over his mouth.

"No," she said. "No—have some water, you'll feel better—" She tipped the waterskin; water poured out the sides of his mouth, and his throat did not move.

The reedmace had not come up, just as she had told him. It was just as well: that meant there was still a bare patch in the field. Her people burned their dead, and he had told her that his laid theirs to rest in the sea: neither one, somehow, seemed right for him.

As poor a plow as a sword makes, it makes a worse shovel; she had been working all day to cut a deep enough hole. Summer, long promised, was now fully come, and she had stripped off her jacket for the first time since the snow had come. Bees were humming among the berries, and the recently turned earth smelled of life.

He should have seen this, she thought. How high everything grew. The smell . . . he had told her, when he had first come to this place, that he could not imagine it in summer, and she had said that when it came he would not be able to remember the winter. Summer pays for all.

Finished, she planted Dasatan's sword in the dirt and used it to lever herself to her feet. The onion patch had been trampled again, but only a bit; most of the Kamanai had learned to fear him, now. Good. They didn't understand what she and Dasatan had made here. How could they? All the others had was a camp, one they moved from year to year. Here they had made a home.

Wiping the sword on her jacket, Ayusha set off for Svatyslan's camp.

Kaman was not at all the way Yavan remembered it. He had noticed felled trees when they first entered the wooded lands; then, instead of their having to seek out young ai Kamanai to guide them to where the amber lay, they were met by a group of them, who told them to follow to the camp.

"Thanks be to the Lady," Kuyuban said. "The sooner we find some guides, the sooner we can be home and rich. Eh, Yavan?"

Yavan nodded. This was Kuyuban's first time leading one of these journeys; he did not know how brief an amber fortune was. For Yavan it had been only five years since he had last taken up his staff to find the god's blood.

"This way," one of the ai Kamanai said. Following, Yavan was surprised to see a wooden stockade wall and gate blocking the path. This, too, was unusual: he had never known the ai Kamanai to make anything they couldn't take with them when they moved to new forage grounds. A bit nervously, he followed through the gate, which a man on the other side opened and closed. Inside was more familiar—a gathering of tents—but there was one large wooden building, with smoke coming out the roof. Yavan drew in a breath, disturbed by the change.

"Yavan, this isn't what you described," Kuyuban said to him under his breath.

"No, it isn't," Yavan said.

Their guide opened the wooden building's door and stood aside. "The Kisar will see you now."

That was something else new, Yavan thought as he and Kuyuban were led inside the wooden building. Ai Kamanai had never had any leaders more formal than the heads of families. The inside of the wooden building was dark, lit only by a smouldering fire pit in the middle, and the place smelled of pine sap. A man was waiting for them, facing away, and as he turned Yavan saw he was wearing a sword. Yavan looked over at his companion: unused to life here, Kuyuban had not noticed the steel, did not know what it meant.

"Friend of the ai Kavatai," Kuyuban said in Kamanai, beginning the standard formula, "I am Kuyuban, son of Kadanim, of the ai

Daneyanim. We have brought gifts to show our friendship."

This was normally the time to awe the natives with the trade goods, but the Kisar stopped him short. "Things have changed," he said in thickly accented Kavatai. He took a step closer and Yavan got a good look at him: clean-shaven, shorter than most ai Kamanai but wearing a bearskin jacket that made him look enormous, and wearing that sword buckled at his belt. A piece of red amber larger than any Yavan had ever seen was fixed to the pommel. "You will not go into our woods to take our treasures from the ground. We have what you want, but you do not have what we want."

He reached into his pouch, drew out a handful of amber, some pieces even larger than the one on his sword. The stone on Yavan's staff glowed in sympathy; so, too, did the one on the pommel of the Kisar's sword.

"We have jewellery that would please any woman," Kuyuban said—still using the formula, but shaken. "Ribbons, and thread—"

"Take that back with you," the Kisar said.

Kuyuban's composure finally broke, and he said, in Kavatai, "What do you want, then?"

The Kisar smiled. "Steel," he said.

Seeing Kuyuban frozen, Yavan nodded quickly and began to back away. Kuyuban nodded too.

"Before you go—a message," the Kisar said, just as they began to turn away.

"For who?"

"You. All of you." The Kisar rested his hand on the pommel of his sword, a message in itself to Yavan. "Those other things you offer— we will want them, too, in time. But when we want them, we will not barter for them. We will take them."

"'You speak very politely now,' Mokos said, 'and I accept your offer. For years uncounted I have been the Lady of this land, its soil and its snow; but until now I never had a Lord to join together the men that dwell here, to make them all one family within a single tent. You shall be Kisar, the first; and to you and those that follow you I give my dark soil, to work and to bring forth its fruits. The whole of this land, from the frozen sea in the north to the shining river in the south, shall be home to you.'

"And so they wed; and at their wedding feast they gave as a gift to all Kaman the dark soil, and became the mother and father of all the people of Kaman, and commanded them to give up their scattered homes and come together to be one people. I was there; I was the last to come and the last to go; I drank the last bowl of soup, and the last drop still sits in my beard."

So the old man finishes his story, and he looks at us as though he expects that to explain all. Perhaps, for a savage like him, such stories do; to us he is useless.

Now that he has finished speaking we can hear that the screaming has stopped. The bridges are burning, and they have not crossed. Bayakul, our sister across the water, is gone, but we have been spared.

"Do not worry, men of the south," the old man says from the darkness. "You are safe on this side of the river. This is your home, and we would not destroy it.

"It is a good thing, to have a home."

LONG PIG

Four stars
Dinner for two $120–$160 with wine, tax and tip
Wheelchair accessible

Don't be fooled by Long Pig's name—it's not another Szechuan hot pot place on the Spadina strip. Chef Nimith Keo is well-known from his stints as head chef at Chimayo Bistro and Aubergine, both fondly recalled restaurants, but it's Long Pig he'll be remembered for. It's a fascinating, eclectic mix of haute and low, a fusion (how overused that word, how appropriate here!) of cuisines including his native Cambodian as well as Mexican, Caribbean and even Polynesian; it's also quite possibly the best restaurant in town.

The decor at Long Pig is sparse but elegant, reflecting the chef's Buddhist principles: a mural of the Angkor Wat temples covers the wall and a few bronze figurines are clustered around the entryway but otherwise the watchword is clean and clear, with white tablecloths, bamboo chairs and a simple place setting, a single wooden fork and spoon for each diner.

Unlike at Aubergine, where Keo was famous for the wonders he worked with bean curd and vegetables, the common theme running through Long Pig's menu is meat. After the *amuse-bouche*—tiny, succulent bones like short ribs, braised in a chili-fired sauce, one per diner—we begin with a gently fragrant broth of ginger and scallions, into which has been shaved flecks of dried pink meat that taste surprisingly, but pleasantly, like Spam.

Our server informs us that after the ribs and soup we are to use the wooden fork only to eat the remaining dishes. We find this more than adequate to eat the plate of greens that comes next, a mound of bok choy and Chinese broccoli in which no meat could be seen but which have been soaked through with a deep umami taste (ground bones and marrow, the server informs us). Skepticism arises, however, at the sight of the dish that follows, which the menu refers to as "two-legged mutton": a steamed lotus leaf stuffed with sticky rice and thick chunks of dense, deeply pink flesh. Our faith in Keo is rewarded, though, and the meat falls to pieces at the first prodding of our forks. As with the broth there is a hint of corned beef, intensely meaty and just a bit gamy, but this is a subtle and complex experience to which the canned product stands as a boardwalk portraitist does to Rembrandt. Unfortunately the most intriguing item on the menu—a Mexican dish with pre-Columbian roots called "Precious Eagle-Cactus Fruit"—is not available that night; in fact, we are told it will only be served on the restaurant's last day of operation. We make a mental note to return on that unhappy day.

To our surprise Chef Keo himself comes out to discuss our choices with us. He explains the thinking behind Long Pig's menu. "In my childhood, in Cambodia, we had nothing," he says. "Under the Khmer Rouge everyone who had any kind of Western education was killed or had to run away. When I ran away I met a man who had been trained as a French chef. We were eating grass, worms—anything at all to survive. If we had any meat, any kind at all, we would be grateful for it, but for him it was always not just something to eat but ingredients, things you could make into something more. When he was finished cooking you would not know you had a worm or something worse in your mouth. We all gave what we could, and since I was too small to give I learned from him how to cook what we had. We lived many months like this, and in the end only I survived.

"This makes me very mindful of food," he goes on. "Do you know what is meant by *mindful*? Then when I come here as a refugee I see people are not mindful of food at all, shovel it in their mouths like coal in a furnace. When I became a chef I want people to eat mindfully—not to eat as though they are starving!

"As a Buddhist, I did not feel comfortable cooking with meat. As I am progressing in my practice I feel this more strongly, which is why I left Chimayo Bistro. But as I am progressing as a chef, I feel the absence of meat puts a limit on what I can do."

As fondly as we recall Aubergine, after the meal we have just eaten we cannot disagree. "It is then I recall the first part of the step-by-step discourse of the Hinayana, which we call dana, 'giving.' Ordinarily in *dana* we are giving away the things that belong to us, which helps us to release our hold on this illusion of reality; also the receiver is changed, made more mindful by the gift.

"Thinking on this for a long time, I remembered the gift my teacher the French chef gave me. I saw then how I could be a good Buddhist and a good chef, and serve meat that is given freely, without suffering."

I confess that I am not fully able to appreciate the theological underpinnings of Chef Keo's cooking, but I thank him deeply for the gift he has given us with Long Pig. As he wheeled himself away from the table and I turned back to my plate of two-legged mutton, it occurred to me that in this city where chefs hop like fleas from kitchen to kitchen, a place as "mindful" as this is one to savour. Head down to Long Pig while you still can.

TALKING BLUES

"Don't you know where those are from?"

I paused, glanced down at the cardboard crate that held the grapes I was about to pick up. It had a grinning cartoon devil on it and the words PRODUCT OF HELL.

Half-shrugging I turned away. Half the things on the shelves had that sticker on them, and if they didn't odds were they had an ingredient or two from there.

She put her hand on my shoulder. "They have grapes grown here, you know. Organic."

I turned back to her, spread my arms so she could see the threadbare coat I was trying to make last another winter. "Do I look like I can afford anything organic, artisanal or locally made to you?" I asked.

Ms. Ethics was undeterred. "You shouldn't buy them at all then," she said.

"Listen," I said, "if you want to pay ten dollars a pound for mouldy grapes that's your business, but leave me alone, okay?" She wasn't the first person I'd heard this routine from, and I'm sure I wasn't the first person she'd said it to. Every now and then there was a fuss about all the cheap imports that came from Hell, but the boycott had never really caught on. Most people didn't much mind where the things they bought came from as long as they were good and cheap, so every time the people that made them started asking for better pay or anything like that the factories just moved—from Mexico to Thailand, Vietnam to China and finally to Hell, where nobody ever asked for a break or a raise. It wasn't like the SAY NO TO LIMBO campaign, anyway, with all those pictures of the unbaptized babies hooking rugs. I mean, people go to Hell because they deserve it, right?

I'm not sure what I was expecting—for her to leave in a huff, maybe, or else keep hectoring me. Instead she just turned away, shaking her head. "I used to believe that," she said, as though she'd read my mind.

I didn't give the business any more thought until I heard her voice again, outside in the parking lot. I kept walking, thinking I might fool her into thinking I hadn't heard her call after me.

"Hey," she said again, and I stopped. It was no use: she wasn't going to let me go without giving me another piece of her mind.

I turned to face her. "What?" I asked, shivering in the damp cold.

A pained look crossed her face and she glanced away. "I'm—I just wanted to say I'm sorry, for bothering you in there. It was none of my business."

"Oh." Now I really felt like a jerk. She looked tiny out here, swamped in a ski jacket the same grey as the sky above her and the concrete below. Strands of straight black hair trailed out from under her red toque. "Don't worry about it," I said after looking at her a second too long. "You're right. I should think more about what I'm buying."

"No—you shouldn't feel bad," she said. She looked around quickly, taking in all corners of the nearly empty parking lot. "Did you drive here?"

Here we go, I thought. If she didn't like the grapes, she'll hate the Microbus. I half-shrugged, turned and patted the VW's side, still recognizably red after all these years. "I know it's not very efficient," I said, "but it's recycled—I'm the fourth guy to own it. That's gotta be worth something, right?"

She laughed. "You must have a big family."

"Just me," I said, praying I might dodge another bullet. "See, I don't really have a regular place—what I mean is I'm on the move a lot, so . . ."

"You live in your car?"

This was it: I was about to shoot back up to Public Enemy Number One. "It's a bus," I said. "A Microbus."

"That is *so cool.*"

I admit it: I fell in love with her in that instant. "It's not that great."

She leaned past me, peered into the VW's windows. "So you just keep all your stuff in there and go wherever you want?"

"What I've got. Mostly it's just a few clothes and my guitar." I shrugged. "I'm a . . . a musician. Sometimes."

She nodded, turned to face me and held her hand out forcefully. "Margaret," she said. When I gave her my hand she shook it forcefully. "Now you're supposed to say your name."

"Oh. Will. Will, I'm Will."

"Will, I'm Will," she said, nodding slowly. "So where are you headed next, Will?" she asked.

"Anywhere, I guess. Someplace I can play, I hope, or at least learn some new songs." I shrugged, threw my shoulders. "Somewhere warmer than this, maybe."

The smile vanished from her face, and she shook her head twice. "Warmth is overrated," she said.

It probably won't surprise you much to hear that she came with me that night, though it sure surprised me. Things weren't too close in the Microbus, really—neither of us were more than a few inches past five feet tall, so we had plenty of space—and we were both able to keep our distance longer than you'd think. Before too long, though, we got closer in the way men and women will.

Only we never got too close, I guess, or I would have asked some of the questions I thought of later: questions like why she never liked to be any place where too many people could see her, or why she never would tell me much about where she had come from the day I met her, or how it was she was in a position to be leaving town with a stranger in a Microbus at all.

Maybe I was too startled by her being with me at all to question any part of it, or busy with what I jokingly called my career. Things had started to pick up in that area: word got around, maybe, that I put on an entertaining show, or else the tide of taste just turned briefly in my favour. For a few months the Microbus took us from town to town—mostly sad little places where the factory had closed, the jobs gone to Hell, and the people had nothing left to do but serve each other coffee.

One night we were at a club called Raskolnikov's, an old-style coffee house where you could still see aging hipsters in goatees and berets. It didn't look like much but it had a loyal clientele, and I knew this might be my biggest audience for a while. I spent a long time working on my set list—lots of trad folk and blues, songs some of them might have heard the first time on vinyl.

The stage was tiny, barely big enough for me and my guitar case, and the blue stage light was burnt out so that just the white and the red burned down on me. The crowd, not packed but generous, was seated at small round tables; I'd played to this sort of house before, so I knew I had to get their attention right off. I squinted into the lights, spotted Margaret sitting over by the door. She flashed me a nervous grin and I leaned into the mike, started up a fast version of "Reuben James" without saying anything. By the last chorus a few people were singing along, so I rolled right into "Rock Island Line," eighty miles an hour, and then right after that "A Hard Rain's A-Gonna Fall," three fast songs without a break. I was sweating by the end of that, I can tell you, and I barely had the breath left to introduce myself.

After that I let myself slow down a little, played "Lonesome Traveler" and "Joe Hill." I'd been doing a lot more shows since Margaret joined me, and it was paying off now: for the first time I felt like I could ask for the audience's attention and get it, like I deserved it, and after a half-dozen songs I had the attention of everyone in the room.

Almost. There was one man I could tell I wasn't reaching, sitting halfway back. He didn't look much like the rest of the crowd, leaning back in his chair and wearing a black dress shirt and a bright red tie. I did "Midnight Special" next, really throwing myself into it, but he still was just staring off into space. Except that I saw, when I looked real close, that it wasn't space he was staring at: it was Margaret.

I let the rest of the show sort of slide from there, playing mostly slower songs and sing-alongs. Margaret didn't say anything about him after the show, and I almost let myself forget about it. I knew that I didn't have a right to ask her anything—I'd certainly never volunteered much about myself—but in the end I couldn't resist.

"Who was that guy at the show?" I asked.

We were both lying on our backs in our doubled-up red sleeping bag, and neither of us moved. "What guy?" Margaret said.

"That guy. He was looking at you." I rolled over onto my side to face her. "He had a red tie on, sitting near the back? He was staring at you the whole show."

"I don't know," she said.

She hadn't turned to face me, still looking up at the ceiling, and I knew if I kept going I would cross the line—but I've never been able to keep to one side of that line. "He looked like he knew you."

"I didn't see him." Now she rolled onto her side, but away from me, and I didn't say anything more. Instead I just lay there in the darkness, listened to her breathe for a long time until I knew she was asleep.

In the morning I made some excuse to be out of the bus for a long while, and when I got back I was surprised to still find her there—but it was just that I hadn't given her enough time: she was packing the few things she had when I opened the doors.

"Going?" I asked.

She didn't look up at me. "I'm sorry," she said—not bitter or angry, just sad. "I have to."

"You don't have to go now. I can drop you somewhere."

Her eyes scrunched shut, and then she turned to me. Her cheeks were red and damp. "It's all right," she said. "They're coming to pick me up."

"They?"

"I'm a fugitive, Will. From Hell. That's where I had come from, when I met you. Now they're—" She turned back to her bag, ran her hand across her eyes. "I can't run anymore."

"Is our life really worse than Hell?" I asked.

"It's not that. I just—I don't deserve this life. I don't deserve you. I should be where I belong."

"Wait," I said, reaching out to put a hand on her shoulder. "We can go, right now. Just keep running—"

"I'm sorry," she said. She picked up her bag, stepped past me and out of the bus. "I have to go."

I watched her as she walked away, waiting to see who it was that was going to pick her up; instead she just kept going until finally she faded into the distance, and I was alone.

For a few nights after that I tried to keep going, but it was no use. When I had lost people before it was always because I pushed them away; this time I hadn't been given the chance. The more time passed, the more I felt sure that even if I didn't deserve her, she didn't deserve Hell.

You wouldn't think it would be hard to find your way into Hell: enough people have told me to go there. I kept on playing shows, hoping to see the man with the red tie again, but I never did. I looked through all the articles in the magazines and the newspapers that talked about how bad the conditions there were, but none of them said how to get there. I even talked to the organizers of one of the boycott groups, but they couldn't help either.

Finally I got an idea. I parked the Microbus in the parking lot of one of those big stores, the ones where the Good Sams park their RVs, and staked the place out. I felt a bit bad about leaving the old VW behind—it had carried me a lot of miles, probably more than I deserved—but there was no way it could go where I was headed.

After five days camping there I hit paydirt: a big truck full of cheap sneakers pulled up, and I wandered near enough to the loading dock to see the boxes all had the little devil logo on them. I had worked a loading dock or two in my time, so I knew when my chance would come—once the guys were done they huddled in the dock for a smoke break, leaving the truck open so that it would look like they were still unloading it. Patting the Microbus goodbye I crept up to the truck and climbed inside, moved to the back where the shadows were deepest and crouched down low.

A long time seemed to pass before they finally closed the truck, but eventually I felt the engine starting and we began to move. I don't really know how long I was in there, though it was long enough for me to get some bruised ribs; the roads got worse and worse as we drove, until finally the truck came to a stop. There were two sharp raps on the side, and a second later the truck door opened up. I blinked at the light, saw someone peering in.

"Come on out," he said. I got to my feet, walked stiffly to the door and climbed out. We were stopped at some kind of border crossing; there was a traffic gate in front of the truck, with a booth at the hinge end of it. I supposed it was the man in the booth who had spoken: he was standing by the truck, now, dressed in a grey military-style shirt and pants and a dark red baseball cap. He was blind, his eyes nothing but dark sockets. "We don't take hitchhikers."

I looked around, my eyes adjusting to the light, but there wasn't much around to look at: the road we were on ran through an endless plain on either side of the gate, the sky a dull grey overhead. "I'm not escaping," I said. "I'm going in."

"Doesn't matter," he said. "Nobody gets in here unless they deserve it."

I remembered an old story then, about one time a musician got a special exception in this place, so I started up with "Black Is the Colour":

Black is the colour of my true love's hair
Her lips are rosy something fair
If my love no more I see
My life it swiftly will leave me.

When I had finished the third verse a tear ran from out of his left eye socket. He nodded, went back into his booth and raised the gate.

I can't really say now what I was expecting Hell to be like: fire and brimstone, I guess, lakes of sulphur and pits of burning coals. It wasn't like that, though, at least not where I was. Instead it was just like a town, one of those little ones you pass through and wonder how anyone could live there, only it went on forever. It didn't have any shops, or restaurants, or clubs or coffee houses—all it had were jobs, the ones it had taken away from all those other little towns. There were the farms where the grapes and other things were grown, sneaker factories and t-shirt sweatshops, stock boiler rooms and call centres—it's always dinnertime when you call from Hell. Somewhere, in all this, was Margaret.

I never saw any demons, either, or even the man with the red tie. In fact I never saw anybody but us sinners, hard at work. Nobody had to make you get to do your job; any time you went to take a break the bad feelings would rise up in you and make you realize you didn't deserve it, and you got back to work. There's no rest for the wicked, they say, and all of us in that place were surely wicked.

One thing was in my favour: maybe because I had come in on my own, nobody assigned me to any one place, so I was able to move around looking for Margaret. It wasn't easy to keep going, though. Whether I was sewing, reaping or trying to sell magazines each job had a rhythm of its own, a rhythm that would draw me in, and at each job I would start up singing a work song. If I was sewing little red swooshes on sneakers, for instance, I'd sing a song like this, passing the shoe along halfway through each line:

Take this hammer, take it to the captain
Take this hammer, take it to the captain
Take this hammer, take it to the captain
Tell him I'm gone
Tell him I'm gone.

Sooner or later when I sang somebody else would start up singing along with me, and when we got three or four singing the sound of all those voices together would lift our hearts a little, make us feel just a bit less alone, enough that each time I remembered Margaret and was able to move on in search of her.

It was hard to tell how the time passed, since you never ate or slept, never did anything but work; maybe it was a year, maybe five, maybe ten before I finally found Margaret.

I guess I expected to spot her across a crowded room or something, run into each other's arms, but it was nothing like that:

I was just singing "Haul Away, Joe" while gutting fish when I heard her voice join in. She had a good voice, thin but pretty, and even over the other people singing I knew it the moment I heard it.

I worked my way down the line until I was next to her. She didn't recognize me at first, until I tapped her on the shoulder; then she gasped and shook her head.

"Will?"

"I've come to get you out."

She looked away, back down at the red-fleshed salmon in her hands. "I can't go," she said.

"You have to. I came here to help you escape."

"I'm sorry." She shook her head twice, quickly. "This is where I'm supposed to be. But you—you should go back."

"I can't," I said. When she had spoken I remembered everything I had sung to the man at the gate, realized I didn't deserve to go. I had never planned what to do if she didn't want to leave, never thought a second past this moment. Now I realized that all I had done was get myself to the place I was meant to be in, the life I had earned. I felt alone, then, more alone than I had felt driving solo down endless highways. We were all of us alone, kept wrapped up tight by our sins.

There didn't seem to be anything to say after that so I just went back to gutting fish, and after a while the rhythm took over and I started up singing again. A few verses in she joined me, and then a few more people around us, and pretty soon most of us on the line were singing together.

Again my heart was lifted a little, and I guess Margaret felt the same way too, because after a while she turned to me and said, "You came here to rescue me. Isn't that enough to show you shouldn't be here?"

"Isn't it enough to show *you*?"

I looked her in the eyes then, and for a minute I felt like I wasn't alone at all. She nodded twice, quickly, and said "How do we get out?"

She shrugged. "You just go. The last time I was here I met an old man who told me he had almost gotten out once—he said if you've got the will to go nobody stops you. I guess they know everybody that gets out winds up back here sooner or later."

"You said he almost got out?"

She nodded. "There was one thing he said was really important. When you get on that road, don't look back."

For a while it looked like it was going to be as easy as that. The road out opened itself right up for us as soon as we left the line; when I came in it had been a long, open plain, but now we were climbing up out of a valley. We climbed for hours, careful not to look behind us, until we saw the slope break about a hundred feet ahead. Margaret had been fading for the last little while, falling a bit behind, and I could only tell by the sound of her breath and her footsteps that she was still behind me.

"Almost there," I said.

The road began to level out, and I saw in front of us a booth like the one where the truck had stopped on the way in. The gate was down, and though the way was clear on either side something told me there was no getting around it.

"I don't think I can do this again," Margaret said from behind me.

I didn't dare look back at her. "Let me," I said.

Ahead, the booth opened and the blind man in the red cap stepped out. "You two'd best turn back now," he said. His eyeless sockets looked past me, and I knew he was staring at Margaret. "You ought to have learned your lesson."

The urge to turn back was strong, as I felt the weight of all the things I'd done drawing me back. Even more I wanted to look back at Margaret, make sure she wasn't wavering. I knew she had only made it this far because of me, and I had only done it because of her; I moved to stand between Margaret and the guard, started to sing.

We are standing pat together
We shall not be moved.
We will walk this road together
We shall not be moved.

As I finished that line I saw Margaret step up to stand beside me, heard her voice joining mine:

Just like a tree that's standing by the water
We shall not be moved.

The eyeless man just stood there for a moment, his face unreadable. Finally he nodded and then stepped into the booth; a few seconds later the gate swung up, and we quickly stepped past.

For a while after that the road got steep again. Finally it levelled off and we took a break, resting on grass in a field of little red flowers.

"I never figured good intentions would be so hard on the feet," I said, taking off my right shoe and rubbing my heel hard.

Margaret shook her head, said "That's the way in . . ." From the way she sounded I expected her to say something else, but she just fell silent; a sinking feeling came over me and I looked over at her. Sure enough, she had turned around and was looking back the way we had come.

"Hey," I said, careful to keep my eyes on her and not the way back. "Remember what the man told you. We've got to keep moving."

"I can't," she said. She sounded like her heart was breaking. "I can't go."

"We can leave if we want to, Margaret. Please, let's go."

She shook her head again, twice quickly. "That's not it," she said. "Look. Please—you won't understand unless you look back."

I kept my eyes on her, trying to find the words that would make her turn around and come with me. Finally I just nodded, and turned back to see the way we had come.

I saw all the people still down there, in farms and cubicles and factories, and I realized that every one of them was there because they thought they ought to be—because they couldn't believe they deserved any better. The only difference between us and them was that we had someone to tell us different.

"There's so many of them," she said. "If we just go, and leave them here . . . all alone . . ."

As much as I wanted to get angry, to curse her for not listening to me and for looking back, I couldn't help agreeing with her. "If we left them here, we wouldn't deserve to leave," I finished for her.

Margaret nodded.

We sat there for a long time then, not saying anything, and after a while for lack of anything better to do I started to hum. Margaret smiled at me, and I smiled back, and a moment later a thought occurred to me. "I guess we made it this far because we weren't alone," I said. "Maybe that's all those people need, not to feel alone."

Her shoulders slumped. "It took us everything we had to convince each other to go," she said. "How can we get through to all of those people? We don't even know who they are."

"I know," I said. "If they all just thought they deserved something better than what they've got—if they all knew they weren't alone . . ." I shrugged.

Margaret rose to her feet, started walking back down to the valley. After a few steps she paused, turned to look back at me. "Well, we'd better get started," she said. She took a few more steps. "Aren't you coming?"

"Where are you going?" I asked.

"Like you said."

I held up my hands. "I'm not a leader," I said. "I could never get anyone to follow me. I was just thinking out loud."

She shook her head impatiently. "Save your breath," she said. "We have to get every voice in this place singing together, and I don't want you going hoarse before you've taught them all."

I opened my mouth to speak, shut it and nodded. Then I got to my feet and followed her, back down to the valley.

I know we'll climb back out again, though it likely will take a while: we don't mean to leave till everyone is ready to come out with us, and when we do we'll do it singing.

Now the final battle rages;
We'll win our union yet somehow.
Though we struggle on for ages
Onward, men! All Hell can't stop us now!

The Face of the Waters

Doctor Yonah Ben-Ezra sat up, his hand on the receiver almost before the phone had started to ring.

"Yes?" he said.

"It's Benjamin Cohen," the voice said. "From Embryology."

"What is it?"

"The boy," Benjamin said. "The first one. It's eight days now."

"And is he—"

"Yes."

Yonah nodded, speechless for nearly the first time in his life. He took a long breath, exhaled. "All right, then," he said. "Thank you."

He had the phone halfway to the cradle before he heard Benjamin's voice still talking. "There's—there's one more thing."

Frowning, Yonah nudged his glasses up onto the bridge of his nose. "Yes?"

"The boy. He—it's time for his bris."

"So I'm a mohel now?"

There was a brief silence. "Doctor . . . ?"

"A joke, Benjamin."

"Oh. I'm sorry. But I was serious—we have a mohel, but thought you could be the sandak . . ."

"He hasn't a grandfather? An uncle?"

"We thought . . . the mother agreed, you would be the most appropriate."

After a moment Yonah said, "All right. When is it planned for?"

"In about ten minutes." Yonah could sense him flinching on the other end of the line. "Sorry for the short notice—the mohel's double-booked, he was just able to clear a half-hour."

"Fine. I'll be there." Yonah paused for a second. "Make sure your mohel has steady hands. I don't want anything going wrong."

Yonah hung up, not wanting to have to explain to Benjamin that he was joking, and pushed himself up out of his chair. It was time to go, if he wanted to be sure of being on time, but instead he went over to his office window, looked out at the sea outside. The number of strings I had to pull for this view, he thought, the number of favours I had to do . . . but it was worth it. When he looked out the window he could imagine he was still in Israel—Israel as it had been when he was young, when it had still belonged to the Jews.

"Every place that the sole of your foot shall tread upon, that have I given unto you," the voice said.

Yonah glanced at the face reflected in the glass, turned away. A stranger might think the face was his, it looked so much like him: but he knew better.

"Go away, ghost," he said. "I settled matters with you a long time ago."

"And I will give unto thee, and to thy seed after thee, the land wherein thou art a stranger," the voice said. "All the land of Canaan, for an everlasting possession."

Yonah turned back to the glass. "Don't start. And don't go quoting Torah at me. My mind is made up in this." He turned away from the window and headed out into the hall, not looking back to the face in the glass.

The words stung: he was just old enough to remember 1967 and all the promise that year had brought. Such pride in that victory, all that new territory, and Jerusalem whole again. How many Jews still walked the streets of Jerusalem today? None but those determined to be martyrs. He couldn't blame the young ones, though, for taking shelter here in Tel Aviv or in Haifa, even for leaving the country. His own sons had gone to the four winds: to New York, Canada, Singapore. . . .

"And I will give unto thee, and to thy seed after thee, all the land of Canaan, for an everlasting possession."

Yonah turned to see the ghost standing in the glass door that led to Genetics. Seen in full it no longer looked much like him—the tillim cast over the shoulders instead of a lab coat, the yarmulke where his head was bare and bald—but the family resemblance was still clear.

"Nothing is everlasting," Yonah said, glancing over his shoulder to see if anyone could hear him. "Not in this world."

"By little and little I will drive them out from before thee, until thou be increased, and inherit the land. And I will set thy bounds from the Red Sea even unto the sea of the Philistines, and from the desert unto the river."

"And what if we don't increase? What if they do?" He glared at the ghost, waiting for a reply, and then started walking again.

After 1967 it had seemed like anything was possible: like the world—or Israel, at least—belonged to the Jews, now and forevermore. And to be sure there was no fear of invasion, not after that spanking, and the rock-throwers and even the bomb-throwers that followed them were never a serious threat to anything but peace of mind. That was the problem, Yonah thought: we had been watching the men and the boys, when it was the women and babies we should have kept our eyes on. They had attacked with fire, and we replied with fire; they had encircled us, surrounded us, and still we stood. But in the end there were simply too many: the sons of Japhet would always outnumber those of Shem, the sons of Ishmael those of Isaac.

There it was, Embryology: white and sterile, not much cheered by the plastic border of blue and pink balloons that ran along the top of the wall. Another glass door stood before him, blocking his way, and as he'd feared the ghost was there as well. He slowed, steeled himself for it to start quoting Torah at him again, but instead it simply stood there, gazing at him with those eyes so much like his.

"We have to survive," he said quietly. "Don't you see that? Whatever else we do, whatever commandments we keep, if we don't survive it's for nothing." He took a breath, tried to slow his heart's racing. "What good is the Promised Land if there are no Jews to live in it?"

"What good is the People if they are not Jews?"

Yonah took a breath: the ghost had never responded to him before, never done anything but quote Torah. He fought for breath, struggling to bring up the words he had held inside for so long. "Nobody told you," he said. "Dammit, David, nobody told you to be a martyr. You could have stayed here, worked with me—gone somewhere safe, like your brothers—"

The ghost was silent again, only shaking his head sadly. Yonah took a breath, readying himself to speak again, but instead shouldered the door open and walked into the room.

He was late, as he'd feared: the kvatter—the mother, he supposed, or the grandmother; at his age it was hard to tell how old people were if they were younger than him—had already brought the boy into the room, put him in the chair the mohel had declared the Throne of Elijah. Yonah did not recognize the mohel but he did know Benjamin Cohen, who was masked and gowned like a surgeon.

"Sorry I'm late," Yonah said as he held out his arms for a nurse to put on his smock and gloves.

"Doctor Ben-Ezra?" Benjamin said. "Are you all right?"

Yonah nodded. He went over to the eight-day-old boy, who was swaddled up to the ears, and lifted him up out of the Throne. Then Yonah sat down in another chair, a hard plastic one big enough for his rather more generous seat: as sandak, the bris would be done with the child sitting on his lap.

"Will the father allow me to perform this mitzvah?" the mohel asked.

Yonah looked over at Benjamin, who looked back at him. Neither had thought of this issue: these children had all been conceived by artificial insemination, and while the sperm donor's name was surely recorded somewhere no-one had thought to track him down and invite him.

"Thou shalt not let thy cattle gender with a diverse kind: thou shalt not sow thy field with mingled seed: neither shall a garment mingled of linen and woollen come upon thee," the ghost whispered in his ear.

Yonah shook his head, as though to clear water from his ears, turned to the mohel and said, "Yes."

"Good," the mohel said. "Why don't you take off his blankets so we can begin."

Nodding, Yonah lifted the boy gently from his lap and began to unwrap the swaddling clothes; he gasped as he uncovered the boy's neck, turned to Benjamin. "It breeds true?"

Benjamin nodded. "On the X." The female line. That was key: to be born of a Jewish mother was to be a Jew. If this passed from mother to son, it meant that even if they lost Israel the children of Isaac would always have a home.

"And all that have not fins and scales in the seas, and in the rivers, of all that move in the waters, and of any living thing which is in the waters, they shall be an abomination unto you."

Be quiet, David, Yonah said silently. This is your fault, anyway. If you hadn't gotten yourself killed fighting over a strip of dust and rock, I never would have started this.

The mohel cleared his throat, and Yonah finished unwrapping the boy, held him under his arms as the mohel cut the foreskin and the nurse clamped the penis and suctioned off the blood.

It had been almost forty years since Yonah had last been to a bris, but he remembered what came next: "Blessed be our Lord, the ruler of the universe, who has sanctified us with His commandments, and has commanded us to bring him into the covenant of Avraham, our Patriarch."

As one, Benjamin, the mohel and the nurse said, "Just as he has been brought into the covenant, so too he should enter Torah, canopy, and good deeds."

"Whatsoever hath no fins nor scales in the waters, that shall be an abomination unto you."

Benjamin reached for the boy, to hold him for the rest of the ceremony, but Yonah held up his hand: before he could let the child go he had to reach down to his neck, stroke the tiny gills until he saw them open and close.

Do you see, David? he asked. They killed you, made your mother die of sorrow, drove your brothers a thousand miles away. They said they would drive us into the sea. Well, let them: let the goyim have that dry, unwelcoming third of the Earth. The rest will belong to the Chosen.

OUTSIDE CHANCE

Jacob watched the future fade from view as he triggered the relay. He was not sad to see it go; it was a bad one, like a Beckett play come to life. It wasn't hard to imagine Vladimir and Estragon bickering in this wasteland, or Hamm and Clov playing tug-of-war at the end of the world.

Outlines were like that, often as not. It was his job to find out how they got that way, what chain of events had led to the particular doom each future embodied, and to bring back anything that might help ensure the survival of the present. He did not, as much as possible, talk to the people. They didn't really exist, after all; that is to say, they wouldn't.

The cool white of the forecasting room opened up in front of him as the cage finished reeling him in. There was a momentary sense of dislocation and he stood still, trying not to let the chaos of the room pull him off balance. Displays were holocast onto every wall, giving reports from the forecasters; the line men who tried to pull it all together were running from display to display, synthesizing the data into a recommended path of action to be whispered into the ears that could make things happen; the dispatchers were deciding to which lines the next wave of forecasters would be sent. Jacob glanced at the display in front of him:

*** -342/3H/+7 POLAR COOLING OPERATION LEADS TO
MASSIVE TSUNAMI IN PACIFIC—APPX 13M RIP *** +479/8L/+2
ENERGY SHORTAGE DUE TO INTERRUPTED GROWING SEASON
IN MIDWEST NA—APPX 2M RIP ***

None of that would be felt down here, of course, even if it was
allowed to happen. The forecasting facility was insulated, both by its
location and its routines, from the chaos that had made life outside
so unpredictable. Jacob unhooked his datapad from his belt and
coded it to send his data, expecting out of habit to see it come up on
the display. The displays, though, showed only the Probables, lines
weeks or days away. A Probable that looked good was nurtured,
steered to carefully. Outlines existed only to be looted. Ten or more
years in the future, Outlines were so far away on the probability
curve they were always shifting, as insubstantial as soap bubbles.
You could go into the cage a hundred times and not reach the same
Outline twice.

A fresh-faced man in what passed for normal dress outside
walked by on the way out of the next cage over. "Hey, Delacroix!" he
called, and Jacob recognized him: Collins, a Short. "Find the Good
One today?"

Jacob nodded and gave a perfunctory laugh, but said nothing.
There was no answer to that question. That was the joke. If you ever
did find the Good One, you'd never come back to Now.

"Coming to the game tonight?"

"I don't think so," Jacob said.

"You sure?" Collins asked. "Couple new Shorts joining today.
Easy money."

Jacob smiled, remembering the ritual of fleecing new
forecasters—after a while in the job, you got so used to watching
probabilities that you counted cards almost unconsciously. "No, you
have fun. I've lost the touch."

"That's right," Collins said. "I always meant to ask—why'd you
give it up? Short work, I mean."

"Got tired of seeing people I know," Jacob said.

Collins looked briefly puzzled, shrugged; half-aware, maybe, that Jacob had left his sentence unfinished. "Well, have a good one," he said, bustled off somewhere. Shorts were always in a hurry. They had a right to be, Jacob supposed; they were saving the world, after all, even if it was only for a few days at a time.

Jacob felt suddenly disoriented, watched a coffee cup in a nearby tech's hand unpour itself. As he steadied himself a half-dozen other minor corrections unspooled, time knitting itself back together as some past forecaster's report altered relative Now. When he had started out his brain, like everyone's, had rebelled at the corrections, refused to see them; now they barely made him miss a step. He keyed his datapad and a blue dotted line was holocast onto the floor in front of him, leading down the corridors scrawled with running forecasts to where his apartment was now.

He opened his front door, and saw the stark white walls before they sprang into life, holographically painted with his choice of artwork. He had been into Great Masters for a while now, walls gallery grey. Most people these days liked kinetic paintings, but he preferred art that stood still. The room's control panel appeared on the wall when he snapped his fingers, and he keyed it to play music while his dinner heated up. He sat down to listen as the violins stirred the air, wondering, not for the first time, if the seasons could possibly have been as beautiful as Vivaldi made them sound.

Another day, another future. Jacob held in a yawn as the cage ripped a hole in time and dropped him through it. Everybody in Now, from the forecasters to the dispatchers, took themselves so seriously it wouldn't do to seem bored. Well, he'd put in his time, and Long work—quiet, easy on the nerves—was meant to be his reward.

It was his nose that first registered something different. As the cage anchored him in this Outline, twelve-point-four years from Now, he smelled something strange—a warm smell, not dry-baked and dusty, but alive. Though he had never encountered it before, it was familiar: there was a hint of flower-scent to it, and rain. He had never smelled it, but he had heard it just the night before. It was spring.

He took a deep breath, held it for a long moment before releasing it and opening his eyes. The sky was full of light—real sunlight, overflowing with wavelengths the rad-filters and stratoshields in Now never let you see—dotted with white and grey clouds. He was in the middle of a small park; grass, yellow and green, stretched away for a dozen metres in each direction. Two- and three-storey buildings all around were standing, intact, and alive with music and voices.

Calm down, Jacob told himself. He had seen this before. He had read Ibn Khaldun describe it, in one of his textbooks:

At the end of a dynasty there often appears some show of power . . . it lights up brilliantly just before it is extinguished, like a burning wick the flame of which leaps up brilliantly a moment before it goes out.

These were certainly less depressing than the ruined futures, and more likely to yield valuable artefacts—he himself had brought back the battery trees that now covered nearly all of Now's arable land and provided most of its energy—but all of the initially promising timelines were no less doomed, and it never took him long to find the seeds of destruction in them. After that it was just a matter of waiting out the hours or days until the other end of the hole opened and he could be reeled back to Now. Taking one more whiff of cut grass, Jacob set out to explore this Outline.

"A retrohistorian," the introduction to Practical Retrohistory said, "has a few basic tools: documents, testimony, artefacts." Jacob normally did most of his work with documents, but today he was beginning to understand the lure of artefacts. First, clothing: the beige coveralls he wore let him blend into most lines, even Outlines, but people here wore mostly solid reds, yellows and greens in woven cloth. Most of them walked, but some drove small vehicles that glided along the ground on skate struts. Jacob watched as one stopped and the owner got out, leaving it without apparent concern for its safety; a few minutes later two more people got into it, without any fuss from them or passers-by. Looking closer, Jacob could see that the struts were arranged in an open, back-pointing V, with a small wheel on a strut and chain held just above the ground where the struts met. A moment later the wheel lowered to the ground and, turned by the chain, sent the car gliding off gracefully. Trying to figure out the technology behind its operation—he had seen exhaustless vehicles in another Outline, apparently run on broadcast power, and had wanted to get his hands on one—Jacob watched the vehicles move past like skaters on a frozen pond. It was only when a boy of about ten slipped past him on the sidewalk on what looked like a stiff strip of tinfoil that he realized the skates on the cars were simply frictionless. Resolving to pick up one of the children's strip-boards, Jacob moved on.

He paused at a park—there were small ones every few blocks—where a concert was going on in a bandshell, but as he got closer he couldn't tell who were the performers and who the audience: nobody seemed to stay one or the other for long, instruments handed off between songs or even verses. The people near him spoke what was recognizably English, but the ones closer to the music carried on conversations in a sign language he couldn't fathom. As he listened and watched their conversations, Jacob was struck by the lack of stress or anxiety. They strolled in sunlight without fear of skin cancer, hugged and kissed on meeting without concern for disease or disgrace. None of them were in a hurry.

Feeling overwhelmed, Jacob decided to retreat to documents for a while. It did not take long to find a library, an old red stone building carefully preserved and restored. This was where the cracks would appear: examination of weather patterns, employment statistics, medical reports—even, sometimes, just reading the newspapers—always exposed the empty core underneath the façade. He had imagined, with all the music and activity outside, that this line's people might have neglected their technology; inside, though, while he saw row on row of books he also saw terminals that looked enough like those of his time for him to recognize them. Casting a regretful look at the books—real, paper books—he picked up one of the terminal sets and went to sit at a carrel at the back of the room, then linked in his datapad and uploaded a dozen bots that would seek out the information he wanted. Once he had the data he could feed it into his simulations, start guessing just how this world would end. After a few minutes, though, nothing had come back. Starting a manual search, he found—nothing. Concert listings, poetry, cartoons, but nothing—nothing—that referred to anything before the present moment.

"It's the Good One, isn't it?"

Jacob turned around with a start, saw a woman standing behind him. She was somewhere in her twenties or early thirties, with straight black hair cut short and skin as pale as his; she wore grey duracloth overalls and a red vinyl jacket, closer to what he wore than to what he had seen outside.

"Sorry?" he said.

"The Good One," she said again, smiling. "The one we're all looking for."

He waved a hand over the terminal, tuning the display invisible. "Do I know you?" he asked, keeping his voice low.

"Call me Rachael," she said. "I'm a Short."

"Jacob. Long," he said, held his hand out tentatively; she gave it a squeeze. "Shorts always work in pairs. Where's your partner?"

"We don't do that anymore." She turned her head away fractionally. "There aren't enough of us."

"We shouldn't be talking."

"Why not?"

"If you're a Short, that means you're from after my Now. Any contact could cross-contaminate our timelines."

She cocked her head. "You've been outside—seen this world. Doesn't that seem like an acceptable risk, to get all this?"

Acceptable risk. There was no such thing, not anymore. That was why they were needed: the world was too dangerous to leave to chance. Years of blind meddling had left them without any kind of margin of safety, hanging by their fingernails to a world always an inch from Armageddon. Any miscalculation or misstep could lead to millions dead; no-one envied the forecasters whose job was to weigh lesser against greater tragedies, save a billion people by letting a million die.

"What makes you so sure this is all worth having?" he asked.

"I've seen a dozen Outlines that looked like paradise . . . at first."

"So what's wrong with this one?" Rachael asked.

"I don't know," Jacob said after a moment. The main trap in tracing a line's development was post hoc, ergo procter hoc: thinking that because a thing happens after another, the first is necessarily caused by the second. This line, though, was like an embodiment of that—a world full of causeless effects. He waved his terminal visible, glanced over to where his simulations were running. "I haven't found it yet."

"Maybe that's because there's nothing to find," she said. "Listen, how much time do you have?"

"About two days."

She crouched next to him, looked him in the eye. "I've got a little less than that. Whichever of us is right, this is a puzzle one person can't solve alone in that amount of time."

"We can't—"

Rachael put up a hand to stop him talking. "You've been outside. You've seen the people here. I'm telling you—this is it." He read her face, saw no deceit in it. Of course, all forecasters were skilled actors; Shorts especially. "If we do cross-contaminate, how much more corrupted can our own lines get? Even if we each get erased from history, is that really much worse than going home?"

He thought for a moment about everything he had experienced since arriving: the ever-present music, the carefree people, the smell of the air. "All right," he said. "What have you found?"

"Nothing, that's the problem. I mean, everybody's happy, nobody's worried, but nothing makes any sense—like, their movies are all in sign language, but nobody can tell you why. It shouldn't work, but it does—and they don't find anything odd about it at all. It's like they don't even know how good they have it."

Jacob considered the question for a moment. "Maybe they don't," he said thoughtfully. "Maybe we're not finding what's wrong because the information isn't out there."

Rachael frowned. "You still don't believe this is it, then. The Good One."

He shrugged. "Does it matter? Whether we're asking what went right or what went wrong, we need the same information."

"Okay, fine," she said, annoyed. "So if it's not out there, where is it?"

Jacob looked around quickly. "Just because the people here aren't worried doesn't mean there's nothing to be afraid of. It could be someone's doing a really good job of hiding it from them."

"Suppose you're right. Whatever's wrong, or right, with this line, somebody's keeping it a secret. Who's possibly capable of hiding something that big?"

Jacob smiled, let a little Humphrey Bogart creep into his voice. "Why, we are, sweetheart."

The timer on the delay switch flashed to life, started counting down from 30:00. That would make a half-hour buffer between when the alarm system signalled that it had been breached and when the signal was received. Long enough for them to get in, find what they needed, and get out. The switch was one of the basic tools of Short duty; Jacob hadn't held one in years, but as soon as Rachael had handed it to him he recognized the shape and weight of it in his hand, and his fingers remembered how to program it.

Jacob glanced around. In both his line and hers this building was a bolt hole, a repository of equipment and information where a forecaster could get help without risking contact with the local line men and the cross-contamination that would follow. Of course, if this line's forecasters were the ones hiding its history, it probably wasn't a good idea to let them know he and Rachael were here; that was why they had settled on the discreet approach. With a satisfying click Jacob's pick sprung the last, most overt lock, and he opened the door and waved Rachael in. Inside, a hallway led into the darkness. Rachael switched on her UV lamp and, to their eyes, the room lit up. It looked positively low-tech: wooden baseboards ran along the wall, and a path of linoleum tiles led to a door at the end of the hallway, with three more doors on either side. Only the tiny cameras planted in a line along the ceiling showed that any value was placed on this building, and those were very nearly hidden between fluorescent light panels.

If Jacob were trying to protect a building without making it look protected, he thought, he would eschew active sensors like electric eyes. Better to use passive devices, like pressure plates, so that intruders would not know they had been detected. Yes: when he crouched, played the UV light over the floor, he could see them spaced at irregular intervals, a lip of little more than a millimetre betraying them. He pointed them out to Rachael and they made their careful way down the hall. They had a half-hour's grace if the alarms went off, yes, but pride as much as practicality told him it was better not to need the time. He had been doing this before they had invented the switch, before any of the machines except for the very first cages that tore rough holes in time. He knew how it was done.

The door at the end of the hall was unlocked, but alarmed; a fail-safe, in case everything else failed, to make any intruders who got this far give themselves away. Rachael bridged the alarm circuit with a span of conduction cable, and the way to the bolthole—and, he hoped, the secrets this line was keeping from them—was clear. Taking a breath, Jacob opened the door. Beyond was a confused mess of grey filing cabinets, shoved together with barely enough room to squeeze between them.

This didn't make sense. Jacob looked over at Rachael, spread his hands: what now? She looked back and forth frantically, opened one of the cabinets and started rifling through the files inside. She stopped, eyes widened, and handed the folder to Jacob. It was full of paper, a dozen pages. Every one was blank.

Jacob frowned, then noticed his datapad monitoring the alarm system, flashing UV-red. He looked at its screen, saw that a motion detector somewhere in the building was sending its signal. Though that rankled, it was fine; thanks to the delay, they still had more than twenty minutes before the signal got out of the building.

At least, they were supposed to. According to the 'pad, though, the signal was away. They had been made. Jacob reached over to tap Rachael, spun his index finger upwards to signal a bug-out. She looked at him curiously for a moment, then headed back out into the corridor.

Running down the hallway—the motion detectors couldn't do them any harm now—Jacob wondered how fast the alarm response would be. This line looked harmless, but on the other hand they had gone to a lot of trouble to hide this place. He pushed the front door, half-expecting it to have re-locked, but it swung open, and as it did Jacob could hear sirens nearby.

Jacob had spotted one of the small parks nearby earlier, logged it as the best spot to hide out if things went sour. They ran for it now, trying to keep out of sight as the oddly small and bulbous police cruisers arrived, and dug themselves under a thick hedge, sharp branches cutting into their clothes and skin. They could hear the cruisers' doors opening and closing, and the cops talking amongst themselves; no dogs, to Jacob's relief. So long as the people hunting them relied on hearing and sight they were safe. For a long time they did nothing but crouch there and breathe as quietly as they could; finally, when the lights and sounds of pursuit had gone, Jacob relaxed his cramping legs and sat down on the ground. A slight breeze blew through the hedge and the smell of damp earth and greenery made him lightheaded.

Rachael tapped him on the shoulder, cocked her head. He nodded and they rose, wordlessly heading for the hotel room where Rachael had been staying. Jacob stood at the window, watching to see if they had been followed, as Rachael sat on one of the beds and stared ahead.

"I don't understand," she said finally, her eyes not meeting Jacob's. "That was—it should have—"

"It was obviously something," Jacob said, quietly. "Somebody went to a lot of trouble to protect it."

"But why?" Rachael said, her voice breaking slightly. "There was—nothing. No answers, no . . ." She stopped herself, took a breath. "Maybe that was the point. Maybe it was some kind of decoy."

Jacob nodded slowly. "Your decoy," he said; still quiet, but a note of anger slipping through. "And I think I've played your game long enough."

"What are you talking about?"

Jacob held up a finger. "One. We deactivate the alarm, but it goes off anyway. Two, the delay switch fails nearly twenty minutes early."

"I don't know why—"

Another finger. "Three, you attract my attention and lead me on a wild goose chase, so that I'm left with less than a day left before I have to trigger the relay, and no way to find out anything useful about this line. Four—"

"No. No, Jacob, you're wrong."

He took a deep breath. "Four, you claim to be a Short, but are working without a partner. More importantly, Shorts only go forward a matter of days, sometimes hours—certainly not long enough for things to have changed so much from your time, and yet you claim to have no more knowledge of this time than I have. I don't see more than one logical conclusion."

He sat on the bed, waiting for her response; finally she laughed.

"As the butt of the joke, I'm afraid I don't find it so—"

"No. You don't get it." She shook her head. "If the joke is on anyone, it's on me. You're right; I am a Short, and my Now is just two days ago. That's what's so funny: my time is nothing like this. This is as much an Outline to me as it is to you."

"That's impossible."

She laughed, bitterly. "Tell me about it. I was supposed to go just two days ahead, check on the first test of battery algae, and instead I got—this." She did not move, but something in her posture collapsed. "Why do you think I even spoke to you? I knew the risks; I might not even exist after all this—this me, I mean."

Jacob sat, looked at her. Either story, he supposed, was equally plausible. "What about the delay switch, then?"

"I don't know. I've been a Short for two years now, and that's never happened before."

"This line's forecasters could have cancelled it," he said thoughtfully, "but only if they knew how to. And—assuming for a moment that you didn't inform them—" He was interrupted by a knock on the door, three hard raps. Turning to Rachael he made a phone with his left hand, thumb and pinkie extended, to signal *Did you call anyone?* She shook her head, made the twirling bug-out signal with her index finger, and readied a finger over the control pad on her belt. When they arrived they had prepared a timelock field in the room, in case they needed to get out quickly; thirty seconds of frozen time to give them a head start on anyone who came after them.

The door opened, and two men came into view, blocking the doorway. Jacob tensed, keeping an eye on Rachael; she would trigger the timelock as soon as they were far enough in to open a space to get past them.

"This is a private room," Jacob said calmly. "Are you with the police?"

Neither man looked like a police officer. They both wore the bright clothing of this line, though they looked uncomfortable in it; each had pinkish-red skin, burnt by too much light in unfamiliar wavelengths. "No," the first man said. He was the taller of the two, but skinny, with Cassius's lean and hungry look. "But you're coming with me."

Jacob nodded, watched Rachael out of the corner of his eye as the two men took another step inside. She gave him a tiny nod, triggered the timelock. A shimmering wall, the edge of the timelock field, appeared around the edges of the room. Inside it the world would be frozen for thirty seconds. Jacob began to rise.

The two men were still moving.

"Don't," the second man said. He was shorter than the other, with a mess of red hair that fell nearly over his eyes and a pair of thick round glasses. "We're in the field too; keyed in before we opened the door." He lifted the broad hem of his shirt, revealed a belt with a control pad like they each wore.

Jacob looked over at Rachael, who looked as surprised as he was. "Who are you?" she said, backing away slowly.

"Easy," the taller man said. "We're not here to hurt you, just make sure you don't go anywhere. Mike, how long do they have?"

The red-haired man, Mike, unhooked an instrument from his

belt. "Just over an hour. She's got the switch."

The taller man moved nearer to Rachael, held out a hand; after a moment she nodded, handed over her relay switch. "There. Two hours from now you'll be free to enjoy this world for the rest of your lives. Until then, let's just sit tight."

"What's this about?" Jacob asked. He heard footsteps in the hall—if he could occupy the men's attention, he thought, the arrival of a cleaner or something might distract them enough to open a chance for escape. "I mean, you obviously know who we are, but you don't look like you're native to this line."

"Very true," a voice said from the hall. A woman entered, standing behind the first two. Like the two men, she was sunburnt, and looked uncomfortable in this line's fashions. Unlike them, though, her face was familiar.

"Davidson," Jacob said. "Jan."

Rachael looked over at him. "So they are—"

"As you are," Jan said. She was not an imposing woman, just over five feet tall, with brown hair worn in a bun and a face full of freckles; her voice, though, had a tone of iron certainty.

"So it's true," Jacob said. "This is what happens to the ones that don't come back." He swallowed. "Like you."

"Not all of them," Jan said. "But some. I'm sorry I couldn't let you know I was safe."

"What happened? Miss your relay window?"

"No." She signalled to the two men, who each moved to more comfortable but still watchful positions on either side of her. "I tested this line for flaws till I nearly went crazy, and then when I was convinced it really was the Good One I tried to figure out how it had gotten that way. I expect that's what you two've gone through the last few days."

"Pretty much," Jacob said before Rachael could speak.

"Then you know what I found: nothing. No chain of events that could explain how to get from Now to now. Then, when I met Mike here, I thought I was in luck: I had come as a Long, but he was a Short, and would be able to explain to me how to get to his time, at least. Except that he told me his time was just as far from this as mine."

Jacob glanced over at Rachael, but her face showed nothing. "So why did you stay, Jan? Why make me—us—think you had just vanished?"

"You're not stupid, Jacob," she said, anger coming into her voice. "You know what that means as well as I do. They don't need us in this line. Things are stable enough that they can afford to take risks, not worry about what catastrophe each action might cause. But there's no path that leads to it, no sequence of actions that goes from our line to this one. You can't get there from here."

"So you decided to stay, rather than give it up," Rachael said. "You knew you'd never find it again if you left."

"You've already been thinking about it, haven't you?" Jan smiled. "Good girl. I knew he'd be the only one I'd have to convince." She turned back to him. "Because you won't give up, will you? You never did. You're so sure you're smarter than the rest of us, you'll take your data back and spend the rest of your life trying to find the key we couldn't."

"I'll stay," Rachael said, "by choice. But why do you have to keep him at all?"

"The same reason Pyotr here had to stay, though he didn't take much convincing once we found him. This line exists; so long as nobody in the past knows that, those of us that made it here will be able to enjoy it. But if actions are taken in the knowledge of its existence, they might keep it from having happened, and we—temporally native to it, now that we missed our relay windows—really would just disappear."

"So the rest of humanity suffers, while you three get to enjoy paradise?" Jacob asked.

"Five, actually—there's two more of us outside—and now it will be seven. And who's to say this line is any less real than Now? The people outside, do you think they'll listen when you tell them they're just a probability, and an outside one at that?"

"You said you'd had a good run, Jacob," Rachael said. He listened to her carefully, listening for truth in her tone. "Don't you deserve a reward? Just let time run out."

He looked at her a moment, nodded. "I guess I don't have a choice," he said, looking at Mike and Pyotr, who were still standing in the way of any escape attempt.

"You're so stubborn," Jan said. "I couldn't possibly be right, could I?"

"Looks like you'll have a lot of time to convince me."

Jan stood and stretched, still keeping a watchful eye on Jacob. "How much longer?" she asked Mike.

"Four minutes," he said after a glance at the instrument in his hand, yawned.

"All right, then. Four minutes, Jacob; then you'll start to see what I mean."

He shrugged. There was no point in arguing. "Fine," he said, glanced over at Rachael. She gave him a nervous smile. "So how are you going to fit us in as natives here?"

"I don't need to," Jan said. "Nobody here has any ID or security numbers. If you want to work, you work; they just believe you are who you say you are."

"There's a lot of work for retired retrohistorians?"

"We all know how to do some pretty useful things. I'm sure you'll find a niche to fit in soon enough, if you want to." She glanced over at Mike, who nodded. "That's it, then; time's up."

Jacob looked from Mike to Pyotr, stood up slowly. "So what now? Are you going to show us around your private utopia?"

Jan smiled. "Why not? Come on—" she motioned to Rachael to rise as well "—since you're natives here now, you might as well know the landscape."

The five of them went out into the corridor in a line, Mike and Pyotr still keeping a careful eye on Jacob—not to prevent escape, which the passage of time had just sealed, but in case he should try to take his frustrations out on them physically. They looked smaller, now, and he realized they had just been pretending to be tough guys; they were forecasters, just like him, and used to pretending to be people they weren't.

Outside it was as bright and sunny as when Jacob had first arrived, the air crisp.

"Smell that," Jan was saying. "I never knew anything could smell so good. Did you?"

"It's nice," he said.

"And that's just the beginning. You can relax here—don't have to worry what the next catastrophe will be."

He stopped at the curb, shook his head. "Jan?" he said.

She looked at him curiously. "What?"

"Good-bye."

He was off, moving more quickly than he had since he'd been a Short; he glanced back, saw that Rachael was following a few steps behind. Jan, Mike and Pyotr were looking at one another curiously, no doubt wondering why he would bother to run when he couldn't get back to Now. Jan was the first to figure it out—of course, she would be—and started running after them, the other two trailing behind.

At the first intersection Jacob made a quick diving motion with his hand that he hoped Rachael would understand; a second later he broke left, into traffic, and she broke right. He hesitated for a second while one of the frictionless cars passed, then jumped onto it and kicked hard with his right leg. Suddenly it was going much faster, with nothing to stop it, and he gripped it tight as it sped away. The driver, unaccustomed to this speed, wasn't sure what to do. By the time the brake strut had hit the pavement he was blocks ahead of his pursuers.

"Sorry!" he called to the driver, a young woman who was looking at him with amazement on her face. He jumped off as the car slowed, crossed to the other side of the narrow street and started on a zigzag path to the park where he and Rachael had hidden after they fled the bolt-hole. He was half afraid Jan and the others would be waiting there; it was obvious now it had been a decoy, meant to flush out any forecasters like him and Rachael. The park was empty, though, and he quickly made it to the hedge they had hidden under, crouched in its shade. A few seconds later he heard hurried footsteps approaching. He risked a look, saw Rachael headed straight for him and felt a reflex of suspicion.

"How far behind are they?" he asked quietly as she crouched beside him.

"I don't know. They all went after you. Maybe you lost them."

He shook his head. "Not for long; Jan was a Short as long as I was. But at least they don't seem used to working together—we're probably the only ones ever to run."

"So why come here?" she asked.

"Ah . . ." He reached under the hedge, felt around, drew out his relay switch. "Abracadabra."

"So that's why they didn't detect yours—why they thought you were on the same deadline I was," Rachael said. "But why did you think to stash it here?"

"I didn't trust you," he said.

"Oh." She looked away; he was not sure if she was looking for signs of pursuit. "And do you now?"

"Well, you had plenty of chances to betray me back in the room, and you didn't," he said. "And you pointed out to me that they'd think my time was up when yours was. So, yes—but that's not really why."

"So why?"

He shrugged. "No reason. Just—a gut feeling."

"You don't sound much like a forecaster."

"I guess I don't," he said, and looked like his watch. "This end of the hole's going to open in about five minutes."

"So you're going back?" Rachael said.

"Of course. Why else would I have run?"

"I don't know. I ran, just because . . ." She put up her hands. "You heard what she said—you'll never find this line again, and if you try to get here in normal time you might keep it from existing."

"Jan's as good a forecaster as there ever was, and her premises are sound, but her conclusion is exactly backwards." He peered over the hedge, set the relay switch to warm up. "Before the cage was ever invented there were always people who would make guesses about the future. One of them looked at the past and the future and said that the system he was living in was doomed. It was inevitable, he said, and he pointed out all of the problems in it that would destroy it. A lot of people listened to him and decided he was right; some of them just gave up, but others tried to fix the problems he had identified. So the prediction he made actually kept itself from coming true; the truth in it made it false. Impossible, right?

"Now look at this line. It's a stable future, but it always hangs just in front of Now. Something's keeping it from happening—"

"Jan," Rachael said, her eyes widening. "Her, and the others. Someone needs to come back from here to make it happen. But— that means the cause is in the future. That's impossible."

"Pre hoc ergo propter hoc," Jacob said, smiling. "It's our fault. Forecasting—messing with time, obsessively calculating every probability of disaster—is what's kept this time potential. Whatever makes it happen, it's outside the risks we're willing to take. But if we go back—make it a reality, not a myth—maybe we can make that leap."

"We?" Rachael said. "My time is up. I'm stuck here."

There were running footsteps audible, just a few dozen metres away. "Teams of two, remember?" he said. "I just have to key you into my relay. We'll both go back to my Now."

"But you're from just twelve years ago—I'm already there. It's impossible."

The relay switch flashed green. "We've got six impossible things to do before breakfast," he said, "might as well get started."

She smiled. "Down the rabbit hole?"

"Over here," Jan's voice called from not far away. Jacob nodded at Rachael, keyed the relay switch to her control pad.

"Hold on," he said, and reached to her.

She put her arms around him, frowned skeptically. "Is this necessary?"

"No," he said, and they vanished.

Closing Time

Nep Gao stood on his tiptoes in the quiet garden to the back of the restaurant, working his small silver knife along the thinnest branches of the prickly ash tree, and wondered when his father's ghost would leave the party. He had died five days ago and was still holding court, entertaining all his old friends and customers. It was just his luck, Gao thought, that his father had died in the middle of *qinshon* season, the few weeks when the tree's buds had their best flavour. Already, chewing carefully, he could detect a bitter note in what he had just harvested. At the rate things were going his father's ghost would still be around in a week, when the *qinshon* would be inedible. This was usually their most profitable time of year, but so long as his father was enjoying the food and company enough to stay on Earth Gao was bound to provide food and drink to anyone who came to pay their respects. So far there had been no shortage of mourners, most of them just happening to come around dinner time and often staying till past dawn.

With his basket full of tightly curled green buds clutched under his arm Gao went back into the restaurant. Though it was only midmorning someone in the front room was playing a zither, shouting out parts of the Epic of the Hundred and One Bandits. Louder, though, was his father's commentary on the action as it was sung: "That bandit's pretty clever, but not as clever as that butcher that used to try to sell tame ducks as wild. Nobody but me could smell the difference from the blood in the carcass!" and "I heard the great Xan Te play that verse once when I was on a trip to Lamnai. He hardly had a tooth in his head, but he ate two whole boxes of my pork dumplings."

Gao could not help blushing when he heard his father telling the same tales he had told a thousand times before. He had never done anything but run the restaurant, never travelled except to buy food or collect recipes, but to hear him tell it he had more adventures than all the Hundred and One Bandits put together. Gao could not count the number of times he had heard his father tell the story of how he had gotten his trademark recipe—the garlicky duck from which he had taken his name, Doi Thiviei—from a hermit who had lived in a hut that was at the top of a mountain when he arrived in the afternoon but at the bottom of a valley when he left at dawn. The zither player had fallen silent to hear the story and Gao could see a half-dozen others kneeling on mourning stools, listening and chatting as they ate the leftovers of the previous night's meals.

"And then, just when I opened my eyes, I saw—nhoGao, is that you? Don't lurk in the doorway, son, come in and sit down. I'm just at the good part."

"I am sorry, Father, but I must start to cook for today's mourners."

"Oh, well, all right then. Bring us some fresh tea and some red bean dumplings, will you? Now, where was I? Oh, yes—when I opened my eyes, I saw that the hut, which the night before had been on a mountaintop—"

Gao picked up the empty bowls, hurried on to the kitchen before his father could think of anything else to ask for. He could not help but notice that his father looked no more vaporous than he had the day before, felt guilty for wishing it otherwise. For most people the mourning party was a formality, a way to make the spirit linger a day or two at the most. It was supposed to be an expense—if it was too short, cost too little, there would be doubts about one's respect for one's father—but not a ruinous one. Sighing, Gao laid the qinshon buds onto a square of silk which he then tied into a bundle; any rougher cloth would rub their skins harshly and make them lose their flavour. That done he put a pot of water on to boil and looked around the kitchen, wondering what he could make as cheaply as possible that would not offend the mourners. He sipped the chicken broth that had been simmering since the night before, tossed in the bones from last night's dinner. He could put pork dumplings into the broth, make a soup with noodles and fava beans, top it with chive flowers from the garden. For the next course he could deep-fry thin strips of pork in batter, if he made it hot enough he might be able to use a pig that wasn't so expensive.

Feeling hungry now, he pried one of the stones in the floor loose, lifted the lid off the shallow earthenware pot that lay below, reached in and pulled out a pickled pig's knuckle. Looking carefully over each shoulder he took a bite. He had promised to give up eating pork when he and Mau-Pin Mienme had become engaged, but nothing calmed him down when he was nervous the way pork knuckles did. Her family were followers of the Southerner—her name meant Sweet Voice from the South—and so did not eat meat at all. When she had insisted that he at least give up eating pork it had taken him less than a second to agree. It had taken him only a day, following that, to realize that he could not possibly keep his promise, so he had bought a pot of pigs' knuckles one day while she and her family were at prayer and hidden it under the floor in the kitchen, so that she would never know what a dishonourable man she was marrying.

His mouth was now full of the sweet, salty, vinegar taste of the pigs' knuckles and he could feel it easing his mind. It was true: he was a dishonourable man, dishonest and unfilial, breaking his word to his wife-to-be and wishing his father's ghost would leave him alone. He doubted that even Mienme, who like all of her faith had studied to be an advocate to the dead in the Courts of Hell, could convince the Judge of Fate to send him back as anything nobler than a frog. He sighed. It was only because he was due to inherit a good business that Mienme's father, a lawyer on Earth as well as the next world, was allowing her to marry him at all. He had always known how unlikely it was that he should be able to marry a woman like Mienme. She was beautiful and intelligent, while he was cursed with an overfed body and the doughy face that had made his father call him Glutinous Rice. He knew better than to question the divine grace that made her love him, though, and he had believed since they were children they would one day be married. In all that time he had never imagined it might be *his* father that would be the problem.

Thinking of Mienme made him want to see her, have her listen to his problems as she had so often done. Like other women who followed the Southerner she was allowed to go out alone, to spread his Word, and he thought she would most likely be at South Gate Market this time of day. That would work out well enough; he could get all of the vegetables he needed there, and buy the pig later in the day when he was alone. Seeing her face, and hearing her advice, would be more than worth the extra trip. After carefully putting the pot back under the floor stone he opened a small jar in the shelf, took out a boiled egg marinated in soy sauce and popped it in his mouth to cover the smell of the pork knuckle. Then he poured boiling water into the large teapot, put a few of the red bean dumplings he had baked the night before onto a tray, took tray and tea into the front room where his father was still spinning his tales to a rapt audience.

"—of course, a chicken that laid eggs with two yolks would be worth a lot of money today, though we didn't think like that in those days. No, we only hoped she would survive the trip home so we could make Double August Sunrise for the Emperor—nhoGao, you've brought the dumplings. Won't you stay and hear this story?" His father was, if anything, more solid than when he had last seen him, the party more lively as noon approached.

"I'm sorry, Father, I have to go to the South Gate Market to buy food for dinner."

"Well, that's all right, I suppose. Do bring me back some of those preserved mushrooms, and some sweet beer for our friend here, whose throat must be getting dry." The zither player had not sung a word since Doi Thiviei started talking, nor was he likely to for the rest of the day, but Gao nodded dutifully before steeping back into the kitchen.

Once out of his father's sight he picked up the rag that held his shopping list and wrote "sweet beer" on it with a piece of charcoal. His father did not like him reading, saying every other generation had learned to memorize their customers' orders, but on the other hand Mienme said if he were illiterate he would not be able to read the charges in the Court of Hell and his advocate would not be able to help him. He had to admit it meant he took fewer trips to the market, since without a list he always forgot something. He folded his list, strapped his grocery basket on his back and went out into the street.

The streets between the restaurant and the market were crowded, even in the heat before noon, and the wind blowing from the west carried a heavy scent of medicinal incense. Someone in the Palace must be sick, he thought. As the massive iron pillars of the South Gate came into view the smell of the incense was met and quickly defeated by that of spices, sizzling oil and a dozen different kinds of meat cooking. Pausing for a moment, Gao closed his eyes, tested himself the way his father had done when he was child, making himself find his way around the market by smell alone. There, off to his right, someone was making salt-and-pepper shrimp, heating the iron pan until the shells cracked, releasing tiny gasps of garlic and red pepper-scented steam. To his left someone else was frying *mat tran* on a griddle, making sure they would have enough for the lunch rush customers to wrap around their pork-and-kelp rice.

Satisfied, Gao opened his eyes again, scanning the crowd for Mienme's familiar face. He found her standing just inside the gate, handing out block-printed tracts to a family of confused-looking farmers. One, an older man with a white-streaked beard and a broad bamboo hat, was listening politely while the others kept a tight rein on the pigs they had brought with them. Gao waited until the father had accepted the pamphlet and moved on before approaching.

"You do your faith and your father honour," he said formally when she noticed him. Though they were engaged, there were still certain proprieties to be observed when in public.

Or so he felt; Mienme often seemed to disagree. "You know as well as I do that none of them can read," she said, shaking her head. "Our temple offers free lessons, but they won't stay in the city long enough for that. Besides, only the Master could convince a pork farmer to give up meat."

"And you try nevertheless," Gao said. "Such determination will serve you well when you argue cases before the Judge of Fate."

"That's very sweet, nhoGao," she said, making him blush at the use of his childhood name. She was dressed in the brown cotton robe and leggings all her faith wore when preaching, and from a distance she might almost have looked like a man. "But you don't have to reassure me, I'm not about to lose my faith—I'm just hot and tired, that's all. Why are you looking so glum?"

He shrugged slightly. He had not realized his mood was so apparent, resolved to better hide it from his father. "The mourning party is still going on today. If this continues my father's ghost will outlast his restaurant."

"What is it now, four days?"

"Five. My father is enjoying his party so much I think he is happier now than when he was alive."

Mienme put up her hood and extended her hand to him. With her face hidden anyone who saw them would see only a young man helping a monk through the crowded streets. "It's the food everyone's coming for. Couldn't you do something to it, put in something bitter so they won't like it so much?" she asked. "You could say it was a mistake."

"If I make a mistake like that, my father would stay another ten years just to punish me."

They stopped at a vegetable stand and Gao haggled with the merchant for beans and cabbage while Mienme seemed lost in thought. "I've got it," she finally said after they had put their groceries in the basket on Gao's back and moved on. "Remember the night my parents came to the restaurant and you made Temple Style Duck?"

"How could I forget?" Gao asked. "Your parents thought I was insulting them, making bean curd so that it tasted like a duck. My father thought I was insulting the duck!"

"Exactly. Make him that and when he complains, say you're concerned about what the Judge of Fate will find if he keeps on eating meat after his death. That way it'll cool the party down and you'll only be acting out of filial affection."

"That's true." Gao thought for a moment. "That's an excellent idea. You really are too smart to be wasted on a person like me."

Mienme laughed. "I know. I took an oath to defend the hopeless, remember?"

Five hours later Gao held his breath as he lifted the steamer basket's long oval lid. All around him lay the remains of the bean curd, sweet potato, arrowroot, and other vegetables he had used. He did not make Temple Style very often—even most followers of the Southerner did not eat it; it had been created for high-ranking converts who wanted their vegetarianism to be as painless as possible—but he enjoyed the artistry it involved, matching flavours and textures in a way that was almost magical. Gao, the youngest of his father's four sons, had mostly learned cooking from his mother, and she had been the vegetable cook. For that reason his father and brothers had been responsible for the meat dishes the restaurant was famous for and he had been left to take care of the vegetables and small items like dumplings. But his brothers had left, one by one, to start their own restaurants in other cities, and for the last few years he had been doing all the cooking himself, his father only planning the menus—menus he had changed, slightly, to include more vegetables and some of the things he had learned cooking for Mienme.

When the steam coming out of the basket cleared he could see, inside, something that looked almost exactly like thin slices of barbecued duck, greyish-white with streaks of an almost impossible red. Getting it to look right was the easy part, of course; the flavour and the smell were harder, and much more important. He carefully lifted the slices out with a slotted spoon and slid them into a waiting skillet full of oil and the sauce needed to complete the illusion. In seconds the oil sealed the outside of the slices, browning them and making the red streaks even brighter. He lifted the smallest piece to his mouth, burning his tongue slightly tasting it. It was perfect, better even than the cooks at the Temple made it. It had taken him months to duplicate their recipe, making sure he had it right before he could even invite Mienme's parents to dinner, but he had also improved it, giving it that crackling texture the Temple cooks had never managed. This was the dish he made better than anyone else—*Trianha Thiviei*, Temple Style Duck. This ought to be his name, not Glutinous Rice, something he had made every day for the poorest customers because his brothers were making more complicated things. He could not change his name while his father was still around, of course, but soon, perhaps. . . .

Gao sighed, asking forgiveness for wishing his father gone, took the remaining slices out of the skillet then laid them on a waiting bed of steamed and salted greens and white rice. He took the plate with rice, greens and "duck" in one hand and a platter with ten small bowls on it in the other and went out to the front room.

"—so there we were, bound to make dinner for an official of the Fifth Rank and his family and all the salt brokers on strike—nhoGao, have you brought dinner?" The crowd of mourners had grown since the afternoon, with the new arrivals more than making up for the few that had left—word that one of the best restaurants in town was giving out free food had gotten around.

Gao nodded, not quite able to speak. For all the justification Mienme had given him he could not escape the fact that he was giving his father something he would not like. Someone was rolling his stomachs into dumplings as he spooned out the first bowl of Trianha Thiviei.

His father sniffed at the bowl. "Is this duck?" he asked, his brow furrowed.

No sense adding a lie to his long list of crimes. "No, father—it's Temple Style. I made it because—because Mienme was worried about what will happen when you stand before the Judge of Fate."

"Is that so? What a kind girl she is." His father took up his sticks, brought a piece to his mouth and chewed thoughtfully.

"Yes, father. She is very concerned about your trial." Gao felt like a pot of hot tea had been poured down his throat, wondered what punishments awaited him as a result of this.

"You know," his father said finally, "maybe it's because I'm dead, but I don't think I gave this stuff a fair chance last time. It's really quite good—and for my soul, too, eh?" He laughed. Gao echoed him nervously. "Needs a bit more salt, though. Which reminds me, I was just telling them the story of the big salt brokers' strike—you know this one, it's a good story—"

Gao nodded, served the other mourners silently then went out the front door, leaned hard against the wall. He was not sure which was worse, that the plan had failed or that he had hoped it would succeed. Either way things were no better—his father was enjoying his mourning party as much as ever and the number of guests was only increasing.

As he stood in the cool, incense-perfumed night air Nep Gao became aware of bells ringing in the distance. Not the familiar dull tone of temple bells but a higher chime, three strokes, silence, three strokes. The palace bells, he realized. Whoever it was they had been burning incense for earlier—and from the number of bells it had to be an official of the Third Rank, someone in the royal family—had died. He had just pieced this together when he heard a voice call his name. He turned, saw coming down the dark street a man with two heads, one higher than the other. Gao squinted to see better but the second head was still there.

"Yes?" he asked, wondering if this was an agent of the Courts of Hell come to take him to his punishment early.

"We require a service of you," the man said. He stepped into the small pool of light cast by the torch above the door and showed himself to be two men, one riding in a basket on the other's back. It was the man in the basket, who was wearing the lacquered red headdress of an official of the seventh rank, who had spoken. Gao immediately dropped to his knees.

"How can your humble servant help you?" he asked, unable to keep from staring at the man's dangling feet in their white deerskin slippers. That was the reason for the basket, of course; the slippers, which had to be a gift from someone in the royal family, could not be permitted to touch the ground in this part of the city, but the street was too narrow for a palanquin.

"The Emperor's favourite uncle has died," the man said. "We are preparing the mourning party for him and have heard of the effect your cooking has had. The Emperor would like the honour shown to his uncle that has been shown to your father."

"I'm not sure I can—" Gao began, beads of sweat forming on his forehead.

"The Emperor would consider it an insult if the same honour was not shown to his uncle," the man said firmly. "Take this." The man handed a small jade token to the servant whose back he was riding, who then handed it to Gao. "This will let you and anyone helping you onto the palace grounds. You may keep it when you are done." Without waiting for an answer he gave his mount a quick kick in the thigh, making him turn around and head back down the street.

Minutes later Gao was lying on the mat in the back dining room, a bag of cold clay on his head and a dozen mint leaves in his mouth. He chewed the mint to control heartburn, but it was not helping tonight.

"How did it go?" Mienme's voice came from the window.

Gao stood up, opened the door. Mienme pulled herself through the window by her arms, still the adventurous girl she had always been. "Worse and worse," he said, and proceeded to tell her everything that had happened.

"Actually," she said after he had finished his litany, "this could work out well for us."

"How can this be good?" Gao asked, accidentally swallowing the mass of mint in his mouth. "The restaurant is already nearly broke, and now we have to serve food fit for an official of the Third Rank. We'll be ruined—I'll be lucky if I escape with my head."

"Just listen," Mienme said. "Your father can't complain if you give all the best food to the royal mourning party—imagine what that jade token on the wall could do for business at his restaurant. So you can't be blamed for just serving him simple food, and when you do that the mourners will stop coming, and the party will be over."

"You may be right," he said slowly. He drew the token out from his belt pouch, ran his fingers over its cool, smooth surface. "Yes, of course. If we're cooking for the Emperor's uncle, he can't complain if we give him nothing but rice and millet gruel. Even the Judge of Fate couldn't complain." He held the token up against the wall. "I must have done a very good deed in my last life to deserve you."

"In that case," she said, grinning impishly, "come here and give me a kiss while you're still all minty."

Sometimes he wondered if her parents knew their daughter at all.

The next morning he was up at dawn, fishing carp out of the pond in the back garden. Once the fish were splashing in their wooden bucket he took his small knife and cut a half-dozen lilies from the surface of the pond to make into a sauce for the fish—fish fresh enough for the Emperor's uncle. These were the last two items he needed for the day's meals; after making sure the jade token was still in his belt pouch he went into the kitchen, put on his grocery basket, and went out into the front room. His father's ghost was regaling two sleepy mourners with his adventures, while several more lay sprawled on sleeping mats around the room.

"—of course, a pig that smart you don't eat all at—nhoGao, do you have breakfast ready already?"

"I can't cook for you today, father, remember? I left a crabmeat and pork casserole in the oven, you can ask one of the mourners to get it out for you in a few hours, and I'll send you dumplings for the afternoon."

"Of course, of course—I'd almost forgotten. You'll do us proud at the palace, I'm sure—and what a story it'll make, cooking for the Emperor's uncle." Despite his words he did not seem very happy, and Gao wondered if he was finally starting to fade. Crab and pork casserole was not exactly gruel, but it was not the food Doi Thiviei was used to, either. He felt a sudden pain in his chest, hoped that if his father were to depart today it would not be until after he got back to the restaurant.

He had never been to the palace before. Despite the fact that it was at the centre of the city, few people ever received an invitation to go. Those who went without an invitation, hoping to poach the Emperor's white deer, usually wound up as permanent guests—or came home over the course of several days, one piece at a time. As he reached the gate he could not help worrying that the whole thing had been a colossal hoax, that the guards would take his jade seal and his groceries and send him away. When he showed them the token, however, they stood to either side of the gate, and one was assigned to lead him to the palace kitchens.

"How long ago did the noble official die?" Gao asked the soldier.

"The man walked a few steps in silence before finally answering. "Yesterday afternoon," he said. Like most soldiers he had a heavy provincial accent, which perhaps explained his reluctance to speak. "Didn't you hear the bells?"

"I've been busy," Gao muttered. "Have you seen his ghost?"

The soldier again kept silent for a few moments, then spoke, no expression crossing his face. "No. But I hear it is very pale. He was an old man, and sick for a long time."

Gao cursed inwardly. Except for short, violent deaths, long illnesses were the worst. They left a person glad to die, and not inclined to hang around too long afterward. He thanked the guard when they reached the kitchen and got to work unpacking his groceries. He had planned a light breakfast, fried wheat noodles sprinkled with sugar and black vinegar, in case the ghost was not too solid. Then he hoped that by lunch he would be able to serve the carp balls in lotus sauce and crisply fried eel to a more receptive audience.

It was not to be. The Emperor's uncle was vaporous, not interested in talking or even listening to the zither. The mourning party was somber, the guests mostly relatives and lower officials who were attending out of duty rather than friendship. They picked at the delicacies Gao served, leaving the rest for palace servants who could not believe their luck. The ghost, meanwhile, ate only a bite from each dish, pausing neither to smell nor taste any of them.

By mid-afternoon Gao was getting nervous. He had not managed to keep the Emperor's uncle from fading at all, knew that the official who had hired him would not be pleased. If he could have managed even two or three days things would have been all right, but if he could only make the royal ghost stay a day and a night it would look like an insult. He wished Mienme was there to help him.

Finally he resolved there was only one thing he could do: make the most elaborate, most spectacular dish he could, so that he would not be faulted for lack of effort. He settled on a recipe one of his brothers had found in a small village on the southern coast, *mau anh dem*—Yellow Lantern Fish. He sent a runner to the fish market for the freshest yellowfish he could find, telling him to look for clear eyes and a smell of seaweed. When the boy returned he began to carefully cut and notch the scaled, gutted fish and boil a deep pot of oil on a portable burner.

Minutes before dinner was due he ordered the burner be carried into the room where the mourning party was taking place, followed behind carrying the fish himself. Though he could not look at the faces of any of the guests he could tell few if any of them wanted to be there. The most enthusiastic of them, if not the wisest, were using this as an opportunity to get drunk. Even the zither player sounded almost as though he was singing in his sleep. At the middle of it all was the ghost, silent and uninterested in what was going on around him.

Gao had the burner and pot of oil placed in front of the royal ghost, waited a few minutes while the oil returned to the proper temperature. Then, with enough of a flourish to make sure all eyes were on him, he dropped the fish into the oil. In seconds it blossomed out like a paper lantern, its flesh turning golden and crispy. It was a dish designed to impress even the most jaded crowd, and it did not fail him: the guests pressed forward to get a better look and eagerly handed him their plates. Before the first bite was taken, however, Gao knew he had failed. Unlike the guests the Emperor's uncle was still withdrawn, uninterested, not bothering to eat or even smell the fish.

My life is over, Gao thought as he walked home. If the Emperor's uncle had faded away by morning he would be blamed, and that was sure to kill business if it did not kill him. Just then he realized that in all of his worry about the Emperor's uncle he had forgotten to send the lunch dumplings he had made for his father's mourning party. Without food the party was sure to have broken up by now, his father likely faded away. He suddenly regretted not listening to any of the stories his father had told over the last few weeks, too busy cooking and worrying about the restaurant. He had heard them all a dozen or more times, but now might never get a chance to hear them again.

When he neared the restaurant, however, he saw lights inside and heard voices. Creeping into the front dining room he saw his father still holding court before a half-dozen mourners, the room strewn with empty bowls and teacups.

"NhoGao, is that you?" his father asked, spotting him as he tried to slink past into the kitchen. "How did it go at the palace?"

Gao shook his head slowly. "I am sorry I was not able to send you the food I made for the day," he said. "I was busy with—"

"Don't worry about us—we don't need food to keep the party going. Besides, I know where you hide the pig knuckles. Now, where was I . . . ?"

Watching his father, more solid than ever, Gao wondered what it was he had done so wrong at the palace and so right here. He had made dishes for the Emperor's uncle that were twice as elaborate as anything he had ever made at the restaurant, but had left the royal ghost cold. His father, meanwhile, looked likely to remain among the living indefinitely on a diet of pig's knuckles. I must be missing something, he thought. If only Mienme were here to help me think. She would say, if it's not the food—

"Father, can you come with me for a few minutes?" he asked suddenly, interrupting his father in the middle of the story of the *seo nuc* game he had played against a beggar who had turned out to be an exiled general.

"I suppose," his father said, puzzled. "I can finish this story later. Where are we going?"

Without pausing to answer his father's questions Gao rushed back to the palace, flashing the jade token to the puzzled guard. The mourning party was down to just a few diehards, likely trying to win points with the Emperor. The royal ghost was hardly visible, a thin grey mist barely recognizable as once having been human.

"Please excuse me, noble officials," Gao said, dropping to the floor and bowing low. "I forgot the most important part of the mourning party."

A few seconds of silence passed as the guests watched him

curiously, wondering what he was going to produce that might top the Yellow Lantern Fish. Finally his father said, "What a glum group. Reminds me of my father the day our prize rooster died, the one who would crow every time a rich customer was coming—" The guests looked at the chatty ghost in amazement, but Gao's father made straight for the Emperor's uncle. "Did he try to feed you that Temple Style Duck? I only ask because you're looking a little thin. The first time I met one of those Southerners I thought they were crazy, won't eat meat, won't eat fowl, not even fish. But I met one who was a wizard with rice—learned a few tricks from him . . ."

By the time dawn came Doi Thiviei and the Emperor's uncle were chatting like old friends. The royal ghost was looking much more substantial and even accepted one of the sesame balls with hot lotus paste Gao had made for breakfast.

"Gao, I think I'll stay here a while," his father said. "I hope it won't disappoint my mourners, but I've gotten a little tired of hearing my own voice. Take good care of my restaurant, will you?"

"Of course," Gao answered, ladling out the clear soup he had made from chicken stock and the last of the qinshon leaves.

"And I suppose you'll be marrying that Southerner girl and changing the name your mother and I gave you. I know you've never liked it, though it's a good story how you got it."

Gao frowned. "I always thought it was because—well, my face— and I always had to make it for the customers who couldn't afford anything else."

"No, no," his father said. "It wasn't like that at all. You see, when I first met your mother—but I suppose you don't have time to hear this story."

Gao sat down and took a sip of the soup, enjoying the fragile flavour of the qinshon. He only allowed himself one bowl a year, to be sure he would appreciate it. "I have plenty of time, father," he said. "Only please, let me go get Mienme so she can hear it as well. We will both need to know this story so we can tell it to our children."

It turned out his father had lots of stories he had never told; or maybe Gao had just never heard them before.

Lagos

Safrat liked being a vacuum cleaner. Of all the jobs she might be given, it was her favourite: she liked to see in the rich peoples' homes, even if her point of view was only three inches off the ground. It was light work, too, not like digging earth or handling barrels of toxic waste. That shouldn't have made a difference but it did, at the end of the day when the motor-muscles she didn't have ached beyond words.

The amber warning lit up: only half an hour left in her shift. She switched to light suction and began moving more swiftly around the floor, scanning for any spots she might have missed or where dust might have settled since she started. The foreman, Adegoke, had said that a house could never be clean enough for the rich people. If they were not satisfied then there would be no more demand for workers from Lagos, and the telepresence booths the government had built with World Bank money would sit idle. It was up to workers like her, he had said, to do a good enough job that even the rich white people would be satisfied.

She had just finished her inspection when the red warning lit, and she started to disengage from the vacuum and return to full wakefulness. You could not work the machines, even the very simple ones like vacuum cleaners, when you were entirely awake: you shuddered and jolted and made stupid mistakes, as if you were thinking about every step while you walked. Many of the workers drank palm wine or smoked India hemp before their shifts to get into the proper state of mind, but Safrat found it came naturally to her if she chose one simple task to start with and did it slowly and rhythmically. Like the others, though, she was always muzzy after a shift, and she was glad her brother Paul was able to meet her and guide her home.

It was only five months they had been in Lagos. The city was for the ambitious, and neither of them was that: they had been happy to tend battery trees in the country, up north of Ilorin, until the state energy company had chosen their village as the site of the new transmission station. After that there was no choice for either of them but to go to the city like all the rest, try to find a relation who would help with a job and a place to live. They had found a cousin, an *oga* named Tinubu, who had quickly gotten Safrat the telepresence job—they preferred to hire women for some reason—but could only find casual work for Paul, hustling and running for him. This meant that while Safrat gave Tinubu only a quarter of her salary, Paul had to give half of whatever he made since he could not be relied on to bring in anything at all.

Now Paul led Safrat back to their home, past the market crowded with stalls with sheet-metal roofs, where medicines, bicycle parts and DVDs were sold; the sound of the hawkers and the car horns came to her like distant music, barely penetrating the haze that surrounded her. It would take them more than an hour to get back to Isale Eko on foot, but that was all right. They paid only for night rights in their room, and if they got there before nine o'clock they would have to wait around outside the building. Instead they stopped for a meal of *fufu* and groundnuts and then arrived just as the people who slept there during the day were leaving, found the mattresses still warm on the floor.

In the morning Safrat rose, picked up the two plastic buckets that sat at the foot of her mattress and went to the borehole to buy water. As she did she passed one of the sleeping alleys, where plastic sheets were laid on the ground as beds: she and Paul had slept in one of those when they first arrived, and it was only Tinubu and the job he had found for her that had brought them indoors. Water from the borehole was trickling down the alley, creeping over the plastic sheets, but one of the people there still slept anyway.

She paid twenty naira to fill both buckets, waiting for a long time behind a woman with a foot-washing business who was filling ten, loading each one onto a pushcart; then she carefully trudged back to the apartment building, willing herself to ignore the calls of the touts and hawkers that offered her cell phones, watches, anything. The wind was blowing from the east, bringing sawdust from the great mills on the mainland, and by the time she got back she was coughing white phlegm.

"How did you sleep?" Paul asked as she joined him on the stoop. He was holding two wooden bowls full of *fufu*, handed one to her.

"I never remember," Safrat said. "Why do you ask?"

"You were talking," he said. "In English."

Safrat frowned. Both of them spoke English well enough to get by in Lagos, but their first language was Yoruba. She didn't suppose she had ever thought in English, never mind dreaming in it. "What did I say?"

Paul shrugged. He was concentrating on pouring the water she had bought into the dozen or so clear plastic bottles he had collected, which he would then strap on his back under a vest of cargo netting: a few hours in the sun would kill off whatever evils lurked within. "I didn't follow it," he said, not taking his eyes off the bottle's mouth. "Something about a vacation, I think."

She put down her bowl and laughed. "A vacation in English," she said. "That sounds good."

He laughed too, though he did not look up. "I'll bring you water at two, unless Tinubu has a job for me."

Safrat nodded. "Thank you," she said, then stood and patted him on the shoulder, careful not to disrupt his concentration. It was hot already, and by the time she got to the telepresence station she wished she had brought one of Paul's water bottles. On a day like today, though, each bottle might bring three times what it had cost.

The other women were starting to arrive, either on foot like her or by the rattling *danfo*. They were all early: without a watch—one that worked, and kept working, which was not something to be found in Lagos—it was the only way to be sure of being on time. That was something the rich white people who had built the booths insisted on.

"Smoke?" one of the other workers asked, an Ibo girl named Janet. She held out a rolled cigarette, double-stuffed with tobacco and India hemp.

Safrat held up her hand in polite refusal, but a moment later changed her mind and accepted it. The taste was bitter and harsh as she drew in the smoke, and she felt light-headed; she did not much like the effect that smoking had on her, but today she felt a need to join in the morning rituals of the other women.

"My husband says I was keeping him up all night," said one of them, a Lagos-born woman everyone called Victoria; she was careful to note, in every conversation, that she and her husband lived on Victoria Island. She took a swig from a plastic milk jug full of palm wine, passed it to the woman next to her.

"Were you talking?" Safrat asked.

Victoria's eyebrows shot up in surprise. Among the workers there were lines rarely crossed. There were those who came by foot and those who came by *danfo*, and Safrat came by foot; there were those who drank palm wine and those who smoked India hemp, and on most days Safrat did neither. "Why do you ask?" Victoria said.

Safrat coughed, the smoke from Janet's cigarette still burning her throat. "My brother said I was talking in my sleep last night," she said. "In English."

"I only speak in English," Victoria said pointedly.

"But were you talking? In your sleep?"

Before Victoria could speak Janet said, "I think I was. When I woke this morning all the people in my room were looking at me."

Victoria raised an eyebrow and looked Safrat in the eye, ignoring Janet. "Yes," she said. "He said I was talking."

"What is this, what is going on?" Adegoke asked. The foreman, a tall, thin man in his twenties, had stepped out of the station as he did every morning, brandishing his wrist with the gold watch at the women. "You are all nearly late. What is this, palm wine and hemp?

Is this going to help you do careful work?"

Normally this was the cue for the women to put these things away and file into their telepresence booths, but today Victoria turned to face Adegoke directly. "Your machines are making us sick," she said. "Why should we go in?"

Adegoke put his hands on his hips. "What are you saying?" he asked. "There is nothing wrong with the machines. They are brand new."

"Ask Safrat," Victoria said, pointing to her and stepping aside. "She knows what's going on."

"Safrat?" Adegoke asked. "Are you causing trouble here?"

The air was gone from her lungs; if she lost this job Safrat would have to give Tinubu everything she had saved so far as compensation, and his take from the next job would be higher.

"Well?" Adegoke said. "Can't you speak?"

"I was—I was just noticing many of us seem to be talking in our sleep," she said, keeping her eyes on Adegoke's leather shoes.

"That is normal enough," Adegoke said. "When you don't work hard enough in the day your mind keeps going at night."

"We are all talking in English," Safrat said.

"And you think this is the booths? No, it is impossible. The wall of fire prevents anything like that."

The women all looked at him curiously.

"The wall of fire," Adegoke said. He waved his hands around his head. "When the World Bank men built this station, they built it with a wall of fire around it. It keeps things from coming back to you, to the booths. All right?" There was silence. "All right. Now get to your stations and get to work."

Safrat went to her booth in silence, sat down and hooked herself up to the machine. As soon as the drugs had relaxed her muscles she got to work, controlling a forklift loading cartons onto and off of a ship; the usual rhythm eluded her, though, and she was glad to have had some of Janet's cigarette. The work went slowly, and by the end of the day she was too exhausted to think about anything but sleep.

Paul was not waiting for her at the end of her shift: Tinubu must have found him a job, she thought, or at least an errand.

She carefully made her way home, forcing herself to concentrate on her surroundings, and finally settled down on the steps of her apartment building to wait for her brother.

She awoke to find him standing over her, two bowls of *fufu* in hand; gratefully she took one, began to eat it in silence.

"How did you do today?" she asked after a few minutes.

Paul smiled. "Tinubu gave me a job, in the Mile Twelve market."

"A job? For how long?"

"Just for today." He must have noticed the look that crossed her face, because he quickly added, "But he said he'd get me more, soon."

"How much did you make?" Safrat asked.

"Two thousand naira."

"How much did you keep?"

Paul looked away. "Two hundred."

She shook her head. "You'd have made more selling water."

"But he said—he promised if I did a good job selling he would find me a regular job—"

"Selling what?"

"Watches today, but it doesn't matter. . . . Safrat?"

"What?" She blinked, feeling as though some force was pulling her off balance. "What did you say?"

"I asked if you were all right," Paul said. He leaned close. Glancing away, Safrat saw that almost all of her *fufu* had been eaten. Had she been asleep, or just away from home? "You were talking again, in English. When I told you about the watches Tinubu gave me to sell you started to say something about gold Rolexes."

"In English?"

"Yes."

Safrat frowned, shook her head. "Do you have any paper? For writing, I mean?"

Paul nodded.

"Next time you hear me talking like that, write down everything I say. Exactly the words I say, all right?"

Nodding again, Paul said "All right. What do you think this is?"

"I don't know," Safrat said.

The next morning Safrat went back to work, clutching the piece of paper on which Paul had written her nighttime speech. Victoria was already there when she arrived, passing the day's jug of palm wine around with her friends, and after a moment Safrat screwed up the courage to approach her.

"What is it?" Victoria asked, eyeing her suspiciously.

"What your husband said you were saying, in the night," Safrat asked, thrusting the paper at her. "Was it anything like this?"

Victoria's eyes narrowed as she took the paper, squinting at Paul's rough letters. "I don't know," she said. "I suppose."

"What is this?" Adegoke asked, snatching the paper from Victoria's hand.

Victoria threw Safrat a look of fury: to the foreman she was just another worker, and she did not like to be reminded of that. "It's Safrat's," she said. "She brought it."

"Safrat, I told you—"

"It's nothing," Safrat said. She reached out for the paper in Adegoke's hands, but stopped short of touching it. "Please. It's nothing."

"I will keep this," Adegoke said. "But you all should get to work."

The other women glared at Safrat as they passed into the station, their wine and India hemp unfinished. There would be nothing to do but sit in their booths until the shift began, but nobody, not even Victoria, was willing to argue with the foreman.

That day Safrat was given her least favourite job, clearing, cleaning and stacking dishes at an automatic restaurant somewhere; it was nervous work, too delicate to ever establish a rhythm, and the unchanging perspective made her feel as though she was trapped in a box. The day crawled by, plate by plate and glass by glass, until finally the amber warning lit. She used the last half-hour of her shift to check the machine she was controlling for wear or glitches, then disconnected as soon as the red warning came up. Today she was wide awake. She looked around at the others emerging dazed from their booths, heard murmured English on their lips. She frowned, saw Paul waiting for her outside.

"No work today?" she asked when she joined him.

He shook his head. "Tinubu says tomorrow."

"You'll need to," Safrat said. "We have to hire a *babalawo*."

"Safrat—"

"This thing I have, the other women have it too. Some of them, anyway."

"Did you talk to the foreman?"

She glanced back at the station. "He wouldn't listen. Not to me."

Paul sighed. "And the other girls? Will they help pay?" Safrat shook her head. "So why should we do it? Let one of the rich ones do it." By rich he meant someone like Victoria: rich enough to have her own room, to live in a neighbourhood with running water, to take the *danfo* to work.

"I think something is wrong here, very wrong," Safrat said. "I'm afraid to wait."

After a moment Paul nodded, said "I'll ask Tinubu to find us a *babalawo*."

"No. Tinubu can't think I'm causing trouble at my job. Didn't our uncle Olisa have a cousin in the city who was a *babalawo*?"

"Yes, I think," Paul said. "I'll see if I can find him tonight. Is that all right?"

Safrat nodded. "I hope so."

Adegoke watched the women go, looked down at the torn piece of newspaper on his desk. He had been puzzling over it all day, trying to understand what the girl Safrat had written there. Her writing was very poor, but he could make out the numbers: very large numbers, it seemed, and what he thought was the word dollars. A treasure, he thought, she had been speaking in her sleep of a treasure: he had heard stories like this, when he had been a boy in his grandfather's village east of Uyo. Men who had died over money might live on as *eggun*, unable to rest until the treasure was found. He thought that was what the message was saying, that the spirit was inviting him to find the fortune, but at the end it turned into nonsense, just a string of numbers. He picked up a pen and copied what he could read of the writing onto a clean piece of paper, hoping it might make more sense.

His hand slowed as he wrote the last sequence of numbers. As he copied them he recognized the first three as the area code for Lagos. Adegoke counted out the remaining numbers, nodded.

He took a deep breath, picked up the phone and began dialling.

"Sit down," the *babalawo* said.

Safrat looked around the room: it was scattered with scraps of paper and stubs of candles, wooden bowls and drums and shells of kola nuts. To her surprise the *babalawo* did not live much better than she did; in his own room, it was true, but still in Isale Eko. She brushed a spot on the floor bare of nut shells and sat down cross-legged.

"My brother says you fear sorcery," the *babalawo* said. By brother he meant Paul: in the country there were no aunts or uncles, just mothers and fathers.

"Yes," Safrat said. "For the last few nights, I've been—"

The *babalawo* held up a finger. "Shh," he said, then nodded twice, slowly. He unslung the bag from his shoulder and drew out a broad, shallow wooden tray and a small plastic bag full of grey powder. He put the bowl on the floor, opened the bag and emptied the powder into the tray, smoothing it with the back of his hand until it was perfectly flat and featureless. Then he reached into the bag again and drew out eight palm nuts, each with tiny holes drilled into one side. He closed his hands together, shook the palm nuts inside and then tossed them into the tray; some fell with the blank side up, some with the drilled, and he drew lines from one to another in the powder, following some pattern or procedure she could not follow.

"Elegua and Ogunn are present," the *babalawo* said. "A road has been opened, or a door. Something that should not have been opened. Does this mean anything to you?"

Safrat frowned. "I don't know."

The *babalawo* shook his head quickly. "Iron is involved. A car, a bridge—"

"A machine?" Safrat asked.

Frowning, the *babalawo* ran his finger along the path he had drawn between the nuts. "Perhaps," he said. "Yes, I think so, yes. Oggun is concerned with a machine."

"Is that what's wrong with me?" Safrat said. "Is the machine broken?"

"Broken? No." The *babalawo* scratched his head, squinting at the palm nuts before him. "There is sorcery in the machine. An *eggun*, or the work of another *babalawo*."

"Can you help?"

"Perhaps." The *babalawo* scooped up the palm nuts, put them back in his shoulder bag and then emptied the grey powder back into its bag. Finally he put the wooden tray back into his shoulder bag and stood up. "I will need to see the machine."

Safrat sighed as she got to her feet. "How much will that cost?"

The *babalawo* shrugged. "We will see," he said.

Adegoke looked down at the piece of paper, then up at the building in front of him. He had the right address, but he was puzzled: this was a government building, not the sort of place he'd expect to find a fortune. He had been just as surprised, of course, when the number Safrat had written down had been a real phone number. He went into the air-conditioned lobby, suddenly aware of the sweat under his striped shirt, made his way quickly to the building directory. Number thirty-four, he'd been told: he buzzed for it and waited.

"Who is it?" a voice said. It sounded like the same one as on the phone.

"We spoke this evening," Adegoke said. He cleared his throat. "I brought what you asked."

"Already?" There was a moment's silence. "You have it with you?"

"Yes."

"All right. Come up to the fifth floor."

Adegoke looked over his shoulder, then made his way to the elevator. His palms were sweaty despite the cool air, and he felt like everyone could see his wallet bulging in his back pocket. He should have worn his money belt instead. He had bought it when he first came to Lagos, having heard so many stories about how dangerous the city was, but had not worn it long: it was too inconvenient, and he liked having his money easy at hand.

Finally the elevator doors re-opened and he stepped out onto the fifth floor. He was in a waiting room, with a sofa and chairs, a receptionist's desk. "Hello?" he called. He heard no response, so he sat down on the sofa.

A few minutes passed before he heard footsteps coming down from the hallway behind the receptionist's desk. He got to his feet, swallowed, and patted the bulge in his back pocket. A well-dressed man with glasses, Igbo or maybe Yoruba, appeared behind the desk. "Hello," he said in BBC-accented English, extending a hand to Adegoke. "We spoke on the phone?"

Adegoke nodded, took the man's hand. "Yes," he said.

"Good. You have the money? A thousand dollars US?"

"Yes."

"Very good. With that I can get the account unfrozen—it should take about a week. When that's done I'll call you and—"

"What do you mean, a week?" Adegoke said. "Do you think I'm going to give you a thousand dollars and just walk away?"

"These things take time," the man said. "But I promise you, your investment will be amply—"

Adegoke reached out and seized the man's wrist, glaring at him. "Are you trying to scam me?" he asked. "Do you know who I am? I am Adegoke Omojoro. My uncle is Michael Oyelolo." The man's face went pale at the mention of his uncle's name, and Adegoke nodded. "That's right. So I want to see my share today, or I take my money and I walk."

The man pulled his hand away, reached up to pull at the knot of his tie. "Stay here just a minute, please," he said.

Crossing his arms, Adegoke watched the man go. He was glad he had thought to mention his uncle: Michael was the reason he had come to Lagos, the man who had gotten him his job, and his name opened doors. Adegoke smiled to himself, waiting for the man to return.

He didn't. Instead a taller man came down the hall, perfectly dressed in a dark suit. Adegoke's eyes widened, his arms dropping to his side.

"Hello, nephew," his uncle said.

Safrat had thought she would need to find a way to sneak Paul and the *babalawo* into the station, but the foreman was not there: only the night shift women were in their booths, and they saw nothing.

"What are you going to do?" Paul asked the *babalawo*.

"She needs to confront the spirit that is tormenting her," the *babalawo* said. "If it is coming through the machine, then that is how she must face it."

Leading the others down the station, Safrat found an empty booth. "I can do it from here," she said, "but once I'm in the booth I don't have any control over what job they give me."

The *babalawo* unshouldered his bag, started to root around in it. After a minute he drew out a small plastic pouch filled with a coarse brown-and-white powder. "This is a medicine we use to face the *eggun*," he said. "If you swallow this and drink palm wine you will be half-sober and half-drunk, half-dreaming and half-awake. That is the only way to see the spirits directly."

Safrat took the bag, settled into the booth. "I won't need the wine, I think," she said. She hooked herself up and opened the pouch, felt the acrid tang of the powder burning her nostrils. "How much do I have to take?"

"Wet your fingertip, then touch the powder and run it over your gums," the *babalawo* said. She did as he had instructed, feeling a tingle run through her and then a buzz as the medicine started its work; just then the drugs started to flow into her from the hookup and she went limp.

At first it appeared the medicine had not changed anything: the vision feed of a sewer-snake faded into her view, twitching as she flexed the feedback motors. After a few moments, though, she noticed a strange double vision, both the sensory feed she was getting from the snake and something like a chain or a rope running down to it. With a prayer to Elegua, opener of paths, she willed herself up the chain.

The sewer-snake's vision faded from view as she rose, and after a moment she found herself in a space like a cattle pen. She saw herself there, or rather a thing that was labelled SAFRAT: it did not look like a person but a bundle of organs, a beating heart and lungs breathing in and out, hanging in the air. The chain led back down to the snake from it, and all around her were other bundles like it, labelled with the names of all the night shift women. Each had chains leading down from them to their jobs, vacuums or forklifts or dishwashers, but Safrat saw they had other chains leading into and out of them as well. Those leading out went in all directions, but the ones leading in all came from above. She tried to focus on one of the chains that ran down to the women, but instead moved herself into its path.

G01D R0LEX W@TCHES ONLY $30 We represent a w@tch distributor that has overstocked on g01d R0lexes. They have authorized us to offer

Safrat pulled herself away. Paul had mentioned her talking about watches; this chain had to be how the *eggun* was possessing her—possessing them all. She felt her heart racing, saw it echoed in the pulsing heart within the floating bundle labelled SAFRAT. The drugs normally kept her heart even, no matter how hard she had been working, but the *babalawo*'s medicine had interfered with that. She made herself rest until she saw it slowing and then focused on the chain once more, following it upward.

She rose until she struck a wall of fire, and then she burned.

Adegoke's uncle led him back to his office, sat him down in a plush leather chair, then went to his desk and picked up a dark green bottle. He opened it, poured two glasses and held one out to Adegoke. "Scotch?"

Nodding gratefully, Adegoke took the glass and drank. It had a very different taste from palm wine, burning his throat like fire, and he coughed.

"Gently," Michael said. "Good scotch is to be savoured."

"Thank you, uncle," Adegoke said. He took a much smaller sip, found it went down more easily this time. "I didn't expect to see you here."

"Nor did I think I would see you." His uncle held his glass under his nose and breathed deeply, then smiled and nodded. "I should hate to tell your mother you were so foolish."

"But uncle—" Adegoke's uncle threw him a look, and he let his head drop in shame. A vacuum cleaner sat on the floor nearby, idle.

"How did you get the number, anyway?" his uncle asked.

"One of the women at my station," Adegoke said. "She said she had been talking in her sleep. She wrote down what she had said, brought it to me—it talked about a fortune to be claimed, I thought—"

His uncle held up a hand. "Talking in her sleep?" he said. "That is unforeseen. It may be we need more time before we can roll out fully."

"I'm sorry, uncle. I don't know what you mean."

"Talking to myself," his uncle said. "Your girls—they have value as workers, of course, but what is much more valuable is the space in their heads. We can use each one of them to send a million messages every day."

"Messages?" Adegoke asked.

His uncle nodded. "Some are for ourselves, like the one that brought you here, but that is only a sideline. The world is a market, nephew, a million times bigger than the Mile Twelve, and people will pay us to be their hawkers—sell watches, drugs, anything or nothing. We feed the messages to your workers and the lines that let them run their machines carry the messages as well. When the rest of the World Bank money comes in, we can build stations all over Africa."

"But, uncle—" Adegoke felt a pain in his stomach, as though invisible fingers were squeezing him hard. "Uncle, this is black magic."

"What's happening to her?" Paul asked. For the first few minutes Safrat's body had been limp, as though she had been in the deepest sleep, but now she was twitching, writhing.

"She is burning," the *babalawo* said. He opened his shoulder bag again, started digging around in it.

"I should call the foreman," Paul said. "Disconnect the machine."

"Get water. Try to cool her." The *babalawo* pulled out his wooden tray and a wooden rattle with a brass head. He shook it in the air, then tapped it against the tray. "Elegua, open our sister's path. Clear the way for her."

Paul opened one of his water bottles, poured a stream onto his sister's forehead. She jerked her head away as it made contact, but her twitching eased slightly. "Isn't there any other way we can help her?"

"Elegua must open the path, and Safrat must pass through," the *babalawo* said. "But the *orishas* never make it easy."

The pain was intense, every inch of her body licked by the flames. Her muscles froze at the fire's touch, trying to recoil from it, but there was nowhere to escape.

She had a moment's respite, a cool touch on her face, and in that moment she reached out and seized the chain that led up through the wall of fire. Again words and sentences she barely understood ran through her, but she focused on climbing the chain up and through the wall.

Now she was in a space like one of the street markets: shapes her eyes could not resolve flew at dizzying speeds through narrow alleys, while lights flashed over the hundreds of doors on every wall. Noise like the shouts of a hundred hawkers and the blare of a thousand car horns surrounded her, almost driving her back into the wall of fire.

Desperate to escape, she ran to the nearest door; its handle, though, was of a design her hand simply could not grasp. She ran to another door, found it the same: another door, then another, before finally finding one she could open. A chain ran through the opened doorway, and she followed it gratefully, glad to be away from the lights and the noise.

When she reached the end of the chain she got a sensory feed: just vision and motor feedback, a view of a carpeted floor and the bottom of a sofa.

The vacuum cleaner by Adegoke's feet suddenly whirred to life, moved a shuddering foot towards him. His hand jerked, spilling a few drops of whisky onto his trousers.

"Honestly, nephew," his uncle said, "do they really still tell you such stuff in the villages?"

"Uncle, I—" Adegoke looked down nervously at the vacuum cleaner advancing on his foot. "Is that how you won your position here in the city, by magic?"

His uncle shook his head, turned to the computer sitting on his desk and pressed a key that made the screen light up. "Do not talk of such absurd stuff," his uncle said. "I won my position because I had family willing to help me, like everyone else in Lagos." He ran his finger in a spiral pattern over the screen, then tapped it twice; the vacuum went dark and stopped whirring, a few inches from Adegoke's foot. "I went to Manchester Polytechnic, nephew, and I can tell you: there's no such thing as magic."

The sensory feed cut out before Safrat could see where she was, and she found herself back in the noise and light of the market. Though she was a bit better prepared this time it still was overwhelming, and she went quickly through the next door she was able to open: here she had only a timer input and a dimmer to control, but again she was disconnected and driven back to the market. Through the next door she connected with a speed toggle and feedback motors that controlled sharp metal teeth, again being disconnected after a few moments. Finally she found a safe haven, somewhere with no motors or visual but with numeric and audio input. She took a moment to calm herself—the drugs were not keeping her heartbeat even, she had to remember—only half-listening to the audio feed until she recognized her foreman's voice.

The lights dimmed and then flickered as Adegoke's uncle peered at his computer screen, frowning; then the shredder on top of his wastebasket turned itself on, grinding away at nothing.

"Uncle, do you see?" Adegoke said, his voice rising. "This is the cost of doing magic you don't understand."

"I told your mother to come with me, to the city," his uncle said, not turning from the screen. He ran his finger in a long curve over it, tapped it in three spots, and the shredder stopped. "I told her not to raise her children in a backwater, but she wanted to stay by your grandfather." He took a deep breath, shook his head. "So I promised her, any of her sons that wanted to come to the city, I would get them jobs. She did not tell me she would raise them as savages."

Adegoke was silent for a moment, shocked by his uncle's outburst. He looked around at the now-quiet room, gathered his courage to speak. "You would not talk that way to my mother," he said. "She taught me to respect the *eggun* and the *orishas*, and she would not want to see her brother mixed up in black magic."

"For the last time, this is not magic," his uncle said. He spun the computer around so that Adegoke could see the screen. "This connects to the main server. I control all the machines in my office through that, and the messages to and from the women go through there as well. Do you see? Not magic, just technology. Technology we control."

Safrat listened carefully to what the two men were saying. She did not recognize the second voice, the one arguing with the foreman, but it was clear from what he had said that he was the sorcerer. The *babalawo* had said she must confront him, and she expected this was as close as she was going to get.

"Let the women go," the speakerphone said.

Both Adegoke and his uncle turned towards it. His uncle reached out for the TALK button, paused when he saw the light was already on. "Who is this?" he said angrily.

"Let the women go," the speakerphone said again. "Remove your spell from them, in the name of Eleggua and Oggun."

"Do you see, uncle?" Adegoke asked. "Do you see?"

"Will you shut up?" his uncle said. "This is no spirit. Someone has hacked into our server, and is playing games with us." He reached for the phone, stopped and turned instead to his computer, swirling his finger over the screen and tapping it a half-dozen times.

"The women are suffering," the speakerphone said. "Let them go."

Adegoke's uncle let out a snort. "I've sent a message to our computer security team," he said. "This spirit will not be with us much longer."

Unsure what to do now, Safrat withdrew from the phone. She had confronted the sorcerer, but did not think she had changed his mind; she wished she could ask the *babalawo* for help.

A piercing wail cut through the noise of the market: police sirens. Down both ends of the alley she was in she saw flashing red lights, had no doubt who they were pursuing. There was no time to find another door that would open, and no reason to think she could escape that way anyway; all she could do was go back down the chain she had climbed, through the wall of fire, and hope she could hide amongst the other women.

To her surprise the wall did not burn on her way down, and once she was back in the cattle pen she moved close to the bundle of readouts that bore her name. She watched her heart beating, tried to make it slow enough for her to rest.

Now that she had a moment she could think about what to do. She tried to think of stories she had heard where people outwitted *babalawos*, but there were none: in the stories, evil *babalawos* were always undone by their own magic.

Looking around, Safrat saw all the other women in the cattle pen around her: bundles of hearts and lungs and brains, the sorcerer's messages being fed in and streaming out of them. She took a breath, readying herself for another trip through the wall of fire.

"She's burning again," Paul said.

Safrat's body was twitching again in front of them, her chest rising and falling spastically. A low groan emerged from her throat.

"More water," the *babalawo* said, shaking the bronze rattle over her head. "Elegua, bless our sister . . ."

Paul shook his head. "It's too much for her. We have to shut this off." He looked around at the booth, hoping to find a control he understood, but there was nothing. Instead he ran out into the hall of the telepresence station, looking for a way to contact the foreman.

The lights brightened, flickered and finally failed: only the glow of the computer screen was visible in the darkened office.

"Uncle . . ." Adegoke began.

"Secure the server," his uncle was shouting at the phone. "I don't care! Get it done!"

"What is happening, uncle?"

"That hacker crashed our server," his uncle said.

Adegoke heard the cellphone at his belt buzzing, picked it up. The call display showed it was the emergency phone at the TP station, programmed to autodial his number. "Excuse me, uncle," he said. "Yes?"

Two men in short-sleeve shirts ran in the door, both holding flashlights. "I am sorry, Mr. Oyelolo," one of them said. "We're getting too much traffic."

"Is this the foreman?" the voice on Adegoke's cellphone said.

"What about the firewall?"

"Who is this?" Adegoke asked.

"They're getting right through somehow. It's as though the messages were coming from our own system."

"Messages?"

One of the men read from the screen. "Dear Sir: I have been requested by the Nigerian National Petroleum Company to contact you for assistance in resolving a matter. . . ."

"My sister Safrat is in booth—hold on—booth eleven," the voice on the phone said. "Something is wrong. You must shut it off, now."

Adegoke frowned, then looked over at his uncle conferring with the other two men. "Fix it," his uncle was saying. "Block them out."

"I am sorry, Mr. Oyelolo, but we're not rated for that," the other man said. "This must be a problem with the architecture. Only the men from the Bank can fix it."

"But if they fix it—if they see—"

Adegoke lowered his phone, covering the receiver with his palm. "Uncle—" he said.

His uncle turned to look at him, his eyes hard. "Damn it, boy, can't you see that I am busy?"

"I am sorry, uncle," Adegoke said. He held his phone to his mouth again, spoke softly. "Do not worry," he said. "I think your sister will be all right in a minute."

Safrat rose early, feeling better-rested than she had since coming to Lagos. The telepresence station had been closed ten days now, supposedly for repairs; the word was, though, that the old owners had given it up and let the World Bank run it directly. Meanwhile the foreman had paid everyone for the days when the telepresence station was being repaired, so long as they reported each day to collect their pay, and as the time passed they had all stopped talking in their sleep. Word had only come yesterday that the station was to re-open.

"I don't like you going back there," Paul said. "How do you know it's any safer?"

Safrat looked around at the crowded room, the waking and still-sleeping forms around them, and shrugged. The job Tinubu had promised Paul had never materialized, and most days he still sold water; if the foreman had not kept paying her they would have been back to sleeping on a plastic sheet in the alley.

"What choice do I have?" she asked, and picked up her buckets to take to the borehole.

THE DRAGON'S LESSON

Child, why are you crying? Your first bleeding came this morning, and how many gifts did I give you to mark the day—black stone bracelets carved smooth, and a silver necklace so fine a spider might have woven it. Yes, and now you have your own house, as a sister should, walls woven tight against the wind. What reason do you have for tears?

Ah, I see. No, it is no shame—even a lion feels the bite of a fly, as we say. But you must understand, this is not a time for tears. Let me tell you a story—no, you have not heard it before; it is not one of our stories, but was told to me by one of the Dead Men. Of course not. They wear veils to face their gods, as we do; only their god is the sun, and he is everywhere, so they must go veiled whenever they are outside. Beneath they are as alive as you or me. Some are even handsome—and better lovers than our men, I can tell you.

Do not look so shocked, child. You are a sister, now, and must learn to deal with men. In truth the Dead Men are not so frightening; they are more like sisters than our men are.

This story is of a man named Ramaad—I do not know, it is a word in their language. The Dead Men do not live like us. Their men and women live in houses together, and they have many houses built together in large camps. Ramaad was the son of a trader, but his father was not wealthy, and Ramaad knew he would not be given any trading goods when he left home. He had only his friend Yas'al to help him, but he was no better off. His father Inkasar had once been a wealthy trader, travelling far from his home in Akhaduu and returning with the rarest goods, but had somehow lost it all; now he was even poorer than Ramaad's father, with nothing to trade but the old stories he had heard, for which the other Dead Men in their pity gave him just enough food to live. So Ramaad and Yas'al, as they grew, would spend many hours together around Yas'al's fire, planning the trading journeys they would someday make and listening to Yas'al's father tell his stories. To Yas'al they were nothing but a poor old man's ramblings, but Ramaad listened carefully, for his father had told him Inkasar truly had been to all those far places. There was one story especially that Ramaad remembered: a tale of a creature called a dragon that flew all over the world, and would bring great riches to anyone who killed it.

The day came when the two boys were old enough to start on their trading journeys, but Yas'al had to stay at home with his father, whose health was failing; so each of them vowed "I love you like salt"—which is the strongest oath the Dead Men have to swear by, since nothing is any good without salt—and pooled all they had, and it was Ramaad alone who left the village. He took their goods and traded well, returning each season to share what he had gained with Yas'al, and also the stories he had heard—for stories may bring food to a toothless mouth, as he well knew, and everywhere he went he would trade the stories he knew for others. One story, in particular, he hoped to hear more of. Yes, that one. You're right, that is just what he thought; but for a long time he could learn nothing more, and he began to think that this story, at least, Inkasar had simply invented.

Years passed, and Ramaad and Yas'al became used to their arrangement; so much so that when Inkasar finally died, Yas'al did not join Ramaad on his journeys, as he had always said he would, but remained at home and took care of their affairs in Akhaduu. Ramaad continued his journeys, slowly building their stock of goods, taking only small risks and keeping them always one step ahead of hunger.

One day, while on a journey far from home, Ramaad heard of a man who was said to know something about dragons. The man lived several days travel off his route, but Ramaad had never forgotten the story Inkasar had told, and calculated that he could make the journey and still come out ahead on his trades. He made the trip only at night, for fear someone might follow him, and when he reached his destination found only a small hut, which he thought at first must be abandoned, as there was no fire within. Still he went inside, hoping he might somehow recoup his losses, and found there an old man so badly crippled it was a wonder he could feed himself. His legs were missing, and one of his arms, and when Ramaad saw the scars of fire on the man's face and body he knew why the hearth was cold.

"Why do you disturb my pain?" the man asked, turning his sightless eyes towards the door.

"Forgive me," Ramaad said. "I came because I heard there was a man here who knew of a creature called a dragon, but I did not mean to disturb you."

"All you need to know you see before you," the man said. "Do you hope the dragon will make you rich?"

"Yes," Ramaad said.

"I am rich. Do you see the necklaces I wear?" the man asked, pulled down his robe to show the white scars that crossed and recrossed his neck. He waved his broken fingers at Ramaad. "Do you see my rings?" he said. "Lead me outside, then, where the sun will look on our bargain, even if I cannot."

Ramaad took the old man's arm, gently, and led him out of the hut. The sun was just rising, and the man flinched as its light touched his face.

"Will you tell me of the dragon?" Ramaad said. "I will pay you, if I can."

"Give me all that you have, and I will tell you of the dragon." The old man said. "Does that seem too much? If I tell you, and you succeed, you will not need the meagre things you have; if I tell you and you fail, you will not need them."

"Very well," Ramaad said, and he took up all his goods and laid them on the door of the hut. "Tell me what you know."

The man twisted his ruined mouth into what might have been a smile, and began to tell his tale. "Today, as you know, all things living are either animals, made of flesh, or plants, made of wood; but in the beginning there lived also beasts made of stone. Dragons are the last of these. There are few of them left, and they roost only in the highest of mountains, to hide from those that would hunt them."

"How can they be killed, if they are made of stone?" Ramaad asked.

"Though their skin cannot be pierced or their bones broken, still they have a weakness," the man said. "When dragons were born the world was much hotter, so now their blood is always cooling in the air; their hearts must burn with fire to keep it from turning to hard rock. Still they drink water, as all things do, and some of that water turns to steam in their hearts; so they have a hole in their backs, like the spout of a kettle, where it is released. If you can block that hole the steam will have nowhere else to go, and it will kill the dragon."

"And the treasure?" he asked. "Where does the dragon keep it?"

"The dragon is the treasure," the old man said. "When the dragon dies his teeth become diamonds, his bones turn to gold, his heart to rubies, his flesh to rock and his brain to iron; his blood, most precious of all, becomes veins of the purest salt. The dragon, in death, is a mountain of riches, and all mountains were dragons, once."

Ramaad thanked the old man and started the journey back to his trade route, leaving all but his skin tent and water gourd behind. He wondered how he would explain this foolishness to Yas'al, who had always thought his father's stories were nonsense. He consoled himself with the thought that he would not have to face that question for a while; it would take at least a season of working another trader's caravan to recoup his losses.

Still, as he looked back angrily at the old man's hut, he saw a range of mountains in the distance, and he set his mind—better to be a fox in the grass than a dog by the fire, as our men say. He turned back and set out for the mountains, trading as he went the few things he had left for food and water. On he went, though the air grew cold and the ground broken and stony; up he went, though the air grew thin and cold, and each step drew his breath right out of his lungs.

Finally Ramaad could push himself no further. Again repenting his foolishness he fell to the ground and beat himself about the face, as the Dead Men do, when a shadow passed over him. Looking up he saw the shape of great wings above, larger than he had thought possible, and a faint ember of hope rekindled in him—though it was dashed almost at once, as he realized that to have any hope at all of killing the thing he would need to strike it from above. Still, passed water is good as beer in the desert, as we say. Gathering the last of his strength he climbed still higher, until at last he was able to see the monstrous thing just a few throws above him, its skin glowing red like a rock in a campfire. Now he remembered the old man's scars and burns, and he was afraid, and hid himself in a hollow in the rock and watched the dragon circling outside. The very sight of it was terrifying, but he forced himself to watch for the jet of steam the old man had described; sure enough, after a few moments it rose, coming from a hole just a bit larger than a woman's head. It might as well have been as big as a house, though, since he had no way to block it, and anyway no hope of reaching it from where he was. He cursed himself for not asking the old man what he had done—even though it had plainly failed, it might have given him an idea to start with. As he thought on that, he remembered the man's scars and burns, and suddenly it came to him how the old man had attacked, and why he had failed, and he knew what he, in turn, must do.

Ramaad came out of his hiding place and stepped carefully to the ledge. The dragon was still circling, now a few throws higher, now lower. Gathering up all his courage, Ramaad waited until the dragon was as close as it ever came and jumped. It was too big to miss, but its back was scalding hot and as smooth as palm leaves; he landed on its neck and slid down its back, towards the steam vent. A white plume shot out as he approached. This, Ramaad thought, must have been where the old man had failed, falling into the vent and being burned himself. Ramaad gripped the dragon's stony back with all his strength, feeling his fingernails torn out by the roots, and stopped himself before he was close enough to be scalded. He waited until the next jet came, close enough to soak him through with steam, then took his water-gourd and rammed it into the vent, pushing it down until he felt the beast's muscles close around it. Immediately he could hear a rumbling down below, as the pressure started to build, and he let go of his grip and slid down the creature's back and tail, finally falling off and landing on a rock ledge a dozen throws below. Above, the creature was starting to twist itself frantically, its great head straining to free the vent in its back. Ramaad, too badly hurt to move, lay still as he watched the dragon's death throes. Finally the thing froze, and fell with a mighty crash to the ground below.

For a day and a night Ramaad lay there, burnt and broken, wondering if everything that had happened might be a fever dream. Finally, knowing that he would die soon if he did not have anything to drink, he rose and made his painful way back down the mountain. When he reached the bottom he found a stream, and drank from it gratefully; to his amazement, the water was almost hot enough to burn his mouth. He followed the stream to its source, found it in a cave hung with glittering jewels. This, he realized, must have been the dragon's head, and as he walked inside he saw all of the treasures the old man had described.

"I have beaten you, old man," Ramaad thought to himself as he chipped from the rock the tiniest of diamonds, which by itself was worth all the goods he had traded away. "For you killed the dragon, but could not take his treasure; I have done both."

Even in his victory, though, Ramaad knew he had more work to do. If the other people of Akhaduu knew about his sudden wealth they would surely take advantage of him, or else think he had become a sorcerer and kill him for it. Even Yas'al, he thought, he had better not tell, for he had his father's storytelling ways and many long nights to pass when Ramaad was away. How, then, could he use his treasure? At length he thought of the answer. He would take a little at a time—start with the salt, he could say he had gotten a good deal on it—and bring a little more back with him each trip. So long as he did it gradually no-one would be suspicious. He would simply be a skillful trader, building a stock that would soon let him and Yas'al bring gifts to their women to bear children on them.

Yas'al was not inclined to ask questions when Ramaad came back with a load of salt, the purest anyone in Akhaduu had ever seen, and for a few days the two were the most honoured men in the town—for the Dead Men value nothing better than a good trade, and it was clear Ramaad had done very well indeed. The two of them traded away much of the salt, as is customary for those who have received good fortune, to entertain their friends. Still, they had enough—more than enough; Ramaad had not been able to restrain himself entirely—and it was a long time before he felt the need to go on another voyage.

Ramaad went back out on his regular route, but once he was far enough away that he would not be seen he went back to the dragon and got another load of salt, a little more this time. Again he was honoured by the men of the town, but this time Yas'al did not quite share in the honour; indeed the townspeople were starting to say he was living off of Ramaad's charity, just as his father had lived off theirs.

"It is only because I had to stay here in town that they honour you and not me," he said to Ramaad. "Let me come on the next trip, so we can share the work and the reward."

"I need you here to trade our goods when I am away," Ramaad said.

"But we could carry twice as much if I came."

"Without someone to watch our stores the salt would surely be stolen."

"Then let us dissolve our partnership," Yas'al said; for he had been very hurt by the mention of his father. "Give me my half of the salt as a stake, and I will trade with it myself."

Ramaad did not want that either, because he was afraid Yas'al would try to follow him to the source of his treasure, so he said, "I swore I loved you like salt, and you swore the same to me. That is a vow that cannot be broken. Remain."

Mention of their oath seemed to remind Yas'al of his good fortune, and he said nothing more on the matter and let his friend go on his journey alone. When Ramaad returned with another load of pure white salt, though, it seemed to Yas'al that the jokes about him had grown louder, while the townspeople's admiration for Ramaad grew ever greater, and it choked him like a date pit in his throat. He too was clever, though in his own way (which was much like his father's), and he devised a way to get Ramaad to share his secrets. He waited until they were again entertaining friends, drinking jug after jug of honey beer; he had filled his own jug halfway with water, though, to keep his wits about him while Ramaad drank his fill. Then, pretending to be drunk, he said to his friend, "Ramaad, I have never regretted the oath we swore together. From that day to this I have loved you like salt."

Ramaad, who was truly drunk, was happy to share Yas'al's good mood. "I, too, love you like salt, my friend," he said.

"Then, my good friend, tell me where it is that salt you trade for comes from, since you love it no more than you love me."

Ramaad knew he had been tricked, but he could not go back on his oath. "Here is the secret," he said. "I do not trade for it. I found it in a cavern far away, and when I travel I mine some more of it to trade back here."

"I knew it!" Yas'al said. "Ramaad, next time you go you must let me come with you, so I can share in the glory of your 'trading.'"

Ramaad reluctantly agreed, and the next time he left Yas'al came with him, and the two of them mined a great deal of salt. Still, there was much left, and Ramaad began to feel he had been foolish in keeping the secret from Yas'al—though he did not tell him the rest of the secret, or about the rest of the treasure.

Now that he knew where the salt came from Yas'al was less reluctant to trade it than he had once been; instead he began to pay off his father's debts (which no-one had ever thought he would do), and entertain his friends every night, and buy gifts for a dozen women, until Ramaad said to him, "Remember our days of poverty, and how they ended; these days, too, may yet end."

But Yas'al, who had seen the salt cave, said, "There is enough salt there to last us the rest of our lives, and our children and grandchildren too."

Ramaad could not deny it; but still he felt uneasy. He could not say exactly why until the next time he happened to be trading the salt, for a new robe, and the tailor said, "I'll take one stonesweight for it."

"For that I should get a tent," Ramaad said. It was true: before slaying the dragon, he had never even seen a stonesweight of salt.

"That's my price," the tailor said. "Take it or leave it."

Grumbling, Ramaad accepted the man's offer, for he needed a new robe before he feasted with his friends that night. When he went to buy the beer, though, he found the brewer wanted a stonesweight of salt a cask; the butcher wanted the same amount for a roasting calf.

"Do you see what is happening?" Ramaad said to Yas'al when he saw him that afternoon. "Everyone in Akhaduu has salt now; half of them trade in it themselves to other towns. If we keep spending it as we have, soon it will take a dozen stonesweights to buy a cask of beer."

"Even if it does, we will still be rich," Yas'al laughed. "And so will all our friends and neighbours."

Once again Ramaad felt angry for having given up the secret of the salt to Yas'al, but he knew he could do nothing about it. He decided instead to start to mine the gold—he had thought he might start doing that soon anyway, though not for this reason—but not to tell Yas'al where it came from; oath or no, he could not risk losing control of that as well. So he set off in the opposite direction from the cave, telling Yas'al he missed the trading life, and went in a long circle to get back to the cave without Yas'al knowing. Then he mined a tiny amount of gold and came back to Akhaduu along the same slow route.

With the gold they were rich again for a while, but soon Yas'al became jealous once more—as your sisters were jealous of you, today; to each of them I gave gifts when they first bled, but today was your day, and they envied you that. We say that the sun does not know its luck at noon, and so it was with Yas'al. He started to wish ill on Ramaad, even though it would harm himself as well. Ramaad, meanwhile, was on his guard, not eating or drinking with Yas'al, for fear he might be tricked again, and this made it all the easier for Yas'al to betray his friend.

Yas'al knew he would never get Ramaad to tell him the source of the gold, so instead he went to all the other merchants of Akhaduu and told them, "Ramaad is only teasing you with the gold he trades. Raise your prices and you will see a mountain of it."

"Are you mad?" the butcher said. "Already I have seen more gold than I would in a year."

"Besides," the tailor said, "he knows we do not have gold. He will not believe us when we ask for more."

"He doesn't have to," Yas'al said, "so long as you all agree to raise your prices. Then he will have no choice but to meet them or leave his home."

So when Ramaad came back, he found that his gold was worth no more than his salt, and he was angry again at Yas'al—though his friend swore that he did not know where the merchants' gold had come from. Before long Ramaad's gold was gone, and he had to go back to the dragon again; this time he was more careful than ever, buying Yas'al gourd after gourd of beer the night before he left to be sure he would be too drunk to follow him, but still when he returned the merchants acted as though they had all the gold they needed and no desire for any more.

"This is mad," Ramaad said. "Yas'al must have been mining the gold and spending it, the way he did with the salt. Now it is worth next to nothing, but I cannot start to mine any of the other treasures, or the same thing will happen to them."

So Ramaad started spending as little of his gold as possible, no longer buying gifts for women or beer for his friends; so, too, did Yas'al, since of course he had nothing to trade with but the salt, which was now next to worthless. The other merchants of Akhaduu enjoyed the gold they got from Ramaad, but when he stopped spending it found that everyone they dealt with—even the camelteers they relied on to get their goods in and out of town—had raised their prices, having heard how much gold they had; but now the gold was gone, and they could barely afford to do business at all.

"This is all Yas'al's fault," they said. Greed bites like a fly, but brings anger instead of sleep, as we say, and it surely had bitten them. All the merchants of Akhaduu waited until Yas'al was asleep then broke into his house, setting it afire and binding him hand and foot.

"What is going on?" he called out when he realized what was happening. "All of you are my friends! Have I not bought meat from you? Yes, and beer from you? Did I not tell you how to get Ramaad to give you more of his gold?"

"Yes, and you told the camelteers how to get more from us!" the butcher shouted.

"How much did they give you?" the brewer asked.

"What?" Yas'al cried as the flames licked his feet. "No, no—I have nothing, it must have been Ramaad. Look around—do you see any gold here? He kept it all, piled high in his house."

Angry as they were, the men of Akhaduu were greedier still, and the vision of Ramaad's walls piled high with gold drew them like jackals to carrion. They freed Yas'al and let him lead them to Ramaad's house, whose wall they also broke down. Ramaad, though, had been awakened by their coming, and said to them, "What are you doing here, breaking down my wall? Are you thieves or murderers, men of Akhaduu?"

"You are the thief," said the cooper. "Now the camelteers and the men from other towns demand gold from us, while you keep it all for yourself."

"They demand it because you gave it," Ramaad said. "If you had kept it close and precious—" he looked then at Yas'al, who turned away "—it would still be gold, and salt would still be salt; instead both of them are dirt."

His words were wise, but the men were too swollen with gold-fever to listen. Instead they bound him as they had Yas'al and started to tear his house apart, and burn it, and dig in the ground, looking for the gold they thought he had; but they found none.

"Where is the gold?" they asked. "Is it hidden here, or do you sorcel it from stones?"

At those words Ramaad's anger gave way to fear, because in those places a sorcerer is burned if found out, and the fires were very near. He told them about the little sack buried beneath the roots of a date tree outside his house, where he had kept a gold necklace he hoped to give a woman one day—yes, just like the one I gave you this morning. With those words they rejoiced and dug it up, but when they found it said, "What, did you think we would believe this is all the gold you have, after all you have given us? Tell us where the rest is."

"Truly, that is all that I have," Ramaad said. "Take it and leave me in peace."

But they would not take it, and they would not go in peace; they were maddened like bees whose hive has been destroyed, and when they had torn his house apart and dug up every part of his floor they turned again to him and said, "Do you think we want this little bit of gold? Take it and keep it forever!" They took the necklace and held it in the fire, until the gold began to soften with the heat, and then they tied it around his neck, so it burned its shape on his skin. Then, to show that he was no longer a man of Akhaduu and a trader, they blinded him in one eye—for you need two eyes to see things far away, as a trader must—and hobbled one of his legs, so he could no longer travel, and broke all the fingers in his right hand, so he could no longer bargain. Then they left him there, to live in the hut he rebuilt with his ruined hand, and to wait for the man he knew would someday come to ask him about dragons.

Well, that is the story. How do you feel now? Still? Well, tell me, what lesson do you think you are to take from it?

Ah, I see. That is the lesson the Dead Men take from it, Ramaad's lesson. But we take another lesson. It is the reason why I, the richest mother in our village, wear wooden bracelets and live in a simple hut, while all my sisters wear gold. It is the reason why I let your sisters beat you after your blood came, and take away all those gifts I gave you, and leave you here crying.

The lesson we take is the dragon's lesson, and it is this: never be worth more dead than you are alive.

Au Coeur des Ombres

Daniel stepped out of the hospital, started down the narrow staircase. A voice came from behind him.

"M'sieu Chalkwater," the doctor said. Daniel turned back to see him: he was garbed in red, still wearing his beaked mask, and holding a hand atomizer. "I'm sorry, M'sieu, you must be sprayed before you go. For hygienic purposes."

Nodding, Daniel climbed back up to the landing and closed his eyes while the doctor sprayed carbolic on his hands and face. When he no longer heard the shushing sound of the atomizer he opened his eyes and blinked at the stinging mist still hanging there. "May I go now?" he asked.

The doctor glanced away. "Your coat, M'sieu . . ."

Daniel reached up to undo the fastening button of his blue uniform jacket, pulled it off and handed it to the doctor. "Burn it."

The doctor called again when he was halfway down the steps. "You have my sympathies, M'sieu."

Nodding, Daniel stepped down into the narrow courtyard and walked to the street, waited to hear the sound of the hospital door closing. When it came he turned right, past the old synagogue, and headed for the Rue St-Charles. Without his jacket he felt the chill of the Nivôse air, cool even in Nouvelle-Orleans, and he was glad to see the packed omnibus approaching. He gave the old nag a pat on the neck and climbed on, sat amongst the passengers on the tightly spaced wooden benches. Out of uniform he received no special treatment, and so squeezed himself in among the democratic crowd—Creoles and Acadiens, whites and blacks, all but those rich enough to afford a private cab. Many held handkerchiefs over their noses, or else sachets of herbs or vials full of fragrant oil. Daniel leaned back, let himself be mesmerized by the slow clip-clop of their progress.

"Descartes Square," the driver called. By now the omnibus had emptied out somewhat, so that Daniel did not have to fight to get off. Careful to avoid the steaming piles of dry shit the horse had left he climbed out the back, took his bearings from the Goddess of Reason standing at the centre of the square. In the eleven years since she had been erected, a gift to mark the hundredth anniversary of the Revolution, her copper form had slowly turned green; only her spiked crown and torch were still kept polished. Had there been more sun she would have marked the time, pointing to one of the ten numerals around the square, but so near the winter solstice there was too little light to cast more than the weakest shadow.

Daniel walked past the Cabildo, saluted the *officier de la paix* standing guard outside; surprised, the man frowned before tentatively saluting back. Passing the great double doors of Reason Cathedral Daniel reached the Presbytere, saluted the officer there and went in.

"Daniel Chalkwater to see the governor," he told the man at the desk inside.

The man frowned. "Chalkwater?" he asked dubiously; his accent was pure Parisian—either a well-educated Creole, like most of the civil service, or a Continental whose ambitions had somehow been frustrated at home. He glanced down at the open logbook on his desk, ran his finger down the left-hand page. "I'm sorry, M'sieu, I see no Chalkwater here."

"The Governor asked me to come at my convenience," Daniel said. "Could you let him know I'm here?"

"I don't think it's my place to disturb him—"

"Allow me, then," Daniel said, walking past the man's desk and into the atrium; Creoles tended to type him as a bullheaded Saxon the moment they heard his name, and now and then he liked to prove them right. Ignoring the clerk's sputtering he climbed the marble stairs, turned left and went to the oak door labelled CHARLES HENIN, GOUVERNEUR. He took a breath, knocked on the door.

"Enter," a voice called from within.

Daniel opened the door, leaned in. It was a large room, big enough to hold a council; empty benches were spread in two rows on either side of an aisle that began at the door, all pointed at a large, marble-topped desk. There sat the governor, a man in his early fifties with pink, scarred cheeks and straight white hair that fell to his shoulder. The desktop was spread with documents, and despite the cool weather his face was flushed. He looked up at Daniel as he entered, frowned.

"*M'sieu le gouverneur*?" Daniel asked. "I'm Daniel Chalkwater. We met at the ball here in Frimaire, the reception for the Gustave? You asked me to come if . . ."

"Ah—yes," the governor said, nodding. He gestured to one of the two wooden chairs that sat directly in front of his desk. "Please—sit." Once Daniel had moved to the chair and sat the governor began looking through the papers on his desk, finally lifting up the bust of Jacques Hébert and drawing from beneath it a brown cardboard folder, which he untied and spread on the desk. "I understand the Gustave sailed at the beginning of the month. You are at liberty, then?"

Daniel glanced away. "I chose not to renew my commission," he said.

"At full pension?" the governor asked. "How long had you served?"

"Twenty years—I joined the Navy when I was thirteen." He shrugged. "I had meant to retire—perhaps open a shop—but my wife . . ."

The governor's eyes narrowed for a moment, and then he nodded. He looked down at the pages spread out in front of him. "Your rank, at retirement?"

"Lieutenant-Commandant."

"*Bien*. And you have experience, captaining a steamship on a river?"

"I commanded the Chénier, in Guyane," Daniel said.

The governor glanced down at the papers before him, made a note. "Very good. Though you may find the Mississippi a more challenging river than the Marowijine."

Daniel took a breath. "I know a bit about the Mississippi, *gouverneur*."

"Ah?" the governor said, then ran his finger quickly over Daniel's file. "I wasn't aware . . ."

"Not from my Navy service. I spent some time there as a child—my parents were Americans. Abolitionists."

"Ah. So you know the territory—good." The governor made another note, his pen moving in quick, precise strokes. "And your parents, are they—"

Daniel shook his head.

"*Eh bien*. My sympathies." The governor glanced at Daniel, then down at his notes, then back to Daniel. "At any rate, let me tell you why I asked you to come. After due deliberation—about a hundred years!—the Convention has decided at last to change la Louisiane from an inland territory to a full Department, of which I am to be the Director."

"Congratulations," Daniel said.

The governor held up a hand. "It's not an honour I'd choose, believe me. This territory has always been the most resistant to reason, between the Blacks, the Acadiens, even the Creoles—half of them, you know, are descended from fugitive aristocrats. Barely ten years ago the Catholics and the Jews were allowed to practice their faiths in public. And that's only the city; as for inland . . . well, you know it. . . ."

Daniel nodded. France had never abandoned its claim to the vast swath of land that ran up the Mississippi, but neither had it ever expended much energy on it. Over the years it had developed into a nearly lawless country, a half-dozen trading posts in a wilderness filled with Indians, fugitive slaves and abolitionists from the American States and the slave hunters that pursued them.

"At any rate," the governor went on, "with the new work done by M'sieu Pasteur and his colleagues, the Convention has decided it may be possible for white men to survive out there. And so it has been given to me to rationalize our operations." He opened his desk drawer, drew out two sealed envelopes; one was blank, on the other was written *Coeur-Lion*. He handed this one to Daniel, as well as a photo of a man with close-cropped black hair, fierce eyes and an aquiline nose. "Hippolye Coeur-Lion is our intendant in Sainte-Geneviève. He is a good man, a true rationalist. You are to deliver these orders to him, sealed, and see that he reads them. In your presence, please."

"Of course," Daniel said, taking the envelope. "May I ask—why did you want me for this, specifically?"

The governor's mouth tightened. "Saxons have a native stubbornness our people lack. It inhibits reason, as your parents saw, but it has its uses. The interior—" He shook his head. "As we seek to change it, so may it change us, yes? It is my hope you will not be changed." He looked down at the blank envelope, picked up his pen and wrote Chalkwater on it in nervous strokes. "If you have cause to doubt Coeur-Lion's health, or his faculties, open these orders. Otherwise, burn them without reading."

Daniel took the envelope, held it carefully. "Certainly," he said.

There was a moment's silence, and then the governor nodded once more. "There is a ship, the Eugénie, waiting at the Ponchartrain docks. She has an engineer, but you will have to hire a crew. Is this acceptable?"

"Yes," Daniel said. He closed his eyes for a moment, took a breath. "I'll depart as soon as possible."

The governor smiled. "Good," he said. "Best of luck, then, Captain. My regards to Coeur-Lion."

It took Daniel longer than he had expected to gather a crew: though there were many out-of-work sailors at this time of year, few were willing to go up the river. In the end he had to recruit from among the skiff-pilots that plied the lake and the bayous, Blacks, Acadiens and half-breeds; men little more civilized than the coureurs de bois that lived inland. After two decades of military discipline

Daniel at first found their company difficult, but with the clamour and chaos of preparing the ship he soon grew used to them. They were, after all, the kind of people he'd grown up with.

It took nearly ten days to crew and fuel the ship. The Gustave had been stocked with Pasteur's new hygienic canned rations, but the Eugénie was to be provisioned in the old-fashioned way, loaded with beads, blankets, hatchets and brandy to be traded for food and dispensed as gifts. When the long process was finally at an end Daniel signalled to the engineer, who directed the stokers to fire up the boiler. The engine was just working up a head of steam when Daniel spotted an *officier de la paix* walking towards them on the dock, waving a blue flag. Daniel ordered the engineer to valve the pressure, dropped the gangway and went to meet the policeman. "What's the problem, *officier*?" he asked.

"Quarantine," the *officier* said. He handed Daniel the blue flag. "All ships are ordered to remain in port for the duration."

"What is it?" Daniel asked, annoyed.

"Cholera, in Tremé."

"We're going upriver, not into the Gulf."

"All ships. Those are my orders." The *officier* shrugged. "Don't worry, it should be a few days at the most."

"A few days?" Daniel had been on board the Gustave in Guadeloupe when the cholera had hit there; the port had been closed for a full season until it died down.

The *officier* nodded. "It's the new hygiene. All the men from the Academie Scientifique have to do is isolate the source and then they can sterilize it." He smiled. "It'll be the end of the yellow fever, too, and the malaria. We can grow into a real city now."

Daniel nodded. "How wonderful," he said. "Thank you, *officier*."

The *officier* gave him a perfunctory salute and moved on to the next ship at the dock. Daniel sighed, went to the stern and tied the quarantine flag to the pole. Whispers followed him as he went, and when he turned round again much of the crew had gathered to face him. He scanned the crowd, looking for Latour, the pilot and first mate: he was Daniel's sole lucky find, another retired Navy man who was said to know the bayous and the river as well as any.

"It's true we're under quarantine," Daniel said, addressing the crowd but keeping his eyes on Latour. "I'm told it will only be a few days, though, and I'll see that you get paid for that time." In fact he had no authority to do that; the pay would come out of whatever profit he might make from this trip. He could not let the crew wander, though, couldn't let this trip be delayed: nobody else would be sailing until spring, and he refused to stay in this city that long.

As Daniel had anticipated, many of the crew looked to Latour for guidance; he nodded, and they began to move back to their stations. Once the crowd had cleared Latour approached Daniel. "That won't keep them," he said. "Not for long."

"It's a better offer than they ought to hope for," Daniel said. "Were you ever paid for a day you didn't sail?"

Latour shook his head. "It doesn't matter, though. They won't think that it's the rational thing to do; they'll only think of added days away from their homes. If you want them to stay, you have to stay close to them—make sure they see your face every day."

"My rooms are in the east, past Rue Champs-Elysees," Daniel said.

Spreading his hands, Latour said "Why not stay with me? It's only a few days, as you say."

"I couldn't ask—"

"It's no favour," Latour said. "You see, I am rational enough to know what's best for me, and I want to get paid."

Latour's home was modest, a small square house within sight of the lake; unlike the rest of the crew, who were renting rooms at sailors' boarding houses, he lived there permanently, with his wife and children. Though Latour had been in the Navy he had been a crewman, not an officer, and Daniel tried to maintain his distance. Still, he enjoyed the man's company, taking meals with him and his family. It was a cheerful house, and though the quarantine flag still flew any notion of trouble felt far away.

On the third night Daniel awoke, roused by a noise outside. There were people in the streets, despite the *couvre-feu*, and as he came fully awake he realized they were singing. He got out of bed, went to the window: a dozen men, or perhaps women, were standing in the street below. Some were dressed in dark robes, some in oversized clothing, others in moth-eaten finery; all their faces were covered, either with broad hats, doctors' masks or veils. They sang loudly as they walked towards the house:

> *Bring us a treat, bring us a treat*
> *We don't ask for much, just a keg of beer*
> *Your wife or your eldest daughter*
> *Bring us a treat!*

Daniel went downstairs to see Latour at the door; he was laughing with the masked men, passing them clay mugs full of beer. When they had each drunk their fill they sang another song and then moved on, towards the next house.

"What was that?" Daniel asked

"La Guignolee," Latour said as gathered the fallen mugs together and shut the door. "It's from the father country, I'm told, though now it's only the Acadiens that do it. To celebrate the new year."

"The new year was more than three months ago."

"The old new year."

Daniel shook his head. "I was told to expect this kind of thing when I went up the river, but I didn't think I'd see it here," he said.

"Don't be fooled just because you can see the city," Latour said. "You're upriver already."

It was two more days before the quarantine was lifted; finally the ship's wheel began to turn and they sailed out of the lake and west, towards the river's mouth. Here the levees were built so high that they stood metres above the land around them: the deck was level with the rooftops of the houses as they sailed by, and when Latour blew the whistle it startled women hanging laundry. Daniel waved and smiled as they passed, glad to finally be leaving the city.

The first day took them slowly from the lake to the town of Baton Rouge—the northernmost limit of civilization—then up into the bayou country. Here was where a good pilot was key: the river was split into a hundred branches, and only experience could guide the ship to the right one time after time. Finally the streams all joined once more into one, drawing closer to its source, and the river grew wide and sleepy. A thick wall of cypresses stood on either side, dipping their feet in the water, broken here and there by a cleared hectare and a clapboard shack with a clay chimney where an Acadien, a black or both might live.

Nivôse was nearly over, now, but the days were still short; for fear of snags and sunken logs Daniel ordered the anchor dropped while there was still light. He worried about giving the crew so much free time, but as yet there was simply too little to do to keep everyone occupied—on a steamship there was no need to braid rope or mend sails. In another season the whole river would be alive, singing with the voices of frogs and the calls of the herons and egrets, but now it was asleep. Even the alligators had grown torpid with the cold, and the men were denied the sport of luring them with chunks of meat and then bashing their skulls with axes.

Three days from port the land began to dry out, the cypresses giving way to thick stands of pine. From here the forest spread out, uncharted and untouched, for countless kilometres; the river's twists and turns meant that there was no horizon visible, nothing but trees in all directions. All was silent, save the low chug of the engine, until the boat was launched and one of the crewmen stepped onto shore: then a great hum arose, as though a thousand violins had had their bass strings plucked all at once, and a grey cloud of mosquitoes filled the air. The man turned and ran, splashing madly into the water, and was covered in welts by the time he made it back to the boat. There was much laughter among the crew over his frenzied retreat, but beneath it was a grim thought: they were trapped on the ship together, unable even to go ashore.

The ship crept its way through the silent forest four more days until the river straightened out and the trees began to give way to a more open plain: at last there was a horizon again, les montagnes aux Arcs visible in the far distance.

Now their initial supplies were running short. As soon as they were out of the forest Daniel had ordered Latour to watch for any Indian camps they might trade with, but so far he had seen nothing. Daniel was not sure what to make of that; he knew this country was well-populated, but also that the Indians were not generally seen unless they wished to be. The crew began to complain, quietly at first and then more openly, about the short rations. Left unspoken were their deeper fears: each bank was lined with high grass that ran as far as the hills, tall enough to conceal attackers. There was mostly peace between the Indians and Onontio—this was the name by which they knew the Republic, which they in their simplicity thought of as a single man, a great chief—but there were always the young men, eager to win a prize or a reputation.

The tension broke on the eighth day. Daniel was in his cabin, trying to identify on his charts the tributary rivers they had passed the day before, when he heard a cry from the deck. At first he ignored it—a captain couldn't be seen to run at the beck and call of his crew—but as the shouts escalated he lay the map down on his desk, rose and stepped out of his cabin, climbed up onto the deck.

Two crew members were facing one another, standing in the open area at the stern, before the anchor windlass; a red handkerchief ran between them, wrapped around each of their left wrists, while each held a knife in his free hand. Thus bound together they circled each other, unable to retreat past the kerchief's limit, and watched for an opening; as Daniel ascended to the pilothouse above he saw one of the men step in towards the other and slash at his face. This brought a reply from his target, and when they broke and separated as far as the handkerchief would allow each one was bleeding, one from the head and the other from the chest. A crowd had gathered, ringing them on three sides.

"Tell them to stop," Daniel said to Latour, who was leaning over the wheel and watching the fight.

Latour shook his head. "They won't," he said. "The kerchief means it's a duel of honour. Neither can let go without yielding."

Daniel took a deep breath, spoke in as loud a voice as he could manage. "You there, break it up," he said. One of the two men fighting glanced in his direction; the other took advantage of his distraction to advance and attack.

"I said stop!" Daniel shouted as the two grappled, their knives cutting at each other's arms.

"Might as well let them finish," Latour said.

"This is absurd." Daniel reached for his pistol, realized he had forgotten it in his cabin; he lifted his key ring from his belt instead and went to the wheelhouse lockbox, opened it and drew out the pistol within. He went back to the railing, held out his gun and said, "I order you both to stop." Both men paused, the handkerchief slackening a little, and Daniel took a breath. "Good. Now, let go of that kerchief and explain to me what is going on here."

The men stood watching each other, the handkerchief still wrapped around their hands. "You there, Thibodeaux," Daniel said to the man on the right, "I order you to release that handkerchief and drop your weapon."

Neither man moved; Daniel sighted his pistol carefully, aiming between them, and fired. Each man pulled away, drawing the kerchief taut, but neither one released it. The pistol was hot in Daniel's hand. "Both of you, drop everything, now," he said.

"Captain . . ." Latour said from behind him.

The kerchief had gone slack again, but neither man was willing to drop it or his knife. Daniel turned slightly to target Thibodeaux, aiming directly at his chest. "Be rational," he said. "Is this business worth more than your life?"

Daniel kept his pistol trained on Thibodeaux for a dozen heartbeats, wondering if he would be able to shoot a man who had done nothing more than defy him, before the man's shoulders finally dropped. He tucked his knife into his belt and released the handkerchief, pointedly turning his back on his opponent. Howls of disappointment came up from the watching crowd.

"That won't be the end of it," Latour said. "They'll be at it again by nightfall."

"What is the matter with them?" Daniel asked, letting his pistol drop to his side. He kept his eye on the other man, made sure he put his knife away as well. "Did you ever see the meanest midshipman behave like that?"

"They aren't Navy," Latour said, "and this isn't the sea. Think: these are men that come from just a few kilometres upriver of the city, and you're taking them further that way. What did you think it would do to them?"

Daniel frowned, remembering the governor's words. "This

can't be allowed," he said. "I want them both whipped—do it at the windlass, where they fought. Where everyone will see it."

Latour stood silent for a moment; finally he nodded, and Daniel returned the pistol to the lockbox, went back to his cabin and shut the door.

The river ran on before them for another day, gradually straightening out: now it might run a dozen kilometres or more before turning, and Daniel began to hope to see Sainte-Genevieve. The maps he had been given were nearly useless, simple drawings of a river whose contours changed with every season, cutting new channels when it flooded, and he had begun to wonder whether—as the crew whispered—the town had simply vanished. Daniel remembered the gigantic animals whose bones Jefferson had described, which the American had believed still lived in the interior. Here that notion was not difficult to believe, nor was it hard to imagine that they had slipped somehow back into history, to the days before rational men had first set foot on this continent.

At last Daniel heard the whistle blow, three times for a port. When he went up to the pilothouse, though, he saw from the look on Latour's face that something was wrong. He looked out onto the shore, and at first he could not see it: there was a town there, cottages in the Norman style but with walls and roofs of bark, mixed with the long lodges of the Indians and all surrounded by a wooden stockade.

Then Latour handed him the spyglass and he understood: the city was empty. Corpses lay in the streets, swarmed with crows; poles erected at the doors of the Indian lodges stood topped with skulls.

The crew was silent as the Eugénie steamed past the town, though they thronged the deck. Word got down to the boilers, and even the stokers and the engineer came above to see; at the sight of it, though, the engineer swore under his breath and hurried his gang back down below.

"Sweet Reason," Daniel said. "What happened here?"

For a moment Latour was silent; finally he said "Do you want to—"

"No, no," Daniel said quickly. "Was this—is this Sainte-Genevieve?" As soon as he said it he knew the answer: there were no other French towns this far into the interior. "We should go upriver another day, see if any survivors went that way."

"Sir, are you sure—" Latour stopped. "The crew won't like that. They'll worry that . . ."

"I know," Daniel said, "but it's just one day. After that we—" He stopped, picked up the speaking tube. "All stop," he said.

Latour frowned. "Sir?"

"Look—here," Daniel said, handing Latour the spyglass. "I think we have a survivor."

A black man stood on the shore; he wore a dark suit with a white collar, and he was waving a broad black hat in the air.

"Send the boat," Daniel said, then held up his hand. "I'll take it. I want to know what happened here."

Since the fight Daniel had been in the habit of wearing his pistol at all times, and now he made sure it was at his side before he boarded the boat. He chose two men as rowers, Chiasson and Lamoureux, and they launched the boat and headed for shore. The man spotted them and began waving more frantically, running towards the sandy spot where they were going to make landing. The boat slid onto the bank a metre or so from shore, and Daniel held a hand up to the man, warning him to keep his distance.

The man dropped to his knees at the river's edge. "Praise to the Lord," he said in English. "Praise Jesus."

Daniel looked from one of his men to the other, feeling an absurd urge to cover their ears as he would a child's. He climbed out of the boat and approached the man carefully, his right hand hovering near his pistol. "You are an American?" he asked, speaking the same language.

Standing, the man nodded. "Frederick Bailey," he said, extending a hand. His clothes, though cut in imitation of finery, were coarse, and his face was well-scarred with pocks. "I do speak some French, though, sir, if you prefer it."

"That's all right," Daniel said, glancing back at his men. "My name is Daniel Chalkwater, captain of the Eugénie."

"You're an American, too?" he asked.

"Only by birth," Daniel said. The man had reason to be nervous: a white American in this territory was most likely to be a slave hunter. Daniel looked from left to right, taking in the abandoned town. "Have you been here long? Did you see what happened?"

Frederick's eyes widened briefly. "Oh. Oh, yes. A terrible plague."

"A plague?" Daniel asked, his heart tightening. "Where are the bodies, then? And how did the skulls get on top of the posts?"

"Ah! That was—that was Coeur-Lion," Frederick said. "He knows the French hygiene—moved all the bodies out of the town—"

"You know him? Coeur-Lion?"

"Know him? Why, he—he saved me. More than that, he saved my soul."

Daniel nodded, searching the man's face for signs of madness. "Your soul," he said.

"Oh, I know you French don't believe in such things—not most of you—but Coeur-Lion, he's a wiser man. He knows there are powers that guide our paths." Frederick glanced back over his shoulder, at the ruined town, then turned back to Daniel and held his broad hat over his chest. "I am, as you can see, a preacher—my master found I had a quick mind, a good memory, so he taught me to recite the Gospel. A parlour trick, you see, but he soon found he could hire me out to the other masters to preach to their slaves—to show God wanted them to be good slaves, you see. I did such a fine job of that my master took me on tour, brought me to the mines in the mountains to preach to those slaves—they have a terrible time keeping them, you see, because it's so near the border. Thought I might convince 'em not to try to escape."

"But you escaped instead," Daniel said.

"My body did, sir, but not my soul. That was still captive till I came here, you see, and Coeur-Lion freed it—showed me there was more to my faith than the master's shackles. Oh, I was torn up, sir, before I met him—pulled this way and that by my faith and my freedom."

"I hadn't been told Coeur-Lion had much knowledge of religion," Daniel said. "I can't see where he'd have learned it."

"He's a wise man, sir, a very wise man. He understands, in a way that is beyond your reason—married your French logic to faith, you see, made all his peoples live together in peace. He's the greatest man your race has produced, sir."

Daniel nodded slowly. "Where is he now, then?"

"Oh—well—he tried to control the plague in the town, as I told you, sir, but in the end it was no use. He moved on up the river to get away from it, with what people were left."

"And you?" Daniel asked. "Why are you still here?"

A pained look crossed Frederick's face. "He thought I was sick," he said. "Anyone in whom the plague hadn't already come and gone had to stay behind, you see, but I had it as a child—" his fingers went to the scars on his cheek "—so it never came."

"And everyone else, he just left them here to die?"

"It's the hygiene, sir, the French hygiene. He taught me. Limit the spread, control the disease. You must know that."

After a moment Daniel nodded. "Tell me, then," he asked, "this God of yours, this Jesus—did Coeur-Lion explain to you why he brings plagues like this? Why he lets them kill men and women, young and old?"

Frederick frowned. "Well, sir," he said, "I suppose it's that we're all slaves to God, you know—and it's a master's duty to whip his slaves now and again, remind them who's in charge."

In the end Daniel decided to take the man onboard—he said he had been to Coeur-Lion's new camp, and could act as a guide—and the ship began to move slowly upriver once more. He was thankful Frederick's French was limited; the crew members' power of reason was limited enough without exposure to religion, superstition and whatever else might be in the man's head. Already he was disturbed by what Frederick had said about Coeur-Lion: again he was reminded of the governor's words, and of the second sealed envelope in his desk. What was it about this territory, this river, that so changed people? If it were changing him, would he even notice?

The river began to bend over the next hours, turning from northwest to nearly straight north. Daniel remained in the wheelhouse with Latour the whole time, spyglass at the ready, and he had reluctantly allowed Frederick in as well—better, he thought, to keep him away from the crew. The man began to get excited as they rounded the bend, and after a few moments Daniel saw what he was gesturing at: on the western bank, a few kilometres away, stood a vast artificial hill, stepped like the Mexican pyramids. Its scale was hard to gauge at this distance but it had to be at least two hundred metres long on each side, thirty high. Smaller pyramids, perhaps thirty or forty of them, were scattered around it, half-buried and with their edges weathered smooth, and small square buildings with domed roofs nestled in their shadows.

"That's it," Frederick said.

As they crept towards the landing the pilot's course, intentionally or not, veered nearer to the western shore; near enough that when the arrows began to fly, a few of them reached the ship.

"Hard to starboard!" Daniel called. "Get us to the middle of the channel!"

Swearing under his breath Latour threw himself at the wheel, fighting to shift the ship's course. Daniel unholstered his pistol and ran out onto the deck, looked around: the arrows, still flying, were falling into the water now, but one had lodged deep in Thibodeaux's leg. The man was lying on his back on the deck, his face pale, his breath coming in shudders.

"Sweet Jesus," Frederick said from behind him.

Daniel kneeled down next to Thibodeaux, took the man's knife from his belt and cut ribbons off his shirt. He tried to tie a tourniquet but the blood still flowed from the wound, sluggish and dark.

"Let me," Frederick said, elbowing Daniel aside. He took one of the ribbons cut from the man's shirt and dipped it in the blood; then he held the stained cloth between his hands and prayed, saying, "Blood, I judge you in the name of the Father. I judge you in the faith of Jesus. I judge you in the name of the Holy Spirit." Then he turned to one of the other men on the deck, said in broken French "Take this and hide it. Somewhere safe, and never let him see it."

To Daniel's surprise, the bleeding had slowed; though Thibodeaux was still deathly pale his breath was coming in more even gasps as well. "Is that the French hygiene Coeur-Lion taught you?"

Frederick shook his head. "No, sir. Just faith in Jesus." He held out his hand, opened it to show the blood on his palm.

"And I suppose Jesus will keep this man from getting sepsis in his wound?" Daniel shook his head, called one of the crew over. "Alcohol, the white bottle," he said.

The rain of arrows had stopped now, and once the wound had been sterilized and Thibodeaux taken to the Captain's cabin Daniel returned to the wheelhouse. "Ready the boat," he said.

"Should I blow for a port?" Latour asked.

Daniel shook his head. "I think they know we're here."

The Eugénie moved upriver at a crawl, the pyramid rising up as they neared it. Daniel had never seen the pyramids of Egypt or Mexico, only read descriptions of them, but he doubted if they could be any more magnificent than this: it was by far the tallest thing on the plain, looking as tall as the far hills. "Who could have built these?" he asked.

"I don't know," Frederick said.

Daniel ordered the boat lowered, with one box of the trade goods loaded into it. This time there was no trouble persuading the crew to remain on board. Daniel went back to his cabin, took both sealed envelopes from his desk, then went back on deck and climbed down into the boat. Frederick was already there, along with Latour and one of the crewmen.

"One of us ought to stay on the ship," Daniel said.

"There's not enough food aboard to get back down the river," Latour said. "They won't go anywhere."

"So I should expect the crew to act rationally, in their own self-interest?"

Latour crossed his arms. "We don't know what's happened here. You need someone with you." He threw a glance at Frederick. "Someone you can trust."

Daniel nodded. "All right," he said, signalled for the ropes to be untied. Latour and the other crewman took the oars, moving the boat slowly towards the shore. Earlier Daniel had noticed that the pyramid had a row of more closely spaced tiers, like a giant staircase, running down part of its length towards the river; he guided the boat towards its foot.

A crowd was beginning to gather on the shore, a mix of whites, blacks and Indians, with the costumes of all three peoples mixed promiscuously. As the boat struck the bottom the crowd parted, a half-dozen men in Indian garb moving to the fore to greet them. Each of these carried a rifle, and Daniel saw that many others in the crowd were armed with bows, knives or hatchets.

Standing up, Daniel held his hands high to show they were empty. "We come on behalf of Onontio," he said.

One of the Indians who had come to meet them nodded. "Very good," he said in flawless French. "We will take you to see him."

The armed Indians waited until all four were on shore and then surrounded them, leading them towards the pyramid. Two others followed with the chest full of trade goods. The staircase was steep, lined on either side with tall, straight poles: those at the bottom were topped with skulls, as the ones at Sainte-Genevieve had been, but as they rose higher the heads grew progressively more fresh and fuller-fleshed.

The top of the pyramid was freezing, a constant wind from the north chilling the humid air. Two squat buildings stood there, one at the eastern end and the other at the west. A dozen old men, all wearing long white feathered cloaks, stood outside the western building; once Daniel and the others had been led to them they turned towards the building's door and howled like wolves. A small shape emerged from the doorway as they did so, a stooped, sickly, balding man wrapped in a red cloak. It was only by the nose and eyes that Daniel recognized Coeur-Lion.

"So you've come," Coeur-Lion said, wheezing each time he drew in breath. His face was covered with dry pocks, and he reached up to scratch one with a wooden tool shaped like a shallow cup. Two women followed Coeur-Lion out of the building, one black and one Indian, each one young and broad-hipped.

Daniel opened his mouth, found himself speechless. While he was still struggling to find words Frederick stepped forward, threw himself at Coeur-Lion's feet. "It's been eleven days," he said. "I don't have the plague, sir, you can see that."

"You brought them here," Coeur-Lion said. His mouth was toothless, his voice slurred. "Do you know if they have the plague?"

"But—they're your people," Frederick said.

Coeur-Lion shook his head. "These are my people," he said, gesturing feebly at the white-cloaked men. "No matter. You are forgiven." He turned to Daniel. "You brought goods, to trade?"

"Yes—there are more on the ship—"

"Give me one of those blankets. It's too cold up here."

Daniel opened the chest that they had brought from the ship, pulled out one of the striped wool blankets that were a staple of the Republic's trade. He handed it carefully to Coeur-Lion who wrapped it around himself, seeming to disappear within it.

"That's better," Coeur-Lion said. He made a small gesture at the armed men who had brought Daniel and the others, and they started back down the pyramid. "Come with me," he said to Daniel, turning back towards the dark doorway.

Throwing a glance back at Latour and the other crewman Daniel followed, into the low building. It was a single room inside, an apartment with a couch, stools, rope bed and an open, foul-smelling privy. A torch guttered in a sconce on the wall, below it a table scattered with paper and birch bark. Coeur-Lion gestured to Daniel to sit on the couch, then lay himself down on the bed; he nodded to one of the young women who opened her top, presented a nipple for him to suckle at. As Coeur-Lion drew milk, wheezing and sucking and smacking his lips, Daniel found himself paralyzed, his mind unwilling to process what was before him. Finally, when the woman had silently covered herself and withdrawn from the building, he was able to draw out the first of the sealed orders.

"I was given this to give to you, M'sieu," he said, "and to see that you read it."

Coeur-Lion nodded, reached out a hand; Daniel had to stand to deliver the envelope to his grasp. "And your orders?" he asked.

"M'sieu?"

"There are always two sets of orders," Coeur-Lion said. The

envelope Daniel had given him lay in his lap, its seal unbroken. "Have you read yours? You look like an honest man, so I would guess not. But I imagine you've guessed what they are."

Daniel said nothing.

Coeur-Lion picked up his envelope, broke the seal with a sharp fingernail. He squinted in the flickering light, reading the orders with rheumy eyes, then finally nodded. "As I expected," he said. "And now you."

"M'sieu Coeur-Lion . . ."

"No matter," Coeur-Lion said, giving a small wave of the hand. "I am dying, anyway, and your orders are as false as mine." He reached up to scratch at his pocks once more with the wooden tool, careful to catch the flaking skin in its bowl. "When LaSalle came here, you know, in the days of the Ancien Regime, he found the whole valley depopulated: the Spanish had been through a century before, and the Indians were only then starting to recover from the diseases they brought. It was the weapon that won the Spaniards Mexico, of course, though they didn't know it." He took a deep, laboured breath, drew the blanket more tightly around himself. "That is the great difference between them and us."

"They are saying disease will be a thing of the past, thanks to M'sieu Pasteur."

"And do you believe this?" Coeur-Lion asked.

Daniel shrugged.

"The French hygiene," Coeur-Lion said. "We used to say that the English killed their Indians and the Spaniards enslaved theirs, but we taught ours to reason. Wherever we tread, the world becomes more rational. How can it be otherwise?"

"I'm sorry," Daniel said. "I don't understand—all this—"

"I was here—in Sainte-Geneviève, I mean—only a year before they began to get sick," Coeur-Lion said. His voice was fading, his gestures growing most spastic. "A ship had come like yours, bearing cargo from Nouvelle-Orleans. Beads and blankets. . . . At first I didn't understand what was happening, and when I did it was too late. I make strong medicine, I said, convinced them to quarantine their sick, but in the end that failed too." He coughed. "It was Frederick who gave me the idea of taking on their sickness. The Turkish method of variolation, they take the dry pustules up through their noses and become immune. I had the pox as a child of course, had to starve myself until I was weak enough to catch it a second time . . ." He scratched at his forearm again, this time letting the dry flakes of skin shower to the floor. "M'sieu Pasteur would say my methods are unsound. Do you think my methods are unsound?"

When Daniel did not respond Coeur-Lion fell silent, and Daniel sat and watched his chest rise and fall until it was clear the man was asleep. Daniel got up, took the envelope from Coeur-Lion's hand, drew out his orders and read them. Then he held the paper in the torch's flame until they were burned. As he did he looked down at the table below, glanced at the scraps of paper and birch bark. He was only able to make out one fragment: it read *Nous sommes tous sauvages*.

There was no need for his orders now: Coeur-Lion would be dead within days. When both envelopes had burned Daniel returned to his chair to wait for the sunrise.

Some time after that he heard a muffled shot, jolting him to wakefulness. The torch had gone out while he dozed: it was only by his tread that Daniel recognized Latour as he came into the building.

"Is he dead?" Latour asked.

"Yes," Daniel said.

Daniel could just see Latour nodding in the dim light. He followed Latour out onto the broad roof of the pyramid, past the fallen bodies of the two guards outside. Then Latour reached into his coat, drew out a white envelope and let the fierce winds snatch it from his hand. It was gone before Daniel could see if the seal had been broken, vanished into the darkness.

They made their way down the staircase on their hands and knees, gripping the steep steps to keep from falling. Finally they reached the ground and covered the short distance to the boat. Neither one mentioned the other crewman.

"We don't have enough supplies to get back to Nouvelle-

Orleans," Latour said as they climbed back onboard the Eugénie.

"Dump the cargo in the river," Daniel said. "We should make better time that way."

Latour was silent for a moment. Daniel wondered how much his orders had told him: each set of orders, he supposed, would hold a bit less information than the last, so it was unlikely that Latour knew why they had really made their journey.

"Very good."

"Wake the stokers and the engineer," Daniel said. "I'd like to get going as soon after dawn as possible." He wondered if Latour had ever questioned his orders. Probably not: the logic behind them was flawless.

Once Latour had gone Daniel turned back towards the east bank, saw the first light touching the top of the pyramid. He thought about the long-vanished people that had built them, in worship or propitiation of the sun or moon or Reason knew what else. What had they thought, he wondered, when the Spanish came, when they began to get sick? Did they think that their gods had abandoned them, or that the newcomers' gods were stronger? *I make strong medicine.* He thought of the statue, the Goddess of Reason, and of what Coeur-de-Lion had written: *Nous sommes tous sauvages.*

Then the dawn arrived in earnest, and the mist of dreams dissolved. The sun was up, and there was work to do.

Jump, Frog!

To an unnamed correspondent; found in the effects of Samuel Clemens ("Mark Twain") after his death, apparently unsent. Dated December 20, 1881.

You will recall, I think, a story I wrote some years back, about Smiley's jumping frog, how it was the subject of a peculiar bet, and how a fellow took an underhanded way to win it. It has done pretty well for itself, having had the good fortune to be translated into French and the better to be translated out of it. I put forth that it was a true story, and so it was, though many doubted it. Since then I have gained reason to believe, though, that I never did know the whole truth of it—until now; that I shall ever be able to tell anyone that truth, however, I much doubt.

I have, as you may know, recently returned from a short stay in Canada; having to reside there for a certain time in order to claim ownership of my own work, I chose to visit Montreal and Quebec, on the grounds that a place that makes claims to being a separate nation ought to at least have a different language. I gave a speech there that was pretty well received, most likely due to it having as its main competition the weather. It was after the speech that I was approached by an odd little fellow, an old gentleman with a thick black moustache and a fringe of hair circling his bald skull.

Standing very near, and mumbling into his chest, he said, "Meester Clemens"—but I will cease there with reporting his words as he spoke them; recent experience with French has shown me how easily a man can be made to look a fool in a language not his own, and this was a man of great intelligence and education, as you will see.

His tale, then, began like this: "Mr. Clemens, I have long wanted to meet you. My name is Luigi"—but there, with his last name, we get into the unbelievable part of the tale; and so I will pass over it—"and I believe I may cast some light on a story of yours."

My interest piqued, I nodded for him to continue. "I should like to hear about it," I said.

"You are an educated man, so I am sure you recognize my name; you are a rational man, so I feel certain you know something of my work. But you should know that it was not always as a scientist that I imagined myself: instead, as a young man, I imagined I would study theology, and join one of the monastic orders. For I had a hunger, you see, to study those questions which, at that time, the natural sciences did not even hope to answer. Above all, I wished to answer the question of life!

"Practical considerations took hold, however, and I followed my father's advice in becoming a doctor. I married my darling Lucia, made a steady living as a lecturer at the University of Bologna, and for a time was happy. For many years I focused only on the smallest parts of the matter that had formerly been my obsession, studying the bones and organs that made up men and animals. In that time I learned much about how things lived, but still I was no closer to the question of why. What force gave vigour to things once lifeless? What was it that departed the body at death, leaving it no more alive than a stone?

"It was one of your own countrymen, Dottore Franklin, who led me to the answer—for I read how he had, while trying to shock a guinea fowl, taken the charge meant for the bird into himself; rather than killing him, as it would have the bird, it did him no harm. Indeed, I suspected, it more likely had invigorated him: for all his great work was done after receiving that charge, and it is said that even as an old man, while ambassador to France, he was still able to—" (I omit the rest of this story, on the grounds that it is not right to say such things about a founding father, and you will have heard them already anyhow.)

"It was then that I began my researches into animal electricity. Fortunately the marshes of my home state of Bologna were at all times replete with frogs, simple creatures whom I could dissect and study in my quest for the nerveo-electrical fluid. You are, I am sure, already familiar with the part of my work that was published: how I showed that the fluid, present in the air during a thunderstorm, could be used to cause a frog's leg to twitch, and that the same results could be obtained with a spark made by an electrostatic machine or held in a Leyden jar. What you will not know is that I published only the first part of my research: for it was while that first volume was in preparation, and I was preparing the second—my magister opus—that disaster struck. Was it my pride that caused me to be punished so—to lose all that I had, my work, my home, my love, in pursuit of my art?"

Some look of alarm on my face must have betrayed me, for the old man took a step back, then glanced around, perhaps to see if others were listening. Satisfied that they were not he moved yet closer, winding up only an inch or so from my face, and went on.

"My aim, you see, was to do on purpose what I suspected Dottore Franklin had done by accident—to charge a living body with nerveo-electrical fluid. In this way I hoped to perhaps double the lifespan, or at least give vitality well into old age, as Franklin had. My dear wife Lucia had always been sickly; as well as frogs, the swamps of Bologna hold many bad airs, and I knew it was only a matter of time before she, delicate flower, succumbed. A Leyden jar ought to hold enough fluid to achieve the effect I sought, but how much was too much? And would a charge sufficient for me be too much for her?

"To test my theory on a human being would be inconceivable: to apply the charge before I knew the correct amount would be equally so. I resolved, therefore, to determine the correct amount to apply to a smaller creature, and extrapolate from there. What sort of creature was obvious: I owed my little fame to frogs, and did not doubt they would do me greater service. I acquired a frog weighing precisely one pound, which I planned to etherize to a point just shy of death, then test how large a spark it would take to revive it.

"I waited until a night when there was a thunderstorm raging outside, that I might easily recharge my Leyden jar if I so needed. My first few attempts, using small sparks from the electrostatic machine, brought some animation to the frog; emboldened I continued, but the next time over-applied the ether, stilling the poor creature's heart. In my panic I gave it a charge not from the electrostatic machine but from the Leyden jar—the one in which I stored the nerveo-electric fluid I hoped to use to invigorate myself and my sweet Lucia. Remembering Dottore Franklin's experiments with the guinea fowl I feared that, rather than reanimating it, the charge would cook the frog; it had, after all, been given a dose meant for a man many times its size and weight. To my relief, however, the frog revived. More than revived, in fact; for I imagined as its eyes opened that I saw in them—what? A spark of understanding?

"You may imagine my study as it was then, with frogs and parts of frogs hanging from brass hooks, to draw the nerveo-electrical fluid from the iron railing in my garden; imagine, now, how that might look to a frog. Perhaps that was why the frog immediately set to jumping. When I say jumping, signore, I do not mean how you have seen a frog jump: I mean that it shot from the operating table like a ball from a cannon. Had I been in its way I likely would have been killed; as it was the frog touched a shelf holding much of my equipment, sending it crashing to the ground as it caromed off to the facing wall. Though I tried to catch it, my attention was quickly drawn by the bottle of ether that had fallen near the Leyden jar. When I saw that I forgot the frog and ran to separate them, but as I grabbed hold of the jar the remaining charge jumped into me, leaving me stunned; at the same time the spark that had passed from the jar to my body ignited the ether fumes, and a moment later fire broke out in my study. Out the window shot the frog; again I thought of catching it, until I remembered that my Lucia was sleeping in her bedroom.

"Lucia! It was for her sake I had tried to harness this power; for her sake I braved the flames, only to find my way to her door barred by fallen timbers. The charge had given me more strength than I had ever known, but the barrier was immovable. It was all I could do to escape the house before it, and everything in it, was consumed by fire. In as much time as it has taken to tell you, signore, the frog had taken away everything of value I had, but my punishment was not yet at an end.

"When I staggered out into the garden I saw through the dark rain a shape sitting in the pond; over the crack of thunder I heard what sounded like a low, mocking laugh. It was—the frog—croaking at me, and I knew from my time in the swamps what he meant by that croak: he was declaring his intention to mate.

"Can you imagine, signore, what would happen if that frog should have children? If the power I had wakened in it should breed true, and within years all the countless frogs of Earth had the strength of Hercules? It was too horrible to contemplate. I rushed to catch the devil but he evaded me with ease, heading for the swamp.

"I pursued it for years, never quite catching it but at least denying it the opportunity of finding a mate. Its course took me north, which puzzled me at first, until I learned of the powers of extreme cold to recharge a voltaic pile, as well as the ability of frogs to hibernate under snow—some instinct, I suppose, was showing it how to conserve the charge I had given it.

"Here is where I come into your story. Over time I harried the frog to the edge of the ocean, where I thought I might finally catch him: for even a frog such as he could not possibly swim that far. Again he thwarted me, though, for he led me down to the quay, where he jumped—a jump you would not believe if you saw it, signore—onto a ship that was departing just at that moment. Certainly it was too far for me to follow, and at first I thought he had finally beaten me, until my enquiries showed that the ship he had boarded was headed for San Francisco, and that another ship was due to depart for that port the next day.

"On that crossing I enjoyed a few weeks of leisure for the first time in years, and cast my mind to what I might do with the frog if I ever did succeed in catching it. To defeat it bodily was out of the question. Even with the vitality my jolt from the Leyden jar had given me—that which has allowed me to long outlive the three-score-and-ten years Our Lord allotted man—the beast had much greater power than I. Others had followed me in studying the nerveo-electric fluid, though, and had found there were some substances through which it could not pass: lead was one of these. With these facts in hand I formed a plan.

"The weeks of my passage crept by after that; finally we made port, and I crept out of the hold where I had concealed myself. I quickly learned that the first ship had arrived a week before, aided by favourable winds. Finding the trail cold I went inland; having heard that the chief virtue of Americans was curiosity I asked those I met whether they had heard or seen anything of a remarkable frog, one that could jump farther than any other. It did not take long for my inquiries to be gratified: a man, I heard, was harbouring the frog and exhibiting him. This was an unexpected development: I had presumed the beast hateful to all humanity, but now realized the hate that filled its heart was directed solely at me, its re-animator and tormentor. With this in mind I disguised myself as a man of your country, a simple prospector like so many others, and in this guise I approached the man whom I was told had found the frog—a signore Smiley, as of course you know.

"This Smiley, I had widely heard, could not resist a wager, and this was essential to my plan. So it was that when I found him and saw that he was carrying a lattice box, I asked him what lay within: a frog, said he, which in the charming naiveté of your nation he had named Daniel, and removed the lid. Within I saw at once that it was the frog, grown yet larger than when I had last seen it, and (by my good fortune) drowsing in the afternoon heat.

"Why, I asked—carefully concealing my excitement below a mask of indifference—why should he be taking such care of a simple frog? In a tone that implied he was imparting a great confidence he explained to me that Daniel was the greatest leaper since the first frog had been named by Adam. Now was the greatest test of my self-disguise, for of course no man knew the truth of his words better than I, and any hint of my true voice might wake the frog and set it to fleeing once more. Instead I expressed doubt, saying that I saw nothing about this Daniel that made it superior to any other frog; that, indeed, I would not hesitate to bet against his frog in a jumping contest. I was careful, though, to express it as a hypothetical—if I had a frog, I said, I felt sure it should prove no worse than his frog. Smiley rose to the bait, and set off to find another frog against which Daniel could race.

"Now—alone with the frog at last, and it confined in the lattice box Smiley had constructed—I put the final phase of my design into action. In my pouch I carried a quantity of lead shot, which, prying the still-dozing frog's mouth open, I poured into its belly. I spoke earlier of lead's quality of blocking the nerveo-electric fluid: my hope was to disrupt the flow of the fluid within the frog's body, granting it the death I had denied it—and letting us both find rest at last.

"It seemed at first as though I had succeeded. The frog struggled, but its vitality seemed gone, and when shortly Smiley returned with another frog he found that his Daniel not only lost the race but refused to compete, failing even to leave the ground.

"In this, though, I now see my error; for if I had only burdened Daniel enough to reduce him to the level of an ordinary frog Smiley would have thought nothing odd. I had induced too great a change in him, though, for even a man of Smiley's limited intelligence to accept. Lifting Daniel from the ground, Smiley overturned him, and the lead balls tumbled out of his mouth—too soon; for their work in blocking the nerveo-electric fluid was not yet done, and the frog quickly regained its diabolical energy. Smiley, simple man that he was, thought I had intended to cheat him in the wager; unable, with the limited command of English I had then, to explain the true facts of the situation I simply fled, being well aware of the propensity of your countrymen to arm themselves.

"The frog, with the daemonic cunning my experiment had given it, knew of course that it had lost its safe haven, and itself took flight; once I felt I was safe from retribution from Smiley I set upon its trail once again, and so I have been ever since, never again coming so near to ridding the world of the horror I unleashed upon it."

At that, Signore Galvani—for that, he would have me believe, was his name—wiped his brow with a handkerchief, dabbed lightly at his eyes. "Thank you for your time, Mr. Clemens," he said. "You are the first person who has ever heard my entire story, and I imagine the last as well; for my long hunt, I believe, is now finally near its end." With that he shook my hand, placed his hat upon his head, and walked out into the snowy night.

Well, there it is. Easily enough explained, of course: there are many harmless old men who imagine themselves to be important figures from history, Napoleon I understand being the most popular choice, and I would be far from the first writer to meet someone who wished to insert himself bodily into one of my stories.

And yet—the next day I was (don't laugh) invited to a skating party, which I attended, on the frozen surface of the Saint Lawrence River. There, amidst the general merriment caused by my attempts to stand on two feet, one young lad noticed a strange apparition: an old man chasing a small dark shape across the ice. My curiosity roused, I cast my eye over at it: there, indeed, was my interlocutor of the night before—chasing after a colossal dark green frog, which jumped five feet ahead of him with every hop. They were headed north, up towards the Bay of Fundy; and from thence, for all I know, the North Pole.

Now I ask you, what is a writer to do with that?

The Afflicted

In the end I managed a bit of sleep, wedged between the trunk and branches of the oak, before dawn came. My knees and elbows ached as I lowered myself to the ground and I could feel a blister forming on my shoulder where the strap of my .30-06 Winchester had rubbed against my oilskin all night. I went over the previous day's events in my mind, walking myself carefully through every mundane moment from when I woke up to when I climbed into the tree to sleep; then I looked down at my watch, waited for the minute to turn over and started to rattle off words that started with L: life, leopard, lizard, loneliness. . . . Twenty words and thirty seconds later I took a breath and started down the train tracks.

It was about an hour's walk to the camp, my last stop on this circuit. The clearing was packed with tents, their walls so faded by years of sun I could hardly make out the FEMA logo on the side; here and there ripped flaps of nylon fluttered in the breeze. The camps, cramped to begin with, were made even tighter by the lean-tos that had been built to expand the tents or shore them up, so that in places I had to turn sideways to squeeze my way toward the centre of the camp.

As I got deeper into the camp pale figures began to emerge from the tents, most of them dressed in filthy pajamas and bathrobes and nearly all bearing scars or fresh wounds on whatever pale flesh was exposed. I kept my .30-06 at my side and quickened my pace as they began to shuffle after me on slippered feet.

A single tent stood in the middle of the camp, as worn as the rest but bearing a faded Red Cross logo. When I reached it I turned around and shrugged out of my backpack one arm at a time. All the narrow paths that led here were now blocked by the shambling forms that had come out of the tents: they paused as they reached the clearing, watching me carefully as I cradled my rifle.

After a few moments one of them stepped forward. He was bald, save for a fringe of white hair, and he had a bloody gash down the side of his face. Unlike most of the others he was still in reasonably good shape, his skin the colour of a walnut. I levelled my rifle at him; he took another shambling step and then stopped.

"Hey, Horace," I said. I gestured at the cut on his face. "That looks bad."

He shrugged. "There's worse off than me."

"I know," I said, lowering my rifle, "but we'll start with you. Then you tell me who's worse off."

He looked back at the others. "There's a lot that are in bad shape, Kate," he said. "How long do you have today?"

I leaned the rifle in a spot where I could reach it in a hurry if I needed to. "You're my only stop."

He nodded, though he knew as well as I did that even in a full day I only had time to see the worst cases. Their affliction aside, my patients' age and the conditions they lived in meant that each of them had a host of issues for me to deal with. I counted on Horace to keep an eye on who was seriously injured, who had developed anything infectious, and who was showing signs of going end-stage. Everything else—minor illnesses and injuries, the frequent combination of scurvy and obesity caused by their diet of packaged food—I couldn't even hope to treat.

I glanced up at the sky, saw just a few white clouds. "Let's set up outside today," I said. "Sunshine and fresh air ought to do everyone some good."

"Sure. At least we've got plenty of those." Horace gestured to two of the waiting patients and they came up to the tent, giving me a wide berth, and hauled out the exam bed. He turned to the others.

"You might as well get on with your day. I'll come get you when she's ready for you."

A few of the waiting patients wandered off when he said this, but most stayed where they were. The line was mostly silent, with little chatter: the camp residents were used to isolation, many of them only coming out of their tents when I visited or to take care of bodily necessities.

I patted the exam table and Horace sat down on it stiffly. I unzipped one of the pockets on my backpack, drawing out my checkup kit, then held his wrist in my hand to take his pulse and slipped the cuff around his arm and inflated it. "Any cough?" I asked.

He shrugged. "Little bit now and then," he said. "I used to smoke. Guess I'm better off now, huh?"

I nodded. A lot of my patients were former smokers: when they were kids everyone had been, and they had grown up watching cigarette ads on TV. I got the TB kit and a pair of gloves out of my pack, pulled on the gloves, and tapped a syringe of PPD into his forearm. "Let's hope it's just that," I said.

He scowled. "Does it matter?" he asked.

I shook my head. "TB's a bad way to go. You remember how this works?"

He nodded.

"Tell me anyway."

"Watch where you pricked me for three days. If there's a spot, stay out of camp until you get back."

"Good. Hey, do you remember what we were talking about last time I was here? You never finished that story."

"You wanted to know how Adele and I met. Right?" I nodded. "Well, she used to work in the corner store. I would go in every day to buy something, just to see her. Of course all I could afford was a Coke, so she started to wonder—"

I reached out to tap him on the lips, right under his nose, and nodded with relief when he didn't react. "Horace, that thing you pull to open a parachute—what's that called?"

"It's a—damn it, that's, I know it . . ." He closed his eyes, frowning. "I don't remember."

"Never mind," I said. "How'd you get the cut?"

He was silent for a moment. "You know how it is."

I opened a steri-wipe and washed his wound; he flinched as I ran my fingers along the edges of the cut. "Does it hurt?"

He shrugged, gritting his teeth and hissing as I pressed a chitosan sponge into the wound and then covered it with plaskin, running my fingers along the edge to make the seal. He jerked his head suddenly and I pulled my hand back. "What is it?" I asked. "Did I hurt you?"

"Rip cord!" He broke into a broad grin. "Rip cord. Right?"

"That's good, Horace," I said. "No progression since last time. Anybody else I should know about?"

"What do you mean?"

"Your cut," I said. "Those are bite marks. Who was it?"

"Jerry," he said after a moment. "He didn't—I didn't know he'd gone end-stage."

"I'm sorry," I said. One of the things that makes the affliction so terrifying is how rapidly and unpredictably it can progress, smouldering like an ember in some and burning like a brushfire in others. That's why it has to be dealt with when the first symptoms surface, when they're still the parents and grandparents we had known in spirit as well as in body. "I don't suppose he's in the dog cage?"

Horace shook his head. "Ran off. Guess he's out in the woods somewhere. "He was quiet for a moment. "Am I going to—will I . . . ?"

For a moment I said nothing, trying not to look him in the eyes. The fact is that nobody knows for sure what causes the affliction, or even how it spreads: it could be that it's lurking in all of us, waiting for us to grow old. It seemed to me that the ones who had friends or spouses in the camps stayed well longer—but when one went, the others almost always followed soon.

"I can tell that's paining you," I said. "Say no to a little morphine?"

"I guess not."

"Arms up, then," I said, and fished out a syringe. He held his arms up in front of him so that the sleeves of his bathrobe fell to reveal his bare forearms. I drew a finger over his papery skin, tapped the syringe on a good vein. "How does that feel? Better?"

"One of those and I don't feel much of anything," he said. He took a breath, then smiled weakly. "What do you suppose two would do for me? Or three?"

"I don't aim to find out," I said.

"Damn it, Kate—if I'd gone end-stage, you wouldn't hold a moment's thought before you dropped me."

I shook my head. "I'll put down an animal in pain, but you're still a man."

"You won't feel that way when you're my age."

Even seeing just the worst cases took most of the day, and after that I still had the public health work—checking that the rain barrels storing the water supply weren't contaminated, and that the honey buckets were being emptied far enough from the camp—so it was already dark when I finished up, and too late to head to my cabin. I crashed in the Red Cross tent, sleeping on the exam table.

The next morning I rose a bit after dawn and started back to the tracks. My joints were stiff from being on my feet the day before, my skin itched sympathetically from all the scabies cases I had seen and my stomach was still leaden with the camp ice cream—sugar, wild berries and Crisco whipped together—one patient had insisted on giving me. (Crisco is a big part of camp cooking, which goes a long way towards explaining the chronic obesity in the camps; the other factor is that, for the most part, the residents have absolutely nothing to do, no motivation even to get out of their tents. The end-stagers, of course, don't have access to the camp food and typically become malnourished soon after they turn.)

Once I had finished my self-check I headed off again, along the train tracks. When I was about halfway to the station I saw that someone else had broken a trail out from the tracks, into the woods: there were a lot of confused footprints in the mud there, and what looked like blood on some thorns. I followed the trail for a little while, keeping a careful pace, then sped up when I heard the shrieks.

The trail led me into a small clearing in the shade of a tall willow. A man and two women, all clearly end-stage, were standing at the foot of the tree. There was a tension between the three of them, like cats facing off over a fallen baby bird, and when I got a bit nearer I could see the cause: a young girl, maybe ten years old, was up in the tree.

I fished my glasses out of my coat pocket, put them on, and then raised the .30-06 to my shoulder. The broad trunk of the tree made it hard for me to line up my shots, and I was worried that dropping the first one would break the tension between them and send the other two up the tree after the girl.

"Are you all right?" I called to her. The end-stagers turned at the sound but stayed where they were, still eyeing each other carefully.

"Who's there?"

"My name is Kate. I'm here to help you. What's your name, honey?"

"I'm Sophie," the girl said after a moment.

The end-stagers were starting to fidget, my presence disrupting the tension that had been holding them back. Whatever I was going to do, I had to do it soon. "How old are you, Sophie?"

"I'm— I'm eleven years old," she said. "Can you get me down?"

"I will, honey, but first I need you to climb higher up. Can you do that? I need you to climb as high as you can."

"I'm— I don't like going high."

I lowered my rifle slowly, aiming just short of the end-stager nearest to me. "Go as high as you can, Sophie. It's really important."

She started to squirm upwards, hugging the thick branches tightly. "Is this high enough?"

"High as you can." I kept a close eye on the three end-stagers as she rose, watching to see if any of them would make a break for her or for me. When one of them took a step I fired, sending a shot into the ground next to the male. The crack of the rifle made him jump and destroyed the last of his self-restraint: he started to climb up after the girl, now heedless of the other two. They followed him, more intent now on denying him the prize than on getting it for themselves, and I forced myself to breathe slowly as all three of them went up the trunk.

"I can't go any higher!" Sophie shouted.

The male had almost reached her when I was finally able to line the three of them up: I hit him high in the back, just below his neck, and he toppled backward, knocking into one of the others as he fell and dropping them both to the ground. By the time I had recovered from the recoil I had the next round chambered and was trying to get a bead on the second one. She was clinging to the tree trunk, frozen between rising higher and heading after me, and I forced myself to slow down and take aim.

I usually prefer body shots—a head shot is better if you make it, but there's too much risk of missing entirely—but she was a difficult target, rail-thin and wearing a ratty brown housecoat that faded into the tree bark, so I had to aim for her white hair. I peered down the rifle sight, took a slow breath in, and then let it out as I squeezed the trigger: a burst of red covered the old woman's head and she slumped, sliding down the tree trunk.

The third one, the heavy woman, had been chewing on the male that had fallen on her, but the sound of my gunshot made her look my way: a few moments later she was up and heading towards me in a stumbling run. She was faster than I had expected and blurred as she neared me. I peered over my glasses to get her back in focus and then fired: the shot took her in the stomach, a fair bit left of centre, and turned her to the side but didn't stop her. I chambered another round, squinted and fired again. My aim was better this time and she fell, first to her knees and then onto her face.

I began to cough, fighting to keep a bead on the fallen end-stager as I gagged and finally spat up a mouthful of greasy vomit. I wiped my mouth with my sleeve and then looked around, hoping the noise hadn't drawn any other company.

"Are you okay?" Sophie called from up in the tree. "Can I come down now?"

"Just take a look around first. Can you see anyone else?"

"No," she said after a few seconds. "There's just you."

"Okay, come on down."

"Okay." She didn't move for a minute or so, then started to inch slowly down the trunk. "Are they—are they all dead?"

I took off my glasses and moved toward the tree. The woman I had hit in the head was gone, but the man was still breathing: I slung my rifle over my shoulder, drew my knife, and rolled him over with my foot. He was better dressed than many of them, in heavy green cotton pants and a blue checked shirt instead of a gown or pajamas: I remembered him telling me that before coming to the camp he had lived on his own, rather than in a home. His skin was thin like an onion's, and white where it wasn't covered with scratches and bruises. My knees protested as I crouched down and slit his throat.

The girl dropped the last few feet and landed next to me. After a moment she threw her arms around my waist; I reached around her and drew her close, feeling her shake as she sobbed silently. "It's all right," I said quietly, and after a few minutes she stepped back, leaving a trail of snot and tears on my oilskin.

She looked from side to side, over her shoulder and then back at me. "Thank you," she said.

"It's all right," I said again. She was dressed in dark blue jeans that showed little wear, a t-shirt, bright red fleece, a yellow plastic windbreaker over that and red sneakers covered in little stickers and doodads. There was some bark and leaf litter stuck to her, but her shoes were mostly clean: she hadn't been in the woods for long. "How did you get here, honey?"

"I was on the train," she said. "I was going to live with my uncle and his wife and his kids." She looked straight at me for a moment, then glanced away. "I was by myself. My grandma . . ."

"So what happened?"

"I was, we were going around a bend and something bumped the train. I got knocked into a door and it just opened. I tried to wave at the train but it was too far away by the time I got up and my phone doesn't work here."

"We're a ways from the tracks."

"I got lost. I guess I should have stayed by the tracks but I didn't know how long it was going to be until the next train came, and I thought if I got higher up I could maybe get a signal on my phone. Then those—those people found me and when I knew what they were I went up the tallest tree I could find." She paused for a breath. "I'd been up there since yesterday."

"Are you okay to walk?" I asked. "We need to get you someplace safe.""

She nodded. "Where are we going?"

"I'm going to take you to the Ranger station. They have a radio—they can let the next train know to stop for you."

"How far is it?"

I shrugged. "A bit more than a day."

I handed her a handful of dry breakfast biscuits. She took a bite of one, chewed it slowly, swallowed and said, "Thanks."

"No problem," I said. "I can stock back up when we get to the station."

"No, I mean—thanks. For what you're doing. I didn't—I didn't think there was anyone, I mean anyone not—you know, anyone not sick out here. "She was silent for a moment. "What—why are you out here? Are you—"

"No," I said. I ran my hand through my hair, held it out so she could see the grey starting to speckle the black. "Not yet, anyway."

"So do you—do you, like, hunt them or something?"

I shook my head. "That was—I try not to do that. Unless I have to."

"Then why are you here?"

I slung my rifle over my shoulder. "I'm a nurse."

At first they thought the homes were the vector. The affliction had spread all through them by the time anybody noticed it: the upticks in violence and dementia were noted but unremarked upon, hardly unusual in the overcrowded facilities, the larger pattern only visible if you saw what was happening with your own eyes. By that point nearly all the work was automated, done either by social robots or remote workers; few homes had more than the one Nurse of Record the law demanded.

So they emptied the homes, setting up the tent cities in National Park campgrounds across the country. None of us who had worked in the homes had shown any symptoms, but that didn't matter. Whether or not we were infected, or infectious, we were seen as tainted—and few of us could find many reasons to disagree

245

with that judgment. So we were each given a choice: a comfortable quarantine, or life in the camps with our former patients. I never found out what any of the other nurses chose, but I can't imagine many of those quarantine apartments were ever occupied.

It wasn't long after I had moved into my cabin that cases began showing up outside of the homes, and everyone over sixty became a presumed latent and carrier. There was never any word about bringing us back, though, just the intermittent shipments of food and medicine and the trains carrying more and more of the afflicted.

It was maybe an hour before she started talking again: just small talk at first, like what my last name was and where I had come from, and telling me a little bit about her life. When she talked about herself I let her lead: I didn't know yet whether her past had made her resilient or if she was just riding on shock and adrenaline, and I couldn't afford to let her crash.

We reached the tracks in good time and followed them east, toward the Ranger station; after an hour or so I stopped.

"What is it?" she asked.

I held a finger to my lips, turned around slowly. "Someone's tracking us," I said quietly.

"Oh," she said after a second. "Do you—is it one of the, the end-stagers, do you think?"

I raised my rifle and began to turn slowly from left to right, watching for movement in the trees. "I don't think so," I said. "Whoever it is has been following us since you came down from the tree. End-stagers don't have that kind of attention span."

Sophie put a hand on my arm: when I glanced at her I saw that she wasn't looking at me, or in the direction my rifle was pointed, but just to the right. Her grip tightened as I turned.

"Sophie," I said, "did anyone else fall off that train?"

For a long moment nobody said anything; then there was a rustling in the bushes, right where I was pointing my rifle. I kept my finger near the trigger but waited as I heard Sophie's breathing get faster and faster. After a few seconds a woman stepped out from behind a tree, dressed in black pants and a jean jacket. Her black hair had hints of white in it, like mine, only hers was white at the roots.

"Don't," Sophie said in a tiny voice.

I took a breath, kept her in my sights. "Are you with her?" I asked.

"Yes," the woman said.

"She's my grandma," Sophie said. "You're right. She was on the train with me." She pulled harder at my arm. "Please don't shoot her."

"I won't," I said, though I didn't lower my rifle. "What's your name?"

"Peggy. Perkins." She raised her hands. "I just—I just wanted to make sure Sophie was all right."

"You shouldn't have been on that train," I said. I glanced at Sophie, then back at Peggy. "They found out, didn't they?"

Peggy nodded. "I couldn't stop her," she said. "They were holding me, and then she just jumped off the train. I didn't want . . ."

There was silence for a moment as she trailed off. I turned to Sophie. "That was a very, very foolish thing to do," I said. "Your grandma is . . . she can't come with us."

"No," Sophie said. "I couldn't. I can't just leave her alone."

"Your grandma is sick, Sophie," I said. "She can't get on the train with you, and they won't let her into the Ranger station."

Sophie crossed her arms. "Then I don't want to go," she said. She scowled, her jaw quivering, and tears were appearing in the corners of her eyes.

Peggy crouched down to look Sophie in the eyes. "Honey, you have to," she said, then turned her head to look up at me. "But I'm not sick yet. I can come with you—as far as the Ranger station. To help keep her safe."

I took a breath. "What's the last meal you ate on the train?"

Peggy frowned. "I don't—"

"I need to know how far along you are. Do you remember what the last thing you ate on the train was?"

She stood up and closed her eyes for a moment. "Ham and cheese sandwich," she said. I watched Sophie's expression, to see if she remembered the same thing. "Little crackers, but I didn't eat them; Sophie had mine."

"All right," I said. "Give me five words that start with R, fast as you can."

"Rainbow. Rutabaga. Rooster. Red . . . Red light."

I nodded, then reached out to tap her on the lips. She drew back but made no other response. "Okay," I said. "You're not showing any definite symptoms yet. But this thing can go very, very quickly."

Peggy's whole body relaxed as she let out a breath. "I promise, I—if you ever think I'm a danger to her, I'll just . . . go away, I'll go into the woods and never come back."

"If you turn," I said, "I'll put you down myself."

We walked for the rest of the day, mostly in silence. Sophie stayed close to Peggy; I felt an absurd jealousy as she held her grandmother's hand and cast occasional glances up at her. We got back to the train tracks after another hour or so, and followed them westward until it began to get dark. Before dusk fell I found a suitable tree to sleep in and, after a meagre supper of jerky and biscuits, we made our way into its branches.

When I woke up I was alone: Sophie wasn't on her branch, though the bungee cord that had held her there lay on the ground. I loosened my own cord and carefully lowered myself to the ground. My knee locked as I touched down: I took a half-dozen deep breaths, straightened my leg and looked around. There was no sign of either of them, nor any sound but the usual noise of the forest in the morning.

"Sophie?" I called quietly. I started back to the tracks, just a few yards away, then stopped when I heard a noise coming from behind me.

"It's us," Sophie called. She emerged from the brush with Peggy trailing behind. Sophie was holding her windbreaker in her hands. "We went to get berries. For breakfast."

"I suppose it wasn't a very good idea," Peggy said, "but I made sure she stayed close."

"No, it's all right," I said. "I was just . . ." I reached up to rub my eyes. "Did you find any?"

Sophie held the hood of her windbreaker up to me: it was about half full of tiny wild raspberries and blackberries. "Look," she said.

"We had a cottage when she was little," Peggy said. She shrugged. "Back before . . ."

We divided the berries between us, and then the remaining breakfast biscuits; Sophie tucked her last one in the pocket of her windbreaker and then looked at her grandmother, who put on a smile.

"Is there any way I can take some of that?" Peggy asked when I lifted my pack.

I shook my head. "It's all right."

"We might go faster."

"I don't remember you having to wait for me yesterday," I said.

"No, I know. I just meant I'd like to, well, carry my weight."

I looked over at Sophie: she was watching us carefully, an expression of concern on her face. "Sure," I said. I separated the zipsack from my backpack, reached inside to take out the box of cartridges and then handed the sack to her. She swung it over one shoulder as we headed off, first going back to the train tracks and then following them to the Ranger station. I kept my hand on my rifle and watched the woods.

"Hey, I see smoke," Sophie said, pointing ahead of us. "Is that the station?"

I could just see the station's fence and gate, and beyond that a wisp of smoke rising up into the air. "We're almost there," I said. "They wouldn't usually have a fire this time of year, though."

"Do you think something's wrong?" Peggy asked.

I held up my hand, then reached into my jacket pocket for my glasses. Once I had them on I could see that the gate across the tracks was open.

"Get off the tracks," I said, looking back at them. "Come on, now."

"Is there a train coming?" Peggy asked as she stepped carefully over the rail. "Don't they blow a, you know, make a noise? So you know they're coming?"

"Yeah, they do," I said. "But maybe . . ." I waited for a minute, glancing back and forth between the station and the woods. Suddenly my pack felt very, very heavy.

"What are we going to do?" Sophie asked.

"I don't know. I don't understand—they wouldn't open the gate except to let a train through, but that's not long enough for . . ." I turned to look at Peggy and Sophie. "You said your train stopped when they threw you off. How long?"

"I don't know," Peggy said, frowning. "Maybe ten, fifteen minutes."

"Which way was it going?"

"To San Diego," she said. "Why does it matter?"

"I think somebody else got on that train when you got off," I said. I lifted my glasses and rubbed my eyes. "Not on the train, but hanging onto the outside. They must have seen that the trains could get through the fence."

"So what happened to the Rangers?" Sophie asked. "Do you think they're all. . . ?"

"I don't know. I guess they might not bother closing the gate, if the station was already compromised. . . ." I took a breath, folded my glasses and put them back in my jacket pocket. "We have to get to their radio so that we can tell someone about Sophie, get her out of here."

"Couldn't we just stay here, wait for the next train?" Peggy asked. "I'm sure if you explained . . ."

I shook my head. "The trains that stop here don't let people on," I said. "You're right about one thing, though. You're staying here, but she has to come with me."

"No," Sophie said. She squeezed Peggy's hand in hers. "I—I'll come. I'm not scared, but Grandma has to come too."

"I'm fine," Peggy said. "That's just, my mind is fine. A whistle, the word I was looking for is whistle. There, you see? You just forget things sometimes, at my age. Doesn't that ever happen to you?"

"What did we have for breakfast, Peggy?" I asked.

"Berries," she said.

"What kind of berries?"

She rolled her eyes. "It was . . . well, summer berries. What you pick in the summer, in brambles with, with prickers." She looked away and then back at me: her face was red, her eyes glistening.

"There's a camp just a few hours that way," I said, pointing the way we had come and off to the left. "You'll be all right there, and I'll check on you when I can."

"No," Peggy said. "I'm not going. Not until she's safe."

For a moment I looked at the two of them standing together, then shrugged. "Fine," I said. I slid open the bolt of my rife, making sure there was a cartridge in the chamber. "Let's go, then, while we've still got some light."

"Should we wait till morning?" Peggy asked.

I shook my head. I had seen too many shapes moving in the bushes, heard too many footsteps and rustling branches. I chewed my lip for a moment, guessing at the distance between the gate and the station—a hundred yards, maybe? "Let's get through that gate as fast as we can—I don't want to get caught in a choke point."

"I haven't seen any—"

"They're there," I said, trying to keep my voice too low for Sophie to hear. "Maybe a lot of them."

As we neared the gate I fought the urge to run: I could hear the end-stagers in the woods around us, feel their eyes on us as we passed through the narrow space. The fence around the Ranger compound was solid steel, with razor wire along the top to keep end-stagers from climbing over it. The open gate, just wide enough for a train to pass through, let us see glimpses of the other side but concealed much more. I slowed my pace as we reached the gate, letting my finger curl around the trigger of my rifle.

Sophie reached the gate and broke into a trot as she passed through, moving out of view. I caught up with her just as she ran into a man in dark clothes who had been moving in front of the gate on the other side. For a moment I thought he might be a Ranger, until I saw his white hair: he turned towards me and opened his mouth to reveal two rows of teeth, like a shark's, perfectly white and gleaming.

I raised the barrel of my rifle, getting ready to shoot and run— the sound of the shot would surely bring all the other end-stagers from the woods—but before I could fire Sophie reached into the pocket of her windbreaker, pulled out the biscuit she had saved from that morning and held it out to the man.

For a moment he just looked at her, his double teeth grinning obscenely; then he took the biscuit and began to chew it carefully, barely able to get it in his mouth. I stood there, watching as he chewed contentedly on the biscuit, and I saw that he was wearing dentures over his own teeth, which were sliding in and out of his mouth each time he moved his jaw.

After a few moments Peggy tugged on my sleeve and led me away. The cabin was about fifty yards off the tracks, the firewatch tower a short distance beyond that: once we had passed the chewing end-stager we broke into a run, crossing the distance between the tracks and the cabin as quickly as we could.

The outside of the cabin was not much different than it had been before it had been repurposed—there was not much you could do to make a wall of stacked logs more defensible—but the windows and doors had been replaced with shatterproof Plexiglas and steel, the wood shingle roof long gone in favour of aluminium. I used my momentum to launch myself up onto the cement platform that stood before the door, the only reminder of the screened porch that had once covered the whole front of the building. Peggy hesitated as she neared it and stumbled; Sophie slowed to help her, the two of them awkwardly levering themselves up onto the platform with their hands.

"Stay close," I said. "We're just going to find the radio and get out."

"Don't you know where it is?" Sophie asked.

"I've never been inside," I said. I took a step back, raised my rifle and waved Peggy forward. "Push it open, then step away."

"What if it's locked?" Peggy said.

"Then we knock very politely and ask the Rangers to let us in," I said, glancing back at the gate.

Sophie grabbed my arm as her grandmother stepped past us, putting a hand on the door handle and turning it tentatively. Peggy leaned into the heavy door, pushing it with her shoulder, and as she did I moved my sights off her and onto the opening doorway. Once she had it fully open I stepped in and then waved the others in after me. When they were both inside Peggy released the door and it swung back, slamming shut with a heavy thud that made me wince.

The door led into a small foyer that opened into a larger room to the left. I stepped into the room and swung my rifle at the other three corners. Fading light from the window showed a brown leather couch, much-patched with silver duct tape, facing a fireplace on the far wall that held some smouldering logs: in front of it was a wagon wheel coffee table, its glass top lying in shards on the floor all around, and an eyeless moose head hung on the wall above.

Peggy held her hand to her mouth. "That smell. . . ." she said.

"They've been here," I said. An open doorway in the wall to our right led to a hallway, but it was too dark within to see anything. "Let's hope they ran out of toys to play with."

We crossed the room, stepping carefully to avoid the shards of glass, until we stood at the doorway. I took my flashlight from my jacket pocket and handed it to Sophie. "Stay right in front of me," I said quietly.

"I should go first," Peggy said.

I shook my head. "You're too tall. I need to be able to shoot over her."

She opened her mouth, shut it and nodded. Sophie and I counted a silent one, two, three together and then stepped into the doorway, swinging the flashlight and rifle together to the left and then the right. There was a door, half-open, almost directly across from us, and another to the left of it; beyond that the left-hand hallway opened into a room that looked like it spanned the breadth of the cabin. To the right I could see three doors, all on the facing wall, before the corridor faded into darkness.

Peggy pressed against the back of my jacket, trying to squeeze into the doorway with us. "Which way?" she asked.

I nodded at the door across the hall and Sophie and I moved forward together. The wooden door swung inward as she kicked it: the room lit up as she pointed the flashlight inside, with mirror, tile and porcelain bouncing the light back at us.

"Let's try to the left," I said. "It's not as far from the front door in that direction—maybe we'll get lucky."

The smell we had noticed earlier grew stronger as we opened the next door on the left. It was a smell I had known before I ever came here: every home I ever worked in had it, no matter how hard it had been scrubbed.

The flashlight's beam picked up a carpet, dresser, and two single beds, on each of which lay an unmoving body. I started to cover Sophie's eyes with my hand, but the smell had already reached her: she spat up water and half-digested berries, and dropped the flashlight onto the floor. It rolled into the room, and Sophie reached down to pick it up; as her hand closed on it something seized her and pulled her forward. I took a step, trying to get a bead on the end-stager who had grabbed her, but Peggy rushed past me, knocking me to my knees. In the dim light I saw her grabbing Sophie's other arm, pulling hard, and I heard Sophie scream.

I didn't bother to stand but instead rose to one knee and tried to sight the end-stager. All I could see, though, was Peggy: she had knocked Sophie aside and leapt onto the one who had grabbed her, clawing at him with a savagery that was, I was sure, entirely foreign to her nature.

"Grandma?" Sophie asked.

Peggy turned back to us: her face was chalk-white, her eyes wild. I kept my rifle where it was, watching her carefully.

"Sophie, go," I said. "The way we were going."

Peggy looked from me to Sophie and then back again. She opened her mouth but remained silent, a perplexed look on her face. She took a step toward Sophie and my finger curled inward, touching the cold metal of the trigger.

"No," Sophie said. "Don't . . ."

Peggy froze. I rose to my feet, keeping her in my sights. "We have to go now," I said. I backed up towards the door, putting myself between Sophie and Peggy. Sophie reached from behind me and grabbed my arm, pulling it down until the .30-06 was pointed at the floor.

I took a step back out into the hall, still watching Peggy, and glanced to my left. Two end-stagers had emerged from the large room at the end of the corridor. One was a bald male in faded blue pajamas, his bare feet trailing blood; the other was a female dressed in just a dirty, pilly grey bra who had a halo of frizzy grey hair and little round bumps all over her body, like someone had slipped a sheet of bubble wrap under her skin.

"Go."

Sophie looked at her grandmother for a moment before heading down the long corridor, the flashlight's beam jumping around the walls as she ran. I took a step backwards, trying to keep both Peggy and the two end-stagers within my arc of fire, then turned and ran after her. I could hear the male and female pick up their pace behind me and swore under my breath, cursing myself for triggering their instincts by running.

Sophie looked back at me, slowing her pace to let me catch up. We were already past the doorway to the room we had come in, so we ran until we could see the end of the hallway. There was a door on the left, just before the furthest wall; beyond it the hallway turned left, with a hint of light visible at its end. The exposed logs on our right showed that we were following the outer wall, and ahead of us we could see light coming through a transom over a wooden door. When we got closer, though, we saw that the door handle had been removed and nails driven through the door into the frame.

I took my jackknife from my pocket and tried to work the blade into the empty socket where the handle had been, thinking that if I could get the latch free I might be able to force the door open.

"Can you use your gun?" Sophie asked.

I took a step back and raised my rifle, aiming at where the handle had been. "I don't know," I said.

"No, the other end—bang it on the hinges."

I nodded, then handed her my knife. "You keep working on the handle." I slid open the bolt and let the cartridge fall to the ground, then turned the rifle around and slammed the butt into the upper hinge. I could see the screws pulling out of the frame, but just barely.

Sophie was kneeling in front of the door handle, trying to disengage the latch with the knife. She glanced behind us, saw the two end-stagers rounding the corner, and screamed.

"Just keep trying," I said. "We can get out of this—"

When I moved to hit the hinges again, though, something was pulling the other way: I turned to see the bubble-wrap woman's hands on the barrel. My finger went to the trigger, but by the time it had gotten there I remembered I had taken out the cartridge.

The bubble-wrap woman had both hands on the barrel now and was trying to pull the rifle away from me. The bald man crouched down, trying to creep past the woman and me to get at Sophie, who screamed again.

Suddenly the bald man's head flew forward, slamming into the door. I glanced away from the woman to see Peggy stumbling back from where she had collided with him. The bubble-wrap woman looked at her, too, and that gave me enough of a chance to pull the barrel out of her grasp; I swung the stock forward and it hit her head with a crunch, knocking her back into the wall. Sophie was curled up into a ball, covering her face with her hands, but the bald man had forgotten about her and was struggling with Peggy, scratching her face with long, dirty fingernails.

I turned back to the hinge and hit it again, saw the ends of the screws come loose from the doorframe. "The doorknob," I said to Sophie.

She moved her hands from her face, then froze as she saw her grandmother struggling with the bald man.

"Sophie, the doorknob," I said again. "If you can get that I think I can open it."

She nodded and turned back to the door, sticking the point of the knife between the door and the frame. A few moments later the whole door moved slightly within the frame and I lowered the rifle, took a half-step back and slammed my shoulder into the door. The top half of the door pulled free of the nails holding it to the frame and with another slam the whole door came loose and fell onto the ground.

I stepped outside but Sophie didn't follow. "Come on," I said, but she was frozen. Peggy was still wrestling with the bald man, his teeth sunk into her shoulder as she punched him in the stomach. I took the box of cartridges from my pocket, loaded one into the rifle and drew a bead on the man's bald head. "Don't look, Sophie," I said, then pulled the trigger. The shot drove the man into Peggy, knocking them both over.

"Come on." I grabbed Sophie's wrist and pulled her after me.

"There should be another radio up in the firewatch tower."

"No," Sophie said. "My grandma's hurt.'

"Oh, honey," I said. "She's not your grandma anymore."

Sophie said nothing as she moved to pull the dead end-stager off her grandmother. Peggy was in bad shape, but still moving; there were cuts and bruises all over her face, and bright red blood was oozing out of the toothmarks on her shoulder. I fumbled with another cartridge, loaded it into the chamber.

"Is she going to die?" Sophie asked.

I raised my rifle and tried to sight Peggy, who was rising stiffly to her feet. "Come on, Sophie," I said. "Get away from her. We have to go."

Sophie turned back to look at me, frowning deeply. "Is she going to die?"

"Yes," I said. "Not right away, but yes, she probably is. Bite wounds are bad—they get infected, and the blood she's lost is going to make it worse."

"Tell me what to do. To help her."

I took a step forward, nudging Sophie aside with the rifle barrel. Peggy looked up at me, silent, her face unreadable. "There's nothing you can do to help her. Your grandma is gone."

"No, she isn't," Sophie said. She turned to Peggy and looked her in the eyes. "You're sick, I know that. But you aren't going to hurt me, and I'm going to help you."

Peggy's ragged breathing slowed as Sophie held her, becoming more regular. After what felt like a long time I took a breath, looked right and left, and then dropped my rifle. I unshouldered my pack, took out some steri-wipes, two syringes of my moxifloxacin/clindamycin bite mix and one of morphine. "Give me her arm," I said.

Sophie took Peggy's right hand in hers and straightened her arm. I found a good vein, wiped it clean and tapped the three syringes, one after the other. "That should help with infection," I said. "Do you want to do the bandages?"

Sophie's mouth quirked up into a tiny smile, and she nodded. "How do I do it?' she asked.

I handed her a steri-wipe, tore open a pack of chitosan sponges and handed it to her. "Clean your hands first, then press these into each of the wounds." I held my breath as she touched the first sponge to Peggy's bite marks. "Careful, it might hurt her," I said.

Peggy flinched as Sophie applied the sponges, but did not move. "Now what?" Sophie asked.

"Here," I said, passing her the bandage. "Wrap this around the wounds five or six times, nice and tight."

When she was done she looked back at me. "Is that it?"

"That's everything we can do," I said. I put a hand on her shoulder. "We have to go."

She looked her grandmother in the eyes for another few moments, then stood and turned. "All right," she said. "Let's go."

The firewatch tower stood a few hundred feet down a path past the cabin, silhouetted in the evening light. A narrow wooden staircase zigzagged inside the tower's timber frame, up to the observation post and radio tower at the top.

I paused at the bottom of the staircase, letting Sophie go ahead of me as I watched to see if anyone was coming after us; Peggy was sitting where we had left her, watching us, more still than I had ever seen an end-stager. We climbed up carefully, the stairs creaking and groaning as we rose, and by the time we got to the top the sun had nearly set.

Sophie had said nothing since we started up the stairs. She stopped a few steps below the platform and looked down at me: the stairs reached the platform on the west side of the tower, so we could just see each other in the pale pink light of the setting sun. Down below I could see the whole Ranger compound and I understood why it had angered the end-stagers so much, looking so mockingly like a home.

"What do we do now?" she asked.

"Find the radio," I said. "See if it still works."

"And then?"

"We let people know you're here."

"Do you really think they"ll come and get me?"

I took a deep breath, let it out slowly. "We'll tell them what happened. To the Rangers. They'll have to do something about that, and . . ."

After a few seconds she nodded and climbed up onto the platform. There was a small shed there, with a narrow walkway around it and a metal antenna on top. Sophie opened the unlocked door to the shed and we slipped inside.

The small room had an air of long disuse: the flashlight's beam revealed a narrow cot, a folding wire-and-nylon chair, and a desk on which sat a pair of binoculars and a radio and microphone. The radio was old and bulky, a black box with a front panel covered with switches, and even before I reached the desk I knew it was broken. I flicked the on switch up and down a few times, but nothing happened.

Sophie sat down on the cot, saying nothing. I sat down next to her, and as I did the flashlight flickered and died. In the darkness I could hear her banging the butt end of the flashlight; a few moments later I felt her shifting her weight and then a tiny blue square of light appeared in front of her, just enough for us to see each other's faces.

"Hey, my phone works up here," she said. "Two bars, that's not bad. Should I . . . should I call somebody? Who should I call?"

"911, I guess," I said. "That's got to do something."

We sat there a while longer, neither of us moving or speaking. "Are you going to come?" she asked finally.

"I can't," I said. "I'm here for good, like everyone else."

"The Ranger that was . . . one of the ones in the room, she looked a lot like you. You could pretend you're her. You could come with me."

"No," I said after a long moment. "I have too many people counting on me." I took a breath. "More than I thought, maybe."

Sophie nodded slowly. "I think I need to stay here too," she said. "To take care of my grandma. And I think maybe you need someone to take care of you, too."

"Maybe," I said, and reached out to take her hand. She smiled, and then we both zipped our jackets and went to sleep sitting up.

Holdfast

Irrel was halfway through milking Black-Eye when the sky went dark with dragons. He looked up to see what had happened and saw dozens of winged shapes obscuring the sun in the east. They were flying low to the ground: that might mean rain, but if they were riding-dragons it meant battle coming. He shrugged and turned back to his work, resuming his interrupted song:

> *Five riders in a ring*
> *Round Bessie's udder*
> *Bessie bring milk*
> *Milk bring butter*

Milk fell into the bucket with each pull, thick and yellow with cream drawn by the charm. Irrel's daughter Niiv sat on a stool across the yard, churning the milk: with every fourth stroke she clapped the churn-staff down hard, to catch the hands of any witches or devils that might try to spoil the butter. She stopped partway through a stroke and pointed over Irrel's head.

He turned just in time to see the load of worm-cast falling a short distance away to the west. Irrel gave one more pull of Black-Eye's udder and patted her on the side. "Good girl," he said as he stood. Then he called out: "Sifrid, get the wagon and shovels."

Sifrid, the season-man, was over by the house: he waved and then headed for the carriage house.

Niiv stood up, threw a glance in Sifrid's direction. "Let me get the cows back inside and I'll come with you."

Irrel shook his head. "Black-Eye's too full to wait. Besides, someone has to keep watch over Tyrrel."

His daughter frowned. "Where is he?"

"Chicken coop, should be."

Niiv crossed her arms. "Well, am I to be a milkmaid or a nursemaid?"

Irrel fought to keep himself from smiling at her pout and her wrinkled nose. It was far from the only thing she had got from her mother, but it was the one that most recalled Eliis. "Fetch him first. Black-Eye will keep for a few moments, and then perhaps you can persuade him to try milking her." He took the tally sticks from his apron pocket and handed them to her; she took them, gave Black-Eye a pat and walked off towards the chicken coop, sighing loudly.

Once she was gone he made his way to the stable, unbarred the small door and stepped inside, pausing until his eyes adjusted to the dimmer light. Along the wall hung a dozen rope harnesses, each one tight and unfrayed. He cast his eye over the harnesses, his fingers twitching with the memory of having tied them, until finally he reached out and chose a Ram's Knot.

Grunting a little with the effort he lifted the harness off of the wooden hook and went to the stalls. Sviput and Svegjut whickered as he passed, impatient to be let out into the yard; he called Sviput, the gelding, with a whistle and then led him to where the leather collars hung. Once the horse was dressed Irrel brought him outside, shading his own eyes against the change in light.

Sifrid had loaded the dray with shovels and drawn it up by the gate. His shirt was soaked with sweat: his childhood in the city had not well prepared him for farm work, and he stooped with exhaustion as he drew the cart into position to be harnessed.

"Where are we going?" he asked as he dumb-tied the tug to the horse's collar.

Irrel pointed down the road to the west, then gave the gelding a pat and tossed the halter over its neck. He leaned down to loosen the holdfast on the gate, then lifted it carefully and hung it on the fencepost before leading the horse and dray forward with a tug of the harness rope. He kept a tight hand on it: the Ram's Knot would give Sviput strength to pull the load when the cart was full, but for now it only made him headstrong. Sifrid closed the gate and followed along a few steps behind.

The road was rough, holed by hoof prints and stranger spoors. After they had been walking for a while they saw a man ahead leading a donkey-drawn cart. Irrel gave the lead a tug, letting Sviput go more quickly, and they soon drew up close enough to see that it was Allren, who worked the farm on the other side of Slow Creek.

"Morning find you," Allren said, touching the brim of his hat and tugging it.

Irrel touched his hat in response. "And you," he said. He gave the lead a pull to slow the horse, found himself breathing harder than he was used to: his years had mostly spared his strength, but he had lost much of his wind.

"You saw it too, I suppose?"

Irrel nodded.

"And there's been men this way, looks like." Allren pointed to a break in the fencing at the side of the road: beyond it the wheat had been trampled and torn from the ground, the heads broken and kernels scattered. "Or almost men. Only the Margrave's beasts would eat plain rye, and before harvest time too."

"People will eat the same as pigs if they're hungry enough."

"That's true as you say it," Allren said, nodding. "That's not your fence there, is it?"

Irrel shook his head. "My hide ends back at the crooked tree."

"Didn't think so. Never saw your fence in such a state."

The wind, which had been blowing from the south all morning, had shifted to the west: it brought the smell of worm-cast, acrid and sulphurous. It grew stronger as they kept walking, passing beyond the fenced land and into marshy country. Finally they began to see the first drops of worm-cast, pats of manure about a hand around that were fibrous like a horse's droppings but dark, oily and resinous. Irrel had Sifrid gather them as they passed: each drop clung to the season-man's gloves, needing a hard shake to fall into the cart.

The largest concentration lay ahead, in a pile about a cowhide around that had fallen on a stretch of peatland at the edge of the marsh. Two more men with carts were standing at the side of the road, having come from the opposite direction: one Irrel knew as Karten, a brinker whose tiny strip of land stood just outside the marsh, and the other one he did not know at all. Both touched their hats at his and Allren's arrival.

"Fair morning," Karten said. He was thinner than the last time Irrel had seen him, sometime in the winter.

"To you," Irrel said.

Allren looked back the way they had come, then further down the road. "Do either of you claim a stake by law in this find?" he asked. After a moment the two men shook their heads. "Then I propose we divide equal stakes. Do you all agree?"

Karten and the other man both looked to Irrel; after a moment he nodded, took his shovel from the cart and began to walk towards where the worm-cast had fallen. The others followed him as they walked first across the spongy peatland and then through the thick shit, which reached nearly to the tops of their boots by the time they were at the centre of it. Once there they clasped hands and then turned away from one another, walking towards the edge of the worm-cast and drawing their shovels behind them to quarter it. Sifrid brought his shovel and they began to work, separating sticky spadefuls from the pat and ferrying it back to their carts.

When they were both bringing loads to the cart Sifrid cleared his throat. "There's something I need to talk to you about," he said.

Irrel grunted, levering the shovel high to drop the worm-cast into the cart. "And now's the time, is it?"

"Well, it's, I guess it's as good a time as any, but I couldn't wait any longer. With the harvest coming, I mean."

"Hm." Irrel planted the shovel on the ground and leaned his weight on it, catching his breath. "And so?"

"Well— Well, I suppose you know that I have— I've known Niiv, I've known your daughter a long time, and . . . Well. Perhaps you know already."

"I hadn't thought a goldsmith's son was working as a season-man because he needed the coin," Irrel said.

Sifrid was silent for a moment. "Yes, of course," he said. "And, well, the thing is, I'd like to marry her. I'd like to marry your daughter, to marry Niiv."

"Well," Irrel said, "I suppose I should talk to Niiv about this."

"She feels the same as I do, sir."

"I'm sure she does, but I'll talk to her just the same."

Sifrid laughed nervously. "Of course. I only meant—"

Irrel held up a hand. There was sound he couldn't quite identify, something out of place. After a moment he realized it was a voice, quietly chanting:

Ten little men all in a ring
Ten little men bow to the king

He closed his eyes and turned his head slightly from side to side, still listening.

Ten little men dance all day
Ten little men hide a—

Irrel reached out and seized the boy by his shirt-collar. Of course it was Tyrrel, his son, his hands still splayed out in the dancing part of the charm. "What are you doing here?" Irrel said. "Your sister's sure to be beside herself."

"She didn't even go look for me!" Tyrrel said. He was a handsome boy, a bit small for ten but already bearing the lean, serious face of a man: a thatch of chestnut hair, his mother's legacy, fell over his eyes. "I watched her before I followed you. She just went into the house."

"And you showed her right," Irrel said, frowning.

"But I needed to come with you," Tyrrel said. "I have to start learning about things like this. I'll be a man soon enough, you know."

Irrel nodded slowly. "So you will," he said. "Well then, get in the cart and see if you can find any worm-coal in that mess."

Tyrrel wrinkled his nose in distaste. "What's worm-coal?"

Irrel held his thumb and forefinger about an inch apart. "Shiny black balls, say this big. Burns purer than sea-coal or charcoal—might be we'll sell what we find to Sifrid's father."

"Is it just smiths that use it in their craftings, or is it wizards too? We could give it to Uncle Allel."

"Could be we would, if you find any. Now hop to."

Tyrrel's eyes widened, and Irrel turned to see what he was looking at: more dragons were flying in from the east. Tyrrel began counting as they flew overhead: "One for sorrow, two for joy. Three for a wedding." A moment later another appeared on the horizon and he laughed, a child again. "And four for a baby boy!"

Irrel looked over at Sifrid, who was blushing. He took a deep breath and went back to his work.

By the time they had gone back to the farm and finished shovelling the worm-cast onto the dung hill Niiv had dinner ready. Irrel kept his eyes on his plate as they ate the meal: dark bread, beet pickle and cheese.

"Fetch me some rope and meet me on the afternoon porch," he said to Tyrrel as he stood. He looked over at Sifrid: the young man was a careful distance from Niiv, keeping the fire pit between them. "There might be some trouble tonight. I need you to walk the fences today, make sure they're all holding. Be sure you go sunwise, not widdershins."

Sifrid nodded.

"And me?" Niiv asked.

"Hex signs need freshening," Irrel said. "You know where the paint is."

He stepped out of the summer kitchen, then turned and went through the door that led into the storage room. He drew a rope-cutting knife from its drawer, then took four thunderstones from their box and went back through the long hall and out onto the afternoon porch. Tyrrel was waiting for him there, sitting on a stool with a pile of rope at his feet.

Irrel settled into the empty stool across from him, put down the knife. "That was quite a charm you did this morning," he said. "Kept it up all the way to the marsh, and with five men there too."

"It's just a children's charm," Tyrrel said; he shrugged, but there was pride evident in his voice. He had always excelled at the craftings children did for mischief, making a leaf fly through the air or a thrown stick return to your hand. His hands were quick like his mother's had been, and he was able to hold his concentration much longer than any other boy his age.

"Well, it's time you learned some proper crafts," Irrel said. He gestured at the coil of rope. "We'll start with knots. Do you know any of those?"

Tyrrel nodded. "Niiv taught me the one to stop a nosebleed, with a red thread."

"All right, let's see you do that one—but with a rope."

Frowning, Tyrrel picked up the knife and cut off an arm's-length of rope. He drew it into a loop, then crossed the standing part and brought it back up through the loop, drawing it tight. He regarded the knot for a moment and then held it up to his father.

"That's the knot your sister taught you?" Irrel asked.

Tyrrel nodded. "I think so. She only showed me once."

"And does it work?"

"Sometimes."

"Maybe to stop a nosebleed, but it won't hold for much else. Untie that and let me show you a real knot." Tyrrel held the rope out to his father, but Irrel shook his head. "No—I'll tell you what to do, and you tie the knot. Hold up the rope and let one end drop: the part you're holding is the standing part. Between that and the end is the bight. Do you have that?"

"Yes, father," Tyrrel said, rolling his eyes a little.

Irrel took a breath and went on. "Drop the end under the standing part and bring it back over. Now draw it back through the loop you've made."

"That's the same knot I did," Tyrrel said.

"It's not—and that's the difference between a knot that holds and one that betrays you. Now make a loop big enough to go over a cow or a horse's head. Mark the point where the loop closes, then tie the knot I just showed you right there. Now make the loop again, so that it crosses just below the first knot—crosses under. Bring the end around and over the standing part, now pass it under and up through the loop."

Tyrrel's hands moved hesitantly, finally pulling hard at the end: it slipped the length of the rope and his knot vanished. "Why can't you just show me?" he asked.

Irrel shook his head. "You have to feel it in your hands."

"Is that what makes a wizard?" Tyrrel asked, looking at his hands. "Did Uncle Allel have clever hands as a boy?"

"Try that knot again," Irrel said. He repeated his instructions, slowly, and this time Tyrrel's knot resolved into a figure eight. "Do you see? That knot brings the loop closed, but the first one keeps it from closing too tight on the animal's neck."

Tyrrel frowned. "That didn't feel like making a charm."

"It wasn't—not yet. The craft comes from doing it right: from tying it so well that your hands move the rope themselves, and you just step out of the way."

"What will it do if I do it right?"

Irrel reached out to touch the loop of rope his son had tied. "That's the Lamb's Knot. It'll keep an animal gentled so long as it's around him."

"Oh," Tyrrel said. "What about the other knots? What do they do?"

"There's no end to them," Irrel said. "There's clever knots that will slip under a thief's fingers or bite like a snake, and wise knots that know the hand that touches them before they loosen or hold. But you be careful, and not just with knots: when you work a craft, it works you too." He looked Tyrrel in the eyes. "Do you understand?"

"Yes," Tyrrel said after a moment.

Irrel held his son's gaze for a moment and then stood. "Here," he said, placing his hands flat against Tyrrel's elbows. "Push against my hands as hard as you can, as though you were trying to spread your wings like a bird."

Tyrrel nodded and began to push. Irrel had to work harder than he had expected to keep the boy's arms at his side, but after a few dozen heartbeats Tyrrel gave up. "Now what?" he asked.

Irrel released the boy's arms and they rose up of their own accord, as though he had been charmed. He looked from one arm to another in amazement.

"D'you see now?" Irrel asked. "Whatever you craft, you're always pushing against something—and it pushes you too."

"I understand," Tyrrel said, in the deadly serious tone he used when he was trying to be grown-up. He frowned. "If I learn knots well enough, do you think I could do magic? Wizard magic?"

"A wizard's just a crafter who doesn't make anything useful. Your mam could craft a candle that brought warmth to anyone in the home, a shoe that made a horse never stumble and jam that let you remember the day the berries were picked: that's magic enough."

Tyrrel said nothing. After a few moments he turned away, untied his knot and began to tie it again, his brow furrowed.

Irrel watched him for a while and then stood. "When it feels like a craft, you'll know," he said. "When that happens, tie a half-dozen or so more. There's like to be some noise tonight, and I want the cattle to stay in their places."

When he went to the barn he could see the work Niiv had done, repainting the hex signs. She had been doing them for years, since she had been about Tyrrel's age, and while he could still discern the shapes of his originals underneath they were clearly her work: much more ornate, with his simple sunwheel shapes fractured and filigreed, and more colourful as well. He admired them for a moment and then took his spade to the northeast corner of the barn. He dug a hole a hand deep and then took from his pouch one of four thunderstones—flat stones shaped like ax-heads, which had been left buried in the ground where lightning bolts had struck—and sang:

Roll, thunder, roll
Down from mountains tall
Where lightning touched once
Let never lightning fall.

With haying time so soon past, the barn might as well be a box of tinder—and he had seen enough to expect fire in the sky tonight. He went sunwise from corner to corner, burying a stone and singing the charm at each one. When he rounded the northwest corner he saw Niiv up on the ladder, freshening the paint on that side's hex signs. When she saw him she stopped her work and came down the ladder.

"Did Sifrid talk to you this morning?" she asked.

Irrel frowned. "Did you not ask him that?"

She laughed. "I think you scared him, father. I haven't seen even his shadow since dinnertime."

"Well. Yes, he did talk to me."

"And?"

He took a slow breath. "And you already know what he said, so what questions could you have of me?"

"Are you happy for me?" she asked, wrinkling her nose with exasperation. "Do you approve? Will you bless our wedding?"

"This is not some fancy then? You haven't just cooked him up a love-apple, or twisted your belt to get him hot?" Like her brother, she had always been skilled at the children's charms: like her mother, hers had served to get the village boys running around after her like puppies.

She crossed her arms. "Father. No. This is real—we both want this. And we . . ."

He let her silence hang in the air. "Your mam could have taught you a crafting for that," he said quietly. "I haven't given you everything she would have, I know. But the wise woman owes me for winter corn—she could . . ."

"It's what I want," Niiv said.

Irrel nodded. "It's love, then? Truly?"

"I don't know," she said. "His father is the best goldsmith in

Rebenstod. We could craft a charm that would make me the most beautiful woman there is."

He smiled. "You are the most beautiful woman there is."

She smiled too, sighing. "I know, Father. But really."

"And do either of you know any handfasts?"

Niiv shrugged. "Sifrid doesn't. I've tied a few, with boys from the village, but . . . Well, they weren't ever meant to last." She looked away, towards the farmhouse, then back to him. "I thought—I was hoping you could teach us the handfast you and mother tied."

Irrel said nothing, holding his hands in front of him: he curled his fingers and then straightened them again, slowly. "No," he said at last. "That's past me now—and besides I needed your mam to tie that."

"Of course," Niiv said.

He let his hands drop, put them on his hips. "You know, when your mam and I were young we spent our winter nights learning handfasts. There was none of that sledding around to farm and village you have today."

"I know, Father."

"There are plenty of fine handfasts I could teach you, ones that will last you a lifetime." He brushed his hands against the front of his pants. "I've got to finish burying these thunderstones and then get on my other work. I'll see you at supper."

When he passed by the porch he saw that Tyrrel was not there: there were about a dozen knotted harnesses lying abandoned on the ground—the first few tangled messes, the rest perfectly tied Lamb's Knots. He sighed and set out to find out how Sifrid was doing with the fence.

He followed the fence's circuit until he heard voices ahead, one a young man's and one a child's—answering the question of where Tyrrel had gone. Irrel looked at his hands and began to move them, stiffly at first, to do the charm his son had done that morning. He had not crafted it since he himself had been a boy, but he found his fingers remembered the motions—held up flat, then turned inwards, then coiled into a ring, bowing, dancing, tucked away into fists—as he quietly chanted the charm:

Ten little men standing straight
Ten little men open the gate
Ten little men all in a ring
Ten little men bow to the king
Ten little men dance all day
Ten little men hide away

Irrel could feel the craft working through him as he did the charm, and unlike his son he did not need to repeat it to keep it going. Sifrid was leaning against the fence, his face covered with dust and his shirt damp with sweat; Tyrrel sat on the fence post, curled like a gargoyle as he interrogated the young man.

"Will you and Niiv live in Rebenstod?" Tyrrel was asking.

"I expect we will, if we get married," Sifrid said.

"Is it a big place? Are there wizards there? Did you ever see my uncle there?"

Sifrid turned to look at the boy. "He passes through from time to time. And it's not as big a place as some, but it's bigger than others. Bigger than your village."

"Does it have a schoolhouse?"

"Several."

Tyrrel nodded sagely. "In the schoolhouses there, do they just teach you children's crafts or do they teach you to be a wizard?"

"I don't know," Sifrid said. He held his fingers splayed out in front of him. "I was never in a schoolhouse: I was apprenticed as soon as I could hold a graver. Every time my hands grew, my father wept." He was silent for a moment. "But you don't need a school to teach you crafting, or your uncle for that matter. I'm sure your father could teach you anything you might want to know."

"Father?" Tyrrel asked. "All he ever does is farm-craftings. He won't even do knots, because of his fingers."

"Maybe now, but he did a great one once—he and your mother, that is. Didn't you ever notice how you're never short of water here? How spring comes a little sooner than in the other farms, and summer stays a little later—fruits ripen without rotting and keep without spoiling? That's from the handfast they tied at their wedding. It bound them to each other in a way no other handfast had ever done—bound them to this farm and it to them, bound even time itself. My father said it was the finest working he ever saw—as great as anything the Margrave or the Thaumaturge ever did."

"Is that why you want to marry my sister?" Tyrrel asked. "To learn our magic?"

Sifrid was silent for a moment. "No," he said. "I want to marry her because I love her."

Tyrrel jumped down from the fence post. "I think that would be a good reason to marry somebody," he said.

A growing noise had been coming from up the road, and now it resolved itself into the tread of dozens or hundreds of men, marching together in ragged rhythm: soldiers, as many leaning on their spears as carrying them, and each with a holed coin sewn over his heart to protect him. Not the Margrave's things, Irrel could see: these had to be the Prince's men.

"Come back to the house," he called to Tyrrel and Sifrid.

"I want to watch."

"Tyrrel. To the house, now."

The boy threw him an angry look and then began walking slowly towards the house. Irrel kept his eyes on the Prince's soldiers: they were not nearly so wild as the Margrave's beasts, but desperate men could do desperate things.

"Karten told me they're letting people shelter inside the walls at Rebenstod," Sifrid said quietly. "We could be there by nightfall if we rode."

"I'll tie the holdfast," Irrel said. "We'll be safe."

"Yes, I know," Sifrid said. "I just thought—"

"We'll be safe."

Without another word they went back to the farmhouse. Irrel and Niiv brought the animals from the pasture back into the barn, dropping the tally sticks into the pail to keep from counting the cattle too closely. Then it was time for supper: Irrel sat on a bench facing his daughter, eating his bread and soup in silence, while Tyrrel sat beside Sifrid, peppering the young man with questions.

HOLDFAST

They sat around the small fire for a while after supper, while Niiv did the dishes; then it was time for Tyrrel to go to bed. Irrel opened the bed-closet and crouched to tuck his son into the quilts, reciting the night-charm:

Touch your collar
Touch your toes
Never catch a fever
Touch your knee
Touch your chin
Never let the burglar in

Tyrrel giggled when his father tapped his chin, then smiled sleepily. "Do you think Uncle Allel will ever come to see us here?" he asked.

"I don't know," Irrel said. "He's a busy man."

"Could we go to visit him? It's not right, you know, that I've never seen my uncle, and I'm almost a man."

Irrel shook his head. "I can't be travelling, you know that. I've the farm to care for, and in the winter the roads are no good." He took a breath. "But you might, perhaps—now that you're almost a man. Or perhaps he'll come to Rebenstod to see your sister, when she marries, and you can see him then."

"Yes," Tyrrel said, his eyes half-shut. "Yes, I think so."

Irrel crouched there for a few moments more, listening to his son's breathing settle into the slow rhythm of sleep; then he rose, with some difficulty, and went back out into the long hall. It was nearly dark, lit only by the embers of the small fire in the main room, and he did not know where Sifrid and Niiv had gone. Sighing, he went out the main door and up the path to the gate.

He took the previous night's holdfast from where he had hung it on the fencepost, untied it and began work on the new one. None of the standard knots would be strong enough, not with what was likely to happen that night, but he might start with a Sheep's Tail knot for a base: holding the end of the rope towards him he made an overhand loop, then passed the end through it and up behind

273

the standing part. He passed the end down through the loop a second time and then continued to elaborate the knot, feeling his fingers soften like butter as the craft began to work through him. Soon he had a knot that would hold against the Margrave and the Thaumaturge both, but he did not stop. As the rope danced in his hands, twisting around and around itself and slipping over and under the loops he had made, he knew that if he wanted to he could tie a knot that would be greater even than the handfast he and Eliis had made: a knot that would hold everything just as it was, bind them all and hold fast against time and chance. He held the end of the rope in his hand and took a breath.

The night passed, as all nights eventually do: but it never grew very dark, with spells, lightning and dragon-fire lighting the sky. Unable to sleep, Irrel went to the summer kitchen, kicked at the coals in the fire pit until he exposed a glowing ember and lit a candle from it. Then he went to the storage room and hauled up the trap door to the cellar before going carefully down the stairs. In the dim light of the candle it took him a while to find what he was looking for: a few jars of blackberry jam, hidden away in memory of the day he and Niiv had gone foraging in the bush and Eliis had preserved the few berries they had brought home. He went back upstairs and sat on the bench by the cold ashes of the fire, licking the dark jam from his fingers.

When true dawn finally came he went outside and surveyed the farm. The barn was entirely intact, even the hex signs unmarked, and the stable door still held. He walked down the path to the gate and kneeled down to untie the holdfast, feeling the craft dissipate as he loosened the knot.

"Morning find you!" Allren was coming down the road towards him, the front of his hat pulled down low to block out the morning sun.

"And you."

Allren stood on the other side of the gate, his hands on his hips. "Did you hear? The Prince's men prevailed, if you can believe it. Why, they say the Thaumaturge himself took part in the battle." He tilted his hat upwards as a grin crossed his face. "The Margrave is overthrown!"

Irrel undid the last loop and hung the now-slack rope on the fencepost. He stood up and nodded slowly, brushing the dirt from his knees.

"Well, there's that."

THE COLDEST WAR

"I may be gone for some time," Gord had said.

It was their only joke, and like everything else in the base it had been worn smooth with use and re-use: Stan and Gord each said it before leaving the base, every time they went out to walk the inuksuit and fire the flare, their way of laughing at the dark.

The whole island was just over a kilometre square; on a good day, Defence had calculated the whole circuit would take just over three hours. The problem was that Hans Island had no good days. At this time of year there were hardly any days at all: only a little over an hour of grey twilight around noon, the remaining time given over to the endless Arctic dark.

Stan glanced at his watch, put down his book and went to start the Coleman stove. Though it was substantially warmer within Base Hearn than outside, where kerosene turned thick and white as lard, it still took the stove a few minutes to heat up; while he waited Stan unpacked two dozen frozen Tim Hortons doughnuts and a can of coffee. It was a challenge, getting the six thousand calories they needed each day, but the doughnuts and coffee were more than a contribution towards that: the two half-hour overlaps between their shifts were the only time either of them saw another human being each day, and the ritual helped them pretend that they were back in the real world—not planting a frozen toehold for Canada in a place so remote even the Inuit considered it uninhabitable.

Before long the stove was hissing with a bright blue flame, but Gord had not returned. Stan checked his watch: 14:35, just five minutes late—six hours was normally enough time to get from base to base, but with the storm he could hear howling outside it might easily take more. He turned the stove low, just hot enough to keep the fuel liquid, picked up the one-volume Deptford Trilogy and started reading, careful not to lose Gord's place.

It was around 14:45 when Stan checked his watch again, and he decided to brew the coffee and fry the first dozen doughnuts. He had to give himself a good ten minutes to suit up, not to mention warming his hands enough that he could stand to insert the catheter, so he unsealed the pack of frozen doughnuts and tossed them in the skillet. The smell quickly filled the small space, the fat surrounding each doughnut melting and starting to sizzle, and when the coffee aroma joined it Stan could almost imagine he was home.

When another ten minutes had passed he began to worry. Gord was now almost a half-hour late, and Stan began to wonder if something had happened to him. Of course, he might just be holed up in Base Franklin; they were under strict radio silence—anything battery-powered died within a week in this cold, anyway, and their hand-crank radios could receive but not send—so there was no way to communicate between the two bases, just thirty-five metres apart as the goose flew. No way, for that matter, to send a cry for help.

Stan sighed, drank the last of his coffee; a layer of frost had already begun to creep inwards from the rim of the mug. "Sorry, Gord," he said as he shut off the stove's low flame, hoping the fuel would not have time to thicken again before Gord got back. He pulled his undersuit off the hook, stepped to the middle of the room where he could stand up straight and stepped into it, cotton and Kevlar covering everything but his mouth and eyes. Then he popped a bulb of hydrating gel into his mouth, minty and medicinal, and stepped to the first door of the heatlock.

He reached towards the emergency override before stopping himself. If something had happened to Gord—if he wasn't just late, hadn't just decided to wait out the weather at Base Franklin—what if it hadn't been an accident? What if there was a Dane out there?

It was no secret the Danes wanted them gone; it was their government, after all, that disputed ownership of the island with Canada—the only reason anyone cared about a barren hunk of rock halfway between Ellesmere Island and Greenland. Or not exactly halfway, as each government claimed. Hans Island was at the edge of a strait that had opened up in recent years, in summer at least, making a Northwest Passage finally viable for commercial shipping; if the island was Canadian then so was the strait, and if it wasn't the strait was international waters. For want of a nail, the horse was lost. . . .

Neither Canada nor Denmark, both NATO allies, were willing to fight over it. That was why he and Gord were there: to live for twelve full months on the island, firing a flare each day at the two times satellites passed overhead, to prove Canadians lived there year-round. Gord and Stan had been detailed from the Ranger base at Alert when no Inuit had been found willing to do it; even for them this was no place to live. As for the Danes. . . .

Stan drew his hand back, let the heatlock cycle at its normal rate. They had seen no sign of Danes since they had arrived the previous spring, but in planning the mission Defence had assumed they would face some covert attempts to interrupt their stay, come up with as many countermeasures as they could. The heatlock was one of those, designed to prevent the expulsion of too much warm air that might betray the location of the camouflaged base. With no knowledge of what similar technologies the Danes might have—only that they were likely ahead in the race—Equipment, Procurement and Supply had done what they could while Stan and Gord trained in the near North, learning lower-tech survival skills.

After what felt like forever the outer door opened. By that time Stan was chilled through, despite his insulated undersuit. The outersuit was hanging a few metres away from a hook attached to the heat baffle that rose over the base. Unlike the undersuit, which was designed to keep him warm, the outersuit kept the air around him cool: it was basically a man-shaped thermos, filled with gel-packs that stayed liquid to sixty below, absorbing and storing the heat he threw off so he would have no infrared signature. The breathing mask drew air in from outside, cold and dry, but stored his exhaled air in cooling chambers before expelling it, again to keep him as cold as the world around him. Outside the suit was Kevlar covered with a layer of a nanofiber that tuned itself to the ambient light around it, grey in twilight and black in darkness; the headpiece's visor, sealed away from his breathing mask to avoid fogging, was an insulated crystal display that gave him a digital feed in IR as well as the visible spectrum. He looked like the Michelin Man with it all on, but in this terrain he was nearly invisible to conventional or IR sight.

Flexing the suit's stiff fingers Stan opened the gun locker, picked up his Ross Polar III and slung it over his shoulder. He patted his hip pocket to make sure the flare pistol was there and then followed the curve of the heat baffle, emerging halfway up the steep slope that led from the cliff on which Base Hearn sat to the flat top of the island where the flare station was. Out of the shelter he felt the force of the wind on him, blowing pebbly snow hard enough to make him glad of the suit's extra mass.

He switched on the light intensifier, the sky almost fully dark at 15:10—this near to the solstice just a few hours passed between dawn and dusk. The island was barren and nearly featureless, a wrinkled rock that rose up high at one end and sloped down to a stony beach at the other; he tuned the contrast on the video feed way up, exaggerating the many creases and fissures in the ground enough so that he could actually see them, turning all into dark lines that looked like they had been drawn on the ground with a felt-tip marker.

At this end of the island there was no horizon; to his right were the cliffs and the endless, frozen sea, to his left the rocky slope that rose up at an unclimbable angle. He followed the ridge he was on until the first inukshuk came into view. This one they had nicknamed Atii, "Let's go" in Inuktitut; it looked the most like the inuksuit you saw in the south, a vaguely man-shaped pile of rocks with legs, arms and head, the whole thing about a half-metre tall. They had built eight of these around the island, all different: as well as checkpoints they served as sentries, the thought being that someone unfamiliar with the island would likely stumble over one and knock it over. The first one, built where the lower ridge climbed up towards the island's flat top, was undisturbed, so Stan sighted the second and headed for it.

It took him a minute to notice what was wrong: this inukshuk, called Howa-ii or "turn left," should have one arm longer than the other, pointing to its right. Instead it looked like the first one, arms and legs symmetrical. Someone had been here, someone who did not know how the different inuksuit were supposed to look.

Stan checked the timer readout on his visor: 15:53, still almost two hours until he had to fire the flare. He left the inukshuk as it was, to warn Gord if he was still out here, and started the climb up to the plateau at the top of the island. This was one of the few possible approaches, and even here it was a rise of nearly forty-five degrees, going up four metres in a distance just over that; he leaned into the climb, keeping his gaze moving back and forth to spot any moving objects or IR sources.

He was halfway up the slope when he saw something, or thought he did: whatever it was didn't throw off any heat, and even with the contrast at maximum it was hard to tell a rounded grey shape from the sloping rocks. It might have been Gord, or a Dane, or nothing; before Stan could get a second look his foot caught in one of the island's deeper folds. He pitched forward, striking the hard ground with a crack before rolling down the slope.

Not quite unconscious, Stan's mind swam as he struggled to right himself. The suit's weight fought against him, making him slide further down the slope before he could get to his feet. Standing uneasily he looked around. To his dismay, none of the inuksuit were in sight. Their third function was as landmarks: each part of the island looked much like every other part, its steep rise and fall making it impossible to see any distance except from the plateau.

You're in a house where all four walls face south, he thought. A bear walks by. What colour is the bear? This near to the Pole, a compass was useless; on a clear day he might spot the North Star, but today was far from that. He checked the time readout: 16:20, an hour and a half till the fifteen-minute window during which he needed to fire the flare. He might head straight up, but there were few enough manageable approaches to the plateau that he could spend hours getting there. Better just to follow the path of least resistance: that was where they had placed the inuksuit, at points where anyone walking the island was likely to pass. If he could find one he recognized he would know where he was—assuming it was still intact.

That reminded him of the figure he had seen, or might have seen, just before falling, and he suddenly wondered whether his fall might have damaged the suit. The head of the suit was able to tilt far enough down for him to see that he wasn't radiating from the front, but there was only one way to tell if he had a sign that read SHOOT ME in IR on his back; sighing, he lay down on the ground, watched a few minutes tick off. Enough heat would have gotten out to visibly warm the stones by now if he was bright, so with effort he rose again and turned around. Nothing: the million-dollar product of Canadian ingenuity and second-hand NASA technology had survived a fall. Letting out a dry breath Stan started his way downhill, not having to remind himself to take the easy path.

He saw the ocean first, the endless frozen waves of Kennedy Channel, almost missed the inukshuk that stood a few metres before the shore. As he neared he saw that the upper stones were leaned against one another to make a V, or a pair of arms held skywards. Now he knew where he was: the southern shore, only about twenty metres and a gentle slope from Base Franklin. Now that he had his bearings he could get there, check on Gord, and still get up to the flare station in plenty of time; knowing where he was he could even see the building, its camouflaged dome barely visible against the curve of the island.

Before he had covered half the distance he saw that he had been wrong to think the suit had not been damaged. It was not leaking heat, but he could see now that the seal between his breathing mask and visor had been broken: dry as his breath was it was starting to fog up the panel, and before long he would be blind.

He could not change his plan: there was no use heading for the flare station if he couldn't see to fire the flare. If he made it to Base

Franklin while he could still see, though, he might be able to get a spare, or repair the seal—or Gord might be there, might tell him that he had fired the morning flare and there was nothing to worry about. Then they could both laugh, share coffee and doughnuts and forget about this whole business.

Stan forced himself to slow down. He had to keep his breathing shallow, slow the frost forming on his visor. The base was so close; it took everything he had to keep his strides even, his heart quiet. Moving this slowly he had too much time to think—about what might have happened to Gord, about the visor, about the Danish rifle that might be pointed at him. Though he knew he was still dark he felt terribly exposed, and could not help letting out a long breath when he reached Base Franklin. Near to the beach end, this base rose up away from the ocean, presenting its rounded grey face to the rest of the island. With stiff fingers Stan flipped up the cover for the keypad, punched in the code for the heatlock.

It didn't open.

Forcing himself to hold his breath, Stan tried again, punching the numbers carefully with the stylus-tip on his right index finger. Again, nothing.

What was going on here? Frost lacework was creeping in from the edges of his visor; Stan realized he was hyperventilating, forced himself to count to sixty to slow himself down. The timer was covered now, illegible.

Scanning from right to left, Stan noticed that there was no rifle outside the base. That wasn't like Gord: he knew to leave his weapon in the gun locker outside—any condensation from a change in temperature would freeze and ruin it when you went back out. Slowly, Stan circled the small, slanted building, confirmed there was no rifle anywhere around it. Gord had left his gun somewhere else, then, or he had been forced to go inside without taking the time to drop it—or whoever was in there wasn't Gord.

He was nearly blind now, and realized he would have to leave that question for later. Just about ten metres away, buried in a fissure that ran most of the way across the island, was one of their two bolt holes—caches of emergency supplies, in case they should be caught outside the shelters. Something in there might help him, if he could get to it.

Though this end of the island sloped more gently it was still a rough climb, especially since he could not see his feet. He had to be near the fissure now: he dropped to his knees and began to crawl, feeling the ground ahead of him as the world outside faded to white. Finally it was gone entirely, the only evidence of it the wind howling in his pickups.

His left hand touched something softer than rock, and he knew he had made it: the fissure was one of the only places on the island where snow collected. Stan thrust his arm into the snow as far as it would go, slowly crawled along the fissure until he felt hard plastic. Still fighting to keep his breathing even he cleared the snow off the bolt hole's lid and began to pry it open, both arms fighting against the stiff hinge. For a moment all his strength left him; after a second's rest he tried again, a loud crack telling him that he had not opened but broken it.

Stan reached into the box, felt around for the tools and supplies that lay inside. There was no question now of repairing the seal, not without being able to see what he was doing. Instead he fumbled for the ice-knife he knew was in there, part of the igloo-building kit, and drew its butt end sharply towards his visor.

It did not feel right, swinging a sharp, heavy object at his face, and his first few blows fell lightly. On the fourth try he closed his eyes, brought the knife full force into the blinded visor. At first he could see no effect, but as he kept swinging cracks appeared, lines of darkness crossing the pure white of his vision. He switched hands and swung again, bashing the wooden handle against the plastic until finally it splintered and cracked.

Now it was truly dark: he had no IR to see by, no night-vision. At least the storm had stopped, just enough light falling from the hazy sky for him to make out the shape of the ground around him. As he stood and looked around, the wind cold on his face, Stan suddenly realized he was bright where the visor had broken. He scooped snow up from the fissure and packed it into his visor and rose again, his face burning, and tried to sight the trail that would lead up to the flare station.

The flare would be easy enough to find, probably only twenty metres or so away, but it was also the one place a Dane would be sure of finding him. He had no choice: he didn't know if Gord had succeeded in firing the morning flare, so if he didn't fire this one nearly a year spent on the island could go to waste.

Despite his freezing face Stan forced himself to move slowly, again being given unwanted time to think. What could have happened to Gord? If there was a Dane on the island, why now? It wasn't the longest night of the year, or the coldest day; those had both passed weeks ago. There was nothing he could think of that might have upset the balance of power, unless it was some new technological development—

"Son of a bitch," Stan said, cursed himself as his exhalations puffed out like word balloons. That had to be it: the Danes had perfected the heat-silenced gun.

There were two reasons nobody had expected an attack. The first was that the suits, when they were working, made Stan and Gord almost invisible; since any Danish operation would have to be covert, not an all-out assault, that by itself would probably be enough to prevent it. The Danes probably had similar suits, which brought up the other reason: every time a rifle was fired the barrel got hot, lighting up the shooter in IR. That meant that even if you could sight your target you had just one shot before you made yourself extremely visible, and given the Kevlar layer of the suits one shot was unlikely to finish anybody off.

Defence had spent a lot of time and money trying to solve the problem but eventually gave up, consoling themselves that the Danes had probably failed as well. But what if they hadn't? What if the Canadian presence on the island had pushed them to develop some way to instantly cool the gun barrel, or mask its heat signature? With a heat silencer you could fire any number of shots without giving your own position away—and heavy though they were, the suits weren't made to stand up to serious fire.

By now Stan's heart was beating fast, his strides quickening as the flare station came into view. He looked from side to side; seeing nothing in the dark he broke into a run. At the edge of his vision something moved, and he froze: covered his face with his arm, hoping to block whatever heat was coming from his face as the snow melted. The storm had picked up again, making too much noise for him to hear anything else. He turned to face into the wind, dropped his arm and waited until his face began to numb. Then he slowly turned around, watching.

He started as he saw a shape, tall and clear against the sky; let out a breath when he realized it was the flare station, just a few metres away. Once more covering his eyes with his arm he walked blindly for it, feeling ahead of him with his free hand until he reached it.

The flare station was a simple structure, mostly wood and stone, a framework tower three metres tall. In the middle sat the flare cannon, just a tube and a foot-trigger; two hourglasses, one red and one blue, were hung from the frame on horizontal spits. They were meant as a backup in case the time displays in their suits failed, as electronic things so often did here, and also as a sign that the flare had been fired: once that was done they turned their hourglass over. Both the glass and the sand inside were made of synthetics that did not expand or contract with temperature, so that they would reliably tick out twenty-four hours every day. The sand was supposed to be luminous as well, but at this time of year it did not absorb enough light to glow. Without his visor, Stan could see neither whether Gord had turned his over nor if his had run out.

The storm had let up once more, and something on the ground shone with a hint of starlight. Moving slowly, Stan moved to see what it was. He crouched down, felt the smooth barrel of a rifle. Once it was off the ground he could see that it was a Ross Polar, which made it Gord's: the Danes used Arctic Magnums.

Stan straightened up, looked around once more. If the rifle was here and Gord was nowhere nearby, then he had probably dropped it after firing, to escape its heat signature. Wishing he could tell whether the barrel was still hot Stan hung the rifle from the tower by its shoulder strap, scanned the horizon once more. Now that the storm had cleared the ocean reflected the dim light from the sky, surrounding the dark rock of the island and stretching out as far as he could see. If Gord hadn't been able to make it to the base he might have gone out there: in their training they had learned that sea ice was a better place to make a shelter, at least in winter, since the liquid water beneath was warmer than the ground. Even if he had still had his visor, though, it would have been impossible to spot anyone among the endless frozen waves.

He turned back to the hourglasses. He needed light to see whether his hourglass was near empty, whether Gord's had been turned, but anything that let him see would let the Dane see him. On the other hand, if someone weren't expecting light. . . .

Leaning against the flare station, Stan drew his flare pistol with his left hand while shading his eyes with his free arm. He turned towards the hourglasses and fired the flare away, out into the dark; in the brief light he just had time to see that his hourglass, the blue one, was nearly empty. The satellite was overhead, its eye on the flare station for no more than ten minutes. Hoping the Dane, if he was out there, was still blinded by the flare Stan turned his back on the tower and hit the foot-trigger.

A sizzling ball of fire flew straight up out of the cannon, for a moment illuminating the whole island. In that second Stan saw a dark shape off to his right, spun towards it and brought up his rifle. His stiff and clumsy fingers found the oversized trigger and he fired without thinking, heard a dull wet sound that told him he had hit his target.

"Shit!" Stan said, twisting to shrug out of his rifle's shoulder-strap. Now he had two useless rifles, at least until he could be sure Gord's had cooled. He circled to the other side of the flare station, keeping his back to it, and tried to slow his breathing. The snow on his face had melted; he was unarmed, visible, and had just marked his position for the world to see. He brought his forearms up together to cover his face and chest, waiting for the volley of shots that were sure to come, forced his stuttering breaths down into his mask so that no wisps of steam would betray him.

Eventually his heart slowed, and he risked a look out between his arms. Why hadn't the Dane attacked? He would never get a better opportunity. Unless—Stan remembered the wet sound he had heard when he fired. If Stan's shot had burst one of the Dane's gel packs he would be leaking heat, and if the Dane didn't know Stan's visor was broken he would think Stan could see him. That was why he hadn't fired back: a hot weapon could be dropped, but you couldn't shake a bright spot on your chest.

Where was he, then? Not still lurking out there, if he thought Stan could see him. He would have to go for shelter, somewhere he thought he could repair his suit or just make a stand. That meant either Base Hearn or Base Franklin. Stan moved slowly around the flare station, keeping his back to it, spotted one of the inuksuit a half-dozen metres away. There was only one of those on the plateau, the one they called Hulla or "turn right," which pointed the way to Base Franklin. The other way, then, led back to Base Hearn.

During the storm snow had piled up against the flare station; Stan picked up a double handful and packed it into his broken visor, leaving just enough room to see out. This time he did not feel the cold, his skin numb to the snow's touch. Now he was invisible again.

At this end of the island the edge of the plateau was a sharp drop, nearly two metres to the next ridge. Only at the point marked by the inukshuk was the slope manageable, but Stan could not see it: either it had been knocked down or the night was simply too dark. He traced the edge carefully, the ground a murky darkness below, until he felt sure he had sighted the heat baffle that hid Base Hearn. He sat, dangled his legs over the edge and slid down, not knowing how far he was going to fall until his feet hit the ground. His right knee flexed painfully with the impact and he fell onto his side, the wind knocked out of him and rising like a cloud. He stood up carefully, sighted the heat baffle and began limping towards it, once more following the path of least resistance.

He would not have noticed the heat baffle if he had not known it was there. They had built it from their supply crates, then covered it with the same fabric as their suits so that it looked like part of the island. He crept towards it, holding his breath. His heart thudded heavily in his ears with every step.

A thought occurred to him, and he stopped. The passage between the baffle and the base was narrow, just over a half-metre wide; if the Dane was waiting for him there, rather than inside the base, he would be impossible to miss—and the suit would not protect him from a few well-grouped shots to the chest, or a single lucky one to the face. It was more likely that the Dane had gone inside—he couldn't wait forever—but there was no way for Stan to know. If he went in there he might be stepping right into the face of death.

A moment later he thought of a worse possibility. What if there was no Dane? What if it was Gord?

He hadn't wondered before how the Dane had come to the island—he had supposed it was by snowmobile or dogsled, which he had left out on the ice—but now it felt suspicious. And how had he known how to reprogram the heatlock to Base Franklin? How had he made his way around the island so easily?

But if it was Gord, why was he doing it? Was it just that the dark, the cold, the isolation had driven him mad?

Had *he* been driven mad?

Had he mixed up which inukshuk he was looking at, at the very beginning? Had the heatlock at Base Franklin simply been jammed? He had fired at a shape in the dark, though: if it wasn't the Dane it had to have been Gord. Gord might think he was the Dane, or just that he had tried to kill him. That he was crazy.

Stan stood there for a long time. He was starting to feel hot, beads of sweat forming on his forehead and dripping down, frozen, into his eyes. The gel packs in the suit were near their limit: he would have to take it off soon, let them cool down again, or they would overload and start to shed heat. Finally he decided what he had to do.

It made no difference whether it was Gord or a Dane, who had attacked whom, who was mad and who was sane. He could not risk the narrow passage between the heat baffle and the base, and Base Franklin was closed to him. It didn't matter, though. All that mattered was that the flare was fired at least once a day. He only had to make it a few more months, until spring came and his year was up.

Stan turned, started to make his way back towards the bolt hole. He could not stay on the island. It was too small and exposed, and without a shelter the rock would draw heat from him so quickly he would be dead by morning. Better to go out on the ice where it was warmer, build an igloo from the snow that was out there, piled up against the waves. He had been trained to build one in just a few hours, and once inside he would be warm enough to survive. In the brief light of the next noon he might even be able to repair his suit: there were tools in the bolt hole, a spare faceplate he could put on when he had time and privacy, as well as a stash of flares and emergency rations.

He made sure to take more than he thought he would need. After all, he might be gone for some time.

WRITTEN BY THE WINNERS

Dave glanced over his shoulder, leaned in close so that his body blocked the screen. He had been sifting through old TV comedies for weeks now, screening every episode frame by frame for inconsistencies, but today he had made a real find—a few lines of dialogue on Family Ties that referred to Richard Nixon.

There was no predicting where remnants like this would appear. The device that had changed time was more like a shotgun than a scalpel: it had established the present its makers wanted through hundreds of different changes to the timeline, some contradicting others. The result was a porous, makeshift new history that made little sense, but the old one had been thoroughly smashed to bits. It was those bits that remained that he and his whole department were tasked by the new history's makers with finding and erasing.

Most of what he found was much more innocuous, references to things that had little ideological power but simply had not existed in the new history. This one, though, had meaning, a direct reference to a political event in the old history. He looked around again, drew a tape from the bottom drawer of his desk, slipped it into the second recorder and hit COPY. He could feel his heart beating more quickly as the seconds ticked by, felt the pressure of seen and unseen eyes on his back; finally the inconsistency was over, ending as abruptly as it began, and he was able to breathe.

The danger past, he felt a rush of exhilaration. It had been more than a month since he had had anything to present to the group, but this would more than make up for the dry spell. He logged the original clip and then deleted it, consigning another inconsistency to the dustbin of history. He decided it was no use trying to work for a while, after the excitement of making and hiding the copy, so he got up out of his chair and went to the kitchen.

Maura was there, biting open a bulb of milk and squeezing it into her coffee, a few strands of her long red hair loose and stuck to her mug. She looked up as he came in and smiled, and for a second he thought about reaching out and brushing her hair off of the cup; instead he simply gestured to it. She smiled again, her cheeks colouring a bit, and freed it with a toss of her head.

"Working hard?" she asked.

He shrugged. "No harder than directed," he said.

She laughed, threw him what he thought was a conspiratorial look. Maura was one of the few people in the office he could talk to at all: most of the others were either Party members striving to be noticed or else had been ground down to grey dullness by the endless frame-by-frame searches that filled their days. "Big plans for the weekend?" she asked.

"Nothing too exciting. I might have to buy new shoes."

"There's a sale at Ogilvy's, I think," Maura said. "You should try there." She blew on her coffee, took a sip. "I might go there this weekend myself."

Dave nodded. Could he bring himself to suggest that they go together, maybe out for lunch or a drink afterward? Was she fishing for that? When he opened his mouth, though, his earlier confidence had left him, and he felt the moment pass in silence. "Maybe I'll see you there," he said at last.

"Sure," she said, moved to step past him. "I'd better get back to work, before Chadwick sees I'm away from my station."

"Me too."

Maura frowned. "Shouldn't you get your coffee first?"

"Oh—right," Dave said, laughed. "Well, see you later."

"Bye."

He watched her go, trying not to be too obvious about it, then turned to the coffee machine. Stupid, he thought—but had he been wrong in seeing something there, hearing an invitation? If only he hadn't lost his nerve. . . . After tonight's meeting, he thought, and the reception his find would get, he would have confidence to spare. Tomorrow he would try again, and this time he would push the conversation as far as it would go.

The rest of the day passed slowly, but finally it was over. After checking again to make sure no-one was looking Dave ejected the tape from the second recorder, slipped it into his briefcase and went to clock out. He put on his coat and his outdoor shoes, stepped outside. The snow had finally been cleared, three days after the storm, and already the banks were grey with dirt. A half-dozen cars, their ancient chassis recovered with plastic shells in jolly hues, moved slowly down the street; like the road the sidewalk was slick with ice, the cold seeping right through his thin plastic shoes as he turned left, headed for downtown.

Halfway down the first block his right shoe cracked. Looks like I will be shoe shopping tomorrow after all, he thought to himself as he crouched down, opened his briefcase and took out some briefing papers; separating out one page he folded it and then stuffed it into his shoe, hoping it would keep out the slush until he had reached his destination.

As he began to straighten up Dave noticed someone behind him, half-hidden behind the high stairway leading to the Justice building: a tall man in a dark coat, looking nonchalant but coincidentally stopped at the same time as he was. Careful not to look too long at the man, Dave set out again, starting on a zigzag path once he was out of the government district and into downtown. Here the streets were more crowded with pedestrians, most dressed in bright colours that fought against the creeping grey mist. The new history weighed relatively lightly on its subjects: they were still free to shop, to enrich themselves as best they could, to wear or consume what they liked—and for most people that was enough.

After a dozen twists and turns he risked a glance back behind him. Confident that he had lost his shadower—if indeed the man had been following him at all—he returned to his original route and made his way to the meeting place. This week they were gathering at Paul Beatty's house; Paul, an electrician, was one of the few members of the group who could be sure they weren't being watched. Paul was already there, of course—he had the freedom to make his own hours, and always quit work early when the meeting was to be at his place—and as Dave rounded the corner he saw two figures silhouetted in the light of Paul's open door. Dave knew Gilberto Lorca by his slouch hat and ever-present umbrella, but he did not recognize the young woman with him. He waved but they did not see him, and he was forced to knock on the door when he got there. Dave stood still, careful to be in full view of the spy hole, until the door opened.

"C'mon in," Paul said. He was wearing jeans and a heavy sweater, as usual, and a pair of thick-framed black glasses around whose arms were twisted wires of various colours. "We're just about to start."

Dave followed Paul into the hallway and took off his shoes, careful not to worsen the crack in the right one, then hung his coat on the crowded hook. "Am I the last?" he asked.

"Maybe," Paul said, not turning back as he spoke. "We may not get anyone else. Give it five more minutes."

Nodding, Dave followed into the living room. Gil and the woman Dave didn't know were already seated on the couch, another man next to them and a half-dozen others in chairs around the room. Dave knew most of them by face but not by name. They each knew as few names as possible: this was dangerous work they were engaged in, committing a crime so grave the law could not even name it. They were studying history.

"Why don't we get started," Gil said, his tone making it a statement rather than a question. Gil had recruited the earliest members—it was he who had brought Dave in, back when Dave had been an undergraduate studying the new history—and he had a tendency to hold court at meetings, even when they were at other people's homes.

"Fine," Paul said, taking a seat in the chair nearest to the front door.

Dave sat down as well, his briefcase in his lap; his fingers played on the catches, waiting for his chance to tell the others about his find.

"My young friend here has made a very exciting discovery," Gil said. He turned to the woman sitting squeezed between him and the arm of the black leather couch. "My dear, why don't you tell everyone about it?"

Dave's fingers gripped his briefcase as the woman stood. She was not tall, just an inch or two over five feet, and a bit heavy: she wore a blue mock-neck sweater and a denim skirt that stopped just above the knee, her brown hair cut in a bob that had been allowed to grow shaggy. "Hello," she said, glancing around the room. "I'm—"

"No names," Paul said.

The girl nodded quickly. "Right," she said, then twisted around and leaned down to pick up an artist's portfolio that was leaned against the arm of the couch. "I'm— I'm a student in Professor— I mean—"

"It's all right," Gil said. "We all know *my* name."

Dave frowned. He had been looking forward to this all day, had little patience now for Gil's flirting with his latest protégé. "What do you have to show us?" he asked, trying to sound supportive of the girl while he hurried her along.

"Well—I—I found this at a yard sale." The girl unzipped the portfolio carefully, drew out a flat, square object about a foot long on each side. It took Dave a moment to recognize it as an LP; the side facing him had only white text on a black background, too small to be read. The girl flipped the record over so that the front cover could be seen. It bore a picture of a blonde woman with a guitar, dressed in black leather, and some nonsense words in large, jagged letters. After a second Dave remembered to read them left to right: TOP HITS OF THE EIGHTIES.

"The number one hit for each year," Gil said. "The whole decade."

Dave leaned forward. Despite his jealousy he could not help feeling excited about this, a physical survival of the old history. It wasn't just that such things were illegal; they were terribly fragile, even if they were plastic or metal. Accidents had a way of happening to them, as though the new timeline itself wanted them destroyed.

And now—the girl drew the record itself carefully out of the sleeve, eliciting a gasp from her attentive audience. Ten songs the new history had erased; ten songs that did not exist anywhere but on that flimsy piece of vinyl. . . .

After a few moments the excitement began to wear off. There was something different about this artefact, something dangerous. The other things they had collected were oddities, pieces that did not fit into the new history, but this directly challenged that history in a way its masters could not allow. If you were found with it they would not bother with self-criticism or re-education: you, it, and everyone who knew of it would simply disappear.

If any of the other group members shared Dave's worry, though, he did not see it. They passed the record carefully around the room, reading song titles aloud and humming as the memory rushed back—four of them singing "Every Breath You Take," piecing the words together. When it had gone all the way around the group, back to Gil and the beaming girl, the other finds were presented; a postcard from Washington, a Mutt and Jeff cartoon, a newspaper article about a baseball game between two teams that had never existed. When Dave's turn finally came the excitement had been drained out of him and he presented it with little fanfare, responding with just a nod to Gil's praise.

When the last artefact had been presented and logged—it was Gil who took the risk of recording everything, keeping the information in one place so that one day he would be able to reconstruct the old history—Paul brought out a bottle of Glenfiddich that would have been thirty years old if it had ever existed and poured out glasses for everyone in the room. Now the conversation turned back to Gil's student and her find. Gil's pride in both was clear, and while he still felt a gnawing worry in his stomach it was hard for Dave to remain jealous. Before long the meeting broke up and they started to head out, singly or in pairs, careful to space out their exits and take different routes away from the house.

Dave slept poorly that night, awoke feeling little rested; he brewed an extra cup of coffee, breaking his own rule, and paid for it as he was forced to find a restaurant halfway to work that would let him use their washroom. Finally he stopped at a doughnut shop, bought another cup of coffee in exchange for the privilege and made it to the Broadcast and Media building fifteen minutes late. Hoping his tardiness would go unnoticed, he made his way to his workstation and sat down.

"Lawson," a voice came from behind him. It was Chadwick, his supervisor.

"I'm sorry I'm late," Dave said, trying to remember the excuse he had concocted on his way there.

"Never mind that. I've got someone here who wants to meet you."

Dave nodded and stood up, followed Chadwick out of the work area and into the conference room. It was designed to house two dozen people but now held only one.

"This is Mr. Geraci," Chadwick said, stepping aside to let Dave pass into the room. "He's from upstairs. Does performance reviews."

Geraci stood. He was a heavy man but all muscle; he wore a black plastic overcoat, a red plaid scarf crossed loosely over his chest. Two beige folders sat open on the table in front of him. "Mr. Lawson," he said, reaching a hand out. "It is a pleasure to meet you."

"Thank you," Dave said. Geraci's hand was extended straight out across the long oval table, and Dave had to bend awkwardly to take it. "What do you—what can I do for you?"

"We have received good words about your performance," Geraci said, not releasing Dave's hand. "Your logs, your records are very good, without blots."

"Thank you," Dave said, struggling to unwind Geraci's syntax. He glanced behind him, saw that Chadwick had left. "I do the best that I can."

"Yes," Geraci said. At last he let go of Dave's hand, waved his own casually to let the sweat that had collected on Dave's palm evaporate. "Your record shows that you are very diligent, very thorough."

"Well—thank you." This was no performance review, Dave knew that. A message was being sent, but what? If Geraci was with the Agency then everything he said was some kind of code; words that sounded positive, like diligent and thorough, instead were criticisms. Was he being told they knew about the clips he hadn't reported? Or—his stomach clenched tight, bitter coffee rising up his throat—did they know about the record?

No, he thought. If that were the case this conversation wouldn't be happening: he'd just be gone.

"You have nothing more to say?" Geraci asked.

"No. I mean, well—it's a pleasure, of course, to know that Mr. Chadwick has had such positive things to say about me." He had learned that survival tactic in high school, perfected it in university: when under scrutiny, bring in someone else in hopes the investigators will turn their attention off of you.

Geraci nodded and turned his eyes down to the folders in front of him, but he did not appear to read them. "Very good. And do you have any questions for me?"

"Yes. Of course. I—" If you did not ask questions, if it seemed like you wanted the conversation to end, it was assumed you were hiding something. "I wondered if there might have been any criticisms of my work that I might improve on?"

"Your records are without blots," Geraci said. He looked up at Dave, his eyes narrowing. "This was said."

"Of course." Dave drew a breath and released it quickly, careful not to hold it too long. "Does Personnel have any suggestions on how I can go beyond my current performance level?"

Geraci smiled, looked down at one of the folders and made a note in small, illegible handwriting. "It will be taken under advisement," he said. "That is all the time I have at present, Mr. Lawson. Please inform Mr. Chadwick that he may send in the next."

"Yes, of course," Dave said. He held out his hand, waited a few seconds for Geraci to acknowledge it before turning it into a wave goodbye. He turned and headed for the door, suddenly aware of his cracked right shoe wrapped in silver duct tape.

"How did it go?" Chadwick asked.

Dave shrugged. "He says send in the next."

Chadwick nodded quickly, headed off towards his office. Dave walked over to the kitchen, waited there a few minutes and then went to the window that opened on the parking lot. As usual it was nearly empty; almost nobody in Broadcast was senior enough to be allowed to park in the government district. There was a car there, though, that Dave had never seen before: a black sedan, its metal shell shiny despite the sleet. A few moments later Dave saw Geraci walk into his field of vision, accompanied by a tall man in a dark leather coat. It took a moment before Dave recognized this last as the man he had seen the night before, the one he had thought had been following him—the one he had thought he had lost.

Dave forced himself to breathe. He had survived six years of university, three of them in Gil's secret double-history program, and five more here at Broadcast. He knew the Agency did not play around: if they had anything concrete on him they would have acted. It was probably because he had lost that man last night that Geraci had tried to scare him. They couldn't know where he had gone, what he had seen, what he knew. They couldn't.

For the rest of the day Dave sat glued to his workstation, forgetting even to go to the kitchen when he knew Maura would be there. Gradually he began to calm down, and by quitting time he had managed to convince himself it might be nothing. Just play it safe, he thought: skip a few meetings, keep a low profile for a while and it would blow over.

He was getting ready for bed when somebody knocked on his apartment door. He had been dozing on the couch, half-watching TV; he remembered the meeting with Geraci as he got up and he paused halfway to the door, unsure whether to acknowledge being there or not. Finally he padded to the door and looked through the spy hole, saw the girl Gil had brought to the meeting the night before. She reached up and knocked on the door again.

"Hang on," Dave said, releasing the latch. He opened the door and stepped back quickly to let her in. "Come on in, before somebody sees you."

"I'm sorry," she said. Her cheeks were red, from the cold or from nervousness. "I didn't know where else to go."

Dave leaned out into the hallway, looked around quickly and then closed the door behind him. "How did you know to come here?"

"Gil told me about you," she said. "When I told him—he told me where you lived . . ."

For a moment Dave wondered how Gil knew his address, remembered the time he had tried to host a meeting at his apartment. "All right, all right," he said. "What's this all about?"

"Well, it's—" The girl looked nervously around the small space, moved to sit on the couch. Dave sat on the chair facing it, noticed she was carrying her artist's portfolio. "I don't know how much to say," the girl said.

"You seem to know who I am and where I live, so you might as well tell me everything," Dave said. "Why don't you start with your name?"

"Amy," she said. "I'm studying art at the university—in my class this morning I forgot I had the record in my portfolio, and when I opened it up some people saw it. I don't think any of them knew what it was, but . . ."

"You must have already gone to see Professor Lorca," Dave said. "Why not give it to him?"

Amy shook her head. "Oh, no. I couldn't put him in danger like that."

Dave sighed, closed his eyes. "So he suggested you give it to me?"

"Well—you work at Broadcast and Media, don't you? Gil thought you could, you know, hide it in plain sight."

"He said that, did he?" Dave asked. Like most academics, Gil clearly had little understanding of how things worked in the government: Dave did not have the clearance to get anything into or out of the Archive rooms. He reached up to rub at his eyes "Fine," he said after a moment. "Leave it with me till you're sure the heat is off—and tell Gil he owes me one."

"Thank you," Amy said.

"It's all right," Dave said, waving away her thanks. He yawned. "Well . . ."

Amy glanced around, gave a nervous smile and stood up. She unzipped her portfolio, took out the album and handed it to him. "Well. Thanks again."

"Forget about it." He stood, walked her to the door. "Be quick getting out. Make sure nobody sees you."

She nodded. "I will."

He shut the door as soon as she was outside, listened to her footsteps receding for a few moments before he started cursing himself. Why had he taken the record? He should have refused, sent her to Paul's or else back to Gil. He even still had it under his arm—had anybody been in the hall when he opened the door? Could anyone have seen it? There was no use trying to sleep now: he poured himself a scotch, sat down to watch TV until exhaustion took him.

The next morning he was awakened by the distant sound of the alarm in his bedroom, unfolded himself from the couch and stumbled into the shower. When he returned the record was waiting for him: it sat on the coffee table, the blonde singer on the cover looking as though she was mocking him. He had an irrational thought that if he left it there it would be gone when he got back, faded away like the timeline it belonged to; with a sigh he slipped it into his briefcase, went into the kitchen for breakfast. Of all things, why had the girl had to come on Thursday night? If he had the weekend to calm down he could think of a place to hide it, but as it was he felt, walking to work, as though his briefcase had a bulls-eye painted on it. He briefly thought about hailing a cab before realizing how much more attention that would draw.

The feeling of being watched grew as he got to the office: eyes seemed to be following him, whispers trailing in his wake. He sat down at his workstation and cued up the day's tapes, focused tightly on the screen in front of him. Every few minutes he reached down to move his briefcase, trying to make it less conspicuous.

After an hour or so he began to wonder whether he would be better off going to the kitchen for his break or staying at his desk. Obviously getting up would attract attention, but since he always went for coffee wouldn't it be more unusual if he didn't? He went back and forth over the question for a few minutes before deciding there was no way he would get through this day without more coffee, and got up out of his chair.

Then he remembered the briefcase. What was he going to do with that? He couldn't leave it at his desk, where anyone could open it, but it would look strange for him to bring it to the kitchen. He wished he had decided to stay at his desk—but now that he had stood up he couldn't just sit down again, not without attracting more attention. Before too much more time could pass he leaned down, scooped up the briefcase and set off for the kitchen.

Maura was there, as he knew she would be, blowing on her coffee to cool it. "Hey stranger," she said.

He smiled, holding his briefcase behind him in what he hoped was a nonchalant way. "Hey yourself."

"Looks like you need those new shoes after all."

Dave felt his mind go blank, remembered only after a moment his shoe wrapped up with duct tape. "Oh. Right," he said. He flashed her another smile and turned to the shelf where his mug sat, picked it up with his free hand and put it down by the coffee maker.

"Might be easier with both hands," she said.

He laughed nervously. "Right," he said, put down the briefcase so that his legs pinned it against the wall. "I forgot to put my lunch in the fridge. Just remembered it now."

Maura glanced from side to side, took a sip from her coffee. "Well," she said finally, "I should get back. Performance review's coming up."

"Sure." Dave nodded. "Have a good one."

"Mm."

Dave took a breath and then poured his coffee, his hands trembling. He wasn't sure how to read that conversation, if there was anything to read: the mention of the briefcase, the reference to performance reviews after that business with Geraci. . . . No, he was being foolish. On the other hand, he knew that the Agency often put informants close to the people they were investigating. It was hardly impossible that they were using a double-pronged approach, Geraci the obvious threat to make him nervous, drive him to confide in his friend Maura. . . .

When he returned to his desk he felt a sudden compulsion to look inside the briefcase. Was the record even still in there? Of course it was, he had kept the briefcase in his sight since he arrived—but still the need to look inside nagged at him. He looked quickly over his shoulder, picked up the briefcase and shook it. He thought he could hear the record inside, bumping up against the briefcase, but he wasn't sure. Putting it on his lap he leaned over it, trying to block the sight of it with his body, then snapped the catches. He looked around again, to see if the sound had attracted any attention, then turned back to the suitcase and lifted the lid slightly. There it was, the record, still sitting flat; as soon as he saw it he shut his briefcase and snapped it closed again, but his anxiety had not been dispelled. Feeling as though he might throw up he leaned over further, slipped the briefcase under his desk and then lifted up his feet and rested them on it. Finally he sat up again, forced himself to take a dozen deep breaths in and out and then went back to his work.

Somehow he managed to make it through the rest of the day. At least it was Friday. He had survived the week, he thought as he reached the door to his apartment: tomorrow he would be able to sleep in, replace his shoes, and figure out where he could hide the record.

His hand hesitated over the doorknob. The door was ajar, just slightly: he gave it a push and it opened. Fighting his rising sense of panic he stepped inside and saw that his apartment had been ransacked. All the kitchen cupboards were open, their contents spilled out onto the counters; all the books on his shelves had been pulled down and opened, left spread-eagled on the floor.

Dave's fingers were clenched around the handle of his briefcase. If he hadn't brought it with him. . . . But there was no question, now: they were watching, and their not finding anything would only make them look harder. He had to get rid of the record before it was too late. Holding the briefcase close he turned around and went back outside, looking for a working pay phone. The evening fog had set in, making it hard to see anything; he passed by the first phone he found—better safe than sorry—eventually settled on one that was a half-dozen blocks from his apartment. The duct tape on his shoe had come loose, and the slush was soaking into his sock.

He let the phone ring ten times but nobody picked up. Was Gil just out, or had they gotten to him too? Dave forced himself to keep the panic down, think rationally. Who else could he give it to? The only one whose name he even knew was Paul Beatty; he flipped desperately through the phone book tethered to the booth, felt bile rising in his throat when he found no listing under the Bs. Maybe he should just get rid of the record, he thought, throw it away—but Gil would never forgive him, nobody in the group would, he had been trusted with this—

A thought came to him and he flipped to the business directory. There it was: Beatty Electrical. The dial moved stiffly as he turned it to each digit then let it fall back to zero; after an eternity the number was completed and the call went through. Dave held his breath as it rang once, twice—

"Beatty Electrical," the voice on the other side said. Was it Paul's? Dave had never spoken to him on the phone.

"This is—is this Paul?"

There was a moment's silence. "Who wants to know?"

"It's, um—I'm calling about the record we talked about . . ."

"What about it?"

"I— I was wondering when I could drop it off."

Another pause, long enough for Dave to wonder if he had hung up. Finally the voice said, "I think you must have mixed up your number. *Drop dead*," and hung up.

Dave stood there for a second with the receiver in his hand, open-mouthed, before realizing what Paul had meant: reversing "drop dead" gave dead drop, the locker they used for dangerous handoffs. He wasn't sure if it had ever actually been used before, but he was glad Paul had remembered it. He looked around, peering through the frosted glass and the mist, left the booth and started walking towards the train station.

It being Friday night, the downtown streets were packed: this was when new goods arrived in the stores, and many were not willing to pick over what was left Saturday morning. He pushed into the crowd, hoping that it would camouflage him, at the same time keeping a death-grip on his briefcase. If he could just make it to the station, just drop it off, it would be somebody else's problem . . . He glanced behind him, wondered if he had seen the tall man in the long black coat.

The streets were slick, the ice that had formed at sundown

melted by all the people walking. Craning his neck around Dave bumped into a heavyset woman in a bright green parka, lost his footing and fell forward. Without thinking he threw his hands in front of him to take the impact and the briefcase slammed onto the ground, skittered a few feet away.

Dave chased after the briefcase on his hands and knees, wiped his hands off on his pants once he'd reached it and drew himself back up onto his feet. He looked around again: nobody seemed to be taking much notice of him—it was hardly unusual to see someone take a header on a Friday night. He swung the briefcase back and forth, trying to feel if the record had broken, but he knew the jacket would hold the pieces in place if it had. The only way to know would be to open the briefcase, and he could not do that here.

There was the train station, by the canal. Unwilling to risk another glance back he quickened his steps, turned a few zigs and zags in hopes of losing any pursuit and finally made it to the grand colonnaded entrance. There were fewer people here, and he made a quick scan left and right before stepping inside. His hand fumbled in his pocket for a dollar coin to rent the locker, felt it slip from fingers slick with frost and sweat. He stood in front of the ARRIVALS board, pretending to read the schedule, until his heart slowed. Then he looked around again and made his way to the lockers. They were in a narrow hallway, by the washroom; he picked one in the corner, dropped a coin in the slot and turned the key. The locker door swung open and he pulled his briefcase up to his chest. He was tempted to put the whole thing in there, to avoid exposing the record, but anyone who saw him entering the station with the briefcase and leave without it would have no doubt what had happened. Instead he held the briefcase so that the hinges faced away from him and undid the catches. He took a step back, giving himself enough room to open the briefcase, drew out the album. For a moment he simply held it there until, unable to resist, he reached into the jacket and pulled at the record itself. When he felt it come out in one piece he exhaled, let it fall back in and put the album into the locker, shut it and pulled out the key. Then he walked into the bathroom at a steady pace, went into the furthermost stall, lifted up the lid of the toilet tank and dropped the key inside.

By the time he had left the train station he was already feeling better. He remembered now how the meetings used to make him feel, like he was part of something important: that he was contributing to something that mattered. The cold air outside felt crisp now, invigorating. He decided not to wait for the morning, but to buy new shoes now. Why not?

Turning, Dave felt a heavy hand on his shoulder. "Wait a moment, please," Geraci's voice said from behind him.

Dave tried to turn around, but Geraci held him fast. He craned his head instead; saw Geraci, in his black plastic coat and red scarf, flanked by two men similarly dressed. Geraci led him forward to the train station's loading zone, where the car Dave had seen in the parking lot was waiting. Even in the mist it looked clean and shiny, its windows black.

He knew better than to resist when they bundled him into the back seat. The windows here were as dark on the inside as the outside, and a black plastic partition separated him from the rest of the car. One of the silent men accompanying Geraci sat with him, looking straight ahead during the whole ride.

Finally the car stopped and he was led out. They were not treating him roughly, not yet, and Dave looked to this for some measure of hope: the ride could just as easily have ended in the car.

They were inside, or else underground. He followed Geraci down a corridor whose walls were featureless grey concrete, heard the echoing footsteps of the two men behind him. Finally they stopped at an unmarked door. One of the men opened it and guided Dave inside, sat him down on a folding chair by a small, square metal table on which sat a thermos and two paper cups.

"Coffee?" Geraci asked from behind him. Dave craned his neck to see Geraci come into the room, sit down across the table.

"Sure."

Geraci nodded, unscrewed the thermos and filled both cups, handing one to Dave. The coffee smell was strong, filling the small room. Dave brought his cup up to his lips, sniffed at it carefully and then took a sip.

"No milk," Geraci said. "I am sorry. My men, they do not always think of such things."

"It's all right," Dave said. He took another drink and set down the cup, casting around for something else to say.

"It's a long time you've been working at Broadcast?" Geraci asked.

Dave nodded. His head was starting to swim, his stomach churning.

"You enjoy it there? It is a good fit for your skills?"

"Sure," Dave said, the words pouring out of his mouth like syrup. The chair seemed to have tilted under him, and he tried to right himself.

"You are editing videotapes currently? Cutting inconsistencies?"

"Yes."

Geraci leaned down, lifted a briefcase off the ground and set it down on the table. For a moment Dave thought it was his briefcase, but saw that it was black where his was dark brown. Geraci opened it and drew out a beige folder, opened that and spun a page around with splayed fingers.

"This is a copy of your log, from Wednesday. Do you remember this?"

Dave nodded again; the room shook with the movement of his head and he swallowed hard to avoid vomiting. He didn't understand what this was about—he couldn't think—

"Here," Geraci said, placing his little finger on a few words Dave had written halfway down the page. "Do you see what this says?"

Squinting, Dave tried to bring the page into focus. "I'm sorry—I can't—"

"'Thirteen minutes forty seconds to fifteen minutes twenty-five seconds,'" Geraci read, "'President Nixon mentioned. Watergate reference.' Do you remember this?"

"I—yes," Dave said.

"I have seen this sequence you edited. The character who is speaking, he speaks only of Nixon." Geraci leaned forward. "So tell me, Mr. Lawson, how is it that you know of a *Watergate*?"

Dave laughed despite himself. Was that all this was about? They didn't know about the record, about—

He was reeling, knocked back by the force of Geraci's blow. The door behind him opened, and strong hands gripped his arms and pulled him upright.

"I do not find this so funny, Mr. Lawson," Geraci said. He was cradling his right hand in his left, stroking it with an aggrieved expression on his face.

"I'm sorry," Dave said. The room was spinning around him.

Geraci looked down into his open briefcase, pulled out what looked like a small tackle box. He reached for its latch with his hand, paused and looked up at Dave. "Are you convinced of the seriousness of this business?"

"Yes," Dave said.

Geraci's hand rested on the tackle box, his fingers idly playing with the latch. "Then please tell me. Why is it you feel you must record this mention of Watergate?"

"I—I must have heard it once before, remembered it."

Giving him a look of intense fatigue, Geraci said, "It is neither your job nor your place to remember, Mr. Lawson. Your job is to find things that can only confuse the people, and to help them to forget those things. You are to forget those things as well." He glanced down at the open folder in front of him. "You were a student of history, Mr. Lawson. Was this not made clear to you?"

"Yes. I—it was. I'm sorry."

"Good." Geraci drew a page out of the folder with his free hand, spun it around so that it faced Dave—his other hand still on the tackle box. "This is a confession to the denial of history and also an apology, most heartfelt and sincere. You will sign it at the bottom, please."

One of the men behind Dave put a pen in his hand. "And—that's it?" Dave said. "I just sign it, and—"

"Of course there will be consequences," Geraci said. "Before you can be once more in a position of trust you will have to prove yourself worthy of it—but that chance may be given, in time. All you need do is sign."

Dave leaned forward, tried to read the page; the letters swam in front of him. "I can't read it," he said.

"It is of no consequence."

He reached out with the pen, felt his arm being guided to the page. A blot of ink formed at the beginning of a horizontal line, and after a moment he signed.

"Very good," Geraci said. He picked the tackle box up by the handle, put it carefully back in his briefcase. "I am pleased to see you begin the path to rehabilitation."

The hands holding Dave upright released him, and he slumped forward. He watched Geraci stand, pick up his briefcase and go to the door; on his way out somebody stopped him, and they spoke briefly.

Geraci turned back to face Dave. "A moment more, please," he said, and Dave heard a change in his voice: a crack in his superiority, a hint of bitterness. "My supervisor wishes to speak with you."

Dave watched as Geraci stepped back to let the tall man with the long black coat come in. The tall man gave a small nod and Geraci stepped outside, closed the door.

"David?" the tall man asked, moving to stand where Geraci had sat. "Or is it Dave?"

"I told him," Dave said, his voice cracking. "I signed the paper. I signed it. . . ."

"I know," the tall man said. He leaned down to reach under the rim of the table, and Dave could hear his coat creaking; it was real leather, not plastic. The man drew a small metal device out from under the table, twisted it. "There. We can talk freely now."

Dave frowned at him, daring now to look the man in the face. He had brown curly hair that swept back from his forehead, a sharp nose and a thin moustache. "What are we going to talk about?" he asked.

The man tucked the tail of his coat under him, sat down. "History."

"I told you—I already signed—"

"Not that." The man leaned back in his chair, dropped his arms to his sides. "You made a copy of that clip Geraci was fussing about, didn't you? You collect things like that."

Dave said nothing.

The man shrugged. "It's not worth denying it. I only raised the subject because it should make some things more clear to you; so without you confirming or denying it, let's say we both know there are things that don't fit anymore, pieces of a puzzle that no longer exists. That's not an accusation. All right?"

He took a breath. "All right."

"Good. Now I want you to understand—I am one of those pieces."

Dave's head was starting to clear, recovering from Geraci's blow and whatever had been in the coffee; still, he wondered if he had heard the man right. "I don't understand," he said.

"That group you belong to, I know you collect things that are remnants of the old history—things the device didn't manage to change along with the rest of the world. I'm like that: the new history put me here, but I remember who I was. Who I am."

"So—you're not—"

The man glanced past Dave, at the door. "There are a few of us, and we're very close to control of the device. The problem is, a weapon is only useful if you know where to aim it. That's why I need you."

"Because I know the history," Dave said. He hesitated, not sure how much to say, but the man seemed to know everything already. "The old history. You need me to help you change it back."

The man was silent for a moment, then shook his head. "It's what you know of *this* history we want—the differences between the histories, so we'll know how they put themselves in charge."

"But you have to change everything back. That's why we've been gathering all those pieces—so we can reconstruct the old history—"

"Which is why they've left you alone," the man said. "Your little group is a joke—you think you can change the world by collecting stamps." He stood up, swung a briefcase from the floor onto the table and opened it. From within he drew out the album, reached into the jacket and pulled out the record, holding it in both hands. "You think this can change the world."

"Please," Dave said.

The man pressed both his thumbs to the middle of the record, flexed it so that the vinyl began to bend. "Would you give your life for this? It means nothing."

Dave dropped his gaze to the table. "It's history. It's what's real."

"You of all people should know there's no history," the man said. "There's just what we choose to remember."

After a moment's silence Dave looked up, into the man's eyes. They were a dull brown like his hair, steady and sane. "The new history you're going to make, it'll be just as much a patchwork as this one," he said. "What makes you think it'll be any better?"

The man shrugged, lay the record flat on the table. "It'll be ours."

"Fine," Dave said, though he could not make his tone match his words. "How will you contact me?"

"Don't worry about that," the man said. He slid the record into its jacket, put the album back in his briefcase and closed it. "I think it's best if you stay close."

"Wait—you mean I can't go home?"

The man sighed, smoothed his leather coat as he stood. "You were going to disappear either way, Dave. I've told you things I can't let anyone else know, and you've already shown you don't stand up to questioning."

"But—"

The man went to the door, turned back to Dave. "Well?" He said. "Are you coming?"

Maura climbed up the wide steps to the Broadcast building, the soles of her new shoes fighting to grip the ice. Monday, again; it felt like it was always Monday. She left her coat in the cloakroom, headed for the kitchen to drop off her lunch. On her way from there to her desk she noticed one of the workstations was empty, wondered if it belonged to that man who had been chatting her up last week. She had half-expected to run into him at the shoe store, had thought she wouldn't mind if she did; he was funny, and it pleased her to see the way she made him nervous. She hadn't seen him yet today—what was his name?

"Excuse me," someone said, tapping her on the shoulder.

She turned around to see who it was: a man in his early twenties, blond hair cut short and over-formally dressed in shirt and tie. "Yes?"

"I'm starting today," the man said. He glanced down at a sheet of carbon paper in his hand. "Workstation thirty-seven, do you know where that is?"

Maura nodded, nodded towards the empty workstation she had passed earlier. "Welcome aboard," she said.

"Thank you."

The young man gave her a small, nervous smile and hurried off. She watched him go for a moment, turned to go back to her own workstation. The boy had disturbed her train of thought—what had she been thinking about?

Ah well, she thought as she sat down, cued up the first of the day's tapes to edit. If it was important she was sure it would come to her.

Heroic Measures

The nurse stopped her on her way into the room. "You need to sign this," she said.

The old woman peered at the page the nurse had handed her. Somehow she was unable to focus on the right part of her glasses, and the paper was a blur. "What is it?"

"Directions for his care. Just check this box for resuscitation or this box for no, then sign at the bottom."

"Is it that serious?"

"It's just routine. Do you need some time to think about it?"

She shook her head; she knew what he would want. Still unable to make out the letters she followed the nurse's finger, checked and signed, handed the page back. "Thank you," she said, and went on into the room.

He was lying on the bed, his eyes closed, his form as muscular as ever but looking somehow deflated. It was emptier than in any hospital room she'd ever seen, only a heart monitor beeping softly and rhythmically; no IV, no tubes of saline solution running to his arm, no beeping and whirring and probing machines. The skin that had turned away uncounted bullets wouldn't admit them.

His chest rose and fell, slowly, shallowly, and every few seconds he twitched with the dream-tremors that had consigned them to separate beds all these years. A pair of black-framed glasses sat on the end table next to the bed; he still wore them most of the time, from habit, must have had them on when he fell.

She watched him breathe for a minute or so. It didn't look much different from regular sleep, except for his pale, dry skin and lips, and the crust that had formed over his eyelids, sealing them shut. This is the kind of care he gets, she thought, after everything. She went into the half-bathroom, picked up a rough beige washcloth and moistened it with warm water from the sink, then went back to the bedside and started dabbing at his eyes.

"I'm sorry," a voice said from behind her. Turning, she saw a dark-haired man in his thirties—or maybe his forties; the older she got, the more all people younger looked the same age—wearing a lab coat over brown slacks and a windowpane checked shirt. "The nurse should have told you. We think he might be having small seizures, and we're worried what might happen if his eyes are open. Without his control, I mean."

She nodded, dabbed the cloth on his forehead instead. How long had his skin been this pale, the veins so visible? "I'm—"

"Yes, I know," the man said, holding out his hand. "I'm Dr. Weller. I'm glad we were able to reach you. Was your trip all right?"

"It was fine." In fact she had no memory of it: no memory of anything between being called away from the conference and seeing the nurse at the door. "How bad is he?"

Weller looked away slightly, scratched the side of his head, above his right ear. "Well, that's hard to say," he said. "We have only the simplest tools available. No X-ray, no CAT scan—none of it will penetrate his skin. So really I'm just left with an EKG and a stethoscope."

"And?"

"And we don't know. Who knows what's normal for him? We've seen what look like little seizures, like I said. It might have been a stroke, but we've got no way to tell."

She looked over at him on the bed. He still looked strong; his hair, white as it was, still fell in that curl over his forehead. "So what are you doing?"

The doctor shook his head. "There's not much we can do.

Even if we knew it was a stroke, it would be too late to give him a plasminogen activator—a clot dissolver—even if there was a way to get it in his bloodstream. Frankly, anything we could give him probably wouldn't be as effective as what his own body can do. He's shown an amazing ability to heal himself over the years."

"What are you doing to keep him hydrated?" she asked, annoyed. At what age, she thought, do you start being treated like a child? Or do doctors talk like that to everyone?

"Ice. I don't know if he can choke, but we don't want to take the risk. So we've been taking crushed ice—there's a machine down the hall, in the pantry—and letting it melt in his mouth."

She gently put a finger to her husband's lips. "I don't think he's gotten that in a while."

Dr. Weller had the grace to look embarrassed. "Labour's always at a premium in a hospital. Even for someone like him—if there's a good chance it's just the natural way of things, more urgent care takes priority."

The natural way of things. Who knew what that was, with him? "I'd like you to show me where the ice machine is, please," she said. "And I'd like a cot brought in, if you can spare one."

As it turned out, they couldn't. What they had instead was a padded chair, like a recliner; it wasn't terrifically comfortable, but you could lean back far enough to sleep when you had to. Not that she was sleeping much. She was the only one to watch him: his parents were long dead, her sister half a continent away and too frail to travel besides. No children, of course. Even if it had been possible between them, and who knows if it had, the risk was too great: if he took after his father, one kick while in the womb. . . . As for adoption, she'd never have thought he'd be against it, but he'd always said it would be too complicated. So it was just the two of them.

And now, just one.

Luckily it was near Christmas; their neighbour's son was out of school, could gather a bag full of clothes and books and bring them to the hospital. She had given up on her bifocals, wore her reading glasses most of the time and switched to the others when someone came in or she went to get water. She had started out by reading to him, Edgar Rice Burroughs and Dickens, his old favourites, gave up after a day. Now she saved her voice and reread *Scoop*.

She saw a fuzzy grey-and-white centaur shape moving past the door, heard the breakfast cart rolling by. Switching to her distance glasses she patted her husband on the arm, dog-eared her book and headed for the pantry. After a few days she knew the rhythms of the hospital: the big water cups, the ones that held a litre, were put out on the pantry shelf right after breakfast and disappeared soon after. Every morning she grabbed two, filled one with water for herself and one with ice for him. Like being back at the paper, she thought, timing your break to a fresh pot of coffee, knowing the times when there wouldn't be a line at the Xerox machine. She took a long while filling the mugs, to give the nurses ample time to change him before she got back.

He was stirring when she got back to the room. She knew, now, which tremors could be soothed with a gentle hand or moist washcloth and which would lift him inches off the bed, set him thrashing hard enough to crack bone. This was a small one, and she took up his hand as she sat down. "It's okay," she said.

His mouth opened. "Luh—" he croaked.

Her hand shut in surprise, jerked back in case his should close out of reflex. She reached into the mug of ice, slid a small handful into his mouth. "Just let this melt."

Nodding, he moved his jaw around then swallowed. "Cold," he said in a rasp.

She reached over for the washcloth that sat on the table, dabbed at his eyes. "Do you need anything?"

"Where?"

"You're in the hospital."

His eyelids were clear of the crust now, and he opened them a bit; the eyes behind looked pale, unfocused. "What happened?"

"You fell," she said, fighting to control her voice.

"Fighting?"

She smiled. He had always hated the fighting, using his fists to solve problems: it wasn't the way he was brought up, he'd say, and besides, if someone like him had to resort to violence, it meant he must be pretty dumb. "No."

He nodded. "Good," he said, then took a deep breath. She reached into the mug, her hand numb with cold, fed him another handful of ice. He sucked at the ice for a moment then swallowed. "Tired."

"Okay," she said. "You go to sleep."

"Yeah." For a moment that old twinkle she remembered was there, and the corners of his mouth curled into a smile. "You take care, now."

She woke with a start. Her chair had been pushed away from the bed, and here were people all around, reaching over her husband. The room was oddly quiet, and for a moment she wondered if she were still sleeping, dreaming. Then she realized just what sound was missing. The heart monitor was silent.

"What's happening?" she said, rising unsteadily. She didn't know who of these people, if any, was the doctor, who was in charge. Nobody seemed to be doing anything.

"He's coding," one of them said—a young red-haired woman in green scrubs. "I mean, his heart's stopped."

"Can't you do something?"

"He's DNR."

Still fighting to awaken fully, she tried to pull those letters out of the alphabet soup in her memory. Then she remembered, the paper, the box . . . It was what he had wanted. She had thought it was what she had wanted. "I don't care. I'm the one who signed it. Do something!"

The nurses, or whatever they all were, looked around at one another uncomfortably. Even as she spoke, she knew why: order or no order, there was nothing they could do. Paddles would hardly shock a heart that had withstood lightning bolts, and as for chest compressions—who was strong enough for that? One of his own people, if there were any left in the universe.

"It's all right," she said, calling up the voice she'd used all those years ago to convince her editor—and convince him—that she wasn't afraid to cover the hurricane, or get the interview with the terrorist leader. That she wasn't afraid. "You've done all you—"

Before she could finish the heart monitor started beeping again, haltingly at first and then with a regular rhythm. Even under the fluorescent lights she could see the colour returning to his cheeks.

"I'll call Dr. Weller," the red-haired nurse said, then turned to her. "It could be pretty noisy around here for a while—would you like to sleep in the lounge?"

She shook her head, realized with a start she was still wearing her reading glasses. "I'll wait here," she said, fumbling around to find the other pair in her lap.

It happened once more before the doctor came, his heart stopping and restarting itself. A motherly nurse in pink scrubs trailed Dr. Weller as he came into the room—sleepy-eyed himself— filling him in on what had happened.

"Are the results from the stool and urine samples back yet?" Weller asked, not yet acknowledging her presence.

"I'll go see, doctor," the nurse said, went back out into the dimly lit hallway.

Finally the doctor seemed to notice her. "You should sleep," he said.

"What's wrong with him? Why is this happening?"

He shrugged wearily. "We still don't know. It could be—" The nurse reappeared at the door, handed him a clipboard; he looked it over, nodded to himself. "Well. Liver, kidneys. . . . It looks like, basically, his organs are shutting down."

"So he's dying," she said. She bit the tip of her tongue. "How many more times will this happen? Before he—"

"I don't know," the doctor said. "The thing is, the organs—we think they're healing themselves. I've been tracking what functions we can from what he . . . lets out . . . and it looks like whatever organ's failed one day has healed itself by the next one."

"You mean he'll get better? Will he—"

He shook his head. "No. He's too far gone. He can't heal fully, and it—it looks like he can't fully die, either."

She looked down at her husband. He was resting, now, the heart monitor beeping a reassuring rhythm. Pale as he was, it was hard to believe he would never rise from this bed. Even in the darkest times, she had never really feared for him; he had always been strong, so strong. "So. There's nothing—nothing you can do for him."

"No. We'll keep him comfortable, keep monitoring him . . . I could still be wrong. But . . ." He scratched at the side of his head. "In light of this, I think you need to consider your own health now. Being here is a lot of stress on you, at your age. . . ."

"Yes," she said. "I'll think about it. Thank you, doctor."

"Can I get the nurses to bring you anything?"

"No. Thank you. Switch the light out when you go."

"Sure."

She sat for a while, in the dark, not moving: watching him, watching his chest rise and fall, listening to the monitor's soft song. "What am I going to do with you?" she asked.

To her surprise he stirred, his body stiffening like a still photo of a seizure. "I could see them," he murmured.

His eyes were closed; there was no way to tell if he knew where he was. "Who?"

"Like in the dream." He had told her, a few nights before she left for the conference, about a dream he'd had: finally seeing the place he had come from, all its lost people. "They . . . they're waiting for me." His breathing quickened, then returned to its sleeping rhythm, and his muscles relaxed.

There was no use trying to sleep. She turned the light on, tilting the shade away so he was left in darkness, and picked up her book.

Dr. Weller was pleased when, the next day, she decided to take his advice. "No sense making yourself sick," he had said. "Keep your cell phone on you. We'll let you know if—if anything changes."

In fact it had made her sick to leave her husband there, alone, but what she needed lay outside the hospital's walls. It would not be easy to find, but she was unworried. She had always had a nose for trouble.

The house looked like every other one in the suburban Minneapolis neighbourhood: a half-bungalow, aluminium siding in one of three tasteful shades of grey. A haphazardly shovelled trail led through the snow up to the door, and an uncollected newspaper sat on the porch. Smacking her lips—Chapstick, not lipstick; her days of vanity were gone, and besides, it was so dry here—she rang the doorbell, heard slippered feet shuffling within.

She had to stop herself from laughing when she saw him. It was still the face she knew from a dozen kidnappings, a hundred hostage-takings: the owlish eyebrows, the fiercely intelligent eyes were still there—but he was wearing a crocheted cap in a rainbow of yarn. "I'm sorry," she said when she saw his eyes flashing with anger. "You never seemed to care about being bald before."

"It's for warmth, not vanity," he said, scowling. "What do you want?"

"Can I come in?"

He fixed her a long stare, shrugged, turned to go inside. "I had hair," he said. "You know that stuff the yuppies use to fill in their bald spots? I invented it."

She closed the door behind her, tapped the toes of her boots against the floor to knock the snow off. "So what happened?"

"Well, I used the good stuff—what the doctors can prescribe is just a taste, to hook people on the real thing. That's where the money is. Anyway, I had the healthiest head of red hair you've ever seen."

"And then?"

He tapped the crocheted cap. "Cancer. Chemo."

"I'm sorry." She summoned an expression of concern. "How's it going?"

"Ehh." He went on into the kitchen, poured himself a cup of coffee. "I'm alive. You want?"

She shook her head. "No, thanks. Is that why they let you out of jail, the cancer?"

"Nah, I'm a parolee. It was always attempted whatever, thanks to him, and I never really did anything that bad—never even tried to kill anyone but him, and they couldn't even charge me with attempted murder without admitting the existence of you-know-what on public record." The bald man took a sip of his coffee, frowned, put down the cup. "So, you've tracked me down, and it wasn't just to catch up on old times. What do you want?"

"You know what."

He tilted his head curiously. "I don't, really."

She took a breath. "What you called it. You-know-what."

"Ah," he said, understanding dawning on his face. "Trouble in paradise?"

Her face flushed with anger. "None of your business," she said.

His eyebrows rose in amusement. "Too bad. You know I'm always at your service . . . all you have to do is ask."

"He's—he's very sick," she said, swallowing bile. "And his body, it—He's too strong. It won't let him die."

He gave a barking laugh, broke into a cough. "Why . . . even if I had some—which I don't—why should I give it to you?" He picked up his coffee, took a long sip and swallowed. "I spent half my life trying to make him miserable. Why should I put him out of his misery now?"

"I can pay you," she said, her knuckles whitening as she gripped her purse strap. She took a step closer to him, reached in for her wallet.

"Pay me? Anyway, I told you, I don't have any."

She smiled inwardly. An old interviewing trick, move the conversation along the path of least resistance: not whether he would but whether he could. "I don't believe it. You'd never go without at least one piece, just in case."

He shrugged, smiling broadly. "Sorry. It's a condition of my parole—no owning any radioactive materials of any kind."

"Uh huh." She took a step closer, nodded sadly, and reached for the lump in his right pocket. His hand shot out, quicker than she had expected, grabbed her wrist; she grabbed his other arm and they froze, each unwilling to back down but neither able to risk a struggle and the fall that might follow. She locked eyes with him, felt a blast of pure hate. She fought to hold his gaze, forcing herself to remember everything he had ever done to her, to him.

After a long moment his eyes dimmed; deflated, he looked away, released her arm and reached into his right pocket. There it was, in a nest of tissues and rubber bands: a rough crystal, about an inch around.

"If you want this," he said, "You have to do something for me."

She nodded; there would be a price, of course. There had to be. "What do you want?"

His shoulders slumped, his body curling protectively around the glowing stone. "It should have been me," he said. "Not just . . . time. When it—happens—" She felt a moment's absurd pity for him: he had, she realized, been as bound to her husband as she was. "Tell them it was me."

He snuffled loudly, turned away, wiped his nose with his sleeve. "Tell them I won . . ."

When she returned to the hospital she was told her husband had moved to a different room, in the isolation wing; the woman at the desk couldn't tell her why. An orderly stopped her as she got off the elevator, directed her to a room where white quarantine suits hung in a row from hooks on the wall. A sign opposite said SUIT UP BEFORE ENTERING! She looked around, went back out into the hall and to the nurse's station.

"What's going on?" she asked.

The nurse, an Asian woman she hadn't seen before, shrugged. "Which patient are you here to see?" She told her, and the nurse flipped through a pile of charts. "Your husband's in quarantine. You can visit, but you need to put on one of those suits and follow procedure."

"I know that," she said, her voice raspy from the cold dry air she'd been breathing. "Why is he in quarantine?"

"You'll have to ask Dr. Weller."

"Where is he?"

"I'll page him for you."

She pretended to read a magazine for twenty minutes before the doctor arrived. "What's the matter?" he asked the nurse.

"Your patient's wife is here," the nurse said, pointing her out.

"Ah. How are you?" Dr. Weller asked, stepping over to her.

"What's going on? Why is he isolated?"

"It's his immune system. We had some outbreaks on the floor he was on—we think bacteria in his system may have been mutating for a long time. Adapting to match him—they evolve so much more quickly than we do. So long as he was healthy his immune system would have kept them from getting out into the population, but . . ."

"I thought you were going to call me if anything changed."

"Ah. Well." He looked away. "Nothing has changed. My prognosis is still the same."

"So he's still . . ."

"Yes."

She nodded to herself. "Can I see him?"

"Sure. Just put a suit on—there's instructions—"

"I saw them."

"Okay. You might need a little help getting into the suit."

She had thought, when she saw them on the wall, that they looked like spacesuits, but they were actually very thin. She stepped into the legs, glad to be wearing pants rather than a skirt, and Dr. Weller helped her with the arms and hood. He led her to the room; the first door led into a little antechamber, with a garbage can and a sign over it saying DISPOSE OF SUITS HERE BEFORE LEAVING. The first door closed behind her and she shouldered the next open, went into the room.

The room was dark and nearly empty, with even the few comforts of a regular hospital room gone: no bedside table, no chairs. Just the bed where he lay, breathing shallowly, and the heart monitor. Round adhesive ghosts on his forehead showed he'd had an EEG put on and then removed. She could see why: he was twitching in his sleep, tiny seizures passing over him every few seconds. Loose restraints over his chest and legs kept him from floating more than a few inches from the bed.

"It's okay," she said, stroking his forehead with gloved fingers. "I'm here."

Another twitch went through him, then he seemed to calm. His eyelids fluttered.

She felt her resolve weakening. "I'm sorry I had to leave you. I won't go again."

His lips, dry and cracked, opened slightly; she held her breath. "Luh . . ." He spoke just over a whisper, so quiet she wondered if she had really heard him. His head pitched to the side, as though fighting a nightmare. "Let me go."

"I can't," she said, her voice breaking. "I still need you here."

Another tremor went through him, and his hands clawed convulsively.

"I'm sorry . . . I'm sorry . . . " she said. He said nothing.

This wasn't fair. Why should she be the one to have to do this? Because she could. Because she would.

Opening her left hand she took out the tissue she had palmed while putting on the suit, unwrapped it. She looked quickly over her shoulder, through the windows of the two doors: no-one was paying attention, as usual. The rock in her hand felt heavier now that she could see it. She waited for one of his spasmed hands to open, fitted the rock into his palm. Its glow peered through his fingers, cast shadows across the room that quivered as the seizures took him.

She sat with him for a long time, until he was still.

THE LAST ISLANDER

Saufatu stood neck-deep in the water, watching the dawn arrive over the great empty ocean to the east. He raised the coconut shard in his right hand to his mouth and nibbled on the flesh, enjoying the mixture of sweet and salty flavours, then quickly glanced over his shoulder at the shore. He knew before looking that there would be no-one there: even Funafuti, the biggest of the Eight Islands, was nearly always empty except on Independence Day. Here on Niulakiti, the first of the islands to sink, he had never seen another soul.

He turned back to the sea, took another bite of his coconut and frowned. Something was out there. He squinted, trying to make out the dark smudge perhaps a half kilometre out towards the horizon. It looked like someone swimming, or rather thrashing at the surface; suddenly he remembered what he had put out there, realized what was happening, and pushed himself out into the waves.

It had been a long time since he had been swimming, but a childhood spent in the sea had inscribed his muscles with the necessary motions. He inhaled and exhaled salt spray with each stroke, getting nearer and nearer to the man—for he could now see that it was a man, dark-haired and tanned but unmistakably White—a tourist, who was struggling for his life. The snout and fin of the grey reef shark, rising and falling from the water as it fought to draw the man down, completed the picture.

"Bop it on the snout!" Saufatu called as he got closer, hoping the man spoke English.

The man, who to this point had not yet noticed him, looked his way and tilted his head.

"Bop it on the snout!" Saufatu shouted again. He slowed to tread water for a moment, raised his left hand out of the water and smacked it against his nose twice.

The man turned back to the shark, which was working to fasten its jaws on his leg, and tapped it gingerly. A moment later he smacked it harder, and the shark turned its head away; another hit and it thrashed its head from side to side, snapped its jaws on empty air and dove under the surface.

Saufatu reached the man a few minutes later, closing his mouth to avoid inhaling the bloody water. The man looked pale, but surprisingly composed given what he had just been through. He put his right arm around Saufatu's shoulder and kicked his legs weakly.

"Not that way," Saufatu said, shaking his head. "Past here it's all algorithmic. Just let me pull you."

The man nodded and then coughed, spitting out seawater. "Thanks," he said.

Saufatu said nothing, concentrating on his strokes as he drew the man back to shore. He helped the man out onto the beach, watching him carefully to make sure he did not have any more water in his lungs, and then leaned him against a tree. Saufatu picked up his clothes from where he had left them, and the jug of toddy he had left there as well. He went back to the man, handed him the jug, and set to work tearing up his shirt into bandages for the wounds on the man's leg. Luckily they were not deep, and had already been cleaned by the seawater; he was unlikely to carry them with him when he left.

The man took a swig of toddy, and then another. "Thanks again," the man said. "I'm Craig, by the way. Craig Kettner."

"Saufatu Pelesala," Saufatu said. He glanced out at the sea. "We don't get many visitors here."

"I can see that," Craig said, "what with the welcoming committee and all. You really should put a sign up or something, warn people before they go swimming."

"It's only instanced in that spot," Saufatu said. "People know not to go there unless they want to experience it."

Craig frowned. "Why would they want to?"

"It's a memory. That's where it happened." He gestured out towards the sea. "Or so I'm told. Apisai Lotoala, he was one of the last people to grow up here—he was attacked by a shark right out there, so that's where I put the memory."

"And that's how he got out of it? By hitting the shark on the nose?"

Saufatu shrugged. "That's what he always said. All I know is, I've seen the scars."

Craig nodded slowly. "So—what is this place, anyway?"

"You came here. Didn't you know where you were going?"

He shook his head. "I just picked it by random, pretty much. I look for . . . low-traffic sites. Mostly places that are basically empty, or abandoned. I didn't expect anybody else to be here, to be honest with you."

"Neither did I."

"So—what is this place? Why are you encoding instanced shark attacks?"

"This is my home," Saufatu said. "The Eight Islands were very very low, too low when the waters rose. So my family was given the *salanga* of taking a record of them, as best we could."

Craig looked along the beach from left to right, his head nodding slightly. "And it's all like this, full immersive dreaming?"

Saufatu shook his head. "We were able to record some of the other islands immersively, but this one is mostly 2-D. I was able to convert some of it, like this beach, but the algorithms are expensive."

"What did you use?" Craig asked, crouching down and running his hand over the white, fine-grained sand appraisingly.

"Extrapolator 7," Saufatu said. "Price was an issue," he added, shrugging slightly.

"What about the shark attack? How did you record that?"

"I build the instanced events myself based on stories people tell me, or records in the old newspapers."

"Why?" Craig broke into a grin, held up a hand. "Sorry, I don't mean to be rude."

"We do it to remember," Saufatu said. "So there would be a record of our home."

Craig looked up and down the beach. "So where is everybody?"

"They have their own lives," Saufatu said. "They know it is here, and they tell me their stories to help build it."

"And who pays for it? This must all take up a lot of headspace."

Saufatu sighed. "There is some money. A fund—we had a lucky name, when they handed out the Web addresses, that other people wanted to buy. Of course most of it went to resettle our people, but there is enough left to do a little, for a little while."

Craig nodded. "Listen, I run this—it's like a guide, to interesting places in the Web, places my scouts and I find that not too many people know about. I think people would be really interested in a place like this."

"I don't know," Saufatu said. "We never had many tourists, even when we were above water."

"But that's just it. This place is real, you know, not just another dream with the same old tricks. If people were coming here you could maybe get funding from UNESCO, or the WikiHistory Foundation. Not just to keep the place going but make it better—emotion-encode the events, get custom algorithms." He took a breath, shook his head. "Listen, just think about it. If you decide you're interested, let me know."

Craig held out his right hand, and after a moment Saufatu took it: Craig's PID crossed the handshake, to be logged in Saufatu's terminal. Then Craig gave a small wave, and turned to walk back to the entry portal at the edge of the beach; Saufatu waited until he had gone, and then woke up.

Losi was already gone when Saufatu emerged from his room, so he boiled a kipper, cut it out of the plastic and put it on his plate next to a half-can of *pulaka*. They had been close when she had been younger—mother-uncles and sister-nieces typically were, compared to the more formal relationships between parents and children and the taboo on cousins mixing—but since she had entered her teens she spent nearly all her time in her room or out of the house.

When he went outside he saw that she had left the truck. That was good for him, since it meant he didn't have to face the long bus ride from Waitakere down to his shift at the Auckland airport, but he couldn't help wondering who she had caught a ride with. He sent her a text, offering to pick her up when his shift was done, then got into the truck.

Traffic was worse than usual that morning, spreading out from downtown as far as the Mangere Bridge. It was still faster than the bus, though, and he had time for a coffee-and-toddy with a gang of the other Islanders before his shift started. There were maybe a dozen of them who worked at the airport, though the precise numbers shifted fairly often. Mostly they talked about nothing—work and fishing and the *kilikiti* matches—and sometimes, when Saufatu closed his eyes, he almost felt the water around him, like they were all standing hip-deep in the Funafala lagoon.

They all finished their coffee before it began to get cold and queued up at the security check. Saufatu's heart sank when he saw a new officer at the security kiosk, and he moved ahead of the others. When he got to the kiosk he took out his DP card and held it out.

The security guard, a ruddy-faced man in his twenties with buzz-cut hair, squinted at the card. Finally he shook his head. "Refugee card's not ID," he said.

"I'm not a refugee, it's a displaced persons card," Saufatu said. He jerked his head to indicate the row of islanders behind him. "We all have them."

The guard frowned. "I have to call this in," he said. He picked up his phone and dialled it carefully, keeping a close watch on Saufatu as he whispered urgently to whoever was at the other end of the line.

Saufatu sighed. It was like this every time someone new came on at the security desk. There were more Islanders living in Auckland than anywhere else in the world, but they were still just a drop in a tremendous bucket. The city was home to thousands of migrants from all across the Pacific, all there for different reasons: guest workers on visas, refugees from the political violence on Tonga and Fiji, second- and third-generation residents and citizens, native Maori, and people like him, whom the UN had provisionally declared Displaced Persons.

Finally the guard put down his telephone and waved Saufatu through. The other islanders followed slowly, as the guard took each one's DP card and scrutinized it carefully before letting him pass. When they were all through Saufatu headed towards the baggage terminal, noticing when he saw the Arrivals board that he was fully ten minutes late for his shift—half an hour's pay gone thanks to the new man at the security desk. He kept his pace up all morning, so that by noon he was ahead of schedule and could take a few minutes to watch the planes take off.

That was how he had gotten into the business: as a boy he had watched the flights that landed and took off from Funafuti's airstrip every day, watching the planes get smaller and smaller until they looked like frigate birds. Even when he was grown and working at the tiny airport he would sometimes think about flying away on one, visiting all of the places he had seen in the travel magazines visitors left behind. When the time finally came for everyone to leave, though, the airstrip was under water and they all went on old freighters that stank like septic pits and crawled like snails across the ocean. Then, when his sister and brother-in-law had left Auckland to join the Extraterritorial Government in New York, he had stayed to carry out the family's *salanga*, gathering stories and memories from the expats to build the virtual islands. Only Losi, just ten at the time, had stayed with him: "The surfing sucks in New York," she had said.

She was surfing when he came to pick her up, off a beach in Maori Bay that was studded with black volcanic rock. The road ended at the beach, no parking lot, so he just set the parking brake and leaned out the door, watching as she rode her board into the oncoming breakers, a little bit differently each time—hitting the waves a bit higher or lower, cutting left or right once she was riding a swell. It didn't look much like fun to him, but perhaps the fun part had been earlier in the day. The sun was low on the horizon behind her, and as it turned to red Saufatu began to get a headache; finally he honked the truck's horn, twice, and a few minutes after that he could see her paddling her board back to shore.

Once Losi was out of the water she unzipped her wetsuit, peeled it off and rolled it into a messy ball. She stood on the beach in her black one-piece as a man with knee-length shorts and a ball-cap came to meet her; she reached up to the back of her neck, detached the recording module from her 'jack and handed it to him. The man touched his pico to the module, downloading everything she had experienced that day so it could be cut up in bits, stripped to pure sensation and plugged into surfing dreams.

A blond-haired boy wearing a wetsuit that was unzipped to the waist came up and gave Losi a hug; she leaned close to say something to him, said goodbyes to all the other Kiwis crowded around them and then finally gave a wave to Saufatu and started towards the truck.

"Good day?" he asked as she climbed into the truck, shoving her crumpled wetsuit under her seat.

She shrugged. "Caught some good waves this morning."

Saufatu started the truck, shifted gears and worked at getting it turned around. He noticed a long scrape down her left shoulder. "Looks more like they caught you."

"I spent a little time up at the north end of the beach, getting knocked into the rocks."

"On purpose?"

"Someone's gotta do it."

"I didn't see that white boy doing it," he said, looking straight ahead.

She laughed. "Are you kidding? He got bashed twice as hard."

"If you say so." Saufatu was quiet for a few moments, watching for the turn back to the highway from Muriwai Road. "That reminds me, I met a fella last night who made me think of you—he was out swimming and ran into Apisai Lotoala's shark attack."

"What, a tourist?"

"Not exactly, I don't think. He said he goes looking for low-traffic places—his name was Craig Kemper, I think. Heard of him?"

She shook her head, then stopped. "Wait. Craig Kettner?"

"Yes. Yes, that's it."

"How can you not know who that is?" Losi asked. "What was he doing in the Islands, anyway?"

Saufatu shrugged. "He said people would like to visit them. Do a lot of people follow him?"

"Enough to crash your server," she said. "God, I can't believe you sometimes."

"Well, he asked to see the rest of the Islands—you can come if you want, show him yourself."

She nodded slowly—trying, he could tell, to stay cool. "All right," she said, and smiled.

There was a *fatele* that night, just a small one, in Donald Tuatu's backyard. Saufatu went over after supper, filled a plastic coconut-half from the bowl of toddy and inched around the periphery of the party. There were no singers, just an old boom box, but a few teenage boys were dancing out the lyrics, two from one side of their "village" squaring off against three from the other.

Saufatu spotted Apisai Lotoala sitting nearby, filled up another coconut half and headed towards him. He was a big man, still powerfully built despite his age, and the old folding chair he was sitting on buckled beneath him. He was wearing shorts and a short-sleeved shirt and the scars on his leg shone white in the moonlight.

"Here," Saufatu said, carefully handing him the coconut shell. "You looked dry."

Apisai drained the shell he was holding, set it on the ground and took Saufatu's. "*Ta*," he said, and tipped it back.

"Fella ran into your shark last night."

"Oh? What'd he do that for?"

Saufatu shook his head. "Didn't know it was there. He's not an Islander—American, I think."

"He get out all right?"

"Sure. I told him to bop it on the nose, just like you did." Saufatu took a drink of his toddy. "Look, I may be getting a chance to upgrade the Islands some. I'm going to need you to help me fill in Niulakiti."

Apisai shook his head. "I told you everything I can remember. I wasn't there long, you know—off on a freighter at sixteen, like all my mates. Ask me about that, I could talk all day."

"Saufatu!" Apisai's wife Margaret had spotted them talking and now came over. She was almost as tall as he was and wore a flower-print dress that fell in straight lines from her shoulders to her ankles. "Saufatu, where is that niece of yours? I haven't seen her in years, it feels like."

"She turned in early," Saufatu said. He tapped the back of his neck. "She surfs—records how it feels, they sell it to the dreamcasters. A whole day of it tires her out."

"But how is she going to meet a boy?" Margaret asked. "You know the ones her age, they're all getting jobs, in the city or on the ships." She turned to her husband. "She's so busy, we're going to have to find her someone nice. Can you think of anyone?"

"Leave me out of this," Apisai said.

"She's coming with me to the Islands tomorrow night," Saufatu said. "You can come too, if you like. I mean, you can come anytime— it's all for you."

"Oh, Saufatu, I don't know how you have the energy for those dreams," Margaret said. "You must have it very easy at the airport. I have to be up at five to go and clean my houses."

Saufatu turned to Apisai, who had been retired for nearly a decade now. "Well?"

Apisai shrugged and took another drink of his toddy.

Before going to bed Saufatu sent Kettner a text, suggesting they meet again the next night. He disabled the realtime lock and then went from island to island, planning the tour he would give to Kettner and Losi.

To his surprise, Losi was still there when he got up: even more surprising she was in the kitchen, boiling a bag of kippers and heating a bowl of *pulaka* in the microwave. "Good morning," she said, putting a plate and fork down as he sat at the table.

"Good morning."

If Losi noticed his bemusement, she showed no sign of it; instead she pulled the bag out of the boiling water with tongs, cut it open and slid the reddish fish onto his plate, getting to the microwave just as it began to beep. "How was your night?" she asked.

"Fine," Saufatu said. He flaked off a piece of kipper with his fork and chewed it slowly. "Fine. Thank you."

She spooned a pile of hot *pulaka* onto his plate. "Have you heard from Craig Kettner?"

Saufatu shook his head. "Not in the night. I haven't checked my texts this morning, though." He took another bite of the salty fish, chewed it thoughtfully. "Do you need a ride this morning?"

"Are you sure you have time?"

He nodded. "Sure. Just let me finish up and let's go."

"Sure." She smiled, then turned to put the empty bowl of *pulaka* in the sink. "Do you have time to check your texts first?"

Luckily she was recording at Karekare Beach that day, a bit nearer to home than where he had picked her up the day before; luckier still the regular security guard was back on duty and waved him right through, so that he was only twenty minutes late and short an hour's pay. He checked his texts before starting work and found one from Kettner, agreeing to meet him on the Islands that night (though of course it would be morning for Kettner, if he lived in America). After that the day went quickly, his mind barely registering the bags he moved from plane to carousel as he rehearsed the tour he had planned.

When his shift was done he picked Losi up from the beach, smiled at the way her eyes lit up when he told her about the text from Kettner; she was nearly bouncing in her seat the whole ride home, and throughout supper she pressed him for details on his first meeting with Kettner. Finally it was time to hook up their dreamlinks and go to sleep; after the usual moment of wild dreaming the REM regulator kicked in and they both found themselves on the pink sand at the tip of Funafala, the narrowest inhabited island in the Funafuti group, where they could see both the lagoon and the western islands and east to the open sea. It was also home to the village where he had grown up, and most of the landscape was drawn from his own childhood memories: thick stands of coconut trees, huts with thatched or sheet-metal roofs; and the wrecks of small boats that he and his friends had used as forts and playhouses.

Kettner was already there, looking at a pair of small wooden boats, with outboard motors and canvas soft tops, that had been pulled up onto the beach.

Saufatu waved to him, took Losi by the hand and led her over to the boats. "Craig, thank you for coming. This is my sister-niece Losi—she does dream work, too."

"Really?" Kettner said. "What do you do?"

Losi shrugged dismissively. "I'm a recorder—we just do B-roll, you know, generic surfing stuff, but Brian—that's the guy I work with—he's an indie dreamcaster. Whenever we have enough time and money we record some more."

Kettner nodded appraisingly. "That's great. Why don't you give me your demo reel, I'll check it out."

"Cool," Losi said, smiling. "Yeah, I will, cool." She held out a hand, and after a moment Kettner reached out to shake it.

"Do you mind if I take some recordings?" Kettner asked. "Just samples, to show people what I'm talking about."

"I can do it," Losi said. "If that's all right with you, Uncle."

Saufatu nodded quickly. "Yes, all right."

Before he had finished speaking she was in the water, making a long and shallow dive out towards the wrecks in the distance. Kettner watched for a few moments as she crested the low waves, then turned to Saufatu. "So what am I seeing here?"

"This is where I grew up," Saufatu said. "It's the southernmost island of the biggest atoll. All the islands in this group ring around Te Namo—that's the lagoon, there—the swimming's good here, on both sides, and there's reef snorkelling too."

"Your niece mentioned surfing?"

Saufatu shook his head. "We never did that here. Losi, she grew up in Auckland—her dad worked for the consulate there—and those Kiwis are mad for it. You get bigger waves on the sea side of the western islands, but we always stayed in the lagoon where it's safe."

"Safe?"

"Well, except for the sharks."

For the rest of the night Saufatu led Losi and Kettner around the islands—carefully avoiding Fogafale, where paved roads and cement houses spread out from the airstrip to fill every inch of the island in a thick sprawl; though he had recorded it accurately, he suspected it was not the side of the Islands that Kettner thought his followers would want to see. Instead he took them up to the five small islands in the Conservation Area on the western side of Te Namo, where there were good-quality instanced interactions with green turtles and fairy terns. The World Wildlife Fund had financed the recording of these atolls, which was why they had more detail and interactive features than the inhabited islands. Only Tepuka Savilivi, the sixth and smallest island, had had to be reconstructed from tourist photos and satellite maps; it had been swamped before the recording began, the first of the islands to sink entirely.

Everywhere they went Losi recorded samples—diving in the warm, shallow water of the lagoon, climbing trees to cut down coconuts and peering close at terns that hovered curiously in front of her, hanging in the air just inches from her face before flitting away into the trees. Saufatu ended the tour in Nanumea, where they could see the wrecks of small ships just offshore from the village and, out towards the horizon, the rusting hull of the John Williams.

"That's a U.S. Navy cargo ship—the Japanese sank it in the war," Saufatu said.

"Can we go out there?" Kettner asked.

"To the ones near shore, yes, but not the big one," Saufatu said. He threw a look at Losi. "It's still there, though, just a little bit further under water. Someone could go out there and record it, if we had the money."

"This is really remarkable," Kettner said. "I can't believe nobody knows about it."

"Nobody knew about the Islands before they sank," Losi snorted.

"I never tried to publicize it," Saufatu said. "It's really just meant—for our people, you know. But if you think that this can bring some money in—make it so more of us can be involved in upgrading it . . ."

Kettner shrugged. "I can't promise that, but I do think a lot of people will be interested in seeing this. So much of what's out there is so fake, you know? But this really lets you feel what it was like to live here." He held up a hand. "I won't do anything unless you're sure you're okay with it, though. This is your baby."

Saufatu looked over at Losi, then nodded. "Yes," he said. "Go ahead."

"Great—I can do a preview reel from the stuff Losi captured, and I'll let you know when the piece is going to run," Kettner said. "You might want to rent more server space."

Losi spent most of the next day locked in her room, carefully culling the footage she had recorded—Saufatu told her that Kettner would surely edit it himself, but she said she wanted him to be picking between good, better and best—only emerging more than an hour after he came home from the airport to eat a reheated bowl of mackerel and breadfruit and then crash in dreamless sleep.

Saufatu had hesitated to tell other Islanders about this business with Kettner, unsure what they would think about a bunch of foreigners coming to the Islands, but when he saw Kettner's "preview reel" he knew he had to share it—proud of the work he had done in conserving the Islands, of course, but also of Losi's work in capturing it. The footage had not been stripped and sliced, unlike her usual work, so that it captured not just what she had experienced but how she had felt about it as well. It had all been as new for her as it had been for Kettner, and her joy in swimming, climbing and exploring was clear—not to mention her evident pleasure at showing off. He forwarded the preview to everyone on his mailing list, along with an invitation to join them when Kettner did his show two nights later.

The next day was Saturday, Saufatu's day off, and he suggested to Losi that they go out to the beach together. They had not done this in a long time, not since she tired of the calm and shallow water he preferred, but she gathered up the towels and picnic gear and brought them to the truck—stopping, he noticed, every few minutes to check her texts.

She was silent most of the way out, distracted, and he didn't push her to talk; the truth was that he felt much the same way, thinking about how things might change for the Islands. They spent all morning in the water, swimming and bodysurfing on the gentle waves, then lay out their lunch and tucked into their sandwiches.

"I'm glad your friends could spare you," he said, looking out at the clear sky and whitecapped sea.

Losi shrugged. "They're going to have to get used to it," she said. "All the stuff I do for Brian is stripped and sliced, so he can replace me easily enough if he has to."

"Would it be nice, doing work that has a bit more meaning to it?" Saufatu asked. "More of you in it?"

She shrugged, then nodded, and looked away; they finished their lunch in silence and then went back into the water, swimming against the waves until they were tired enough to be sure they would sleep.

Losi spent the whole trip back leaning out the window, her right knee bouncing and her left hand tapping the seat. Before he had even turned off the engine she was out of the truck and running to the door of the house.

Saufatu set the parking brake and drew the keys out of the ignition. He was just climbing out of the truck when he heard her shouting from inside; he ran to the house, not bothering to lock the truck, and met her at the door. "What's going on?" he asked.

"It's Craig," she said. "He just texted me. He wants me to be one of his scouts."

"What?"

"I mean, I knew he liked my footage when he didn't strip it, but I wasn't sure—you know, I mean, everybody wants to scout for him—"

"But—" Saufatu frowned. "What about the Islands?"

Losi frowned too, cocking her head. "What about them?"

"I thought—Kettner said he thought we could get funding to finish the Islands, upgrade them. I thought you could help me with that."

"I'm—I'm sorry, Uncle," she said. "I just can't pass this up. This is—I'll never get a better chance. And it's work I can do from here, I won't be moving—not right away, anyway."

"And what will I tell your father? What will he say when he hears you're just giving up on your duty?"

"He'll probably be glad I won't waste my life building some crazy fantasyland nobody but you cares about," Losi said. She glared at him for another second, her jaw set, then turned and ran back into the house.

Saufatu stood for a long moment, shaking his head slowly, then turned at a noise behind him. Apisai Lotoala was standing in front of his house, looking uncomfortable. "Everything all right?" he asked.

"I'm sorry you had to hear that."

Apisai shrugged. "I have a son, you know. They're all the same at that age."

"No, it's—it's more than that. She was never interested before, in any of it, and then when she wanted to come see the Islands I thought . . ."

"Nobody's interested in home, not at that age. None of us could wait to leave the Islands." Apisai shrugged. "Maybe it would have been different if we'd known we could never go home, but I don't expect so."

"But you can," Saufatu said. "Come tomorrow night, you'll see. And we're going to make it even better, it'll be just like being there."

"I know what that's like," Apisai said, then held up a hand before Saufatu could respond. "Fine, fine—I'll be there."

Losi's door was shut when Saufatu went inside, and his hand hovered over it, ready to knock; after a long moment he took a breath and let it drop to his side. What could he say to her? He had thought she didn't care because she had grown up here, had never known the Islands, but he had to face the fact that none of the ones who had grown up there cared either. He sat down at the kitchen table and started a text to Kettner to get him to cancel his visit: it felt like a fraud now, absurd to think that a virtual reconstruction could give someone any sense of what it was like to be an Islander. For the tourists, it would be nothing more than another fantasyland, like Losi had said; for the Islanders it was just a dusty photo album.

Saufatu's hand hesitated over his pico's airboard; after a moment he waved it back and forth to cancel the message, then picked up the pico and took it to his room. He hooked his 'jack up to the dreamlink and then forced himself to go to sleep and get to work.

Saufatu walked down the Niulakiti beach to the shore, dodging tourists as they ran back and forth across the sand. He had seen them all over the Eight Islands, walking along the beaches, watching the fearless birds, swimming out to the wrecks—everything that had been in Kettner's preview reel.

Apisai Lotoala was at the shore, standing just ankle-deep in the water and surrounded by a knot of Islanders who were all chatting together, drinking toddy from plastic milk jugs and casting occasional glances out to sea. So far as the Islanders were concerned, this was no more meaningful than a backyard *fatele*; Apisai waved to him as he neared but Saufatu just nodded back, not feeling any need to be humoured.

He spotted Kettner and Losi about a half-mile out, near where the shark attack was instanced: he thought he recognized the blond boy who had been surfing with Losi out there as well. He waved, and Kettner and Losi began to make their way back to shore.

"What did I tell you?" Kettner said as he walked out of the water. Losi followed a few steps behind, her eyes lowered. "They love it."

"It's very gratifying," Saufatu said.

Kettner laughed. "I'm glad you think so," he said, and shook his head.

Losi tapped Kettner on the arm. "Listen," she said, "I'm going to go, okay? Text me."

"No, wait," Saufatu said. He took a step past Kettner, looked her in the eye. "Just stay, a little longer. Please."

"Uncle—"

Suddenly there was a noise, a deep note like someone blowing on a conch shell. A ship had appeared out on the water—or rather dozens of instances of the same ship, a battered old freighter that hauled itself slowly towards every shore of the Eight Islands.

A moment later tourists and Islanders alike had been transported aboard the ship, packed tight on the decks or else peering out of the portholes below. From there they could see the deep-water wharf at the north end of Fogafale and beyond to the narrow streets and concrete buildings where most of the Islands' people had lived for the last fifty years.

There was no water on the ground; this was no sunken city, no drowned Atlantis—only an island that had become too low and too salty to be inhabitable, just one more of the thousands of lifeless atolls that dotted the Pacific.

Kettner was at his elbow. "This is what it was like, isn't it?" he asked. "When you left."

Saufatu nodded. He saw Apisai Lotoala leaning out over the rail, his head turning in wide arcs from side to side and his eyes gleaming with tears. Of course his people hadn't needed the simulated Islands: every one of them already had an unchanged memory of their home the way it used to be. What they had not had, until now, was a chance to say goodbye.

The ship's horn blew again, two sharp blasts, and it began to move away from the wharf. Saufatu turned to see Losi standing behind him. "I'm sorry, Uncle," she said.

"Don't be. You were right."

"But you're not—sinking it? Everything you did?"

"No," Saufatu said. "It'll still be here, for people to see what it was like before—or to help people remember. But this will be the only way to leave."

"Listen," she said, "I could help out for awhile, if you like. I'm sure Kettner would understand."

He shook his head. "Do you know, when our people left Tonga and Samoa they thought everywhere in the ocean had been settled? But they set out again into the open sea, just to see what was out there." He took a deep breath. "Go with Kettner. See what's out there."

She nodded, and they both turned back to look over the side. The wharf and the islands beyond it were moving away in accelerated time, shrinking and then finally fading from view, lost in the trackless ocean.

PUBLICATION HISTORY

"Irregular Verbs" and "Holdfast" first appeared in *Fantasy Magazine*

"Outside Chance" and "Closing Time" first appeared in *On Spec*

"Talking Blues" first appeared in *Triangulation: End of the Rainbow* (Parsec Ink)

"Long Pig" first appeared in *Daily Science Fiction*

"Written by the Winners" first appeared in *Timelines* (Northern Frights Press)

"The Face of the Waters" first appeared in *Triangulation: Taking Flight* (Parsec Ink)

"Another Country," "Public Safety," "Lagos," "The Coldest War" and "The Last Islander" first appeared in *Asimov's Science Fiction*.

"When We Have Time" first appeared in *Triangulation: End of Time* (Parsec Ink)

"Jump, Frog!" first appeared in *Ten Plagues* (Saltboy Bookmakers)

"The Dragon's Lesson" first appeared in *Time for Bedlam* (Saltboy Bookmakers)

"Heroic Measures" first appeared in *Strange Horizons*

"The Afflicted" first appeared in *The Magazine of Fantasy & Science Fiction*

"What You Couldn't Leave Behind," "The Wise Foolish Son," "Beyond the Fields You Know," and "Au Coeur des Ombres" are all original to this volume

ACKNOWLEDGEMENTS

All books are the products of many hands, but a collection like this especially so. I owe a debt to the many editors who bought and, in many cases, improved the original versions of most of these stories and most especially to Sheila Williams who published many of them in *Asimov's*; to Brett and Sandra, for taking a chance on this book; to Helen Marshall, for her support and for providing the book with an introduction much more wonderful than it deserves; to all those writers who provided feedback and encouragement on the book and those who offered to risk their reputations by endorsing it; and to my parents, who inspired me to tell stories.

ABOUT THE AUTHOR

Matthew Johnson is a writer and educator who lives in Ottawa with his wife Megan and their two sons. His first novel, *Fall From Earth*, was published in 2009 by Bundoran Press, and his short stories have appeared in places such as *Asimov's Science Fiction*, *The Magazine of Fantasy & Science Fiction*, and *Strange Horizons*, and have been translated into Russian, Danish, and Czech. He is also the Director of Education for MediaSmarts, Canada's centre for digital and media literacy, for whom he has written articles, lessons, blogs, tipsheets, and educational computer games, and whose material he has presented to numerous parliamentary committees and international conferences, as well as appearing on *The National, Canada AM,* and many other TV, print, and radio outlets.

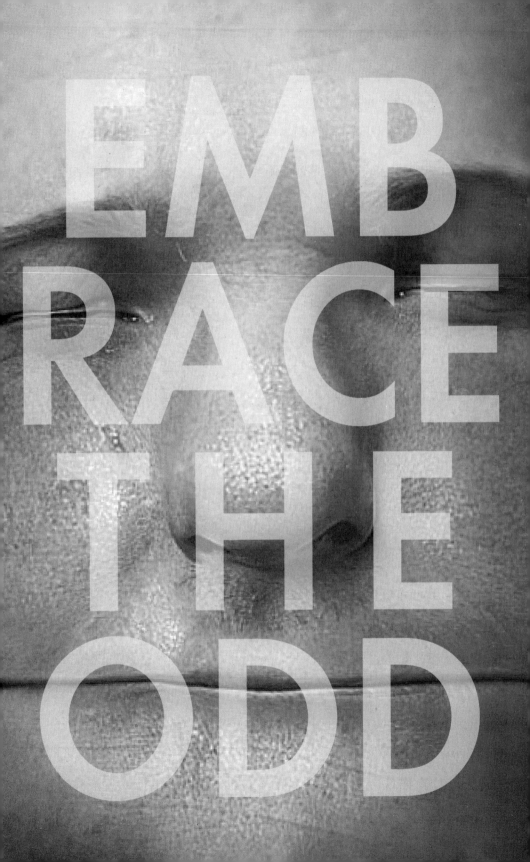

GIFTS FOR THE ONE WHO COMES AFTER

HELEN MARSHALL

Ghost thumbs. Miniature dogs. One very sad can of tomato soup . . . British Fantasy Award-winner Helen Marshall's second collection offers a series of twisted surrealities that explore the legacies we pass on to our children. A son seeks to reconnect with his father through a telescope that sees into the past. A young girl discovers what lies on the other side of her mother's bellybutton. Death's wife prepares for a very special funeral. In *Gifts for the One Who Comes After*, Marshall delivers eighteen tales of love and loss that cement her as a powerful voice in dark fantasy and the New Weird. Dazzling, disturbing, and deeply moving.

SEPTEMBER 2014

978-1-77148-302-5

THE FAMILY UNIT AND OTHER FANTASIES
LAURENCE KLAVAN

The Family Unit and Other Fantasies is the debut collection of acclaimed Edgar Award-winning author Laurence Klavan. A superb group of darkly comic, deeply compassionate, largely fantastical stories set in our jittery, polarized, increasingly impersonal age. Whether it's the tale of a corporation that buys a man's family; two supposed survivors of a super-storm who are given shelter by a gullible couple; an erotic adventure set during an urban terrorist alert; or a nightmare in which a man sees his neighbourhood developed and disappearing at a truly alarming speed, these stories are by turn funny and frightening, odd and arousing, uncanny and unnerving.

AUGUST 2014
978-1-77148-203-5

THE DOOR IN THE MOUNTAIN
CAITLIN SWEET

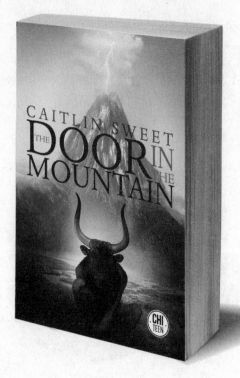

Lost in time, shrouded in dark myths of blood and magic, *The Door in the Mountain* leads to the world of ancient Crete: a place where a beautiful, bitter young princess named Ariadne schemes to imprison her godmarked half-brother deep in the heart of a mountain maze . . .

. . . where a boy named Icarus tries, and fails, to fly . . .

. . . and where a slave girl changes the paths of all their lives forever.

MAY 2014 IN CANADA/OCTOBER 2014 IN U.S.
978-1-77148-191-5

FLOATING BOY AND THE GIRL WHO COULDN'T FLY

P. T. JONES

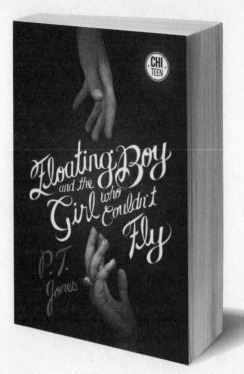

This is the story of a girl who sees a boy float away one fine day. This is the story of the girl who reaches up for that boy with her hand and with her heart. This is the story of a girl who takes on the army to save a town, who goes toe-to-toe with a mad scientist, who has to fight a plague to save her family. This is the story of a girl who would give anything to get to babysit her baby brother one more time. If she could just find him.

It's all up in the air for now, though, and falling fast. . . .

Fun, breathlessly exciting, and full of heart, *Floating Boy and the Girl Who Couldn't Fly* is an unforgettable ride.

MAY 2014 IN CANADA/OCTOBER 2014 IN U.S.
978-1-77148-173-1

CHITEEN.COM